# A PRA MARTIN



RICHARD JOHN THORNTON

A PRAYER FOR MARTIN

DEDICATED TO FAMILIES EVERYWHERE

# PROLOGUE

I can vividly recall the scene at home from all those years ago.

I watched the elder boy as he sat quietly in the armchair.

For some instinctive reason I was always watching him.

His face was expressionless as he observed the view through the lounge window.

He was a quiet, passive child.

Undemanding and seemingly disinterested in the company or affection of others. He was never inclined to display a temper like many young boys. He would show no interest in playing games or playing with any of the albeit few toys we had.

He always seemed at peace; content to keep his own counsel.

Mealtimes were interesting.

He would only ever eat fish fingers. Nothing else would tempt him.

Indeed, he would verbally yet very eloquently criticize our mother for providing anything else.

Unless of course fish fingers were the only option on the menu.

I never really considered that possibility before now.

In hindsight, our mother and father had neither the patience nor the capacity for the kind of love that their eldest son required.

They left him to his solitude and accepted his set ways.

He would rock gently backward and forward in his own world.

Finding his solace in being surrounded with the limited familiarity.

Blissful in his unwitting ignorance regarding the brutal future that lay in wait.

Yet years later as I watched him study the neon flashing high above, I could see that he had changed.

He craved adventure and was tempted to sample the unknown.

He now needed to be challenged by those things that had not been provided in his upbringing.

Although now a fully grown man, my brother is still a child in essence.

And in the end, his true essence was to be his salvation...

# I
# THE CALLING

# 1
# REFLECTION

It never made any sense until the very end.

Like one of those three-part TV dramas that only reveals the answer in the last minute of the last episode.

Only, this wasn't a fictional story.

This was my life, and the life of my brother.

How we survived the early years of anguish and uncertainty, God only knows.

Talking of which - I didn't used to believe in God. Not until I really needed to, anyway. Then it became vital that I stuck with him. And that he stuck by me. I needed God to get me where I am today.

I suppose we all need him, whether we admit to it or not.

I don't know who God is or what he looks like, but one thing I do know is that when I finally meet him, I'm going to hug him and take him for a bloody good drink.

He deserves it.

And so do I for that matter.

My name is Jamie Andrews.

Not a particularly unusual name or a name that trips from the tongue with a semblance of ease or difficulty.

A name of total indistinction.

However, I think by the time you've experienced my story it may well be embellished on your mind for a long time to come.

At least I hope so, because my story is not one you are likely to forget in a hurry. I want you to remember this tale forever. I want you to tell your children about me, and then they can tell their grandchildren in years to come.

As I said, I hope so.

Hope is the one virtue that we all base our lives on. Every hour of every day. Every week of every year, our existence is plagued by the notion that things can and will improve in one way or another.

Most people hope to get a better job; hope to win money; hope to stay healthy. Most people have control of most aspects of their lives. They make their own decisions founded on what they're facing and what they've learned from the past.

I've got little time for that dictum. The majority don't know how lucky they are.

So *what* if you don't win the lottery? From what I can see, those blessed few who have become overnight millionaires seem to wish they'd never put a bloody ticket on in the first place!

They become the targets for beggars and lowlifes; the small-time wannabes who grasp for material possessions that really mean very little in the great scheme of things.

In my personal experience, hope gets you nowhere.

Any positive change is more aligned to the one facet of existence that most of us take for granted throughout our sorry time on God's Earth.

That facet being LIBERTY.

That's the only privilege that *really* matters.

Freedom of mind; freedom of will. If you haven't got that, you've got nothing as far as I'm concerned.

Most people grow up never knowing what real living is truly all about.

They plod along in their insular worlds, counting the pennies. Content to accommodate the toil of routine. The manacle of conformity is inherent centuries of past generations.

Pay the bills. Pay the milkman. Pay the bailiffs.

Pay, pay and keep on paying some more.

*****

It wasn't until I reached my late teens that something happened inside my own head to make me view the world from the outside in, as opposed to the typically selfish human perspective of inside out.

Once you have become familiar with my life, you might say I was fortunate to discover the meaning of liberty at such a relatively young age. You might be right. Strangely, it is only with the benefit of hindsight that I can truly appreciate my process of evolution.

Nowadays, everything seems so clear.

Back then, childhood was a persistently fogged scenario.

It's taken me most of my teenage hood to piece together the dishevelled origins of my upbringing and somehow make it link up with the existence I enjoy today.

A compilation of disturbing images still jumps to the forefront of my mind if I contemplate the past, even for a second.

The nightmares have stopped though; more or less.

Ironically, my bad dreams weren't based on the actual events of my formative years.

It was as though my brain decided to go into a state of paranoia when it felt my head hit the pillow.

Visions of suffering tormented me for what seemed an age. To the point where I almost accepted them as normal. These visions were barely definable in terms of what I was seeing in my mind's eye, but no less scary for it.

I plucked up the courage to seek help from the church to see if I could attach any significance to what was going on inside my apparently crazy nut.

The diagnostic theory was that I had adopted the deep-rooted fears of my brother, and it was in fact *his* sufferance that was manifesting inside my conscience.

I never went back for further counselling. I didn't need to.

The priest had nailed it on my first visit.

Cut and dried. Sorted.

It was at that point that I knew my brother needed me.

My destiny was ordained at that precise moment. I needed to find my older brother, Martin, and rescue him.

Lord knows, though unbeknown to me at the time, he had given me all the hints I should ever need.

I still kick myself to this day for the fact that I couldn't recognise his cry for help sooner.

But then, how was I supposed to identify the distress signal? I hardly knew the guy! I was eventually seventeen-years-old when I decided to find him. Martin was twenty-six. I think.

The only evidence that I had in my possession to confirm his physical existence was a photograph of a youngster on his first day at school - adorned in over-sized blazer, shorts that were too long and a tie apparently borrowed from a neighbour.

He did look cute, bless him. But it was hardly an ID picture, was it? The Martin Andrews I was looking for would be a fully-fledged adult, at least in appearance.

You see, Martin and I were taken away from each other at a young age. Mum said he had 'learning problems' and therefore had to go and live with our father somewhere else.

When it all kicked off in earnest, I was little more than seven.

Mum reluctantly filled me in with some sketchy details as I got older, but I could see that the subject was a source of great distress for her.

Well, of course it was. She had effectively lost her firstborn.

I suppose 'lost' is the wrong word.

Yes, 'lost' is *completely* the wrong word.

As time went on, I discovered that it was Mum who had willingly surrendered Martin into another life. It was *her* decision to send him away, because she couldn't cope with his autism or my father's bitter disposition on the matter.

Mum's thinking was so naively twisted that she convinced herself my father's drinking habit and generally abusive nature made him an ideal companion for Martin as far as she was concerned.

It was of course an unbelievably, incredulously heartless, and misguided decision. Yet she seemingly held little reservation in packing them both off together.

It was killing two birds with the same stone, almost literally.

In Mum's eyes she had rid herself of her two major problems in one swift stroke.

Yet perversely, despite her success in eradicating the two factors in her life that made her unhappy, I firmly believe she lived the rest of her days with a broken heart.

Mum was forever remorseful that she didn't carry the inner strength to see to her family's needs as a fit and able mother figure should.

She took the easy option. The path without diversion.

The simplest and most convenient choice, yet the choice which deposited the biggest probability of regret.

I suppose that my unexpected arrival put the coffin lid on my parents' relationship. Long after my father had left home, Mum said that he used to refer to me as 'the accident'. If you ask me, he had a bloody cheek! It was *him* that was clueless regarding his rightful responsibilities as a grown man and parent.

Yet I copped the blame when I popped out in the delivery room! Charming! If you ask me, my father was a walking bleeding accident. His mother would done everyone a favour had she been on the pill.

If there was such a concoction in those days?

As it turned out, as well as being a woefully inadequate role model, he was also an unprincipled, vicious, and violent bastard.

A wild animal, no less.

Yet even after all these years and now possessing a much better grasp on what he was truly like, I find it very hard to refer to my father in such terms. It hurts me to even say the words.

Go ahead and try it for yourself.

For sure, most dads are grumpy, moody, and unsociable for the great majority of the time. That's okay. That's understandable because it's generally true.

Everybody says things like that about their dad. Don't they?

But never, ever did I imagine myself saying his name in the same sentence as phrases like sadistic bully, immoral drunk or even, evil psychotic. It's a sad fact that all three are appropriate descriptions of the person who was my father.

It's as though I've had to live life in a retrospective mode. Hence the reason I recall events for you mostly in the past tense. It's been a gruelling task trying to scrutinize the pieces of the jigsaw in an effort to fit them together.

Although it was always as if my jigsaw came ready finished in the box, and I've had to take it apart to make sense of it.

Most people gather the pieces as they go along the path of life. They are free to make their own puzzle in any form that takes their fancy. My particular conundrum was set in stone from day one. There were no instructions with it, either. Only personal acumen has enabled me to figure it out once and for all.

Though, rather than attaining a feeling of contentment on eventually reaching a satisfactory conclusion, I still feel resentful that this was ever my puzzle to solve in the first place.

I'm glad for Martin, of course.

He is now mostly free of the binding shackles that held him for so long. Sometimes those shackles were physical - not just psychological.

The state of imprisonment that forced him to exist in isolation rather than be able than live life as the man he now is leaves me feeling hollow as his sibling.

Subsequently, the gut-wrenching sorrow that still haunts me intermittently is the ever-present realization that Martin's prime years were never his to enjoy.

But of course, for the best part of thirty years, Martin didn't know any different. His very being was enshrouded by terror.

He was a mere movement in the background of my father's life.

A scratching in the shadows.

My brother was the afterthought that nobody seemingly cared about.

Well, I concede that's not completely true.

There was always his girlfriend, Bobby.

Don't panic. You'll meet her in person later.

The sheer waste of Martin's younger life is the issue that weighs heavily around my heart to this day.

I occasionally observe my brother now he's a free man.

He laughs at cartoons and sings along to Top of the Pops.

Especially when Bon Jovi are on. Our father's favourite rock group, apparently. In some quarters that would be classed as our father's *only* redeeming feature.

Martin is fantastic at quiz shows, especially the arithmetic rounds on Countdown. He'll say nothing as he mentally searches for the answer. Then he'll write it down - always well within the thirty second time limit.

I can't compete with him. He walks all over me.

He'll also sit engrossed in rubbish like soap operas. It infuriates me that for saying he possesses such a capable brain, he doesn't half digest some shit.

Yet I get the nagging sensation when I watch him doing these things, that he's living the life that should have been his so many years ago. It's like he's playing a game of catch-up that's been started too late.

If I think about it for too long, I get genuinely upset.

He saw me crying once when he first moved into our new home. I don't even know what set me off. It was a few weeks after I'd rescued him from that grimy hole he shared with my father. I think the joke says it was the kind of place where you wipe your feet on the way out.

He had been forced to live in squalor. It wasn't fit to house a gang of rats, not that it stopped rats moving in, mind.

Anyway, we had got him settled into his new surroundings back in Nottingham.

On entering his room, I found him sitting on the bed just looking around at the walls, floor and ceiling. The décor was pastel blue. He gazed at the framed pictures hanging on the walls, especially the poster of the two dolphins. You know the sort - arching from the surface of the ocean, smiling their silly heads off.

Someone must have made a bloody mint out of that photo. Martin won it at a funfair. He was transfixed from the second he laid eyes on it.

He felt a connection with the image. He seemed to empathise with what he saw in the picture. It soothed him. It represented mental freedom; physical liberation; unrestrained energy and absolute joy.

The things he'd watched everybody else practice for years.

His expression was vague and ambiguous as his eyes scanned the interior of the room. I still find it difficult to determine what he's thinking even now.

His face doesn't reveal emotion as most of us would do. A grimace can resemble a smile. When he's happy, he sometimes frowns. As his articulacy has gradually improved, he makes things easier for me.

I walked in and sat next to him on the bed, wondering if he'd even noticed my presence. After a minute or so, he turned to me. I immediately noticed the glistening of a single tear as it nestled on his cheek.

I didn't speak immediately, sensing that he had something to say of more importance.

He simply said: 'Safe now.'

What can I say? I was in pieces! I held him in my arms and wept uncontrollably. He didn't know the reasons or circumstances for the existence he'd previously been forced to endure.

He hadn't been in any position to question things.

Yet he recognized that he had been brought to a better place, with kinder people who would look after him.

To me, his acknowledgement of that fact alone would be enough to placate me for the rest of my days.

The restrictive routine he had accepted for twenty-odd years had been impressed upon him as normal.

He didn't have the option of choosing an alternative lifestyle before.

This is what I mean about liberty.

The ambition and facility to change and re-select. What choices did Martin ever have until they were presented to him by me?

Bloody *none*, that's what choices!

The overwhelmingly gratifying aspect was that he had distinguished his new beginning as being preferable to the past.

I wanted him to generate and nurture his growing inner happiness.

He fully deserved to feel good about being alive.

I was ecstatic for us as brothers reunited.

I still smile to myself when I recall his response to seeing me weep.

He placed his arms around me and whispered in my ear:

'There, there, Jamie. Better now.'

It was the same display of affection I'd seen him convey to his teddy bear all those years ago.

That same teddy bear that he takes to bed with him every night.

Yes, even now.

# 2
# IMAGES FROM INFANCY

As is the case for most people, memories of my formative years are not very comprehensive. Apparently, I was born a healthy five pounds eight ounces and had been blessed with all necessary faculties.

Blondish-brown hair, olive skin, blue eyes; all the looks that would impress the girls!

Obviously, at such a young stage, I had little indication that my considerably elder brother was not so fortunate. At the age of five, Martin was supposedly diagnosed with autism by so-called experts.

Well, specifically it was suspected Asperger's.

But I don't believe he was diagnosed at such a young age. I'm not sure he had officially been addressed by a doctor at all until he attained genuine adulthood.

It did not become apparent until later in his life that my parents were determined to remain totally ignorant of their eldest son's suspected affliction and subsequently were unaware of the consequences that autism could incur on his life if they didn't accommodate the issue.

Alarming in this modern age of therapy and treatment, isn't it?

I know what you're thinking. How can a mother and father *not* have knowledge of such a situation regarding their own son? Well. The honest answer is I have absolutely no idea! As stated earlier, I've had to contend with piecing things together for most of my life.

There were very few answers - just an endless stream of frustrating questions.

Autism presents itself in a variety of ways from a very young age. The brain is by no means deficient in terms of capability. It simply reacts differently to things that most minds accept with ease.

Mum said that Martin would regularly astonish his teachers with profound displays of knowledge for a youngster.

Other times he would refuse to speak in class for days on end.

The condition is readily identifiable. If, of course, someone takes an interest and knows what they're looking for. Yes, you are quite correct, dear reader. The problem should have been confronted at the earliest opportunity. I totally agree.

However, the fact is that despite the rumoured official diagnosis, Martin's condition remained concealed from the outside world for a long time.

As did Martin, for that matter.

Our mother and father were seemingly disinterested in paying any constructive parental attention to his progress. School teachers weren't much more use. They didn't even suspect that something was amiss when he refused to use the correct end of the crayon to draw with and began to eat it.

He said to me once that he couldn't even write his own bloody name at the age of twelve, yet he could pronounce foreign phrases in dialect and spell words backwards!

Probably screaming from Martin's very core was the vital call for help.

Yet tragically, his impediment affected his casual speech also. Asking for help was, by default, impossible.

As I've stated, Autism isn't a slowness of the brain. Far from it. It manifests itself more into the social side of life. Interaction is rarely controlled or predictable in an autistic person. They will talk about *what* they want, *when* they want, often with little relevance to the conversation at hand.

I've done a bit of investigative work over my time and been given the excuse that historically, schools weren't so well-equipped to deal with individual problems such as Martin's. To my mind, that's rubbish.

I knew kids at school that dealt with reading and writing difficulties quite admirably. In fact, one of them is now a bloody bank manager! I also knew people in my year group that had to go to special appendix schools to help them develop at an equal rate to their peers.

The options for assistance were available, should they have been pursued.

My parents seem to have been the obstructive common denominator in most of Martin's affairs. They always chose the path that caused the pair of *them* the least inconvenience.

Suffice to say, my conclusions are that they were perfectly content to remain blissfully unaware of the fact that their eldest son needed help.

There is of course, the other sinister possibility.

There is always the chance that they were perfectly attuned to Martin's wants and needs yet decided to actively ignore his plight.

For my own sanity I cannot accommodate this theory. It opens a whole new can of mental worms for me as you might well imagine.

I prefer to think that my mother and father were simply selfish.

That they were both inherently stupid people who had little clue about anything. The thought that they would willingly prolong their own child's sufferance is the stuff of nightmares. And I've had more than enough of *those*, thank you very much!

But then, it takes me back to the appointment with the priest. He told me that the visions in my head were projections from Martin's mind.

So, maybe my brother *was* under forced constraint?

Maybe he *was* the subject of mental and physical abuse?

Analysis of one's own situation throws up many alternatives. That's why I decided to reach the conclusions that appeased me most.

There are strains of fact in my findings regarding Martin's upbringing. Times, places, dates, people. Yet, thankfully, nobody has confronted me with the unbearable, hard truth about what he had to suffer. I have come to believe that such a prospect would be too painful to contemplate.

Hence, I comfort myself with my own, albeit limited, investigative discoveries.

My brother has always been a distant enigma to me. Yet I behold vivid early memories of him from before he left the family home. Before the vital bridges that could take him to help, were forcibly burned down.

It registered with me, even when I was just two or even three-years-old, that Martin was treated differently at home. Although detecting the actual problem was intellectually impossible, I can recall the evidence of the symptoms being readily apparent.

Martin's position within the family unit did not seem, to the casual observer, particularly undue or unfair. In fact, to the uninitiated, he probably appeared to be a normal and healthy child. However, by this time, the tension between my mother and father must have been palpable.

And I am sure that Martin and I were the cause.

I didn't initially attribute the breakdown of their marriage to a dual resentment or even denial of their own offspring.

Yet to this day I struggle vainly for an alternative cause.

There were times as a youngster that I can recall a vague resemblance to a normal family existence.

We would take shopping trips to the city on a Saturday afternoon. Play cricket together in the garden or on warm summer Sundays. Perhaps venture to Wollaton Park in Nottingham for an ice cream. That wonderful place is the backdrop for the first distinctive memory.

It was when I noticed for the very first time that Martin was somehow being excluded from the enjoyment and attention that I was privy to.

Our early relationship was all too brief and typically uncommunicative, yet I can visualize exactly the way he looked at me on that day.

It did not suggest fraternal jealousy - or to quote the modern psycho-analyst's term, *sibling rivalry.*

No, it was more of a questioning gaze; perplexed and yet curious.

The occasion was a hot air balloon festival.

I would say I was around three or four-years-old, Martin perhaps about twelve. I lose track of ages and dates. You'll have to bear with me on this.

The event itself was a wonderful display of colourful exhilaration.

A child's dream. The one lingering image I have of that day is of Martin sitting in the pushchair - yes, at the age of twelve - as he watched the three of us rise high above in the basket. We were tethered to the ground, of course. It was only a chance to sample the feeling. A quick up-and-down thrill job.

We'd queued up for ages. I was too young to appreciate such a treat and remember screaming my head off at the experience until my throat went sore.

It only struck me many years later, that it should have been Martin standing in that basket - not me!

*He* should have been the one up in the sky, breathing the clear air above the tree line. Seeing the city of his birth from a different perspective. Yet there he remained on terra firma, strapped in the push chair, blankly observing our ascent.

He had no say in the matter; no way to express his whim. A situation pre-ordained by my parents. And yes, I know he was way too old for a push chair. But who was around to question it? Even now, who knows why he was deprived of that special feeling of flight?

He was bound by my parents' will.

Literally and figuratively.

We've never spoken about our time together as youngsters. I still don't know what he was thinking in those dark times. As I said, it's difficult to tell. He was fully entitled to be angry for not being party to the balloon ride that I was invited to sample.

He was also likely to be fearful for our safety as he watched us grow smaller above the trees. It wouldn't surprise me if that were the case.

He is a naturally considerate person.

His own position in the scenario may not have given him any cause for analysis, either. It was the way of things. There was no need for reasoning or bemusement. His place was on the floor, in the pushchair. He wasn't told why. He just obliged my parents' wishes.

That's how uncomplicated life was for Martin.

No thoughts of his own to venture; no personal consultation on any single aspect of his own being was entered into by him.

No freedom of choice or will, you see. That was how it was.

I vaguely remember my father owning a car once.

I couldn't tell you the make or model, only that it was white. He must have bought it before I was born, though again, I haven't found it necessary to find the actual answer.

He used to let me sit on his lap and pretend to drive it. All kids have done it, for Christ's sake! I must have been a baby. Mum used to sit in the passenger seat and Martin in the back.

Again, you notice the exclusive arrangement. I never once saw Martin take the wheel. We didn't have the car much longer after my birth. I don't know if it was sold because we were short of money. More likely it got repossessed if my father's financial acumen was anything to go by. That's if my father *did* buy it. It could well have been stolen. It might now be sitting at the bottom of the River Trent for all I know.

Another facet of our early family life was that we hardly ever seemed to play host to any visitors. I've since discovered that it is customary for every boy and girl to spend the first ten years of their life trying to decipher who their uncles and aunties were as opposed to their grandparents. Then of course there remains the juvenile problem of deciding which set of grandparents belong to which parent.

These issues usually go hand in hand with the fleeting appearances of cousins, nieces, and nephews. The whole scenario is part and parcel of growing up. Discovering one's place in the great scheme of things. Developing a sense of proportion to build your little world upon.

For Martin and me, it seemed that we had no relatives.

It was as though they had either been banished from our existence or had opted to give the Andrews clan a wide berth. Either way, the regular friendly greeting of a loving familiar face was something we were not accustomed to.

In conjunction with this was the absence of friends and neighbours. This is of course, solely dependent on your parents being on sociable terms with any friends or neighbours. Many mothers would refer to their closest acquaintances as *aunty this* or *uncle that.* The child would slowly learn who these 'false' relatives were by a process of discrimination.

The faces and names would eventually fall into place.

Not in our house, though.

I have learned that it was my father who was the main reason for such a situation occurring. He was unflinching in his distrust of other souls. He was aggressive and unjustifiably wary of social contact.

Apart from when he was propping up the bar of course.

Then he was *everybody's* friend. Until the fighting started.

The hold he had on his wife and sons was totally constrictive and had eventually brainwashed my mother into thinking that it was the true way of things.

We were destined to be the family on the island, so to speak.

She wasn't allowed to have outside associations and my father had albeit banished her from communicating with her own family. Bearing in mind she had lost both parents as a youngster herself, my mother sensed no great loss aside from pining for her elder sister on a daily basis.

However, fear had kept them both apart.

Fear of my father.

Fear of the consequences should they try to overrule his command.

The reader may now be assembling some sort of mental picture as to the situation at number fifteen, Lodge Close. That was our home address until I was seventeen-years-old.

I don't think I'm wrong in saying that for the first few years in that humble abode, the total number of visitors - to my recollection - was minimal. Perhaps three or four.

The reader may be entitled to think that I would be far too young to assimilate such circumstances, yet they would be wrong.

The mind becomes very adept at registration when it has little other distraction. The memory banks function perfectly from birth and are quite able to hold any amount of information. In a house of silence and generally absent of frolic activity, my brother and I became experts at observation and digestion of our environment.

Undoubtedly, there must have been speculative knocks on the door over the years. However, we were never actively involved in contact with them. I grew up as a child believing that there was only the four of us. It was an insular existence for sure, but not one of our choosing.

The parameters had been enforced by the patriarch.

There was little alternative to his regime.

We were effectively imprisoned by his wrath.

The family on the island. Yes, good phrase, that.

Other aspects of our untraditional upbringing are a little more obscured by time. I cannot reminisce about my favourite family holiday because I don't recall one. Birthdays were something that seemingly mattered little - to my father anyway.

My mother and I tended to celebrate my big day with a little more vigour after my father left home. I afford a little joke with myself from time to time that I had my first birthday at the age of nine. It was only at this time I realised my birth date was the twenty-eighth of March.

It was blindingly obvious that my father's eventual departure triggered something in Mum that said: okay, we're alright to be happy now.

Bloody ironic, isn't it? But also, incredibly sad that she must have lived with such inhibited misgivings of the man she once supposedly adored and willingly married.

After all, she had made him her lover, her husband, and the father to her two sons.

Even more tragic is the idea that she was willing to dispense with acknowledgement of her eldest son if it meant she was rid of his father. I would even go as far as to say that she must have hated him intensely to proceed with such an unpalatable plan.

Having discovered the more unsavoury traits of his character since Mum passed on, I have nothing but sympathy for her decision. It was the wrong decision - let us be clear on that. However, I must admit that I understand her motives.

I must reiterate that my early memory of Martin as a person is nondescript. There are only certain elements of our first period of brotherhood that come fleetingly to mind. And I think I've mentioned most of them already.

Single instances; not even complete events. Literally, flashes from a dim and distant past. They hold little substantial reference to our bond today. He was a just a face from my history - though thankfully that is no longer the case.

I'll never know if he feels the same about me.

His identity would not leave me, though.

It was only after attaining something close to adulthood that I began to question who and where Martin was.

He was a part of me that I could not ignore.

When the priest confirmed my own belief that Martin was calling for help, I had only one purpose in life.

The irony was that I was by then completely free to make my own decisions.

Sure, I was still at school studying for my A-levels. I wanted to go to university. Yet I was prepared to dispense with that side of things.

It was at that particular time that I could have done with at least one parent to help me make my mind up.

We all need a sounding board; however old we are.

Uncertainty is a cross we all must bear.

# 3
# PARTING OF PARENTS

The passages preceding this juncture are a very limited resume of the first stage of my life. They are intended as a guide for the reader's benefit. A gentle immersion into the background of the Andrews family. There should be nothing overtly shocking or giving cause for alarm. Not yet anyhow. It should simply serve as a collage of memories pasted together.

Although the content may be regarded as slightly unorthodox in its depiction of my early years, the fact that my memories are scant is perhaps not so unusual.

Human regurgitation of data is a selective process.

The mind will file everything, yet only a certain proportion is retrievable, typically at a much later stage than when the event occurred.

The build-up to my parents' separation is one such period that offers very little in the way of identity. I was seven or eight; Martin was sixteen or maybe seventeen. Yes, I'm guessing again. I'd barely begun school and Martin was past leaving age. Barmy, isn't it?

After years of playing out the charade, my mother and father were tired of the game of marriage. Though I was never told so in verbal terms, it is my belief that my father totally regretted having children.

His status in the family as father figure was an act.

To the outsider, it was a very convincing act.

However, he had carried two burdens for the best part of his marriage - his sons. Three burdens if you count Mum. He was extremely bitter about the fact that Martin's affliction - albeit allegedly diagnosed and treatable - had been a problem that someone had supposedly placed on his shoulders.

In other words, Jim Andrews believed that God was punishing him by presenting him with a son who was not conventionally perfect. Unbelievable stuff, isn't it?

My father was far too engrossed in his own self-pity to consider the ramifications for Martin. So as time went on, nothing was done.

Jim Andrews came to believe that he shouldn't have to carry such a charge and was content to allow Martin to go for periods without attending school. But only just long enough to distract any curious observers. A few days here, the odd week there. Firstly, because my father was ashamed to be associated with his son's supposedly unwarranted condition and secondly because he didn't want the authorities to intervene.

He considered any genuine concern from others to be uninvited scrutiny. My father possibly believed that Martin's condition would miraculously cure itself, on its own. The situation never let him rest. He secretly rankled with it for years.

In time, his solutions in dealing with his own demons would become progressively unhinged.

My mother, as you may have already presumed, was not allowed an opinion. No doubt she had one, but it was forbidden for her to convey it. She sat quietly through the years and watched her husband gradually succumb to his own twisted mindset. He didn't want to confront problems and wasn't going to let his interfering wife confront them either.

Well, she was only the mother after all.

Then of course, I came into the equation. The accident. My conception was certainly not planned. At least, that's the notion I've managed to glean after all this time. So, my father's frustration only set itself deeper after my arrival.

Yet he successfully concealed his true feelings as we grew up. He fooled himself into thinking that everything was going to be alright, even though he knew full well that such a train of thought was disaster-ridden.

He couldn't handle the responsibility of bringing children into the world. Especially one that he adjudged to be mentally imperfect and the other that he hadn't made provision for. That policy is fine if you're mean enough and self-centred enough to admit to it.

Not many men are.

Far better to be honest with oneself and one's family than spend a lifetime consumed by hatred and remorse.

Yet again I draw a line under these assumptions with the statement that nobody was around to question what was going on. There was effectively only the four of us party to this entire situation.

By the time my parents' relationship had irrevocably broken down, my father had relinquished his job at a local factory and hit the bottle big time. They had always argued. Raised voices were in earshot from the first moment I was laid into the cot. Yet the rows had become violent towards the end.

Even at such a tender age, I could detect my mother's spirit being ebbed away.

Her soul had all but been destroyed. She didn't seem like a person anymore, let alone a mother, wife or even a *woman*.

One day as a spritely infant I rushed out of the house when I heard the clanking of pots and pans. This was usually indicative that they would be leaving the cupboard and be assuming new roles as missiles.

I could never tell who was throwing what. It became so bad that being at home could be like a war trench. Tin hat country on a weekly basis.

It was on this particular occasion that I chose to retreat to the garden and hide inside the coal bunker. We never used the thing for coal, so its appropriated use as a fall-out shelter was very convenient.

I crawled into the dank shadow of that cold concrete box and listened to the muffled screams and shouts. My mum was usually doing the screaming; my father more often than not doing the shouting.

I had become quite adept at hiding from view when the arguments began. I had also become able to spot the symptoms of a brewing scene, rather than be caught out in mid-battle.

The minutes passed as I crouched in the darkness among the cobwebs. The verbal volleys from the house were relentless. At the time I never knew what my parents were rowing about. Now I can say with some assurance that it was their offspring.

I stared aimlessly into the murk, hoping I wasn't about to be discovered by some great hairy spider who wanted to use me as a landing pad. Suddenly I detected a shuffling sound outside. I could see shadow against the thin shaft of sunlight from the garden. Then without warning, the heavy door of the coal bunker was pulled aside with some considerable force.

I instinctively shut my eyes in expectation of my father's hand on my collar, pulling me clear of my refuge.

As the realization dawned on me that it possibly wasn't my father, my eyes opened again.

There, crouching in the bunker doorway, was Martin.

The look of sheer terror on his face was enough to encourage me to welcome him inside. He had obviously witnessed my escape and thought it timely to follow suit.

Although considerably larger in size, my brother dutifully crawled up next to me and we shut the bunker door behind us. And there we remained until our father's voice carried from the front of the house.

The resulting slam of wood entering frame signified to us that he had left the scene, probably to drown his ever-increasing sorrows at some local watering hole.

On our eventual return to the house, Martin and I discovered Mum in the bathroom.

She was hastily applying make-up to a bruise on her left cheek just below the eye socket. It was the size and colour of a plum. We stood in silence behind her as she intermittently wiped the tears away before adding more cream foundation.

It was another telling sign that the end was nigh for Mum and my father. The strange thing is, I could never decide who she was trying to hide the evidence from. As I stated, we didn't have any regular contact with friends, neighbours, or other family at this time.

I don't think she would be bothered about displaying my father's handiwork to us. After all, we were accustomed to seeing her injuries. I have convinced myself over the years that she was attempting to hide the bruises from herself.

Her own reflection repulsed her. She didn't want to have to see the person that was suffering in the mirror. She would rather run away and cover the problem up, than confront it like a real adult.

This same policy of inaction was evidently instrumental in the development of Martin.

It seemed that her brain would not acknowledge his plight, so in turn she was permitted in forgetting Martin had a plight in the first place.

The option of least inconvenience.

The one aspect to all this that has prevented me from hating Mum as much as my father was a constant belief that this policy was not of *her* creation. It was *his*. My father controlled her absolutely by fear.

Subsequently, we all felt the effects of her lack of resistance.

My father was invariably drunk most afternoons. He never worked again after leaving his job at the engineering company. His days revolved around long lie-ins, afternoon piss-ups and late-night card games with his selection of cohorts. And of course, the occasional fist fight.

Consequently, my mother received little or no housekeeping budget in trying vainly to hold our clan together. However, I believe that even with all the money in the world, we were destined to fail as a family unit.

The Gods were not on our side.

They changed allegiance eventually, but not for a long time.

For many months and years Mum dealt with her lot as best she could. Physical and mental abuse from an alcoholic layabout of a husband only deteriorated our home life.

Until one day, when she had decided that enough was enough.

The final straw came when she discovered that my father had been having an affair with some tart connected with the pub he frequented.

That's what finally ignited my mother's resolve.

Throughout her marriage she had been willing to forego the abuse; the constriction of freedom; the lack of choice regarding the family situation and submission to how my father wanted to 'handle' things.

She had been willing to ignore the fact that her eldest son had a very treatable affliction for which she was forbidden to seek help.

She had lived in acceptance of this out and out villain that had professed to the world that he was a dutiful husband and father, when in effect he was neither.

Yet, despite all the factors that she was open to accommodate, the one thing that Mum couldn't handle was the thought that he should wish to find pleasure in the arms of another woman.

The whole thing stinks of hypocrisy.

I didn't think Mum could ever claim to be a woman who placed a deal of faith in loyalty. After all, she hadn't shown much loyalty to her sons, had she? When she relayed events to me in my teenage years, it still didn't fully register exactly what a sham our family existence had been.

The unnecessary destruction of four innocent souls - two of which could have been avoided if they'd not bothered having kids.

I didn't hate Mum for initially trying to withhold all this. I'm glad she did in a way. She eventually thought it best to give me her side of the story, although it was a case of being reluctantly drip fed information rather than a serious line of adult discussions.

Why had she felt compelled to throw my father out of the house along with her eldest boy? Why had she endured his reign of terror for so long, only to suddenly adopt some moralistic principled stance when he starts knocking off the village bike?

Her last wish of my father was that he opted to return to his hometown. A vocal declaration of hope that resonated through the window and into the street for all in proximity to analyse.

*'Take your slapper and fuck off back to the coast where you came from!'*

As the tales were passed down to me over the years, it only ever contained two major elements.

The two chief protagonists - my parents.

There was never a mention of my brother who I hadn't seen for several years. It was as though Martin had never existed. I hadn't forgotten him, though. Out there somewhere was someone I loved.

I hardly knew him, but that wasn't my fault.

As the time went by, my yearning to repair the damage done to us only grew stronger.

The final, lasting image I had of teenager Martin was from the day he and my father left Lodge Close forever.

As the taxi pulled him away into an uncertain future, I watched from my bedroom window as my mother wept uncontrollably in the front room. She could not bear to watch.

But I could.

I was witness to their departure.

Martin knew I was watching, too. Just before the car disappeared around the corner, he looked out from the back window of the cab, and I am sure to this day he was looking for me.

When he finally spotted me waving frantically behind my glass screen, he did the same from behind his. It would be a long time before I could see that light in his eyes again. Although when I mention this episode now, he claims to have acute memory loss.

But he can capably recall every F.A. Cup winning team from nineteen seventy-one through to nineteen-ninety-five?

I made a secret pledge to myself that I would meet my brother again.

I didn't know when or how, but something inside me had been implanted.

It was a sense of duty that I silently nurtured into adulthood.

Two weeks before my ninth birthday my life had entered a phase of drastic change as half of our family left home. What the immediate future held for me was not clear, but at such a young age I had no control over events.

Instinct told me however, that this sudden change would hopefully be for the better.

# 4
# A NEW BEGINNING

The atmosphere surrounding my father and Martin's departure may have subsided quickly. Or it may have remained for an age. I am unsure.

I was too young to ascertain my mother's feelings at watching her husband and eldest son leave home, possibly never to see either of them again.

She told me in later years that she had absolutely no inkling of where they had gone, though this would turn out to be a total falsehood, probably to prevent me from asking her intrusive and awkward questions.

Whatever the actuality of his whereabouts, I was told even before turning ten-years-old that I no longer had an older brother. That he and my father had gone away to find a different place for them both to live. Being at such a tender age, who was I to question such a situation?

Mum and I continued to live together at Lodge Close, which served us as our family domain quite adequately, despite all the ghosts of yesteryear that undoubtedly inhabited its structure.

My school life had been interrupted at various times until this point, but fortunately I would maintain progress at the same rate as my peers. Mum decided almost immediately that the only way we were going to survive financially was for her to go out and find a job.

Not the conclusion of Einstein, you may say, but you must remember this; Mum had been forced to exist in practical isolation for most of her twenty-year marriage. Social interaction was not a facet of life that she was overly familiar with.

Nor was it an option that she relished.

However, it was the only path that lay before her if she were to maintain a roof over our heads. She refused to claim social security on principal. We got some help with the rent when my father and Martin left but being on the dole was not Mum's way.

Ours was only a council house, and the weekly rent was not unattainable by any standards, as I discovered later, when she would send me with the rent card to the post office. I was, and still am, amazed at how comparatively cheap it is to rent from the council as opposed to private tenancy.

The downside of course, is that many council estates, especially around us, had an unsavoury reputation among the supposedly more refined local communities.

The stigma being founded on the assumption that families growing up in such areas are somehow less civilized because they haven't got an income high enough that allows them to take out a mortgage.

I can't answer to that theory even today.

Suffice to say, we kept ourselves to ourselves.

The outside world was simply ignored. Activity in the street did not bother Mum or I one iota. We had each other. We needed each other. We needed nothing more than that. And that was all that mattered at the time.

Lodge Close and its surrounding streets, as I would eventually learn, had indeed acquired a somewhat negative reputation as I suspected, although thankfully I was never party to any trouble.

In my early teens I clearly recollect walking home from school and seeing broken windows in front rooms that would remain so for many weeks. Cars without wheels that stood on bricks in front gardens. Skips that were delivered empty and within a day were filled to overflowing with all kinds of refuse. And would never be collected.

There was litter all over the place. Gangs on street corners that never abided their curfews left law-abiding residents in a constant state of nervousness. Snarling dogs roaming untamed and scavenging, leaving their links of muck everywhere.

Yes, the stereotypical council estate contains many unpopular images. I can assure you as a thoroughbred council house lad, the stereotype is totally founded.

Having made her pledge to earn a crust, Mum managed to pluck up the courage and go to the job centre one day. She told me how petrified she was of talking to strangers in the outside world.

I clearly remember the morning of her initial interview. Yes, dear reader, my mind even at ten-years-old was very aware and I pride myself on a reliable memory regarding pivotal events.

Certain aspects and incidents never leave us, especially concerning the actions of our parents.

Anyway, she spent an hour pulling a brush through her hair - this was a first in itself - and spreading make-up all over her face. She wanted to create the right impression. She wasn't very good at make-up, though.

It requires a sensitive touch and an eye for symmetry. Not that I'm expert. She had become accustomed to trowelling it on to hide her bruises, as opposed to applying it carefully to accentuate her features and impress the onlooker.

She kept me off school on the day of her induction at the job centre. She said she needed some reassurance as she was very nervous.

The only person she could ask was me. We walked quickly through town and on reaching the centre with its gaudy orange frontage, Mum crouched down and gave me the tightest, longest embrace I've ever had from her.

I could feel her shaking as we stood there in the drizzle. She was nervous alright, but so brave in fighting her self-doubt. In we went, introduced ourselves and were shown into a room full of clerks, desks, and telephones.

It was very alien seeing all those people in one office talking at the same time. All those voices. All that noise.

I sat next to Mum as she spoke to a kindly looking lady about her details, background, and ambition in terms of the kind of job she was looking for.

The clerk must have been quite taken aback by Mum's response. She proclaimed that she would be willing to do anything within school hours and could go for an interview that very morning. After a few phone calls and with little more to be said, we spent the morning knocking on the door of a handful of local companies that were waiting with appointments to talk to her.

The job she was to eventually take had hours that suited, tolerable rates of pay and was conveniently located. At least, that's what Mum told me a couple of years after she had started working there. Mason's Packaging was the name of the company. It was the only job Mum ever had. She stayed loyal to them right to the end.

I think it was the best thing to have ever happened to her in her life - and I mean that in all sincerity. Yes - even including me!

The signs must have been good when she was offered the job, because I distinctly remember us going to the local café to celebrate. That was a real treat. I had a sausage roll and a glass of orange.

I clearly recall sitting opposite Mum in the café, watching the enormous smile of relief that she adorned. The rain was relentless by then, but it was no longer raining so much in her heart. She had taken the first brave step toward rebuilding her shattered life.

Only God can tell the extent of the hurt that she had endured over the years, and in that moment of pleasure in the café, I can see her begin to discover herself once again.

I've realised I've been too hard on her in previous passages.

I apologise.

Incredibly courageous, was Mum.

The first few years as a one parent-one child family were comparatively uneventful. Our lives settled into an ordered routine. We had not heard from my father or Martin since the day they left Lodge Close.

As far as we were both concerned, they were history. We had no indication of - or inclination to discover - where they were and how life was treating them.

My local comprehensive was a tough secondary school, but I was achieving in my own quiet little way. To be honest, I quite liked school. I played for the football team and enjoyed my time in the drama group. By the time I was fifteen, teachers were very hopeful that I would make the most of a capable brain and a bright future.

In the space of five years, my Mum and I had vanquished much of the sorrow from our memory banks regarding the former existence we had been resigned to.

I wouldn't say we were both deliriously happy with life, but we had moved on to a large extent. The previous list of problems that had plagued us as a family of four had now been reduced considerably since we re-teamed as a duo.

It was during the build up to my mock G.C.S.E. exams at Christmas time that I became aware of girls - or to be more accurate, they became aware of *me*. At fifteen, I didn't figure I was a particularly late starter in that department, but I had spent the initial stages of my adolescence concentrating on what mattered.

Mum mattered. I mattered.

Girls, up until that point, did not matter one bit.

However, physically and mentally I had matured early and looked somewhat older than many in my age group. I could have passed for eighteen easily and was one of the first to shave in our tutor group. At over six feet I was also one of the tallest in the school at the time.

And whilst liaisons with the fairer sex had been non-existent until this point, I was enjoying playing catch-up. Indeed, female attention was becoming a pleasurable daily occurrence.

Now, its perhaps still the case in this modern-thinking age that many pubescent boys of fourteen or fifteen would typically run for cover if confronted by a girl. At least they still did in my day. But I must confess that youngsters have no qualms about very much at all.

Nowadays the biggest concern for teenagers is where to get hold of a few free condoms. In fact, I retract that suspicion. Most of them aren't even bothered about that these days.

When I was a young man though, we were generally more reserved in our approach to such things.

It's all a part of growing up; becoming self-aware and gaining confidence in yourself as an individual. As the cringe-worthy saying goes - if you don't like yourself, how can you expect anybody else to like you?

But it is generally true.

Well, I'll let the reader in on a surprising little secret. I was more than happy with myself. I had become self-motivated and confident. I didn't judge myself against others and you may also be surprised to learn that I was not intimidated by anything or anyone.

This unexpected evolution in my personality did not occur overnight, but it did take hold rapidly after reaching my teens. Perhaps that's why I liked drama so much. I was experiencing a knee-jerk reaction to the years of suppression.

Now, there was no holding me back.

Watch out world - the *real* Jamie Andrews is coming!

Looking back, I was possibly a big-headed so and so, but that touch of conceit and self-conviction seemed to act as a drug to the female contingent at school. I had my pick of admirers, like a kid in a sweet shop. I could talk to girls all day long about everything they wanted to talk about. And it didn't bother me one bit.

After years of being a spectator of Mum's insecurities and deep-rooted uncertainty, I had become very adept at understanding the feminine psyche, and it shone through like a beacon to many girls.

I discovered very early doors that they didn't want the clunky, mouthy type who thought that young ladies were impressed by watching lads smashing a football around and swearing all the time and staring in mirrors.

They wanted my type - sensitive, caring and with all the looks! Well, I told you I was a big-headed sod! Nottingham's answer to Clint Eastwood. Well, I felt entitled to be, anyway.

This was *my* time, now. Fuck history and the associated hang-ups it provides. Get on with life.

There's little in the way of an alternative, after all.

Anyway, I digress - back to girls.

The ironic thing was, despite my natural born talent for chatting them up, I had absolutely no desire to attain a girlfriend whatsoever.

How weird is *that*?

Sure, I could appreciate a gorgeous-looking female alright and talk the legs off her, but I was not interested in making up an item with anyone.

I suspect I was the subject of both envy and hatred at school among the other lads, but I didn't catch on at the time. That's not to say that I wasn't distracted from my studies through daydreaming about women, but my priorities were aligned.

Education was a massive issue. I was ever-thankful I hadn't missed the boat because of the domestic mess of my younger years. I was determined to do well at school and stay on at Sixth Form to do my A-levels.

These mock exams were a vital step forward in that direction. At times I felt like the only pupil in the school who seemed to grasp this concept. Education should be the paramount consideration for any teenager. This doctrine is even more potent nowadays.

Anyway, back to women, again.

If I'm totally honest with you - and taking the dozens of other lusting girls out of the equation - the one single person that I did develop special feelings for at this time in my life, was Alex.

Alexandra Lawley was infinitely different from the other girls, in as much as she reminded me of me. Obviously not in terms of physical appearance, but in the way she conducted herself.

Her manner; her poise; her demeanour; her indifference to trend; her evident refusal to join her peer group in the queue to go out with Jamie bloody Andrews!

Ironic, isn't it? My life's full of ironic little situations as you will become aware. I wanted to befriend the *one* girl in the school that wasn't bothered in the slightest about *me*. She was unusually striking in looks. She had brown wavy hair. Hardly wore make-up. Plenty of freckles. Doesn't sound to you like the girl of a man's dreams? Well, so fucking what? And what do *you* know, anyway?

I really liked her.

No, I mean…I *really* liked her.

*Admired* her, in fact. And thankfully as time went on and I caught her eye and smiled back often enough, I got the impression she liked me too.

At this stage Mum was working regularly long hours.

She barely had the energy to discuss her *own* day, let alone ask as to how life was treating me. So, it's understandable that she never pressured me to go out and get a girlfriend or mix more sociably in general. Probably because she wasn't interested in the slightest.

Mum never enquired about my studies, either. She never really asked about my school routine at all. She had enough on her plate keeping her own keel even.

It was as though she was content to wallow in the peaceful existence we now had together. I suspect she had a subconscious fear that if she asked certain questions, she may not get the answers that suited her frame of mind.

Yes, dear reader, despite her personal leaps and bounds, she was still blighted by a severe neurosis. A permanent memento from her marriage. Mum's eternal lack of confidence was tragic. Even more mystifying then that I should have matured so quickly and easily.

Despite settling into the responsibility of working for a living - which became an easier task for her once I was old enough to let myself in and out of the house without supervision - Mum still harboured wounds which would never heal.

Even by her mid-forties, she still found it impossible to mix with anybody on the most basic of communicative levels. For the most part she had remained on the family's self-imposed island. The job at Mason's was akin to just dipping a toe in the water, as opposed to diving in for a swim. Yet I am not - nor should I ever be - critical of her policy.

She seemed content with her solitude. I on the other hand was changing month by month, developing wants, needs, and tastes that I was eager to confront, explore and satisfy.

I kept my inner resolve and passed the following summer's exams with flying colours – two A's, five B's and a C. I was privately thrilled to bits. I went to collect my results alone as Mum was at work. It was toward the end of August if memory serves.

I'd spent most of the summer earning money at the local supermarket stacking shelves and doing the odd bit of warehouse work. I loved it. I had more cash than I could spend and gave a fair amount to Mum for housekeeping.

My immediate boss was a scouser called John Harrison.

He liked the bottle far too much, however, and I got him out of the shit a few times by covering his arse with the store's general manager.

John always appreciated that I would have his back if a problem arose. So much so that when I asked if I could nip out for half an hour to collect my results, he told me to take the whole day off with no loss of pay.

In all honesty I hadn't given anyone from school a momentary thought since my last exam in the June. Yet a spontaneous plan was agreed on before saying farewell on the final day, that involved us all going to the pub to celebrate our results.

I stood in the foyer of the visitor's room at school looking at the slip displaying my grades. I was inflated with pride for myself, and for Mum. It was as though I'd achieved these results for her more than me. Sixth Form awaited. Perhaps University after that?

Now I could *really* start to nurture ambitions.

Suddenly a familiar voice carried over my shoulder as I studied the computerised piece of paper containing my results.

'Who's a clever boy, then? Congratulations, Mister Andrews!'

I turned round to see Alex Lawley peering at my piece of paper from behind me, her wonderful smile complementing eyes like crystal. I always thought her eyes were like crystal because they were a very light blue, almost colourless. Continuing the conversation seemed like the easiest thing in the world to do.

I threw my cheekiest yet hunkiest grin to accompany the response.

'Cheers, Alex. How are you? How did you get on?'

'Oh, pretty similar to you. Enough to get me out of retakes and onto A-levels, anyway. That's what I was aiming for.'

I'll let you into a little secret, dear reader.

There and then, as we stood close enough to breathe on one another in the school reception area, the thunderbolt hit me full on.

At that very moment, for the first time in my entire life, my heart missed a romantic beat and my legs buckled. This girl had me helplessly excited about her. And I didn't truly appreciate just how *much* she excited me until she leaned even closer and put her chin on my shoulder to look at my grades again.

I was in absolute paradise.

Of course, just like Clint Eastwood, I didn't reveal it to her at the time.

I thought that playing it cool was the wisest, most sophisticated option. So, I decided to leave it until we went back to school. Stay patient. Keep her guessing. Make her sweat. It was only a couple of weeks or so. She could take it.

But could I?

So, like all arrogant fools, I kept my feelings concealed as we ventured across the road together for the self-congratulatory booze up.

I can see myself now, covertly watching her in blind adoration as she entertained the group of fellow sixteen-year-old students with her enchanting stories and addictive laugh. And oh, *that* smile.

I was well and truly hooked on Alex by the time the landlord called time on the lager session three hours later. He was a good sort and kept the front door closed. He didn't care that we were all under-age drinkers. So long as we were drinkers. I don't know to this day how he kept his licence.

I returned to the supermarket the next morning full of zest and brimming with excitement for the future.

My shift boss John had swiftly noticed this sudden surge of vigour and enthusiasm.

I caught him smirking at me as he watched me work and naturally, I smirked back at him.

'What's so funny?' I asked.

'You are, Jay Jay! I'm only guessing, but there's got to be a woman involved!'

'Piss off, John!' I chuckled.

I couldn't wait to see Alex again at the start of the next school term.

So much for not being bothered about girls.

# 5
# DEAR OLD HENRY

To say that Mum and I kept completely to ourselves during our second chapter of life at Lodge Close isn't strictly true. Adjoining our road was Glenfield Avenue, which played host to several two-bedroom bungalows.

As one may correctly presume in this unfortunately dismissive age, these bungalows housed many elderly residents of the estate. I had walked past these blocks every day of my life since I could remember.

Many of the inhabitants were wary of passers-by. However, one particularly sociable veteran regularly offered a polite word in the morning to both Mum and I should we happen to be in his presence.

He was usually found leaning against his front fence with a wooden pipe secured firmly in his mouth, steel framed spectacles and grey hair swept back with a handful of what I assumed now to be gel, though I think it was known as 'hair lacquer' back in the golden age.

Well before I attained teenagehood, he would always stop us on our way to town or school and comment on the weather and ask us if we were doing anything nice that day.

Or indeed if we were returning home, he would ask us where we had been and if the weather behaved itself for us.

I think the weather summary gave him an opportunity to open a conversation. Mum said his wife had died many years earlier and she suspected that Henry Thompson, for that was his full name, was rather lonely.

Like most youngsters I couldn't initially be bothered with passing the time of day with a pensioner. I know that sounds quite cruel to admit, but it's true, isn't it? Kids don't generally respond to the older generation. They always think they've got better things to do with their time. When in fact, the opposite is true. It's a sad indictment of life that I fell into that group, but it's not my fault, okay?

However, I did not bank on Henry Thompson being so persistent. It is no exaggeration to say that every time I passed his front garden, he would be there or there abouts, ever eager to strike up a chinwag.

It was blatantly rude of me to consider ignoring him every day and I didn't feel comfortable with the idea of pretending to be in a hurry each time we crossed paths.

Wearing a disguise was also out of the question.

So, over a period of months I accepted this quaint old character with growing affection.

The penny dropped that I ought to treat him with the respect that he undoubtedly deserved. After all, he was one of the few people in life that had ever contemplated giving me the time of day, even if that is what he literally wanted to talk about.

It was during the summer of passing my exams that I finally conceded to myself the fact that I really liked old Henry. He had always taken an interest in my comings and goings and was willing to offer advice on any subject. Be it school, family, jobs, girls, football, weather…

As my confidence progressed, I found myself talking to him at length on a daily basis. I would actively seek out his opinion. One day I felt brave enough to ask him about his wife and the reasons for her premature passing.

As usual, Henry was forthright and unflinching with his answer.

He looked me in the eye and gnawed his pipe as he spoke.

'We'd been married for eighteen months. We were both twenty-two at the time, Jamie. It's a young age to lose someone so dear. We think she was knocked off her bicycle on the way to work by a drunken idiot of a driver who hit her and ran. Nobody saw a thing. Absolutely nobody! The milkman found her body at the side of the road at six-thirty in the morning. I never got over her, Jamie. As far as I'm concerned, she's still with me, even though she's been gone all this time. I'll always love her. Always!'

It was his sentiments about the loss of his wife that really widened my eyes as to what Henry was all about. He had taken a real interest in me since I was a youngster. He was watching me turn from a boy into a man. I was filling a void in his life and, as I would come to appreciate, he was becoming a reliable friend to me.

He had pledged never to marry again in honour of his late spouse, and subsequently he remained childless. As such, he genuinely enjoyed the opportunities to watch me grow up. He wasn't simply being a curious neighbour. He was very fond of me for all manner of reasons.

My realization that he was possibly very lonely struck a chord that still resonates in my soul to this day.

In hindsight, I now see that he wanted to be a distant father-figure to me.

Unbeknown to me at the time, Henry had been informed by Mum of our own family break-up and the supposed reasons behind it. Yet he never once asked me to reveal my own feelings or breach the boundaries of what he considered to be my private business.

I believe this was due to the respect he had for us as people in recovery.

It stood to reason that as a widower in his sixties with no offspring of his own, he rightly viewed me as being the nearest he would ever get to having a son. I felt somewhat protected by this surrogate spirit. I was content to be covered under its loving and watchful shroud.

Mum remained aloof, however.

Even though she had openly revealed our plight to him in the early days, she tended to keep her distance as time went on. To her, Henry was *my* friend - not hers. It was symptomatic of the way her thought processes had evolved over the years since the departure of Martin and my father.

Looking back through my teens, it was an increasing struggle to converse with her on any level in any depth on any subject. She was quietly following her own path with the blinkers on. Henry was avidly following my progress, however. And it was comforting to know that he was subconsciously guiding me along every step I took.

He was really pleased that I had secured myself the supermarket placement at the beginning of the holidays. After sitting the exams in the June, I realized that I had time on my hands and that I was broke. Henry came up with the idea of getting a part time job.

I had bravely followed his advice by simply walking into the shop and asking for the manager. The next stage was to enquire as to any available vacancies. And that was it. I was set on there and then.

I wouldn't have done that without Henry's encouragement. He urged me to be polite yet direct. He had faith in me to pull it off. It was an infallible plan.

The work was enjoyable and altered daily. I effectively worked full time during the summer even though I was only contracted to twenty hours a week. Once John Harrison saw my value and growing enthusiasm, he threw overtime at me left, right and centre. I wasn't complaining.

It got me out of the house and put money in my pocket. He also let me unload lorries on the fork-lift truck. Well, he couldn't do it even though he had a licence. He was always over the limit. It goes without saying that I hadn't passed my fork-lift test, but in John's eyes if I didn't drop any pallets then no one would be any the wiser.

Henry also encouraged me to try and save what I had earned for a rainy day - whilst not forgoing the chance to enjoy a little bit of my weekly wage as well.

He taught me about the fine balance between overspending and over saving. The difference between value and worth.

Much of my money went towards helping the household bills, but I respected Henry's concerns. Another 'first' in my life occurred at sixteen-years-old - opening a bank account and depositing some cash into it!

Henry was also the first person to wish me luck on the morning that I collected my exam results. Mum didn't even give it a mention beforehand. She just offered her usual vacant goodbye before leaving for work and leaving me to lock up.

After Alex, Henry was second to congratulate me when I showed him how well I'd done. I was fulfilling a role for him in his own relatively empty existence. But I didn't resist that one bit. Someone was watching over me. It was a very nice feeling.

He was becoming a role model and a father figure. During that summer, he became one hundred times the man my real father had ever been.

Yet it was during my ridiculous deliberation over asking Alex on a date that Henry really came into his own. As I said, I had talked very briefly to her on results day. We went to the pub just like most others. I recall my emotions twitching uncontrollably - well, even the coolest of cool cats can lose it now and again!

I had made my mind up that I wanted to make Alex my first proper girlfriend. I was secretly hung up on her. But I had no idea what to do about it.

The mission was all set up in my mind for the first two weeks of our initial term as Sixth Formers. She could say *no* if she wanted, but I had convinced myself through blind arrogance that she would say yes.

After several years spent talking with Henry on a regular basis, we felt suitably comfortable in broaching any subject to each other. When I mentioned the fact that I fancied a girl at school he nearly dropped his pipe from between his lips with shock.

'What's brought this bugger on then, our Jamie?' he asked.

It was the first time I had revealed my romantic intentions to anyone. I was comforted by his response. I could tell that he was as surprised as much as he was pleased. But I needed some suggestions on how to tackle the wonderful Alex.

'If you want my advice, and obviously you do, I would be as bold as brass and ask her face to face as soon as you see her. Be honest with her. That way she'll be obliged to be honest back. Don't leave it, Jamie. Don't hesitate any longer or someone else might get in before you.'

Henry's words only served to confirm the sensation that had already blazed through me many a time in the previous fortnight - the need for urgency. I too had nurtured the nagging feeling that I would miss the boat if I waited any longer.

This was another reason that I had taken to Henry. He was very perceptive of me as a person in general. He wasn't often wrong about much. As events would turn out, he would be spot on in this case as well. I thanked him for his opinion and stored it away in my mind ready for use on the first day of the new term.

The days ticked down until it came to crunch time - the return to school. I had hardly slept all night due to the impending duty that lay ahead. It felt strange not having to wear uniform, but casual dress had become an accepted perk of being an A-level student.

So, jeans and t-shirt it was, then.

Mum could tell my mind was not on the job as I struggled to eat breakfast. She didn't bother to scrutinise the reasons, though. She left for work before me as usual. By then, I was used to the responsibility of making sure the house was secure before I went to school.

It was around this time that Mum herself had been struggling to sleep. She said she had been suffering with bad dreams that kept disturbing her in the night. She would wake up sweating, sometimes shouting out.

Her voice had carried through to my room on several occasions during the summer. Not enough to fully wake me, but enough to let me know that her nightmares had become a regular occurrence.

When I asked her about it, she didn't seem overly concerned about the possible cause. She claimed that her mind had become obsessed with a vision. A distant voice. It was calling her for help, yet she felt powerless to do anything. Once she had awakened, the calling would all but vanish.

Yet this clouded image would not leave her conscience.

It was during the night prior to the first day of Sixth Form that Mum's nocturnal shouting became an all-out scream. I'm surprised she didn't wake the whole street.

A piercing, shrill bleat emitted from her bedroom and startled me from my typically intermittent slumber. I jumped out of bed to find her on the landing in her nightdress.

She couldn't remember a thing about her nightmare.

Yet she kept saying that she was needed somewhere, but by whom, where or why was not revealed.

Anyhow, we parted the next morning without further discussion on the matter. My head was full of Alex, anyway. Mum's insomnia was not priority number one, selfish though it sounds to admit it, now.

Predictably, Henry wished me luck as I strode past his front garden on that warm early September morning.

Cockily, I responded with a wink.

'Don't need luck, Henry. Not when you're me!'

I could hear Henry's guffaws as I turned the corner and headed for the main road. It would normally take me about half an hour to amble to school with one or two of the lads. We were never usually in a hurry, as one can imagine.

However, that day I had set a pace for myself. I checked my watch as I entered the school gates. Nineteen minutes door to door! A record! I observed a lot of unfamiliar faces belonging to the new Year Seven pupils. They all looked so small and scared just as I did all those years ago.

I registered myself into the Sixth Form complex and settled down in the common room with a music magazine, which was of course a cover so I could secretly scan everyone entering the vicinity.

Not long now.

# 6
# DISCOVERING ALEX

I couldn't recall ever being so nervous in my life. I certainly couldn't concentrate enough to even pretend to read the NME. I wasn't even into music! Through my sheer masculine bravado, I'll say it was mainly because I was persistently interrupted by the 'hellos' and 'how are yous?' of my fellow returning A-levellers.

But the *real* reason my head was all over the shop was because I was on absolute tenterhooks waiting for *her* to show up. After nearly an hour of lounging around, during which my new form tutor had appeared and then vanished, the thought plagued me that I still not clapped eyes on Alex.

I cautiously asked around, being careful not to arouse suspicions as to my motives for the curiosity.

One very worrying rumour went about that she had opted not to join Sixth Form after all and had gone off to some college or other. I discounted this possibility immediately.

Having finally been acquainted with my tutor group in the period before break and now brimming with despair, I entered the playground to join some mates in kicking a football about.

Then, halfway through our ten-minute match, I saw her.

She walked down the exterior stairway of the Sixth Form complex and offered a little wave. She had spotted me gawking at her straight away. I watched as she placed herself directly in my line of sight on a distant bench behind one of the goals.

Then the child in me took over the reins.

Now, I know this is going to seem immensely hypocritical, but I'm afraid I opted for the sporting lout act. Yes - exactly the kind of egotistical character that only a couple of chapters ago I claimed turned girls *off*.

And as well as ignoring my own advice, I also ignored Henry's. Despite his much better notion to employ the clear cut and direct policy, I went for the one approach that I have already declared resenting others adopting.

My inappropriately loud vocal contribution to the kick-about was matched only by my hapless attempts to repeatedly knock the ball towards her seat. This plan would first entail me scoring a goal - not something I was adept at doing.

Eventually after straining my voice, my groin and potentially my reputation, Alex finally looked up and our eyes met once again.

Her responsive smile was the signal I needed.

'Erm…I'm a bit out of practice, lads. I think I'll take a breather.'

With a united front of disinterested mumbling and likely inner relief, the others continued with the game as I sauntered over to the bench behind the goal. Sitting cross-legged, Alex smiled again as I approached. Her brown wavy locks looked wild, especially as she had opted to complement her hair with a short black skirt and funky red polka dot socks.

It was the first time I had seen her for a fortnight. My heart began to race once again. As if by instinct, she moved her bag to make room for me to sit down.

'How are you, Jamie? I was running a little late this morning! Not a good start to the term!'

Positioning myself next to her I prepared my build-up routine. The immediate priority was to continue the conversation in accordance with what she had just told me. Just to confirm to her that I was actually listening.

'It didn't matter. Our tutor was an hour late as well. Someone told me you weren't coming at all. I got pretty worried for a moment.'

All seemed fine. I was playing it calmly - not being too adventurous. I sympathised with Henry's tactics, but right then didn't seem the time to strike. Alex observed the football game as I studied her elegant profile. She knew full well that I was watching her, and eventually she turned to face me again.

'So, what have you been up to this summer, Mister Andrews? Anything to get me excited?'

'Well…I told you on results day I got a job at the supermarket stacking shelves and un-wrapping pallets. It doesn't pay much but it helps Mum out with the bills.'

I could tell by her expression that she had forgotten the conversation from just over a fortnight ago, but she was impressed by my attitude to helping with the finances at home. Yet she was evidently a little confused also.

'Don't your parents go to work then?' she asked in all innocence.

It would be fair to inform the reader at this point that my family background was not a subject of general knowledge among my peers at school.

Throughout my five years in secondary education, I had pointedly avoided talking about what my history had incurred. Alex wouldn't have had a clue about my previous life, quite simply because up until that time I had deemed it to be nobody's business but mine.

Yet she was asking out of a genuine curiosity, and I felt duty bound to be straight with her. I told her briefly about Martin and my father and the fact that I lived alone with Mum.

Alex seemed rather saddened by the bleak depiction of events, but I didn't want sympathy. I wanted fun and laughter. And I wanted Alex! Not to spend my time dwelling on my miserable past.

She understood and showed her appreciation of my honesty with an apology for supposedly over-stepping the mark.

'Don't be sorry, Alex. And don't ever pity me. I don't ever expect you to do that.'

We continued to watch the football, mutually debating the next acceptable line of dialogue. I followed her example.

'So, enough about me…what did the summer bring you, Alex Lawley?'

Taking a deep breath she smirked and leaned forward, as lights flashed behind those twinkling crystal eyes.

'Well…my family and I went to Cyprus on holiday. It was stiflingly hot! Have you ever been? It's so picturesque and we…'

As I watched her lips move, I suspected she felt uneasy. She suddenly sensed that her wonderful family holiday may not be of remote interest to a poor lad who lives alone with his mum on a council estate. But she didn't know about that until one minute ago, so I didn't take any offence.

'…I'm sorry, Jamie. Tell me to shut my boring mouth.'

I grinned and shook my head. *Now* was the time to strike.

It came so naturally in the end.

'There you go again, apologizing for no reason. Do you have any idea how long I've yearned to be in this situation, Alex?'

She stared into me. She looked beautifully perplexed.

I enlightened her as to how I felt.

'Alex. I've wanted to talk to you for so long. I've watched you for months. I don't want those other girls. I've been attracted to you for a long while…it's only now I've got the guts to admit it to you. I know you think I'm some big-headed prat with all the attention and stuff…but I'd really like a date with you. If it doesn't work, we'll forget it. But you've got to let me try…just once…then we'll know…won't we?'

I could tell she was dumbfounded.

And on observing her initial reaction I kicked myself for employing Henry's two-footed *get in there* approach. She went quiet on me. *Shit.* I thought I'd ballsed it up. I tried to imagine it from her point of view, and it seemed even worse.

One minute we were exchanging pleasantries at school break time.

The next she was sitting next to her potential boyfriend.

However, if I thought she was surprised or possibly repulsed by the idea, her eventual response hit me between the eyes like a bullet. A few seconds of silence preceded her reply.

She sighed heavily as her crystalline eyes looked directly into mine.

'Do you know how many times I've dreamed about *you*, Jay? How many times I wished that you would look at *me* instead of that group of tarts that swarm around you all the time. I used to rush past you to avoid eye contact, secretly hoping that one day you would cast them all aside and ask me out. I'll give you this much…you don't half take your bloody time!'

With that remark we both fell about laughing.

A combination of euphoric delirium and immense relief washed over me. For the best part of a year, she had been covertly observing *me*, whilst I had tried to be careful about revealing my own desire for *her*.

Yet again, the irony surrounded me. I could have had my wishes granted ages ago and didn't even know it! What a pair!

We edged closer together on the bench. Break time was over, but it didn't matter at that precise moment. We didn't even concern ourselves that there may be witnesses to our wonderful union. I took her right hand in my left and moved my face close to hers.

I had overcome the biggest barrier. The difficulty I faced now was putting the final sentiment into words. I fluffed it initially, like all boys, but she got the message alright.

'Does this mean now then that…are we actually…you know…together as a couple, then…?'

She said absolutely nothing. Gently cradling the back of my head, she pulled my lips to hers. And held me firm. It was Heaven on Earth on that football court.

Not a bad fifteen minutes' work, I thought to myself.

My head spun, my legs shook, and the blood surged through my veins.

I'd gone from inept Sixth Form footballer to accomplished love god in one giant break time leap. My chest was almost exploding.

I had been courageous and had emerged from the other side unscathed. As we parted to attend our lessons, I whispered in her ear that she had made me the happiest person in the school.

Nay - in the whole world.

Yet that wasn't my only thought.

One other person encroached into my mind as I entered the bustling classroom floating on air.

Good old Henry.

I couldn't wait to tell him.

How chuffed would *he* be?

# 7
# SOMETHING LIKE NORMAL

Life for me in my first term of A-levels was beginning to resemble the comforting stable format that most of my peers had enjoyed and taken for granted for many years.

My studies were fine, although I suppose I could have put in a little more effort at times. I had chosen English Literature, History, and Art. I was enjoying all three. Alex was more of a mathematician than a creator.

Of the pair of us, I deemed myself to be the more stylish half of our union. In allowing me such a jibe, Alex returned volley by claiming to be the intellectual contributor to the relationship.

I couldn't argue with that.

I fell in deeply love with her very quickly. I've got no qualms admitting it. It soon became common knowledge at school that we were dating, and it seemed we started a bit of a trend in the Sixth Form block. Several other couples emerged from the woodwork over a period of weeks. As with all A-level groups, our social lives were becoming a distinct priority over our schoolwork.

We would invariably meet up during afternoon free periods in the pub opposite the school grounds. It was called the Tiger Inn. It had certainly seen its fair share of wild animals - particularly at throwing out time! But as I intimated earlier, the landlord loved us being in the place. I felt part of a great camaraderie.

Alex was not an extrovert in any way, but she instantly blossomed in the company of others. Literally like a flower opening once she sensed genuine interest in her from others. She enchanted the group with her humorous tales about being an infant and her childhood experiences, which in turn encouraged others to reveal their own embarrassing moments from the dim and distant past.

Needless to say, I remained resolutely silent in my earnest appreciation of these annals. And the fact that I had no pleasurable memories from growing up that warranted sharing in public.

Yet it was strangely gratifying to listen to fellow Sixth Formers' stories. I was envious of their obviously loving family backgrounds. All of them different, yet all carried the themes of intimacy with parents and fondness of their formative years. One recurring subject that always amused the group was of how cruel they thought they all were to their little brothers and sisters.

I could only try and empathise. I had nothing to contribute to the think tank. Alex didn't pressure me, and the others picked up on her protective vibe.

She understood me perfectly.

She *always* understood.

Those first few weeks were blissful. Both of us were sixteen-years-old, full of energy and vigour. We wanted to do so much together and talked eagerly of aims and ambitions.

I admired Alex because she was her own person with her own identity. I had noticed it straight away even way back in Years Eight and Nine. She didn't conform to what others expected of her.

She was in sole charge of her own destiny.

Almost the opposite scenario to my own.

Although the great majority of our time spent together centred around school, we still did the things that all young couples do when they can't bear to be apart. Luckily, we had money to spend due to her generous parents and my job at Savers.

We had only been an item for two months when she dropped the first - albeit predictable - bombshell.

Alex told me she would like to meet my mother.

I had purposely steered clear of that particular avenue. But it was inevitable that Alex's interest in my family would grow. And it was only fair that if she was keen to learn about my history, then I should indulge her.

It's called trust, I think.

By that point she knew most of what I could remember about Martin and my father. Now she wanted to meet the woman who had made it all possible.

For most teenage lads, having their mother meet their first girlfriend is perhaps not the most daunting of life's tasks but it does carry that vibe of awkwardness. Ultimately though, the hinging factor is that they are usually proud to show off their chick to their parents at the first chance. I was certainly proud to be Alex's boyfriend.

And anyway, the problem wasn't with Alex in any way shape or form.

The problem was with Mum.

Work was providing her only source of regular contact with the outside world.

Darker nights had crept in, and she had seemingly resigned herself to another long, lonely Winter at Lodge Close.

I had mentioned once or twice that she ought to try and make an effort if Alex should want to come around for an evening. It was only natural for a son to want his girlfriend and his mother to get along with one another, wasn't it?

In my euphoria of the previous weeks, I had not paid so much attention to Mum. I hadn't really noticed how much weight she had lost. She wasn't eating regular meals. Nor was she sleeping. She was dog-tired and working from dawn until dusk.

One morning - it could have been late October or early November - at the breakfast table, she made a statement that would influence the rest of my life, although I was relatively unaware of the implications at the time. I observed her pallid features and sunken cheeks.

Now was my opportunity to ask her what was wrong.

She was emotionally and physically deteriorating before my eyes.

At this point, the reader must understand that Mum was never the most vibrant of personalities for obvious reasons. Her condition before now would have been best described as barely stable. Somewhere along the line in the previous months, the wheels had well and truly come off.

I hadn't really seen the signs until they hit me smack in the face across the box of cornflakes that day.

I asked her if she had considered going to see a doctor. She couldn't keep this pace up. She would struggle to be around at Christmas if she didn't recognise the origin of her stress. Her gaze was centred on the tabletop. Her reply was tinged with deep-rooted fear. The cause of her anxiety was duly announced, albeit cryptically at first.

'Find someone to help him, Jamie.'

I totally sympathise with your anticipated response, dear reader. An incomprehensible answer, which in no way allayed my concerns about her health. I pressed her to expand on her thoughts.

'What are you talking about? *Who* needs help, Mum?'

She looked me directly in the eye. It sent shivers down my spine as the word passed clearly from her lips and registered with my brain.

It was a name that I had not heard her say with any strand of emotion for several years.

'Martin.'

I searched frantically for some meaning to attach to the situation.

Why would she mention him? She wanted nothing to do with Martin, did she? She had turned the final page of that chapter long ago. I had even been forbidden from mentioning it.

I continued to probe Mum. She hadn't given me enough to go on. My brother's name wasn't adequate. I needed more of her thoughts. I was becoming seriously concerned for her state of mind.

She never seemed to go to bed. I never even caught her cat napping on the sofa. I had witnessed her opening a full bottle of Scotch - the small size, mind - just before midnight on more than one occasion. I would come down the following morning to find the empty bottle in the bin and a note scrawled on a piece of paper for me.

The message always read the same:

*Gone to work, love. See you 2nite x*

How she didn't get sent straight home again for being drunk on the job I'll never know. She must have had a bloody lenient boss.

My concerns had begun forcing me to check on her during the middle of the night to see that she had come upstairs to bed. She was never there. I would always find her downstairs, slumped in the armchair in a drunken stupor.

Back across the breakfast table I continued to scrutinise.

'Why don't you sleep anymore, Mum?'

Her gaze moved slowly upward from the unused cereal bowl on the table and rested on me once more.

'I'm too scared to sleep. If I close my eyes, I see it clearly. It's too much.'

With that statement Mum rose from the table and went to dress for work. She said nothing more about it. The following day was when Alex first enquired about the chance to meet her. I felt a dual sensation about Mum at this time.

Firstly, serious worries about her changing personality and emerging lack of self-worth. Perhaps she had always been like it. But being sixteen years of age and seeing your own Mum totally adrift from reality is not pleasant. I don't expect you to understand.

Just take my word for it.

It's terrifying.

Yet the secondary sensation was one of which I can only describe as embarrassment. My Mum was like an alien at that time. It was hard enough for *me* to get through to her just passing the time of day. What chance did anyone *else* have? I didn't really want Alex seeing Mum like that.

My motives were purely selfish, of course. If Alex suspected for one minute that I had originated from a family of nutcases, then she would have been fully entitled to give me the elbow.

The fact that I was beginning to believe Mum was cracking up was not something I felt happy to share. Not even with Alex.

However, it was not fair to keep Alex totally in the dark about my life at home. I had far too much respect for her and beheld ultimate faith in her powers of discretion to even consider keeping it a secret for long. We discussed the situation one evening after school as we walked to her house.

I can recall the scene as though it was yesterday.

Autumn was in full swing.

Seasonal change was in evidence as we ambled through the local rec - East Park - swishing red and brown leaves with our shoes. Linking her arm in mine, I gave a much-deliberated response to her perfectly normal wish to meet Mum.

'She's not well, Ally. She hasn't been for some time. It's not nice to look at. It's not you meeting her that I have an issue with. It's Mum's unpredictable temperament. And just her general demeanour. I'm worried for her. It may not be safe for you to be involved with her just yet.'

As always, Alex listened to my every word. She considered my point of view as the leaves continued to crunch underfoot and a chill wind danced around our ears.

Finally, she spoke.

'What is she afraid of, Jay? Has she said what it is that is scaring her?'

I thought carefully about mentioning my mother's reasoning. It would sound ludicrous to her, but again, it was the truth that Alex deserved to hear.

'It's my brother, Martin. She claims that he needs help. She's had loads of bad dreams about it recently. But we've had no contact with him or my father for nearly seven years, Ally. None of it makes any sense. So far as I was concerned, I was encouraged to forget the first half of my life. Now Mum has done a U-turn on me.'

It was perfectly understandable that Alex did not fully grasp the situation.

Quite naturally, it was not a domestic scenario that she was regularly acquainted with. Crazed parents and brothers that vanish and then cry for help via nightmares! Incredibly odd, to say the very least.

But I was certain of one thing. Whatever response Alex offered, I knew her reaction would be at least earnest and genuine even if a little baffled. I didn't mind. The point was that she sympathised with my concerns and offered the advice that my own mind had already deemed unavoidable.

'Get her some help, Jay. Don't sit watching the problem grow. Help her to help herself. For your sake and hers.'

I was pleased that I had been able to speak honestly with Alex about things. She was absolutely right. Of course, she was. I couldn't shake off the sinister implication that if I did nothing then Mum would somehow find herself too far gone to be assisted.

Relief in sharing the burden was outweighed by the harsh knowledge that Mum's mysterious condition was likely to get worse with time, not better.

The following day I had a free period and opted to go home early to catch up on some assignment or other. I passed Henry on Glenfield Avenue and was met with one hundred and one questions about Alex. I promised him that I would bring her round to meet him soon. I intended to keep the promise as well.

I had been through the front door for less than five minutes when the telephone rang. It made me jump a little, as bleating phones often tend to do in silent houses. I noticed the kitchen clock reading five past two. I thought it a strange time for anybody to ring, particularly as there was never usually anyone at home during the day.

Tentatively, I lifted the receiver.

'Hello?'

The caller's voice was unknown to me.

'Hello, Liz? Is that Liz Andrews house? It's Steve. Steve from Mason's Packaging. Just wondering why you aren't at work, love. Hello? Are you there? Are you okay?'

Immediately I began to panic.

If Mum wasn't there, then where the hell *was* she?

I thought quickly on my feet to appease the caller.

'Hello. Steve. Thanks for calling. This is her son, Jamie. Mum's not here, either. I'll find her and get her to ring you back, okay?'

The caller did not respond for a few contemplative moments.

Then came the warning.

'Oh, hi Jamie. This is her foreman, Steve Vickers. Tell her to come and see me as soon as possible. please. And tell her she's on thin ice with the gaffer.'

I didn't fully understand and asked for him to explain.

'Why, Steve. What's Mum done?'

'It's what she *hasn't* done, Jamie. Your Mam's not put a full week in since the middle of summer. I don't know what the matter is, but I've spent enough time trying to talk sense into her. I can't cover her back forever, son. Tell her to get to get back to work tomorrow or I can't have any control on how things go. Okay? Goodbye.'

Her job was obviously in jeopardy due to bad timekeeping, but where she could have been on these days off was a total mystery.

It made me realize at that moment just how little I knew about Mum's affairs.

I had seen her every single day for sixteen and a half years, yet now I was becoming engulfed in the sensation that my mother was in effect a stranger in many ways.

How could I have known she was skipping work? She never *talked* about anything.

How was I supposed to know important things about her if estrangement had become the basis of our entire relationship?

Later that night I was in bed when the front door opened and in she walked. Or should I say staggered. Mum was freezing cold, bedraggled, and pissed out of her face.

Now I am sure that you as the reader are totally perplexed as to why I didn't go screaming around the neighbourhood looking for her at an earlier stage, or at very least called the police.

The honest answer being - nor do I.

It wasn't a matter of not caring about her. More a case of having a different instinct to the majority. Somehow, I knew she would come home, albeit the worse for wear. It never entered my seemingly tiny mind that she would be in distress or in need of assistance. Mum just wasn't that sort of woman. She certainly wouldn't appreciate becoming the centre of a missing persons chase.

She looked at me forlornly as I watched her stumble upstairs toward me. Now wasn't the right time to talk, either.

Yet the words she eventually spoke chilled me to the bone and left me restless all night. As she passed me on the landing, Mum kicked off her shoes and threw down her coat as she opened her bedroom door.

Before entering, she turned to me in the semi-darkness. Even in the half-light I could see her eyes were red and raw. She had evidently been upset at some point earlier. In the murk of night, she looked more fatigued than ever.

'I couldn't find him, today. I couldn't…find him.'

Before I had chance to answer, she slammed the door behind her and presumably collapsed onto the bed.

Yet again she had left me in a state of bewilderment. Who had she been looking for? Why was she missing work? What the hell was wrong with Mum?

I felt I had only just drifted into sleep when I heard the scream. It tore into my conscience and roused me in an instant.

I bounded out of bed and threw open Mum's door.

She was out of her own bed, crouching like a baby under the windowsill. Her wailing was unrestrained. It was a sound of utter despair, grief, and pain, all combined into one outpouring that seemed to have taken a complete physical hold on her.

I switched on the bedroom light and went to pick her up.

Untold sufferance was etched into the face that looked back at me.

The weeping eventually subsided as I held her in my arms.

My mind was made up.

Mum needed serious help.

I had sat and watched and done nothing for too long.

Just as Alex had warned me *not* to.

Now it was time to act.

I had to find some answers, and quickly.

# 8
# TAKING INITIATIVES

I had slept next to Mum for the remainder of the night. To be honest, it was for fear of her own safety that I dare not leave her alone. In addition, it was surprisingly comforting for me to have her close by. I felt like a small child who was both protector and protected.

Not a sensation I was readily accustomed to from years gone by.

As usual we rose for breakfast at around six. Normally she would be ready to leave the house for a quarter to eight, but not this morning. She was hesitant. It was as though she knew that she would be in for a hard time at work.

My main concern was not her attendance at Mason's. I was far more curious as to her whereabouts the previous day. And all the other days when I had wrongly presumed she had been at work but instead she had decided to go AWOL.

'I just went looking, Jamie. Looking for clues.'

That was her answer. Straight and simple. But for me, it wasn't sufficient. I told her about the previous day's phone call from her foreman. She shrugged her shoulders and explained to me that she would go and sort it out. I could not get the images from the previous night from my mind. Her tears. Her search for this elusive source of torment.

I pressed for answers that I wasn't sure I really wanted to hear.

'Mum, what are you looking for? Who is it that keeps appearing in your dreams?'

She sat in her pink dressing gown with her hands clasped in her lap. I felt a sudden sense of déjà vu. I recognized that it was highly unlikely that she would produce a reply that I would find understandable or acceptable.

This time, she did not look me in the eyes when she spoke. Evidently, she also knew that I was becoming frustrated with her conduct over the past month. It was a cross that I could only bear for a finite amount of time.

'It's Martin. He needs me.'

With that, I lost my temper.

'Mum! Martin is not with us anymore! You don't know where he is, do you? How can you begin to go looking for him? You're obsessed with the past! These ghosts are trying to finish you off, Mum! And from what I can see, they're succeeding rapidly!'

She glanced upward.

Her face showed little emotion for such an emotive subject.

'I see lights, Jamie. Coloured lights. He's striving for them...to reach them.'

Again, my patience was being tested.

'Right, that's it! I'm getting you to a doctor. You need help, Mum. Can't you see you're having delusions? You are worn out and your mind is fraying with fatigue. And the drinking must stop. It's affected every part of you. And now it's affecting me. I'm sick of it. I can't even bring my bloody girlfriend round to meet you!'

Mum didn't flinch as I stormed from the kitchen and into the hallway. I grabbed the notebook from next to the phone and scanned the time on the wall clock to confirm that the local surgery would be open in an hour.

It would prove to be a long sixty minutes.

*****

The formalities ensued in a short conversation which ended with me slamming the receiver down and returning to the inert form of my mother sitting slumped in the dining chair.

'Tomorrow morning at ten-thirty. Okay?'

Now at last she began to respond with a modicum of rationale, even though I was well past the point of listening to her claims.

'I'm not going to the doctors. There's nothing wrong with me!'

'Well, I don't believe you, Mum! And if the doctor tells me there's nothing wrong with you then I won't believe him, *either*! You're going, and that's that!'

I left her to dwell on the prospect as I ran upstairs to change for school. I needed a shower but couldn't be bothered. I didn't even kiss her goodbye for the first time in ages. Walking out into the cold November air quickly sharpened my senses and unfortunately made me question my own instincts.

Was it right to force her to go and see a professional? Was my perception of her behaviour exaggerated? I was now very confused.

I couldn't wait to see Alex. She'd understand my decision. Alex would make it all seem so simple.

With double English out of the way I ventured outside at break time.

The vibrant atmosphere of the Sixth Form common room was a little too stifling. I wanted to feel the tingling of the frost-laden air on my face. I stood on the exterior balcony listening to the distant shrieks of laughter from the playground below, as the throng of excited pupils grew steadily larger.

I sensed a presence behind me.

Alex moved close and wrapped her arms around my waist.

'Hello, you. How's life?' she whispered.

I didn't answer right away. I continued to stare into the grey skies that met the nearby rooftops and the distant horizon. Rude maybe, but under such wonderful scrutiny I was on the verge of upset. Now was not the time or place for pleasantries.

But I answered her eventually.

'How's my life? Well, apart from you, Ally, it's a bit shit just now. I had a right night with Mum. I think she's lost the plot. I'm taking her to the doctor tomorrow. At the very least he can give her something to knock her out at night.'

I finally turned to face Alex and kissed her on the lips. I could see the thoughts racing around her amazing brain, yet she offered no initial response to my plan. Well, it was originally *her* plan, not mine.

I opted to change the subject.

'Do you fancy going out tonight, Ally? Just for a drink? Or to eat if you want? I can walk you home after. No problem.'

I could tell that Alex was still contemplating the issues surrounding my mother. She wasn't ready to divert her thoughts to a possible pizza supper. I wanted her opinion, yet I felt that she probably ought not to be fully involved in - what was, after all - *my* problem.

Naturally, she looked concerned for me. I didn't want her to be worried about something she couldn't remedy. It brought out the frown lines on her forehead.

However, Alex's sense of perspective had reliably allowed her to consider her next statement carefully.

There was no strand of flippancy when she spoke.

I loved to watch her mouth when she did so.

'Jay…what if your mum *isn't* going mad?'

I heard the words and let them descend slowly into my mind.

However, I didn't fully understand the motive for the question.

'What…you mean if someone *was* calling for help in her dreams? Don't be ridiculous, Ally.'

Alex released her embrace and stood back a pace.

Her expression was one of commanding sincerity.

'You trust my opinion, don't you, Jay?'

The answer to that question needed little forethought.

'I trust you with my life, Ally. But all this crap Mum keeps churning about my brother is doing my fucking head in. It's rubbish!'

Alex remained unmoved and slowly shook her head.

'Yes, I can see your struggle. But that's what I'm pointing out. What if it's *not* rubbish? What if your mum *is* seeing your brother? You're not able to say either way, are you? You're just dismissing her as going cuckoo. It isn't fair on her. She's got no earthly reason to make any of this up as far as I can see.'

For the first time ever, I could feel myself getting annoyed with Alex. Perhaps it was *me* that was cracking up and everyone else was perfectly sane. It felt like it at that precise moment.

Alex fortunately interrupted my evolving frustration.

'What happened last night, Jay?'

We continued to speak on the balcony. I relayed the events of yesterday. Mum's vanishing act; the call from Mason's; Mum coming back drunk; the scream; the tears. It all came horribly back into view. Like a phantom that I thought I'd vanquished.

'If truth be known, Ally, I'm scared shitless about what's going on inside Mum's head. It's all come out of the blue since the summer. I thought she was happy. Either she's going to see a doctor about *her* sanity, or I am about *mine*!'

We smiled and kissed again as my anger subsided.

I held her close again as she whispered in my ear.

'Don't automatically disbelieve her, Jay. Give her all your love. God knows, she deserves it. Did you ever consider the possibility that she maybe more scared than you are?'

The bell to signify the end of break resonated around the walls of the outbuilding. Time to go to lessons.

We parted with a pledge to speak again at home time.

I collected my bag and walked through the school corridors oblivious to the frantic activity around me.

Perhaps Alex was right.

Maybe I was being too hard on Mum.

It surely wasn't her wish to be subjected to such torment.

Then the vision re-entered my head of seeing her in a crumpled, weeping mess at the side of her bed the previous night.

Hopefully the doctor would make some logical judgement on it all.

*****

The end of the school day was enshrouded in near darkness as I approached the front gates where Alex was waiting. She looked very stylish in her large woollen hat, fluffy scarf and long, black coat. Dressed for the weather, Henry would call it. Him and the bloody weather!

Then it occurred to me. I had made a promise to old Henry.

It also occurred to me that I'd better keep it.

I kissed Alex on the cheek and took her hand for the walk home. Her smile instantly lit up the grey early evening. We ambled along the canal that flanked the main road. The shadow of sycamore trees was intermittently lit by the steadily increasing amber glow of the streetlamps.

'So, Mister Jamie Andrews, love of my life…how was the *rest* of your day?'

I liked it when she called me that. It made me feel totally invulnerable. I was untouchable so long as Alex was around.

'Oh fine. Did you still want to meet for that drink later?'

'Well, I thought it is a little cold to be wandering about. Is it okay if I say I've got to wash my hair tonight?'

I chuckled and wrapped my arm around her. I was happy again.

She was always able to make me forget the bad stuff.

'Okay, but there's someone I want you to meet before I walk you home. It's only a short detour.'

*****

Standing at the front door of number thirty-two, Glenfield Avenue, Alex and I waited in the glow of the porch light for Henry to answer. Finally, we saw movement through the porthole of frosted glass. Then we heard a scuffling sound from the other side of the door, which was followed by the click of the latch.

A curious face peered over spectacles through the chained gap. Henry's eyes widened as he recognised the good-looking young lad and his very attractive girlfriend.

'Ayup, it's our Jamie! Blimey, you look frozen stiff! Just a minute, lad!'

Henry released the door, and we were both invited into the warm domain of the hallway.

I could not resist the chance to begin the banter.

'You do the right thing, keeping that security chain on at night, Henry. Never know *who* might be dropping by!'

I winked at Alex, expecting a cutting reply from my old friend which was duly delivered with the timing of a pro as he shut the front door behind us.

'Yes, well you never know if any of them Lodge Close scumbags are passing. Can't stand 'em. Well, *most* of 'em, anyway!'

Laughter ensued as Henry offered me an embrace.

He then looked Alex up and down with a grin that the Cheshire Cat would have been proud of.

'Henry, this is Alex. Alex, meet Henry. Second in line only to you, he's my best friend.'

Alex flashed that wonderful smile that would melt the hardest of hearts. The strangers shook hands. Henry could not take his eyes off her. Had he been forty years younger I might have felt threatened. As it was, I was inflated that two people who meant so much to me had finally crossed paths.

'Your hands are cold. Miss. I'll put the kettle on unless you both fancy something stronger to warm yourselves up?'

'Coffee's fine thanks, Henry.' Alex beamed as she removed her coat.

Within minutes, Henry and Alex were totally at ease in each other's company. The fleeting thought developed. How odd it was that we were in his house, when my own home was only in the next street. But I could not take her there?

Not yet anyway.

The three of us enjoyed a most pleasant hour talking about school, love, football…and yes…the weather.

Inevitably, my own domestic situation reared its ugly head. I was not looking forward to talking about Mum and her troubles, but secretly I wanted Henry's opinion on her dilemma.

'Funny things, dreams. Some say they are predictive. Some say they are an actual representation of reality. Some say that it's the mind playing tricks with its own history. Who knows?'

Alex and I listened intently to Henry's verdict as he perched in his fireside chair and fiddled with his pipe.

We dared not interrupt as he continued.

'But don't fall into the trap of telling your mum she's losing it, our Jamie. If you keep telling her that then she'll start to believe it *herself*. Then, who knows what she'll do? Sort her out a prescription tomorrow and get her back to work. It's lack of sleep that's causing her to be muddled. She'll be fine, lad. Take my word for it. But don't dismiss her claims. They are founded somewhere in her head.'

I looked over at Alex who offered me a knowing smile. She didn't need to say *I told you so.* I could feel it being telepathically transported. I needed another drink and entered the kitchen to re-boil the kettle.

Henry and Alex continued the discussion without me. Both were sensitive to my position and were careful to avoid treating the subject as a trivial matter.

I strained to hear what was being said as the kettle worked its wonders. Another half-hour was pleasantly passed before I decided to take Alex home.

We wrapped ourselves up for the walk back to her house. She kissed Henry on the cheek, and I shook him by the hand with a word of appreciation.

'Thanks for your time, Henry. I'm glad I spoke to you.'

Henry's gaze fell once again to Alex who gleamed like an angel in the porchlight.

'I'll be here for you so long as you need me, our Jamie. I'm on your side, son. Look after your mum. She needs you to by the sound of things.'

Alex and I moved beyond the porch to be greeted by a seasonally sudden drop in temperature, our breathing instantly forming clouds of frosted vapour.

Henry hadn't quite finished with his orders.

'By the way, Alex. A delight to have met you. Jamie…look after this lovely lady of yours. She's on your side as well. You've picked a good 'un there. Be mindful of the fact. Look forward to seeing you both again. Goodnight.'

It was only on leaving Henry's that she revealed a sliver of the sentiment he had openly expressed to Alex.

We strode briskly in the freezing air and were at the front gate of Alex's parents' house in a matter of twenty minutes.

She turned to face me. I thought it might be to offer a kiss.

'Thanks for taking me to see Henry. He's a lovely man. He's very fond of you as well, Jay. He looks on you as his own son, doesn't he?'

I nodded in agreement. I was tired and wanted to get to bed, even though it was still only half past six. I resigned myself to the impending ritual of returning home.

'Oh well, I'd better go and see who Mum's been trying to find today.'

With that comment despatched, a disapproving Alex raised a pointed forefinger and addressed me sternly.

'Oy! None of that, Jamie Andrews! Your mum needs *you*, not your cynicism! You and I will have words if it continues!'

I smiled and drew her closer as she giggled lovingly.

'I know, Ally. I know, Come here.'

We kissed for what seems like minutes on end. It probably was. I immersed myself in her warmth and the fragrance of her perfume. I didn't want to leave her at that point. I wanted to stay with her all night long.

But I couldn't, and so I didn't.

Our moment of tenderness was spoiled by the opening of her front door and a silhouette with a deep voice.

'Alexandra, are you coming in? You'll catch your death out here!'

Alex responded in the affirmative and turned back to me.

'Sounds like Dad's in a mood. Nice change. I'd better go.'

'Okay, I'll meet your parents next time, being as you've met Henry.'

'It's a deal.'

Our lips met for the final time that evening.

On parting, Alex uttered the phrase that is often used, yet so rarely understood.

I had gotten as far as the pavement across the road when she caught my attention with a short whistle and a loud whisper.

'Oy!'

I turned and smiled at her.

'What's up?'

I couldn't quite see the look on her face when she spoke, but it was the first time I could recall that anybody had said those words to me in my life.

'I think I love you, Jamie Andrews.'

# 9
# AN APPOINTMENT

The casual observer should feel obliged to extend a degree of sympathy to any sixteen-year-old son who has to accompany his mother to the doctor's surgery just to ensure she gets there.

Thankfully, Mum was at home when I returned from taking Alex to her door the night before. She had also experienced a relatively restful night. However, her bad dreams did not occur every night. They would no doubt be back with a vengeance soon enough.

The apparent problem she had with the subject of my brother was seemingly taking a respite, though I never believed for a moment that it had miraculously vanished.

Alex's parting words the previous evening were of infinite satisfaction. They provided a most welcome distraction from the impending appointment with Doctor Suitor. As I sat nervously next to my mother in the waiting room, I suddenly realized that I wished Alex was there with me, too. It was probably better that she wasn't, but I wanted her there all the same.

I was also surprised that Mum came to the surgery with little form of protestation. She had changed her tune from twenty-four hours ago. It was as though I was being appeased. I suspected that she may have come only to get an all clear from the GP and go home quietly to resume her insanity. Yet deep down she knew that I was totally justified in making her attend that day.

As she had proved with her job, she didn't have the courage or the discipline to come by herself, that was for sure.

One day I hoped, she might even thank me for making the appointment.

I had rarely been ill in my life. So, it was very unnerving having to sit amongst all those sick people. I mean, who knows what I could have contracted in that fifteen-minute timeslot? I wasn't happy to be there in the first place. A complementary ailment on departure was not something I wanted to take back home with me.

A call from across the room broke my concentration on the matter.

'Elizabeth Andrews, please.'

The nurse beckoned us through with a sympathetic smile.

I ushered Mum to her feet and followed her down the corridor.

I could feel the eyes of twenty other patients burning into me, as if to say - *what does he think he's doing?* If they'd have asked me there and then, I can honestly say that I didn't have the slightest idea.

I could smell the consultation room from a short distance. A mix of chemical cleanliness and sour ointment. Very similar to the aroma found in a dentist's foyer, but without the smoky garland created by burning teeth being filled.

Mum sat in the chair.

The doctor was evidently surprised to see that his patient had an accomplice.

'Hello Mrs. Andrews…'

He then looked at me with more than a hint of suspicion in his tone.

'…and you are...?'

I wasn't about to be involved in a confrontation over wanting to be in the room with my own mother. I hoped that my explanation would suffice to allay any disapproval the doctor may have had with my presence.

'Jamie Andrews…I'm her son…I made the appointment on Mum's behalf yesterday. I hope you'll allow me to remain with her. She needs help, but…she won't bring herself to admit it.'

The thin-featured doctor peered over his spectacles as if to confirm my story with an inspection of its source. He paused for a moment to deliberate on the situation. He wrote something down as he spoke.

'Well…as you may presume it is not my policy to allow consultations to be witnessed by a third party, but I accept your motive and I have no immediate concerns if that is what you wish. Now, what seems to be the trouble, Mrs. Andrews?'

I thought Mum would clam up at this point. Yet it has never ceased to amaze me to this day how eloquently and concisely Mum put her case across. I didn't have to say a single word.

After days of denying there could be a need to even see a doctor, there she was depicting her symptoms with sterling accuracy before making an all-out plea for his assistance.

She briefly included our family background, all possible causes for her state of mind and lack of physical wellbeing. I don't think she omitted any important factors.

She made no obvious effort to conceal anything of relevance. I didn't have to prompt her to mention any vital factor.

Having proceeded to make all necessary physical examinations, the doctor listened intently to her recollections of the nightmares, the intake of booze and the recent insomnia.

And then there was her repeated notion that she was being tormented by the spirit of her eldest son. In all, the doctor asked the pertinent questions and digested her answers studiously. The session lasted for over half an hour before the initial diagnosis was revealed.

'Well, I'm not a psychoanalyst unfortunately Mrs. Andrews, but I can say this regarding your physical status. Your lack of sleep, intake of alcohol and subsequent poor diet provide a potent and damaging combination. Your body is running on empty. I believe your mind is overcompensating for a lack of material sustenance.'

I listened intently to his every word. The words of a professional, no less! Not to be discounted at any risk.

'That is why you cannot sleep. Your body is not able to function normally. It isn't digesting any food. It will be in a constant chemical resurgence due to the alcohol. In other words, your body is craving for normal everyday usage. Eat, work and sleep. It's a pattern that, if seriously interrupted, can take months to reset.'

The doctor glanced over his gold-rimmed spectacles once again and addressed me with his immediate suggestion.

'Mister Andrews, I am going to prescribe a mild sedative for your mother to be taken at night before she goes to bed. It will help her sleep and that in turn will restore her energy levels for the day ahead. In time, her natural body clock will resume. She won't feel as tired during the day because she *will* be sleeping - I guarantee it! Her normal appetite should also return if she's back at work and burning energy. Do either of you have any questions?'

Mum and I looked at each other.

Grossly naive of the pair of us, but Mum and I had expected the GP to go some way in trying fathom out her night visions. Of course, he wasn't there for that. He was a man of medicine - not mystery.

It all seemed somewhat unsatisfactory at the time. With hindsight, I wish I'd adhered to my instincts. As it was, we took the prescription and left the surgery. The nagging feeling in my mind remained that there was something more serious behind Mum's change in condition beside lack of sleep and getting drunk every night. Still, the doctor didn't appear overly concerned, so who was I to question his conclusions?

The cold November air cut through us like a knife as we emerged from the surgery. Even in daylight, the twinkling lights of the High Street were indicative that Christmas was just around the corner.

Thankfully, Mum didn't seem overly objectionable to being treated as some child who needed to be told what was best for her.

I just wanted her fit and well again. Something she needed assistance with on a daily basis. She also needed to get back to work as soon as possible.

I suggested that we take a little detour and looked for ideas for a Christmas present for Alex. It seemed a strange plan of action at that moment, considering that Mum hadn't even met her. Yet she seemed agreeable to explore the smattering of jewellery and craft shops that tempted us with their varying illuminated window displays. Mum was even smiling when she saw how eager I was to pick something nice for Alex.

Then she came forward with her weirdest statement yet.

It was even more disconcerting than the claims about looking for Martin.

I was surprised to find something that Alex would truly like. A pair of silver earrings encrusted with a single crystal each. They reminded me of her eyes, and I couldn't resist buying them there and then. Mum watched intently as I purchased the jewellery, and she followed me out of the shop adorning the widest of grins.

I turned to her amid a genuine wave of curiosity.

She looked me in the eye and the smile never faded.

Her simple comment initially pleased me.

'I hope Alex likes the earrings. You do love her don't you, Jamie?'

It was a relief to talk to Mum about the nice things in life for once.

And a direct question deserved a direct answer.

'Yes, Mum. I do love her. She wants to meet you.'

Then the tone turned remarkably, unexpectedly sinister as we stood shivering.

'I hope she loves you too, Jamie…because you'll need her when I'm gone.'

As I said, my initial reaction was almost one of gratification that Mum finally seemed happy about something.

I paid little heed to her words when she said them.

Then over a period of days, her remarks began to trouble me.

I began to realise that Mum wasn't simply making a wishful gesture. She was — albeit vaguely - informing me of the future. It was as though she had a plan all set in her mind. The further realization gradually dawned that the appointment with Doctor Suitor had been a fruitless waste of time.

Unfortunately, I didn't realize my folly until it was way too late.

The look in her eye was one of wild abandon. Both the doctor and I had missed the signals. There was nothing wrong with Mum that any amount of medicine could rectify. It was her mind that was well and truly screwed up. The charade in the surgery was simply an act of compliance on her part.

She wanted me to be satisfied in my mission to make things right. She loved me enough to want me to stop worrying and she had said the right things at the right time. She had acted brilliantly. Even the professional had been suckered.

I kick myself to this day. I wish I'd have known all of this at the time. As per usual in my life, I was generally the last to know the truth, and only then because I bothered to conjure the effort to discover it for myself.

Mum and I went home after our little shopping excursion, and we ate lunch together before settling in front of the television. Alex phoned to see if I wanted to go to meet her parents. I declined. That evening, I opted to stay with Mum. I promised Alex that we would both go to see her mother and father straight from school tomorrow.

She understood. Alex always understood.

That night, Mum took her medication as prescribed. I truly believe that she hardly slept a wink. I checked on her every couple of hours, which inevitably took its toll on my own rest. I was certain it was around three-thirty in the morning when I last recalled checking my watch and finally drifted into slumber.

The respite from acting as her minder was short-lived.

*****

The screams coming from Mum's bedroom were as though generated from hell itself. Blood-curdling wasn't the phrase.

They were deafening and ludicrously frightening.

Entering her bedroom, I was terrified at what I discovered.

Mum was standing on the bed and wailing at her loudest pitch.

In between hysterically scratching at the wall behind the headboard, she pointed toward me as I stood silhouetted in the doorway.

Having just woken, my vision was blurred so I had to squint into the murk to find the light switch.

As the room lit up, I could see that Mum's eyes were as wide and white as saucers. The life had appeared to have drained from them, yet she was making the oddest, jerky movements with her arms.

I begged her to quieten down and be calm, but to no avail. I had to shout to hear my own voice. Walking over to the bed, I offered my hand to help her down.

She ignored the gesture and continued to scream whilst pointing toward me.

Then came the moment that I found disturbing enough at the time, yet now, much later, it makes me turn cold when I bring it to mind.

I stared at my mother, as her face contorted with terror.

She seemed to be reaching out to me, as though I was somehow beyond her grasp.

I remember thinking at that moment that the doctor was a bloody charlatan.

Then, as I stared intently at her features, I slowly recognized a face that had begun to replace hers.

I shut my eyes tightly before deciding to look again.

I wanted desperately to help her as she squirmed in her prison of pain.

Then slowly, I realized to my horror that I wasn't looking at my mother at all.

Her expression had adopted childish features that I remembered on last seeing from my bedroom window years earlier.

It wasn't Mum that was in the room yelping her head off for the whole world to hear.

It was her eldest son.

I was looking at my own brother.

I was looking at Martin.

*****

I was awakened by my own shout. A howl of urgent distress that resonated throughout the house. My eyes flicked open. I bolted upright in bed. Sweat poured from my body as I tried to ascertain shapes in the darkness.

The next instance Mum pushed the bedroom door open and flicked on the light.

'You alright, love? You've been making a hell of a noise during the night!'

Perplexed and perspiring, I looked up at my mother.

I could not distinguish events of the previous hours.

I asked her what she had been doing standing on her bed.

Mum told me that it was *me* who had been dreaming.

She claimed to have had her best night's sleep for an age. She also declared that the medication seemed to have done the trick.

'I'm glad we went to the doctors, Jamie. I feel a lot better, already.'

I was drowsy and too tired to make any sense of what she was saying.

'I'm alright, Mum. Sorry for waking you. It was just a bad nightmare.'

'Try and grab another hour's kip, Jamie. See you in the morning, love."

Shutting the door behind her, Mum returned to her room.

Just before I put my head back on the pillow, I glanced over to the clock on my chest of drawers.

It displayed the time as being ten past two.

The next sound I heard was the alarm going off as normal at six a.m.

# 10
# MEETING MOTHER LAWLEY

I didn't press Mum for answers the following morning. We ate breakfast and went our separate ways. I went to school and Mum, hopefully, to work.

My mind wound itself around the experience of the previous night. It was bemusing rather than unsettling. Did I actually have a nightmare? Was it Martin that I saw standing on Mum's bed? Was she concealing the truth about her medication? Was it in fact *me* who needed a bloody doctor? Had I been in a trance for six months? I could not begin to fathom an acceptable solution to any of it.

As you may rightly presume, I made it my business to debate the situation with Alex as soon as the opportunity arose. She thought I was very brave for accompanying my own mother to the doctors. Considering the instability of Mum's character at that time, I suppose it was possible that a modicum of insanity could be attributed to my own disposition.

We sat alone in the common room just before break time. It was such a relief to see Alex again. Yesterday had seemed to last forever without her.

I apologized once more for having to refuse the invitation to meet her parents but pledged that we would visit the florists on the way there tonight.

'You can't buy my mother with flowers, Jamie Andrews! She'll think you've been up to no good! I'm afraid you'll have to work harder than that to impress!" she chuckled.

I gazed into Alex's eyes. I could lose myself forever in those crystal pools. Forever and ever in Heaven.

'Ally…did you really mean what you said to me…the other night…outside your front door?'

Suddenly Alex appeared rather sheepish and coy.

Not characteristics I would have normally associated with her. I sensed her ever-so-slight discomfort and attempted to assuage her embarrassment in whispered tones across the desk before she could answer me.

'I thought it was fantastic to hear those words, Ally. You mean everything to me, you know. You must believe me. I think I'd go stir crazy if you weren't around.'

We exchanged a long lingering kiss which was duly aborted at the sight of other pupils entering the room.

It was at that moment that I relayed to her what had happened during the night. She listened as I spoke. As she did so, her expression became distinctly ill at ease with what she was hearing. Especially the part about Martin's features appearing before my eyes.

'You must think I'm bloody mental anyway, Ally. I'm making it sound like my house is haunted, for Christ's sake!'

Alex paused for a few moments before she conveyed her reply with a stern gaze.

'Maybe it is, Jay. Maybe it *is* haunted?'

Yet again she had provided a slant on events that I had only briefly contemplated and then discarded as impossible. However, when she said it as an outsider looking in, everything became somewhat clearer.

Yet still I challenged her.

'But that's ridiculous. Isn't it? I grimaced.

Alex sat back in her chair and indignantly folded her arms.

'Why is it? How do you know that it's *not* the truth? How do you know that the reason for your mother's distress *isn't* down to a ghost? It would be a theory that fits the facts. Unless you just don't believe in ghosts?'

Alex's perception of my largely undisclosed family life carried wonderful wisdom at times. She would take any situation and offer a flip side alternative simply by applying logic. It was refreshing to have another pair of eyes observing events.

Maybe I was too close to it all to gain a semblance of realism. Yet the ghost theory was surely too far-fetched, despite my currently spiritual existence.

I went on to tell Alex about Mum's strange comment in town, regarding her not being around anymore. No, I didn't mention the earrings! This time, Alex portrayed a half-smirk, yet was evidently as puzzled as I was.

'Why would she come out with something like that, Jay? There's no motive for saying such a thing. I take it we have her blessing as a courting couple, then?'

We both giggled before analysing the secondary implication of Mum's odd overview. Alex offered a possible theory.

'Perhaps she's going away for a bit? A holiday perhaps, with friends?'

I offered a wry smile in return that Alex expertly interpreted as *don't be silly, Ally.*

I explained Mum's apparent ease of manner at the surgery.

'It was like she was *happy* to be there. I can't work it out.'

'Well, if she says the sleeping pills have worked, don't dwell on it. Take her word for it. Maybe she'll be on the mend far sooner than you think.'

The bell droned to announce the end of break. I adopted Alex's optimistic appraisal. Yes, Mum was feeling better. She had gone to work on a good night's sleep. I needn't worry myself about it anymore. However, the strain of doubt would not dissipate.

My mind was not at ease. Far from it.

The school day passed quickly, and I remember meeting Alex at the school gates as normal. We walked briskly into the town centre as the early atmosphere of Christmas began to encroach against the slate skies above.

We passed the jewellers where I had been with Mum yesterday. Alex teased herself by studying the price tags. I eventually led her away discreetly and we made for the florists.

'What kind of flowers does your mother like?'

'Expensive ones!'

We always raised a laugh between the pair of us. We had been an item for just over three months and were enjoying discovering the many things we had in common. Such as sense of humour, favourite film, love of animals, our preferred flavour of tortilla chips and dip.

The only negative was that any period of time I spent with Alex seemed to pass far quicker than I would have liked.

Having chosen a moderately priced yet large bouquet, I escorted Alex to her parents' house with a growing sense of inflation.

I felt genuinely proud to be at her side.

As we walked, this feeling was suddenly tempered by thoughts of my mother and whether she had attended work. I had to fight with myself to erase any doubt or suspicion. It only served to make me miserable.

Isn't that tragic, dear reader? The sheer perversion of having to avoid thoughts of one's own mother because it causes misery.

We walked through the gate to Alex's front door. The same place where she had told me that she loved me not so long ago.

Well, okay, she said that she *thought* she loved me.

My heart began to beat a little faster as she knocked on the door and we waited for someone to answer. Eventually, a shadow appeared behind the glass and the door was pulled gently open.

'HI, MOTHER!' Alex shrieked as the porch way became bathed in light from the hall.

'Hello, love! Kettle has just boiled. Good timing as usual.'

Animated introductions ensued and Sarah Lawley seemed genuinely delighted to meet me. She didn't physically resemble her daughter in any way, yet if I shut my eyes and listened, I could hear that same definitive, authoritative tone in her voice.

The first half hour or so was filled with exchanges regarding school, my job at the supermarket and Christmas. I couldn't be sure at the time how much Alex's mother knew about my history, or indeed my current family situation.

It was relieving to think that I wasn't being judged for my past. A cleansing sensation I was not familiar with. She expressed the usual maternal sentiments in joking that she was worried Alex would never find a boyfriend to run away with.

'Well, we're not planning on going anywhere just yet, though Cyprus sounds nice from what Ally said.'

I had fed them both the invitation to talk about their summer holiday. It sounded exciting and adventurous. Riding mopeds in a foreign country; snorkelling over reefs; stopping where they liked for meals; getting drunk and dancing with waiters. It was an alien yet enticing prospect for someone like me. Despite the fact I found myself in the position of non-contribution once again.

I could tell that Sarah was a smart and considerate lady. Stylish in looks and manner. She never once asked me anything that could have been construed as intrusive.

She wanted to know about me as a person. Not the bullshit that I'd grown up with such as my nutty mother, my abusive father, my brother's ghost. For crying out loud how much more ludicrous can it sound!?

Alex prepared some sandwiches in the kitchen leaving Sarah and I alone for a few minutes. I could tell that she was fairly impressed with her daughter's choice of boyfriend.

Well, I told you I was big-headed, didn't I?

By then I had learned to spot the signs when a woman finds you attractive. Their eyes never leave you. They can't look at you without a silly grin under their nose.

Having said that I suppose it would be fair to say that Alex had shot that theory right up the spout!

I'm not saying that her mother fancied me. Not at all. That's a bit sick. Her reaction just struck a chord with me at the time. The inner knowledge that I had made a brilliant first impression. She was undoubtedly pleased for her daughter. Especially at that most festive time of year.

'What a wonderful Christmas you're both going to have. Speaking of which, what are your plans, Jamie?' asked Sarah.

I pondered the perfectly natural query for a few uncomfortable moments. I genuinely hadn't given Christmas Day any thought at all. It was weeks away. I never gave Christmas much consideration, anyway. But this year was different. I thought it high time for a little jest.

'I'm coming here, didn't Alex tell you? I'm bringing my whole family around for dinner. We'll be here about eleven, okay? There are only six of us! Or is it seven?'

Sarah began to giggle as Alex walked in with the sandwiches.

She then gave the reply that I least expected.

'Brilliant! The more the merrier! I'll buy an extra-large turkey! Christmas is far too quiet now that Alex has grown up, anyway.'

'What, Alex…grown up? It'll never happen!' I japed.

Glancing across to Alex, I noticed that she was no longer smirking. Then I looked at her mother whose smile had also seemingly reduced. Maybe mother and daughter had been talking about my upbringing after all. The pair of them had adopted expressions of concern as I relayed my plans for the big day.

'Seriously, I'll probably be stuck at home with my barmy mother. There's only the two of us, so dinner is a breeze to cook! Egg and chips all round! No trimmings.'

Still I looked at mother and daughter Lawley for a semblance of a smile between them. But they now glared back mischievously as if about to reveal some surprise. Alex spoke to break the silence.

I was obviously missing out on something, here.

'Well, I hope you don't mind, Jay, but actually I've already put the pair of you on the guest list for Christmas Day.'

My mouth literally fell open and my lower jaw rebounded off the carpet. Was I hearing things? I was certainly *seeing* things these days, but could I have possibly heard Alex correctly?

Only when her mother affirmed the invitation did I console myself with the fact that my ears were definitely not playing tricks with me.

'You mean...you want me to come *here*...for Christmas Day?'

My mouth had still not closed by this point.

'Yes...and your mum. Both of you. You'd be most welcome.' Sarah proclaimed.

To say I was taken aback by the kindness of the offer is putting it mildly. I think I made up some stalling tactic that I would have to see what my mother wanted to do and that I couldn't give a definite answer there and then. And there was Henry, of course. I wanted to visit Henry on Christmas Day.

'No hurry.' Sarah Lawley reassured me.

'So long as we know by Christmas Eve!' chipped Alex.

More laughter ensued as I tucked into the sandwiches.

The unexpected gesture of generosity had blown me away.

By the time it came to leaving I was in a state of imbalance once more. Thrusting me into this warm, loving family environment, indeed!

Alex Lawley, you had a lot to answer for.

I had truly enjoyed my visit to meet her mum. Sarah was funny and genuine. Alex was so lucky. I thanked her mother for the mention of Christmas Day and would be in touch with a reply. Alex saw me to the door as Sarah shouted goodbye from the lounge.

The air outside was sharp and uninviting. I held Alex close and kissed her goodnight. It was time to go home and see my own Mum. It was a wrench to leave but I couldn't put it off forever.

'I'll see you in the morning then, Ally.'

'Okay, darling. Maybe next time you come my dad will be here as well. He's not very often home from work before six or even seven, though. But I'm sure he'll take to you like Mum has.'

The light-hearted atmosphere vaporized into the freezing night sky.

Reality smacked us both in the face once more.

'Try and sleep tight tonight, Jay.'

Alex offered a hopeful squeeze of my hand.

'I'll try, Ally. God knows I'm ready for a decent kip!'

We kissed again.

Alex opted to send me away smiling.

'I think you impressed my Mum tonight. She couldn't take her eyes off you!'

Time once again for a joke.

'Well, she's only human, after all. I told you the cheaper flowers would still do the trick!'

Alex gave me a playful slap on the bum as we parted for the evening.

I went out through the gate and gave a little wave.

Heading for Lodge Close, relentless uncertainty accompanied my stride.

And the premise of what I might find there quickly eclipsed the joy of the previous couple of hours.

# 11
# AN END TO TURMOIL

Removing the front door key from my pocket, I scanned the windows of the house to check for any signs of activity. I could see that the reading lamp was on in the front room, yet the curtains were closed.

The latch clicked to release the door, in turn revealing a hallway in total darkness. I tried not to shout in case she was sleeping.

Not likely, but I secretly hoped so.

'Hello, Mum? You home?'

There was no response aside from a deafening silence. Flicking on the hall light I closed the front door and ventured into the kitchen. There was nothing to suggest that Mum had been home at all. Everything was as I had left it that morning.

The thought encroached that she may have gone wandering again, though of course there was no note to indicate where she had gone or when she'd be back.

Everything became very clear as I entered the lounge. The fire was full on. It felt like a blast furnace. By the armchair stood a large bottle of whisky. Three quarters empty. Next to that, her sleeping pills. Thankfully my instinct to panic was quelled as I saw that the pill bottle was nearly full.

Evidently, she hadn't been to work. She couldn't have. The time was only around seven. She didn't finish her shift until five. She must have been on the drink all afternoon.

I checked the telephone to see which numbers had rung and to see if anyone had left a message. I instantly recognised the second of the three registered on the caller display. It was Mason's. No doubt now she had opted to avoid work. There was no message left, either. The time of the contact from Mason's was ten-thirty-two a.m.

I continued to confirm the other missed calls. The first of the morning was a 0800 number. Probably window salesmen or insurance brokers. We never even bothered picking the phone up when those numbers appeared.

The third call did not register a number at all. It wasn't even indicated as withheld. Yet there was a spoken message, left at twelve o'clock midday precisely.

I pressed the play button and went to hang my coat on the back of the armchair.

The phone speaker emitted a strange gurgling sound, followed by a clicking noise.

I heard a voice mumbling, but nothing audible was being said.

I listened closely as the caller continued to rustle something at the other end. Then a raised voice in the background could be heard. Perhaps yelling at the caller. It was difficult to tell. And then at that moment when the raised voice could be heard more clearly, the exchange ended.

I don't know why at the time but standing alone in the lounge listening to the answerphone left me feeling distinctly uneasy. The hairs on the back of my neck stood on end. I dismissed it as a wrong number. There seemed nothing particularly unusual about it. Wrong numbers are an everyday event.

It was my body's reaction that concerned me. Not the call.

I trudged upstairs and was only partially relieved to find Mum face down on her bed - fully dressed and dead to the world. At least she was sleeping for once. I was content to leave her to it. I shut her bedroom door behind me and went back downstairs to watch TV for the evening. Mum did not stir at all.

I thought little more about the confused message on the answering machine. Despite my pang of curiosity, it seemed unimportant at the time.

And anyway, Mum was the singular, persistent priority for me.

*****

It was twenty after two in the morning when my nightmare woke me. I bolted upright in a cold sweat with the image engrained in my mind.

Two eyes staring at me in the darkness.

To whom they belonged remained undisclosed.

I stared back at the eyes until they flickered to divert their attention to concentrate on someone or something elsewhere.

Something elusive.

I didn't know who or what. The mysterious presence approached the first image in the darkness. The eyes appearing before me then closed.

Instantaneously, my own vision fought to clear to reveal the interior of my bedroom.

I sat on the edge of the bed and pulled on my dressing gown. I was shivering uncontrollably. I needed the toilet.

Passing Mum's bedroom on the landing I pushed open the door to check she was okay. In the semi-darkness I could just about recognise her drunken form still slouched on the bed. I don't think she'd moved a muscle for twelve hours.

My head began to spin as I urinated. A dizzying sensation that caused me to place a hand on the cistern in an effort to stay upright.

It was only when the feeling of nausea passed that I felt a compulsion to hear the strange telephone message once again.

Downstairs, I flicked on the lounge lamp, lifted the receiver, and pressed the relevant numbers on the keypad.

I concentrated on the weird, muffled voice at the other end, followed by the shouting, the rustling then the sudden cessation of the call.

It was so innocuous, yet there was also something that seemed so poignant about it. I remember turning the call over in my mind as I went back to bed. There was no indication as to the source, yet it all seemed somewhat familiar.

I placed my head on the pillow and drifted back into a deep sleep.

*****

The alarm roused me at six a.m. as usual. Never did I imagine that the events of the day ahead would evolve as they did. Even now in retrospect it is unbelievable. I woke up that day not knowing what it would bring, yet dawn would bring with it the trigger for massive change.

Change that would affect the rest of my life.

I clambered out of bed and shuffled downstairs. The postman had delivered early. I stooped to pick up the envelopes from the door mat. The top one was franked with the Mason's insignia. It was addressed to Mum. I couldn't trust her to read it, could I?

Much as I hoped she would see sense it would have been correct to leave it for her to open.

No, sod that, I thought, and tentatively tore at the seal.

It was from the personnel officer at Mason's. It claimed that if Mum didn't make any effort to contact the company within one working day of receipt of the letter, they would have little option but to consider her contract of employment null and void. The note did not go into detail about the reasons for such a drastic measure.

Back upstairs, I detected little sign of life from her bedroom. She would be in no state to attend work just yet. I dressed quickly and made her a cup of tea. I couldn't expect Mum to respond to the letter as she was still blotto. Nor would she want me to accompany her if she went there to explain.

Instinct told me to go down to Mason's myself and try and save her job.

If anybody could do it, I was sure I could.

*****

Mason's Packaging was stationed on an industrial estate on the outskirts of the town centre.

An old asbestos-panelled building; slate grey in colour and totally uninspiring.

The reception for visitors was basically a rectangular hole carved into the corrugated wall. I spoke into the intercom to introduce myself and an electronic voice acknowledged my presence and opened the door automatically.

I approached the front desk as the lady receptionist looked up and forced a half-smile. It was still only ten to eight, after all. She was evidently not in a sociable mood having to do some work before her shift had officially started.

'I don't usually answer the door before eight. This had better be good.'

I wasn't drawn by her rudeness. I had far bigger fish to fry.

'I'm here on behalf of my mother, Liz Andrews. I need to speak to her supervisor, Steve Vickers.'

I recalled that Mum talked very fondly of Steve during the early days of her employment. He had been portrayed as a fair but firm kind of guy. In short, a good boss. He had sorted Mum out when she needed overtime. He had been lenient when she had found the going tough.

However, I suspected that the situation was now far different. For a start, I couldn't even begin to guess the last time Mum had even set foot in the place.

Steve eventually appeared from a side door and invited me to his office. His smile was bright enough, perhaps to disguise the bad news that he had in store for me. We sat down and he made me a coffee. I remember thinking at the time what a pleasant place it seemed to be to come and work despite the bleak outward appearances.

Machinery droned on the other side of the wall as I sat opposite him, and he explained about the letter and Mum's predicament.

'I know your Mum's had a tough time this year, Jamie. I've done my utmost to keep personnel from badgering her, but things have gone beyond my control. She won't answer the phone. We've sent more than one letter. Your mother hasn't put a full week in since the summer. The company have had enough. If she was covered by a doctor's note, then things would be different. But the very fact that *you're* here instead of her says it all. I can't convince the company she's worth keeping if she won't even turn up! You understand, don't you, lad?'

I couldn't argue with a single thing he had said. He did sound fair. He obviously had a lot of time for Mum. It was her fault that things had come to this. Nobody else's.

Steve continued.

'I've known Liz since she started here. She was a brilliant worker. Abiding, got on well with colleagues, good attendee. What's happened to her, Jamie? What's wrong with your mum?'

I'll always remember the look on Steve Vickers' face as he put that question to me. Until then, no one else had ever asked me.

*What's wrong with your mum?*

His query was evidently motivated from a genuine concern. His interest was sincere. He knew about her booze trouble. Apparently, there had been plenty of evidence lying about at work - a sackable offence - that he had brushed under the carpet.

He knew she'd let herself go during the past year. We both recognised the symptoms. It was frustrating that neither of us could grasp at the cause.

'I can assure you that if she doesn't show up by the end of the day then the company will say to me that they have no choice. They've at least a dozen people on file lining up to fill her shoes. If it was up to me, I'd give her more time to sort herself out. But it isn't up to me. I'm sorry, Jamie.'

I thanked Steve Vickers for his appreciation of the circumstances and decided to return straight back home.

It was still early. Mum had the rest of the day to make peace with her job and I had to ensure that she gave it her best shot.

The deadline had been well and truly set.

All she had to do was meet it.

*****

I hadn't seen Henry for a few days. It had been bitingly cold and with other things going on I hadn't given him a second thought. He was pottering around the front garden in his Wellingtons and thick duffel coat when I passed him on route back to the house.

He spotted me of course and blurted out his greeting from behind a combination of billowing breath and tobacco smoke.

'By heck, lad. You're an early bird. And you're going the wrong way! School's *that* way. I thought you'd have known after all these years!'

'How are you, Henry. It's a tad cold for gardening, isn't it?'

'Aye, well, I like me morning air you know! Helps clear me tubes out!'

I smiled and studied him as he bent down to remove a discarded crisp packet from his lawn.

'Dirty lazy bleeders! Why don't they use a bin? By the way, how's that lovely young lady of yours keeping? She's a cracker! You're a lucky lad! Look after her, or someone else will!'

'Don't worry, Henry. I'll be seeing her in a bit. I'm just checking in on Mum then going back out to school.'

Henry stood to his full height, still with the crisp packet in his hand. He looked puzzled as he sucked his pipe. Uncertainty was a rare occurrence for him. I could tell he was struggling for the right response.

The words he eventually spoke nearly knocked me off my feet with surprise.

'But your mum will be at work by now, won't she?'

'No. I'm afraid not. I've just been to Mason's. She's been threatened with the sack because of her poor attendance.'

Henry took a couple more puffs on his pipe before continuing.

'Well, it seems the threat may have worked, our kid!'

Now it was my turn to be confused.

'What do you mean, Henry?'

'Well, she passed here not twenty minutes ago going towards town. I shouted but she ignored me.'

Now I panicked.

'Are you sure it was her? Did she look okay?'

'Yes, it was your mother alright. She didn't half seem in a hurry to get somewhere. Looks like she'll be keeping her job!'

I looked at my watch. It was only a quarter to nine. Maybe Mum had seen sense at last. Maybe she had woken up and felt motivated by the letter from Mason's. I had purposely left it on the kitchen work-top for her to see. About time, too!

I felt incredibly elated by the thought that she was trying to help herself again.

'Thanks, Henry! I've got to go. I'll be late.'

'Okay, lad. Bring your lovely lady around again soon, won't you? She's a wonderful tonic for an old man!'

I raced home and rammed the key into the lock. The house was silent. Mum's empty bed confirmed Henry's story. The letter from Mason's was lying on the un-made bed clothes, next to the bottle of Scotch - the contents of which looked to have reduced somewhat.

My head began to spin. I hoped against hope that she hadn't turned up to save her job as drunk as a skunk.

That would have been the end for certain. I recall beginning to throw a loose plan together. Did I follow her back to town to try and cut her off? Should I phone Mason's to see if she had turned up yet? Typically, Mum had left no clue as to what was happening in her head.

I grabbed the letter and the whisky bottle and cursed under my breath. I decided to telephone Steve Vickers to tell him that Mum was on the way.

The potential scenario had disaster written all over it.

I bounded downstairs into the lounge and picked up the receiver. As a matter of habit, I checked the message list for any calls that may have been missed.

I was surprised to see that there had been a call whilst I was out earlier on. It was timed at seven thirty-nine. Evidently Mum had answered it and I supposed that she had forgotten to erase the message.

There was no number on the display screen.

It wasn't a withheld number, either.

I pressed play. I soon wished I hadn't.

Silence ensued for a few seconds followed by a sound very similar to interference on a TV or radio.

Like static, but unusually different. I focused my attention. I felt sure I could hear someone breathing. Yes, it was a repeated intake, yet it seemed irregular, somewhat jerky.

Then came the message that immediately cursed my body with terror.

Remembering how I felt on hearing the words for the first time is a moment in my life that I have never forgotten, and it will forever accompany my existence.

The voice was quiet…trembling…familiar…

*'Mummy…Mum…help…me…'*

Four simple words.

Then the caller hung up.

The stark unflinching truth of the matter etched itself into my mind.

My limbs became weak as I dropped the receiver to the floor. I struggled to get my breath and began to sweat profusely. I looked down to my hand which still had the letter and bottle in its grasp.

Suddenly the picture became very clear.

I had to find out where Mum had gone. If, according to Henry, she had been out of the house for about half an hour then she could be at work by now.

It was a challenge to regain my clarity of thought.

I picked up the receiver once again and punched in the number for Mason's.

The miserable receptionist answered with a humourless quip.

'You can't get enough of us today, can you Mister Andrews? I'll just put you through to Steve.'

Steve Vickers confirmed that Mum had turned up at the industrial estate about fifteen minutes after I had left but had been turned away by security as she was obviously under the influence of alcohol.

According to the commissionaire on site, she staggered up to the security lodge and looked very distraught.

Her upset and disorientation were only compounded by the refusal of entry.

Where she went afterwards was a mystery to all.

Any thoughts of school and Alex had been totally overshadowed by the need to find Mum.

The source of the disturbing phone message began to cause me real trepidation. Was this all a sick game to somebody?

Was an unseen force trying to send me stark raving bonkers?

I looked at the time on the phone display. Twenty past nine.

I had to get out and find her without delay.

Slamming the front door behind me, I set off on my mission.

Little did I know that as I left the house for the second time that morning, my search for Mum was too little…too late.

*****

East Park looked glorious even in the early throes of Winter. Bleak bare limbs were simply on standby. Ready for the following Spring to sheath them with foliage. Once the early morning mist had risen, it left a carpet of silver which slowly but surely would evolve into green.

Much of nature's family had long since hibernated into the trunks of trees or made burrows in the banks of the stream that trickled coldly around the perimeter of the parkland. The odd squirrel would appear intermittently to observe the surroundings but would not stay visible for long.

It was a scene of natural beauty.

Autumn's coat of red and brown had long since disappeared. Thick, black bodies of oaks and sycamores formed coverts at varying locations around the acreage.

Shadowy, damp places that even the slumbering animals found uninviting as a resting place.

Amongst one such covert, a small clearing had formed over time.

Spiny limbs criss-crossed overhead, in turn forming a lattice canopy.

Hanging from that canopy today, was a long, white woollen scarf.

Attached to the other end of the scarf by the neck, completely concealed to passers-by, was the body of Elizabeth Andrews.

Mother to two sons; Martin and Jamie.

Limp.

Lifeless.

Liberated.

# II
# THE JOURNEY

## 12
## A PRAYER FOR MUM

The body had been discovered in the afternoon by a council gardener. Mum's name and address details were handwritten on a piece of paper and placed in her coat pocket before she committed the ultimate act.

Almost as is if she wished to assist the process after she was found.

The police made it their business to inform me politely as next of kin, and I identified her body before making a preliminary statement.

Her features on the mortuary slab were almost serene.

Mum looked content for the first time in her arduous life. I felt strangely numb as I stood before the woman who had brought me into the world.

Yet I didn't feel alone.

Alex was there with me, and she was more upset than I was.

I never anticipated that her first introduction to Mum would be under such tragically painful circumstances.

But besides Alex, there seemed to be another soul at the scene.

Rather than a definitive presence, it was more a comforting, yet intangible spiritual witness.

It was during my conversation with the police that I was handed an envelope found at the scene. It was sealed with my name written on the back. I recognised Mum's handwriting. The police said I could open it in my own time, but should they deem it necessary they may need to view the contents.

Alex joined me for the duration of the interview.

Her companionship was incredibly soothing. I missed her terribly when she wasn't around. She held my hand throughout.

She shed tears at regular intervals as the police made their enquiries. I suspected that whilst she was obviously sympathetic to my situation, it was her closeness to her own family was brought to prominence in the light of such events. She loved her parents dearly.

I had only ever really known one of mine, and my love for Mum was never the conventional kind.

We supported each other as mother and son through a period of sufferance. A sufferance that did not conclude for Mum as it had done for me at the age of eleven.

I was happy to be myself and live my life.

But Mum had cowered away from the reality around her.

She constantly ran away from her true self.

Mum had been irreparably scarred by the past.

I can now see that it was only a matter of time before she would concede defeat.

It was a few hours after I was told that her body had been found that the recent incident in the jewellers returned to haunt me.

Her unexpectedly flippant yet concise indication that she would soon be gone.

The signs were all in place. She was trying to tell me.

I just didn't identify them.

Alex stayed with me after the police had left. She was a rock of dependability and loving comfort. I sat on the settee at Lodge Close and stared at the telephone on the table. I dared not tell Alex at that time about the second message.

The police had heard all messages that were stored on the phone memory. They were seemingly unconcerned about pursuing the matter.

Besides, it wasn't appropriate for me to start playing Sherlock Holmes on the day of my mother's death. So far as I was concerned, Alex would remain blissfully ignorant of the strange events that had led to Mum's final farewell.

At least, that is what I intended to happen.

The time was reaching ten p.m. I turned away from the telephone as Alex walked in with coffee for us both. She also had in her possession the mysterious envelope that was found with Mum, apparently on the floor of the covert beneath her swaying feet.

The police suspect that she may have purposely held it in her hand as she ended her life, possibly containing some reference to her final communication. We would soon find out.

'If you don't want me to see what she's written, I'll go. I'll understand, Jay. It's not a problem. My dad will come and pick me up.'

I sat in silence, wanting to respond.

I secretly feared the contents of the letter. Should I share that fear with Alex, or spare her from it completely?

No. That wasn't fair. She was the only person in the world who was taking genuine interest. She didn't deserve to be excluded.

I patted the settee cushion. She smiled in gratitude about the fact that I obviously trusted her and depended on her, and she took her place next to me.

‘I’m scared, Ally. You might be, too.’

‘It’s only a letter, Jay. What could be so frightening?’

I looked her in the eyes. Those wondrous, hypnotic crystalline eyes.

‘You really don’t want to know. It’s freaking me out even thinking about it.’

With that, Alex took my hand and offered me the envelope.

‘Come on. Let’s get it over and done with.’

I put my coffee mug on the floor.

In the envelope was a single piece of writing paper which I duly unfolded. I immediately saw that it was not a long letter in terms of words. However, the message could not have been more potent in meaning.

It looked to be in Mum’s best handwriting, which made a change from her usual scrawl.

With a nod of affirmation from Alex, I began to read the note aloud as a firm lump of trepidation caused my voice to falter.

*‘My Dearest Jamie,*

*My time with you is at an end. This is not my decision. It is the deeming of someone else. Someone unseen that I have perhaps never, nor will ever, meet. I part from you with one last wish. It is not my wish, but the wish of your elder brother, Martin.*

*He is suffering, Jamie. I could not venture to his aid. On top of all the other failings as his mother, that is my final failing on his behalf.*

*You must go to him, Jamie. Retrieve him from his despair and constraint. This is your destiny. It is unavoidable. Fate has always controlled our lives in the most destructive of ways. Change the hand of fate, Jamie. Help me to redeem my mistakes. Put things right for all of us. There is identity to his whereabouts. Look to God, Jamie. He will guide you, as he guided me.*

*Your eternally loving*
*Mother x’*

Alex and I looked to one another in sheer disbelief at what we had just read.

I could no longer retain my composure. The eloquence, conviction and passion of Mum’s words were significant enough to send my emotions spiralling downward into a deep well of ensuing grief.

Alex hugged me tightly as my stomach knotted and my head began to throb. The searing pain of loss was a torture that I never knew existed until then.

A crucifying, relentless assault on all my senses.

As I submitted to the ride into tearful oblivion, I buried myself in the abiding protection of the woman I loved.

We slept in each other's arms until morning.

*****

It was a couple of days later before I found the courage to speak to Alex about the letter and its implications. I replayed her the second '*save me*' phone message.

We were as dumbfounded as each other.

She wasn't so much frightened, as intrigued.

Typically, she was forthright with her opinion.

'Jamie, I think you really need to forget about all this for the time being. My dad has offered to pay for the burial costs. We can afford it. Your priority is to think about the funeral and dealing with that above all else."

Alex was right of course.

I met her father, Kevin, for the first time the following day. It's very discomforting for a man you've never met to offer you the best part of five thousand pounds to allow your mother a proper send off.

Kevin Lawley was genuine in his sympathy and whilst we shook hands firmly on first introductions, the tears and emotion exhibited as I sat with Alex's parents had been sufficient to instigate long, warm embraces by the end of the meeting.

He told me not to concern myself with the details. He would take care of any unpleasantness. That was fine by me.

And even though it may have been judged rather inappropriate by some at such a time, I was also asked to consider an offer of accommodation from Kevin and Sarah Lawley for as long as needed.

The generosity of Alex's parents was unrelenting.

I was smothered in family love.

It was a welcome respite from the years of cold discontentment surrounding Lodge Close.

Although thanking them for their kindness was a sincere response of relief on my part.

But I did not know what decisions I would want to be making over the next few weeks.

The future now filled me with a sense of dread.

All I needed to know was that Alex would be there for me whatever happened.

*****

The funeral took place at East Park chapel and cemetery three days before Christmas. The hiatus had occurred due to a delay in the pathologist's report.

Verdict: suicide.

It was unnerving, not having Mum around anymore.

Yet I couldn't help feeling that a burden had been lifted - from her shoulders *and* mine. Further emotional alleviation arrived when the police confirmed that they were no longer treating the matter as suspicious.

Alex proposed the possibility of informing Mum's elder sister of the arrangements.

I hadn't the feintest idea where to start looking for Aunt Shirley and hadn't laid eyes on her since infancy, so despite its merits, the idea was swiftly deemed by both of us to be a non-starter.

The twenty-second of December is a date of great resonance.

Its significance arises because it was the day I said goodbye to my mother forever.

Christmas has never generated the typical brand of festive excitement for me that it seems to do for most of the world's inhabitants.

The chapel service was short and poignant as one might expect.

But as one might also expect, there was little scope for reminiscence or humour.

Alex and I stood together in the cemetery as Mum departed beneath ground. Alex's parents stood behind us alongside Henry. I was disappointed that there wasn't more attendance from Mason's, though her manager Steve Vickers stood respectfully behind the main group.

I thanked him heartily for his condolence and his efforts prior to her passing. He had tried to help Mum, but alas, it was a vain attempt on all our parts.

I kept my attention on Mum's coffin for a few minutes before Alex suggested it might be time to go.

The four people in the world that now truly meant anything to me were by my side in my time of need.

The sense of general numbness returned that day.

But I didn't weep for Mum.

I prayed.

I wanted her to enter her new life as a different person.

Unshackled; unhindered; free.

That is what I prayed for.

I'll never know if the prayer was answered for her.

*****

The next important date on the calendar was Christmas Day itself. It was supposedly inevitable that Alex's family would welcome me into the festivities at their house, with a view to me staying among them if I felt I wanted to.

I had been sleeping on their sofa for the past few evenings and returning home in the morning.

It was notable that I hadn't experienced a nightmare since Mum's death.

I had made a promise to Henry that I would go and see him before he ventured off to the village hall for his annual Christmas Community Care dinner.

It's a phrase that he always found hard to pronounce when sober, never mind when he was drunk at the end of the afternoon with all his club cronies.

I had put some belongings in the spare room at Alex's house during the build up to the big day.

Similarly, they had placed a few presents under the tree for me. Strange as it may sound, I was looking forward to Christmas despite everything. It would be nice to wake up on Christmas morning to the sound of voices and laughter. Well, I was still a child after all, though by the age of sixteen I had ended my devotion to the theory of Santa Claus.

Alex loved her earrings.

There was so much significance attached to that little piece of jewellery.

Alex was very moved when I explained what they meant to me in offering them as a gift.

And she understood their deep significance.

Alex always understood.

She walked with me to Henry's bungalow after we had eaten breakfast with her parents. The route was coated with a sprinkling of ice. It was a white Christmas morning, even though the snow had opted to stay hanging in the sky.

Henry was so pleased to see Alex. He had seen quite a lot of me over the past few days, but he had always made a point of reminding me to bring her round again.

'What a wonderful sight for sore eyes you are, my dear!'

And Henry was quite correct. She did look absolutely stunning on Christmas Day. Alex didn't wear a lot of make-up as a rule. Yet she was one of those women who recognised that less was more. It was a natural skill. Together with her black winter outfit, she was radiance personified.

Henry kissed her on the cheek as she handed him a greeting card signed by the pair of us. She had also had the wonderful idea of taking him a few mince pies - homemade by her mother. I topped the bounty up with a small bottle of rum. Henry's favourite tipple. We talked for an hour or so and waited until his friends arrived in a car to collect him for dinner.

I can honestly say - though memory may be blurred - that my Christmas that year was the most enjoyable of my life.

How ironic is that?

Even with all the domestic upheaval and personal loss incorporated, I was somehow able to cast the misery to the back of my mind.

I was surrounded by generous, understanding, loving people.

Having finally been prized away from the last connection to my own family home, I was immediately welcomed into the arms of another.

The transition was smooth and natural. I did not feel like an intruder in the uplifting domestic environment that Alex and her parents had offered - far from it.

They all wanted me to get my life back in order and had provided some firm foundation for this.

It would be grounding for me to ascertain how to plan my immediate future.

A solid starting point for me would be recognising that I still had academic potential to fulfil.

I had to get my brain back in gear and attune myself to school once again.

And whilst focusing ahead to the imminent weeks and months, I was just as determined to make the most of my present stability with the Lawley family, and hopefully eradicate from memory the damaging past associated with my own.

# 13
# GOODBYE TO LODGE CLOSE

With the New Year having arrived, I had managed to establish a settled home base with Alex and her parents. The casual observer may say that they were doing what was only right by taking me in.

But I took nothing for granted anymore.

You must remember that reliance on elders - especially family - was not a way of life for me. I fully appreciated everything that Kevin and Sarah Lawley had done. Perhaps if I wasn't courting their daughter then things would obviously have been different. But destiny rules. Fate had its hand in most events in my life.

This time, it was seemingly on my side for once.

I had returned to Lodge Close at regular intervals since Christmas to pick up any mail that may have needed tending to. Over the weeks, I had managed to tie up any loose ends that Mum may have encouraged.

Thankfully, somehow, she didn't owe anyone any money. I anticipated she might have left me with a financial powder keg to navigate. But I was grateful that the burden I had expected, I wouldn't have to shoulder.

Whilst making the visits back home every other day, I had begun to consider whether moving back into the house on a permanent basis could be a probability. The rent was only three months in arrears, and the council had been very generous in their attitude.

Basically, I was given a choice. Move back in alone and pay the arrears as the new tenant, or let the council revoke the tenancy agreement and forego the balance owed.

Taking the house on alone was not a viable option as I was skint. Even though it was the house I had grown up in, I had little affinity to the place. Although I struggled to recall even a modicum of happy memories associated there but it was, nevertheless, my true home. Realistically though, living there again did not appeal in the slightest.

I briefly deliberated the idea of asking Alex to be my co-tenant, but that would be far too disruptive to her. Aside from the hassles of moving her gear into a supposedly haunted house, it would be a struggle to cope in terms of paying our way.

Two full time jobs would perhaps cover bills easily, but I wasn't really prepared - at that stage anyway - to dispense with my education.

We were both far too young and I never broached the idea with her.

There was no way I could expect Alex to make such a drastic commitment.

In the end I opted to relinquish any financial and personal connection with number fifteen, Lodge Close. It was far more convenient for all concerned if I took up the kind offer from Alex's parents. I would owe the council nothing - which was another boon.

I was given one calendar month to vacate the premises. Furniture could go. Scrapped or sold, I didn't care. Kevin arranged for a skip which we filled on a cold Saturday morning in late-February.

Whilst we humped the chairs, table, and wardrobes onto the front pavement to break up, Alex and her mother were inside packing the smaller items into boxes for charity shops. Last to top up the skip were the carpets. By the Sunday evening, the house was a shell.

The Lawley's garage contained some boxes of possessions which I would sort out at a later date. With the help of a committed family team, the job was made quick and painless. As Kevin closed his garage door on a lifetime of trinkets, I decided to pay one final visit to my former home.

I owed it the final farewell if nothing else.

With the keys due to be handed back to the council the following Monday morning, this would be my last chance to occupy the house and pay a spiritual goodbye.

Alex asked if I wanted her company, but I decided to go alone.

As anyone who has moved house will understand, standing within its walls for the last time is a bittersweet moment. The bricks and mortar encompass a history of personal experience, which you must leave there forever. You cannot take your affection for one place and transpose it to another. It is impossible.

I made sure I positioned myself for a few moments in each room, even though there was nothing there to identify with now. My own bedroom was an empty cube. Mum's bedroom was a shadowy arena where ghosts may be reawakened someday.

I didn't overstay my welcome. The hairs raised on the back of my neck in accompaniment to the goosebumps on my arms.

A quick exit was prompted.

I thought briefly of my own dreams as I shut her bedroom door. The mysterious eyes on the wall; the vision of a brother in his mother's body. I had given little consideration of late to the material horror of these visions.

Like Mum, it was all in the past as far as I was concerned.

At the bottom of the stairs, I took one last casting look before opening the front door and walking out for the final time in my life. I pulled the latch and the door swung open. I stepped into the porch and turned to face the dark, featureless hallway.

As I pulled the door slowly toward me, I continued to stare through the narrowing gap.

Something among the shadows caught my eye.

A slight yet detectable flicker of movement; the merest hint of another presence.

I paid it no further mind and slammed the front door shut.

Then a familiar voice startled me as it resonated in my ear.

Henry stood at the front gate, puffing away on his trusty pipe.

'Sad day today, son. I watched you walk past my window earlier. Just wanted to make sure all was okay with you.'

I was grateful at that moment for his presence. It reminded me that I still had some grasp on reality among all the confusion.

'That's it, Henry. I'm not coming here again. In a few weeks another family will be living here.'

Henry ambled up to meet me at the front door.

'You're a very brave boy, Jamie. Strong and defiant. I saw it in you as a young one. I knew you'd pull through. I imagine it's been tough."

I had barely touched on the subject of my family with Henry. Even though we'd spent many hours chatting over five years or so, he had always respected the fact that my private affairs were nothing to do with him.

He had maintained a distant viewpoint throughout, believing rightly that I would be okay. His faith in me as a person was stimulating - and rare.

I was glad to have him at Mum's funeral.

He was a friend to both of us.

'Come on, lad. I'll make you a drink back at my place.'

I felt distinctly uneasy as I began to walk with him down the path toward the front gate. My history began to suddenly pull at my conscience. I could not help but hear my mother and father screaming at one another in one of their violent rounds of argument.

I recalled the silence that followed my father's exit as he threw the door open and stormed off to the pub.

Then, another memory came to the fore.

A wilful compliance caused me to be drawn back up the path and around the side of the house to the back garden. The encroaching darkness of early evening caused me to tread carefully but some aspects cast light on their appearance.

It was now overgrown and unrecognisable as my own playground as a young boy.

'Henry…just wait there for a minute, please. There's one last thing I must do.'

'Okay, lad. Take your time. I'll be right here.'

I walked past the side of the house and then along the ancient asbestos garage and suddenly felt I had reached the place I had been ordained to attend.

There, among yard-high weeds and covered in moss, stood the trusty coal bunker. I approached the bunker and crouched down. I don't know why to this day, but I felt a compulsion to pull open the front panel and look inside, even though visibility was minimal.

I stared into the shadows.

The memory of Martin and I sitting in the alcove cowering from our father's rage was vivid, despite the actual event being almost ten years earlier. It was then that the rain clouds in my mind began to reform and eclipse the mental sunshine that had ruled supreme for several weeks.

Mum's letter had been quite clear in its aim.

Yet I couldn't substantially connect her wishes with any aspect of my own life.

The image of Martin hiding in the shadows was tormenting. The feelings it evoked did seem to have some relevance to the present time, but I had no frame of reference.

The notion that Martin was in trouble of some kind was implanting itself in my head again as I sat crouched next to the bunker. Mum's request had begun to gather some connection to what was to happen in the future.

What I couldn't get my head around was how she knew these things.

*Why* was my brother in trouble? *Who* was he in danger from?

The second part of the riddle concerned his whereabouts.

Mum had insisted that I looked to God. *Why?* There was nothing remotely religious about my upbringing as I could remember. Yet Mum had suddenly placed great faith in the proverbial Lord. She had never spoken to me about God before she died.

When was this great link to faith given any credence? What were her motives in sending me in this direction? What clues did I need to uncover if I were to find this great being on high?

I was in danger of regressing into the past if I persisted in indulging this train of thought.

In essence, my family was gone.

I belonged with the Lawleys, for now.

I wasn't in any position to start playing psychological games with myself over the mystery. I rose to my feet and walked out of number fifteen without looking back. The sight of Henry in the short distance beyond the gate was reassuring.

I now firmly believed that the place had become occupied by something sinister, and I didn't want any part of the negative undercurrent that resided there.

It was a two-sided dilemma.

The house brought back bad memories for me, and I brought bad memories back to the house. My mind would only manifest itself on this situation unless I found a complete diversion.

I made a pledge as I walked away.

I would never again allow myself to be dragged back to the home of my youth.

My destiny was not going to be entwined around this emotional vortex.

However, that's the problem with fate. The decisions are already made for you. You think you make your own choices but in truth you have no influence over matters.

That is destiny's role by default and definition.

The path is already selected.

As such, my pledge to remain distanced from the bewildering debris of my former life was to prove futile.

*****

Back at Henry's I sat quietly in the lounge as he handed me a very small rum in a glass tumbler.

'I know you don't drink it as a rule, but you'll be surprised at its effects. Both calming and medicinal, lad. Just a drop. No harm done.'

I watched him re-light the tuft of tobacco in his pipe before he poked a rod into the coal fire to give it life. It was soothing to watch him in the cosy silence of his front room.

This was the moment when I became alerted that something may have been amiss with Henry himself.

He turned away from the mantelpiece and simultaneously began to cough. Not a normal round of coughing, but a loud, explosive, and seemingly painful process of trying to clear his throat.

Henry bent over double and the reddened expression on his face suggested he was hurting inside. I stood up to help him with the glass of rum in one hand. Henry then removed his handkerchief and placed it to his mouth.

I stood behind him just in case he lost his balance.

Looking over his shoulder, I noticed that the handkerchief was spotted liberally with blood.

The sight shocked me. I had never seen anything as remotely stomach-churning. Whilst the urge to enquire forced itself upon me, I resisted temptation.

Eventually, the coughing subsided, and Henry seated himself. He sipped a little from my glass and regained his composure. The incident was soon out of my mind as the subject reverted to my own situation.

'So, young Jamie…now what? What does life hold in store for you next?'

It was a question that I hadn't even asked myself, let alone considered a viable answer to. I had concentrated all my energies on shutting the door on the past.

I naively figured that the future would take care of itself.

'There are no guarantees in life, son. You must make plans and take opportunities. Seize what is in front of you! Before it's all gone!'

He was right of course. Life goes on. Events will happen. That is certain. Yet I wondered how Henry had managed to continue after losing his wife so long ago. A life alone is a terrible prospect for any man - or woman, for that matter.

I tentatively broached the subject for only the second time in our friendship.

I had not mentioned his late wife to him for a long while, yet at that juncture it seemed highly appropriate. Losing a loved one was now something I understood. Henry stared at me and smiled. I wasn't sure how he might respond to such an emotive question.

'My heart has stayed broken, Jamie. Nearly forty years of unhealed hurt. But we will be together again one day. I am sure of that.'

Such an answer begged my next question about his belief in heaven…and God.

'I just trust that there is a meeting place somewhere, lad. I've kept faith in the theory since the day I lost her. The thought has helped me stay sane through my years of grief.'

But what if there was no afterlife?

What if death *was* the end?

Henry sucked intently on his pipe and stared into the flames that flickered at our feet. As I watched his face contemplate the possibility, as the amber glow from the coals illuminated his weathered features.

'The likelihood I will never see Doris again is not something I have ever considered for a moment.'

I could sense Henry's upset and felt it best to leave him with his thoughts. I finished my drink, bid him a good evening, and promised to see him soon. I will never know the true extent of his discomfort at the absence of his wife. Yet I realised that I had touched upon it for the first time.

It was not pleasant to behold.

It was ironic - ahh, my old friend, irony! - and simultaneously upsetting that whilst Henry was longing for the past to return, I consoled myself with the private proclamation that I had finally turned the page on my own personal history.

I didn't want to reacquaint myself with any of it.

Not then, nor ever.

As ever, of course, it was out of my hands.

*****

I awoke in the dead of night with a piercing wail that seemed to endure forever. I reached over clawing frantically but couldn't find the bedside lamp switch to erase the images behind my eyes.

Constricted breathing; the burning of flesh; a black, loveless heart.

Alex rushed into the Lawley's spare room and embraced me as I shivered uncontrollably.

Perspiration formed in great beads on my body.

Yet this was not my own sensation of trauma.

It was a conveyance of events elsewhere.

It was happening as I dreamed it, but not to me.

Somebody else was trying to tell me of their anguish.

I was soon asleep again as Alex softly cradled my weary head.

# 14
# A SEMBLANCE OF ROUTINE

My seventeenth birthday was celebrated with a family meal. Namely, the Lawley family and myself. It won't surprise you to learn that I'd never eaten proper Italian before. But the positives generated by this very pleasant if untypical event could not divert attention from issues that were persistently creeping over my horizon.

My nightmares had once again become regular and increasingly dramatic by the springtime.

Alex's parents had asked me if I wanted to talk to them about my obvious troubles. They were naturally sympathetic, but understandably wary. Kevin and Sarah concealed it ably, but their patience must have been wearing thin regarding my prolonged residence with them.

Aside from this obvious sticking point, I agreed with them in principle. I too was now beginning to feel as though I *should* be placed under some sort of analysis to uncover the source of my torment.

There was nothing concise about the visions that interrupted my sleep. It was more a carriage of implied distress. Even now, I cannot depict the images for you, dear reader. Frustrating and incredible as it may seem, that is the fact of the matter.

On a welcome lighter note, Alex and I were deeply in love after eight months of being together as an official item. It may have helped that I was living with her in such close daily proximity.

We talked through every conceivable explanation for what was happening in my head. We both put it down to delayed mental trauma over Mum's death which would eventually efface itself.

For the time being, it was a facet of my life that I simply had to accommodate.

I was totally against the use of any form of drugs to appease the problem. The opinion of a medic seemed inappropriate. And my mother's albeit brief encounter with sleeping pills had not left good memories.

Alex had even persuaded me to invest in a mobile phone just to assist ease of contact. I had never seen the point in them before, but she was at pains to express how behind the times I was with modern technology, and it might prove invaluable. Who was I to argue?

In terms of practical arrangements, school and home life presented no apparent problems.

We were due to take end of term mock exams which I had studied hard for by way of a distraction. I had also decided that I was not going to rely on the generosity of Kevin and Sarah Lawley indefinitely. It was high time to earn my keep and my first port of call was back to my old supermarket manager, John Harrison.

To say he was pleased to see me was something of an understatement.

'Well, look what the cat dragged in…how's it going Jay-Jay?'

He always used to call me that.

Why, I don't know, but I had no objection.

We went into his tiny office at the rear of the warehouse. I explained my reasons for not being able to retain any working hours since the end of the previous summer. He was completely sympathetic and listened in silence for a full five minutes.

Anyone who knows John Harrison will tell you what an achievement that is for him.

John originated from Liverpool - a breed not generally reputed for their peaceful disposition and adherent manner. John was no exception. But he had a good heart under the regional mouth.

'What hours can you do for me then, Jay-Jay? Just name anything and I'll slot you in. No problem at all. I might even get you a fork-lift licence so you're legal!' he winked.

It never fails to amaze me how certain people look out for you throughout your life. I supposed that the reasons particular individuals cared so much about me is because firstly, I earned their trust and respect.

Secondly, because I never took them for granted.

Quite surprising really, as my family background had not attuned me to such a practice. Far from it. It was something - like many other aspects of my life - I had discovered quietly for myself. John, Henry, my dearest Alex…they genuinely cared about me…and I was very appreciative.

I arranged to work Saturdays and Sundays and evenings in the week should he require me to cover any absence. John was overwhelmed to have me back, claiming that it was high time he had some quality labour working for him again.

However, there was one little issue I had innocently overlooked and of course, it would trip me up swiftly.

I revealed my news to the Lawley family that same evening as we sat to dinner.

Whilst her mother and father were very pleased with developments, Alex was not so enamoured with my regained status as a shelf-stacker and displayed her disapproval with a dramatic exit from the dining table, which involved the throwing of cutlery and the slamming of two doors.

Kevin and Sarah looked at me lost for words. With Alex being their only child, they were always alarmed if she became annoyed about something.

They were Alex's regularly captive audience.

I however, remained unperturbed.

'I owe you both for helping me out. I'm going to begin paying you board. I need to do this for my own benefit. It's a personal step forward.'

Despite her parents being very admiring of my attitude, Alex was not so easily convinced when I eventually confronted her upstairs in her bedroom.

'So, when the hell am *I* supposed to get to spend time with you, then? Why didn't you consult *me* on your little plan?'

I can still see myself standing in her doorway.

She sat with her back to me suffering from a severe bout of umbrage.

'Look, it's a positive move, Ally. Think of all the nice surprises I can get for you with my wages!'

It is an infallible strategy. Throw the scent of money under a woman's nose and she will agree to anything…within reason.

I continued to justify my decision as she fumed.

'Listen, I've been living here for four months and not paid a bean to your parents. You do understand, don't you Ally? I've got to do this. Plus, I know the boss well. He'll get you a little job if you fancy it. I'm sure…'

I was stopped dead in my tracks by her response.

I had *really* touched a nerve, now.

'Erm, no bloody way, Jamie Andrews! *Me*? Working in a *supermarket*? I don't think so!'

Now I was the one getting slightly annoyed. Of all Alex's personality traits, out and out snobbery was one I had not previously encountered.

'Oh…a bit beneath you, is it? Shop work…yes…I see what you mean, oh, how common! How could I ever expect you to lower yourself to such demeaning standards?'

Silence ensued as we frayed at the edges. We sat on her bed listening to each other sigh heavily. As always in times of such drama, I eventually opted to lighten the mood.

'I think, Alexandra Lawley, that we have just had our first argument, dear.'

Yet again, there was little reaction from Alex as she wavered under her mass of brown ringlets.

I eventually relented and peered under her fringe to discover a broad smile.

God she was beautiful, especially when she was angry.

An emotional, passionate female - there's nothing better in life!

'And you…Jamie Andrews…are cruising very close to a bruising!'

Needless to say, by this point she realised that she had displayed exemplary selfishness, and I had successfully planted the seed in her head about earning some form of income.

Then she gave me *that* look.

The look of a woman in love.

*****

For the following few weeks leading into early summer, life had settled down once again. At least in terms of my day-to-day activities.

However, the bad dreams continued to recur every week or so.

Dark, sinister nocturnal encounters with no significant detail attached.

Sleep was a becoming a regularly troublesome task. It was slowly beginning to affect my concentration at school and at work. I struggled through the mock exams with two C's and a D. Not a fantastic exhibition of academic prowess, but passes, nonetheless.

My rota at the supermarket seemed to slot in just fine with domestics. John was glad to have me back in the team. He was a good boss. He looked after me every step of the way. I enjoyed the work and the money and felt a great sense of contribution by forwarding a proportion of it to Kevin and Sarah. The rest I saved in my current account. In many aspects, my life to the casual observer was knitting together admirably.

I had made a pledge to Kevin that I would gradually sort through some of the boxes of belongings from his garage so as he could use it for putting his car into once again. This I had begun doing after my exams, when the increasingly lighter evenings made it a more amenable chore.

Alex helped me sometimes, usually by insisting that I kept everything that I had moments earlier deemed suitable for the dustbin.

Great hoarders aren't they, women?

I looked through my old toys. There weren't many of them. Clothes that were way too small for me. Some tatty old books and a selection of photographs that looked like they'd been taken in the nineteenth century with a potato.

We laughed together at the sight of me as a tot in my jump suit shovelling breakfast down my front. There was one fine action still of me at the local park sitting in a puddle wearing an expression of discomfort. You know the score. The typical collection of family snaps from a generation ago.

A generation I had now all but forgotten.

There was one particular photograph that I still have in my wallet to this day. Alex found it between the pages of an old comic.

A young boy on his first day at school.

Blazer, socks, tie - the works! Cute and adorable.

Alex waved it under my nose with an unrestrained giggle.

'You were ever so handsome as a young lad. What went wrong?'

She laughed heartily and held her stomach as I studied the boy in the picture. Sure, he was cute. In fact, he was strikingly good-looking for his age. But it wasn't me in the picture.

I looked at Alex as she quivered with delight on her haunches.

'Whilst I understand your merriment at my expense, you should get your facts right first.'

Alex immediately ceased her bout of mirth and looked at me dead pan.

'What do you mean?'

'The schoolboy. I think you'll find that's my brother, Martin…not me.'

Alex re-scrutinised the photograph and adopted an apologetic air which required no vocal accompaniment. We continued to route among the debris of my past in an uneasy silence.

I spent a few evenings in the garage. I didn't want to drag the task out for more than it was worth. I was becoming apathetic about looking at every single scrap of paper. There was nothing remotely significant about much of the paraphernalia and possessions rescued from Lodge Close.

Until the day I found the diary.

There was a small box of official looking envelopes that Alex and her mother had carefully kept separate from the other bric-a-brac. Evidently, they had been knowingly considerate in doing this.

Everything I needed to lay my hands on was in that box.

Unbeknown to anyone at the time, it would become the key to the future.

I was alone in the garage one evening. I think Alex and her mum had gone swimming. Delving indiscriminately into the white shoe box I removed opened brown envelopes and discarded the old bills they contained. Other items included the rent book, our TV licence from four years ago – probably unpaid - and other financial items of little interest or relevance.

As the contents became sparser by the second, the diary revealed itself to me lying in the bottom. There was nothing overtly interesting about its outward appearance. Just a standard pocket diary, maroon in colour, with a small pencil tucked down inside the spine.

Opting for a quick peruse, I flicked open the pages.

It was from the previous year, and I immediately recognised Mum's dishevelled handwriting.

The strange thing was, she had only written entries for the last six months of the year. It was as though she had decided to begin writing it in the middle of July.

My curiosity was now fully engaged, and obeying curiosity's bidding, I began to scan her scrawl.

The entries were bemusing. Simply worded yet meaning nothing to me on initial inspection. I remember Alex returning from her swim and she entered the garage as I read. Obviously, the concentrated frown on my face as I did so, indicated to her that at long last I had found a remnant from Lodge Close that I had deemed remotely noteworthy.

'Look at you…the thinker…does it hurt much?'

I heard her juvenile chuckles but didn't respond. The diary was beginning to take on some pertinence. Every single entry was a brief resume of some kind of appointment.

Some entries appeared twice weekly.

To give you some idea of how it read, I've outlined two or three from memory:

*Thurs 11 Aug – 11am - cup of tea and chat until 1230. Feel a little better.*

*Tues 16 Aug – 1030am – tearful after bad night. Talk about it all afternoon with FC.*

*Fri 26 Aug — 2pm – feel wretched – Father Carroll hypnotises me. No result.*

To say I was a little confounded was an understatement of the highest order.

Entry after entry chronicled the detail of her encounters with this mysterious Father Carroll. I threw the diary over to Alex who was flicking through an old magazine of Mum's.

'Have a look at this, Ally. See what you make of it. I don't get it at all.'

Alex opened the diary and began to scrutinize the contents. Slowly her eyes widened with every line. After five or ten minutes, she averted her gaze from the pages and looked at me.

I returned her glance, expecting a satisfying conclusion from her normally astute mind.

'This is your mother's diary.'

Sarcasm tumbled unrestrained from between my lips.

'No shit, Sherlock! Ten out of ten!'

Alex threw a wry smile and continued with her appraisal.

'Obviously she had been seeing this guy, this priest or whatever he is, as some form of counselling for her troubles. Did she not mention these meetings to you at all?'

Alex was infuriatingly efficient at stating the bloody obvious at times.

My simmering temper got the better of me.

'No, of course not! It was evidently some big secret between her and Father fucking Whatsizname. What the hell did she think *he* was going to do for her that I couldn't? Who the hell does he think he is, anyway?'

I saw the look of disapproval in Alex's face as she simply sat and stared at me across the garage floor. She began to slowly shake her head in response to my outburst, which really wound me up.

I spurred for a fight.

'What, Ally? What the hell is up with you?'

'Maybe *this* is the reason she didn't tell you. Look at you. A cauldron of fury! Calm down for crying out loud! You'll be giving yourself a bloody heart attack!'

Feeling not a little sheepish, I placed myself next to Alex.

We continued to read the pages of Mum's diary together. The entries followed into September, October, and November. All in similar style, revealing very little about what was occurring between Mum and her wonderful counsellor.

Alex offered little opinion on the content. She scanned each entry studiously. I recall becoming frustrated again.

There was one obvious consequence of Mum's liaisons with this guy.

'No wonder she didn't find time to go to work. She was always at *his* bleeding' house! She was probably paying him in kind 'cos she was skint!'

Alex instinctively jumped to defend Mum's honour, which didn't register with any value at the time, but I can see now that it was a very touching gesture.

'Don't be so frigging disgusting, Jay! That is your Mum you're talking about! You don't really *know* anything, do you? Typical of you - exaggerated wild conclusions. Just shut it and think first for once!'

Half an hour passed before we reached the pages pertaining to November. The first week or so disclosed no affecting implication as to what was about to happen to Mum. But I had begun to nurture a stirring desire to find out what exactly had forced her over the edge on that fateful day.

I was not to be disappointed.

Alex and I pulled the little book closer as answers gradually began to reveal themselves in the encroaching dimness of the garage. I look back on the moment now and it all seems like a chapter from an Enid Blyton story.

You know the scenario - the two daft kids with the book of secrets!

However, Enid Blyton, it most certainly was not.

*Thu 10 Nov – 1pm hypnosis works – saw Martin in tears at a window.*

*Fri 11 Nov – 10am under again – Martin still at window, he sees me and calls.*

*Mon 14 Nov – 3pm session nothing seen. Then later terrible nightmares – Martin in tears, calls me again and again.*

*Tue 15 Nov – 9am – try hypnosis to locate Martin. No result.*

*Wed 16 Nov – 9am – hypnotised again, flashing lights, laughter, screaming, a tall tower. Location not revealed.*

*Thu 17 Nov – 9am – Not going back to FC, will go back to work.*

Alex and I finished reading the final entry together. We held in our hands the pieces of the puzzle. Mum had evidently tried to get help through the church. I interpreted it as an act of desperation, though by the sounds of things it looked to have worked to some extent.

Yet for some reason the emerging truth was something she decided to run away from once it came within touching distance.

The date of the last entry, the seventeenth of November, was the day before she was found hanging by her own scarf from the limb of a tree.

It made sense, at least partially. The riddle was at last attaining some form. The onset of dusk shrouded the garage.

Alex and I sat in the murk with a flashlight, deliberating the diary and its contents.

In the half-light I gazed at the woman perched beside me, and I told her why I loved her so dearly.

But questions were beginning to burn away inside my soul.

'Why didn't she tell me, Ally? Why wouldn't she let *me* help her?'

I hadn't cried for weeks over Mum. Yet at that moment, the grief reigned uncontrolled once more.

With her eternally protective embrace, Alex held me tightly until the storm passed.

Alex didn't pass opinion on what we had read in Mum's diary that night.

To the casual observer, it may have appeared as though we were snooping into a dead woman's private affairs and that I had absolutely no right to become annoyed about Mum's prerogative to handle things as she wished.

I suppose some may say that the business with the priest was nothing to do with me either.

But please remember before you judge, dear reader.

I was in torment, also.

Mum's past was now beginning to haunt me all over again.
Every night.
I had felt I had adopted the demons that she fought in vain.
But I was different to Mum.
I would not be prepared to submit to them as she did.
I would not run away.
I would confront them.
I would defeat them.

# 15
# FATHER CARROLL

Despite my resolution to cut all ties with the path I had previously trodden, ghosts of my past were equally determined in letting their continued presence be known.

It was as though they were chasing me in a purposed attempt to upset the balance.

All other aspects of my life were just about perfect.

By the first weeks of summer, I had successfully seen off my first A-level year with a general notion that whilst it wasn't bad, it could be better. I had some money in the bank and a flourishing home life with Alex and her wonderful parents.

As a very special treat, they had booked for the four of us to go on holiday to Cyprus in the coming August. Alex had obviously dropped the hint to Kevin and Sarah, and they had come up trumps for me yet again.

I had begun to compare their attitude to life as being similar to the premise of instant coffee. Every decision they made was done so with speed and efficiency and with a modicum of unnecessary consideration.

If something needed to happen, it would happen in the blink of an eye. Instant, you see? They had become an inspiring influence in my life, and still are to some degree.

Yet even though I was growing and changing in attitude and perception, I still could not relieve myself of the gnawing distractions inside my mind.

Although I was making all the right decisions about the direction I wanted to follow, subconsciously I knew that my fate was possibly in the hands of an unseen force. I could not remember my last decent night's sleep.

In fact, it had gotten to the stage where I actually *feared* sleep because of the phantoms it encouraged.

Teasing and baleful apparitions that ravaged my state of slumber most evenings.

It was so consuming that I was even thinking about my bad dreams during the daytime. I longed for the knowledge that would bridge the gap between my nocturnal communications and the actual truth.

Discovering Mum's diary had done me no favours in my quest to enter a new life and shake the bad memories off. I still could not fathom why she would look to a stranger for assistance in her trauma yet leave me completely unaware about her disposition.

Alex thought I was reacting out of injured pride rather than concern. She believed that I was offended by the notion that another man could assist Mum more capably than me. Admittedly, it was a jagged pill to swallow. But I maintained that it wasn't the reason for my growing unrest.

I had begun to develop a will to follow Mum's own path and destroy the foundations of her misery once and for all. I would be prepared to face the causes of our torment and conquer them totally.

I was not one for cowering in any scenario.

If I was going to play this game, then I was playing to win it.

Alex saw my increasing frustration, but thankfully she was mature enough to accept my reasoning. She loved me. She loved who I was. She would never question my judgement; merely offer her own as a point of balance.

It was her love on which I had depended so heavily for many months. I had no doubt as to her significance in my life. Even if, according to her, I didn't send her loving text messages often enough.

Yet still I carried the burden of needing to exorcise the past. What happened at Lodge Close may have been something I chose not to delve into at the time, but nevertheless, it happened. Mum was gone for a reason. She had evidently endured immense sufferance in the latter weeks of her life.

Somebody knew the answers to all my questions, and I was determined to press for assistance in discovering them.

It was on a muggy evening in July when I attained clarity as to the way forward. I was covering a twilight shift at work - as I regularly did. The nightmares had intensified.

The awareness of another's purgatory was becoming intolerable to bear. My concentration on a daily basis had long been affected, but I was capably papering over the cracks to that point.

John only employed a skeleton crew after six o'clock. Just two or three staff to cover the necessary tasks until closing time at eight.

This particular evening, the store was unusually quiet, and I'd pledged to perform a few stock counts ready for the next morning's shelf fillers.

I was alone in the toiletries aisle counting toothpaste of all things.

Crest Three-in-One! I'll never forget it.

I stood with clipboard in one hand and pen in the other.

The handhelds' server was down - again.

As I got halfway down the stack of boxes, I heard a soft, distant voice.

It spoke out a number; *thirty-two.*

My attention was diverted, and I looked to ascertain the source of the quip and their whereabouts.

There was not a soul to be seen.

I began to re-count the packets. Once again, half-way down the pile, the same voice uttered the same total: *thirty-two.*

I was now beyond curious. I was tired and grumpy. If I was interrupted once more, I would lose my temper.

Right on cue, my third attempt to count was disturbed in the same fashion.

In a fit of anger that Alex would no doubt have disapproved of intensely, I threw my clipboard to the floor and strode swiftly around to the next aisle to uncover the culprit.

There was no one there.

I was alone.

Now, if this little tale is beginning to bore you, dear reader, I offer no apology. For what happened next will certainly regain the interest. I gave up on the stock take and served a couple of late shoppers. It was my turn to lock up and I did so in the normal manner, following the normal routine.

Having secured the roller-shutters out front, I knocked off the lights. Setting the burglar alarm, I then proceeded to step outside and lock the back door of the shop. To the rear of the store is a small car park. I turned away from the secured door and in the short distance across the car park I saw a figure.

He was a male, late-twenties, handsome, smiling. He seemed to know me, though he didn't speak. I paid no more mind to him. Setting off in the opposite direction, I was stopped in my stride by a voice. The same voice as before. I thought it may have been in my head, but it seemed to echo around the walls of the nearby houses.

The words referred to the incident with the toothpaste a while earlier.

*'I told you – thirty-two! Why don't you ever hear me, Jamie?'*

You will sympathize with my initial reaction.

I turned around to see who had shouted. The man I thought I had seen on the other side of the car park had vanished.

I now know that I was looking directly at a vision of my brother. I can also confirm that it was not him in person, but some mental representation of his physical being. It sounds crazy to the uninitiated, but you know by now dear reader that I'm an honest and crazy kind of guy!

The experience severely unnerved me.

I ran to meet Alex - she always came to meet me from work half-way from home. My heart was beating like a drum. Sweat poured from my body. I didn't go into detail with her about what I'd seen - or thought I'd seen.

I didn't really want to discuss anything with her as we walked briskly back to her house.

She would have been justified in being angry with me for not disclosing my feelings, but that wasn't Alex's way.

By the time we had reached the Lawley home my mind had already moved on to the next stage of the puzzle, which I decided to put to her for some feedback as we walked upstairs.

'I'm going to meet the counsellor that Mum was seeing. This…Father Carroll... he holds the key. I've decided, Ally. I can't put it off any longer.'

Alex duly contemplated my words. She was never in a hurry to respond at any time. She wanted to be assured in saying the right thing.

Her eventual reply was as reliable as ever.

'Do you think that's wise, Jay? It's unknown territory. You may not like what you find. He may not be willing to talk to you, anyway.'

Never once had she shown reservation in her support. She didn't let me down then, either.

However, it didn't matter - I had made my mind up.

'What harm can it do to at least try? I really can't feel any more pissed off about things than I do right now, Ally?'

Again, she paused and thought her response through before conveying it.

'Yes, I understand. Do you want me to come with you, Jay?'

I didn't want to involve her in this. It wasn't strictly necessary. I could cope alone. It was for my own peace of mind, after all.

Alex was sleeping soundly at night. I wasn't.

I was seeing people and hearing voices. She wasn't.

'No. There's no need for you to come. This bloke must be affiliated to a local church or parish organisation. He won't be difficult to track down I wouldn't have thought. I'm going to find him...tomorrow. I appreciate your concerns, Ally. But this isn't your struggle. It's mine. I hope you can see my reasoning.'

With a sigh of wary resignation, Alex embraced me warmly.

She understood.

Alex always understood.

*****

The following morning, I kissed Alex goodbye and made for the library. I figured it was as good a place to start as any if I was going to track down a local man of the cloth. I hit the target within minutes of flicking through the relevant register.

Reverend David Carroll was apparently based at a church in a town on the other side of the city. It meant a bus ride or maybe two, but I considered that to be a minor hindrance to the plan.

I set about my forthcoming mission. In the space of one hour, I had made great strides. I hoped to be rewarded with some answers. I had no preconceptions of the man I was about to meet.

I ought to be treating him as a friend, yet I was decidedly suspicious about consultation with a representative of God. It was an alien experience.

It was also a path that had led Mum to her demise.

I would not enter the discussion as an aggressor, however.

Neither would I pretend to entertain any form of wildly exaggerated exposition. This man must know more about my own mother's state of mind than I ever did.

I needed his help. I had to show him respect for the fact that he had tried to assist my mother. Pride was not an emotion relevant to the day in hand.

I wanted to discover the reasons for Mum's decision to end things so suddenly.

It was a situation that did not sit easily on my shoulders.

*****

As a stranger in a new place, I can recall stepping off the bus and asking an elderly lady the way to the church. I remember little about the initial appearance of the building itself.

It had an imposing, ornate frontage with a soaring spire - the usual ingredients. The large wooden door was conveniently ajar, and I walked in without a second thought.

Well, in my ignorance I figured that I was as entitled to enter the hallowed arches as much as anybody else, even if I was a non-believer.

Standing inside the doorway, I hollered for a response, but none came. I moved to position myself among the silent pews and admired the architecture. The dark wood and polished brass. The wooden trusses, stone supports and stout buttresses. The colourful sunlit windows that depicted distorted faces and figures.

I was not comfortable in that somewhat spectral environment.

I recognised the altar, pulpit, and font. All seemed to be in place, aside one thing - the man I had come to see. For minutes on end, I stood in silent, cautious appreciation of this completely foreign territory.

The absence of sound was both daunting and soothing. The building possessed a strange tranquillity whilst boasting a tangible, almost foreboding atmosphere - especially to a lifelong non-attendee such as myself.

And then suddenly, I discovered I did have company after all.

'Greetings, young sir.'

I jumped out of my skin. I spun around to see the source of the echoing voice standing where I had been only moments earlier.

I engaged with his friendly expression as he began an introduction.

'I thought I'd let you browse a while before offering my assistance. Welcome, my friend. A newcomer, I see. I'm David Carroll.'

Father Carroll was a short, stocky man in his fifties. A detectable North-Eastern accent did not overbear his speech. It made him appear affable, especially when combined with his white beard and rose-tinted cheeks. He walked toward me and offered a hand of greeting, which I shook firmly and without reserve.

I was not in the habit of consulting with such figures, and I chuckle on recollecting my first proclamation.

'You've a lovely church, Father Carroll.'

How corny is that?

Yet, he replied with tolerant dignity and humour.

'Thank you, my son. I quite like it. Though, the dusting is a real bind.'

I laughed nervously before clamouring for my reason to be inside the blessed church in the first place. My eyes darted around the walls and ceiling, trying to conjure up an explanation for my presence.

Then, the honour was taken from me.

I had never really believed that leaders of any faith possessed magical powers, although I was aware that the subject was a continuing cause of debate for many people. I simply assumed from a young age that they were trustworthy individuals who had earned respect for a lifetime of doing the right things.

Father Carroll's next words defied any logical, earthly explanation. My preconception of such religious figures was not only about to be challenged, but totally reversed.

'Your mother liked it here, also.'

Not for the first occasion in recent times, the hairs on the back of my neck stood on end. It was like the script of a film. It didn't feel real, but you had to suspend all disbelief for the purpose of effect.

This man I had never met until two minutes ago knew exactly who my mother was, who I was, and no doubt, why I was there.

I was simultaneously frightened and spellbound.

Yet there was nothing objectionable about this individual who had tried to shield my mother from her tormentors. I could immediately see the appeal of this refuge and indeed its keeper.

Already the puzzle began to make more sense.

It was a centre of peace and solace. No one could have hurt her in this temple of protection. I felt suddenly comforted by the presence of the unassuming figure that stood smiling before me.

Yet my reaction to his statement was understandable and natural.

'How do you know who my mother was? You don't even know *me*.'

Father Carroll moved closer and gestured to the nearest pew.

'I recognize the pain you carry. Please, let's be seated. My knees ache these days.'

Despite his apparent air of assurance, I still needed some convincing that he could provide the answers I needed.

'Well, how can you claim to know me?'

Father Carroll placed himself next to me on the wooden bench and spoke softly.

'I didn't say I did know you, did I? I just said that your mother liked to come here. That's all.'

I sensed in my immaturity that he was having a bit of fun at my expense. Not a good idea in my current state of mind. However, I maintained decorum and responded in kind.

'I need to talk to you about her.'

The vicar nodded his head slowly and his features adopted a solemn expression of recognition.

'Yes, you do, son. I'm glad you've come. I suspected the burden would transfer to you after your mother's passing. It's typical of such cases."

Father Carroll seemed quite clinical in his appreciation of my family's history. I had to reluctantly assume at that point that he knew everything there was to know about me. He certainly spoke as a knowledgeable man would do. I posed the relevant query.

'How do you mean, *such cases*?'

'The sufferance of the passed parent often transposes itself onto the child. It's probably been in process for some time. No doubt the signs have been there for you to see. It's just that you couldn't identify them. That's not your fault.'

Father Carroll was beginning to shed real light on my experiences of the past six months. He expressed himself easily and concisely, as though it was something he dealt with every day as a matter of course.

It didn't occur to me at the time, but that was exactly the case.

'What are these signs that I am supposed to see?'

The priest rubbed his beard before explaining.

'The nightmares; the apparitions; the voices. If it's of any consolation, you haven't been imagining them. You're not going mad, son. You're receiving a message. You are a spiritual conduit. That, in itself, is a privilege. Someone is trying to tell you something. All you must do is learn to understand these callings. Don't fear them - that's what your mother did. She ran in fear and eventually buckled. Present the answers to the questions that burden you. Be confident that all will be positive. Active participation - that's the key, my son."

I recall my mind becoming clearer by the second.

Everything Father Carroll said had a resounding impact on my train of thought. It was time to ask him his opinion on my mother's demise.

Firstly, I needed to know how he first met her.

'Why here? Why twenty miles away from where she lived?'

'She entered just as you have done. Elizabeth simply walked in here one day. I did not think it relevant to ask where she had travelled from. I pitied your mother. She had such little resolve. But you're stronger. You've got the heart for the fight, son. I can see it in your eyes.'

I looked into the priest's eyes as he spoke.

The man oozed sincerity and wisdom. I felt guilty about misjudging him prior to our meeting.

'But *who* am I fighting? Who is sending me these terrible visions?'

'Look to your heart, Jamie. You already know, who. The more important questions are...where...and why?'

It was the first time he had used my name. I had made a connection with Father Carroll that would change my life and its order of priorities forever. It would also influence my view of such figures of faith and the vital role they play for many.

Yet I still wasn't satisfied. I continued to pursue an adequate solution.

'Please tell me *where*, Father. You know where, don't you? My mother knew as well.'

David Carroll moved closer and met me firmly eye to eye.

His stern glare never left mine as he revealed his findings.

'Your mother searched for a truth that she didn't *really* want to uncover. You must understand that she asked me to show her the way and I did so. Yet when the path was laid before her, she opted to retreat. She sacrificed herself rather than face her destiny.'

I wanted to challenge him regarding his input into Mum's downturn.

'But you must have had some idea that she would not deal with things capably. She was an alcoholic. She was depressed.'

Father Carroll lowered his voice to just above a whisper.

'They were merely *symptoms* of her troubles - not the causes. She came to me to see the cure for herself. I am no doctor. I don't administer medicine. I don't advise. I create an environment for individuals to see for themselves what they need to achieve. Then it's up to them.'

I became emotional, but in an angry way.

'But she hanged herself! What did she discover that could cause her to do such a thing?'

He leaned closer again until our faces were only inches apart.

'Are you up to the challenge, Jamie? Can you handle the truth?'

The adrenalin surged through my veins as I pursued my fate.

'Tell me where my brother is, Father. Please. I know he needs me. But without your help, I cannot reply to his call. Give me the key to open the door. I beg of you.'

The priest stood to his feet and clasped his hands. For the first time in our brief yet intimate acquaintance, Father Carroll looked uneasy. I sensed his obvious discomfort.

Was the truth really going to be so bad to listen to?

He glanced down to the floor before continuing.

'You may or may not be aware that your mother submitted herself to hypnosis. This enabled her inner mind to come forth. Hypnosis relinquishes the process of inhibition. It's an avenue through which only the absolute truth may pass. Do you understand me, son?'

I nodded eagerly. I silently urged him to tell me more.

'The problem is…that only a small portion of the full facts may reveal themselves at any one time.'

It was at this point that I remembered Mum's penultimate entry in her diary. Screaming; laughter; lights; a tower. I knew what those things were in their individual sense, yet they had little connection with one another.

I asked him what it should mean.

'Ah…your mother kept a diary. Good. I asked her to log her visits and any accompanying thoughts. I'm glad she did.'

'Yes, but what did you help her discover? What do these symbols mean?'

Father Carroll resumed his seat next to me.

'The question is, what do those images mean to *you*, Jamie? I cannot provide the final answer. They must mean something to you *personally*. Symbols that pertain to your family, to your history. I can help you no more.'

He had already been instrumental in building the framework of the entire mystery for me. There was just the one, seemingly unattainable missing link.

Yet the bigger picture was so much clearer.

My visit had already served a great purpose.

The priest laid a hand on my shoulder and spoke with sincerity in his eyes.

‘I am sorry for your predicament, young Jamie. I would like to talk with you longer, but I must oblige my next appointment. Meet your destiny head on, son. Conquer the wrongs in your life. You can do it.’

I thanked Father Carroll for his time. He escorted me to the door.

‘God bless you, Jamie. If you gain the knowledge you seek, and you overcome your hurdles, be sure to come and tell me. This house is always open.’

I bid goodbye with a shake of his hand and left the church grounds carrying more optimism than I had arrived with.

The humidity outside was almost stifling on that day in July.

I vividly remember standing at the bus stop for the trip back.

My mind turned over the events of the past half hour.

Where was this elusive place that Martin was calling me from?

I was certain in my own mind that I now had to find my brother. His torment was now mine. All I needed was the destination - just one more clue to his whereabouts.

Nothing else seemingly mattered as I sat through the bus ride home contemplating my fate, and the possible fate of Martin.

Yet still I couldn’t decipher *why* he was in trouble.

He would be a grown man by now.

Unrecognisable as the adolescent I knew.

But who could want to inflict pain on him?

Why was he hurting?

And who was the perpetrator?

*****

Alex rushed into my room in the dead of night, awakened by the incessant shouting. I sat up shaking and drenched in cold sweat.

She flicked on the bedroom lamp and held me close.

Comforting thoughts were whispered in my ear to ease the distress.

As I retreated into her protective embrace, the answer to the riddle burned at the forefront of my brain.

A searing, incredulous revelation of a truth that had always been present.

As Father Carroll had said, it wasn’t always possible to see the signals.

Now, I had seen them - all too clearly.

I wasn't to know it at the time, but it was the last nightmare I was to have about my brother. It could have been no coincidence that it happened on the same day as my journey to the church.

As I recovered in the refuge of Alex's love, the crude reality of my final vision began to re-emerge.

The stark terror of the sequence depicted was almost too harrowing to bring back to mind.

I was roused from slumber by a vivid, gruesome image of my brother cowering on the floor in tears and in desperate discomfort.

The man standing over him inflicted repeated blows as he unleashed a torrent of rage.

As Martin recoiled in the scene, the onslaught became ever more brutal.

It was the identity of the assailant that then triggered the location of such cruelty.

I awoke from the horror, armed finally with the knowledge I had yearned for.

I now knew exactly where my chosen path should lead me.

The attacker, standing over my brother with weapon in hand, I instantly recognised via his stature and tone.

Then his face briefly came into full view as final confirmation of my worst fears.

And all became crystal clear.

Martin was begging for mercy.

And the tyrant that towered above him?

It was our father.

## 16
## A DECISION

'I've got to go away. I must go to Martin. Mum was right all along. He's in danger. He needs me, Ally.'

We sat in the conservatory at her house, each cradling a mug of tea. Neither of us had slept for half the night.

Alex knew instantly that my outlook on the whole dilemma had changed dramatically.

It was the early hours of dawn.

The mood between us was pensive.

'I wish you would use your bloody mobile. I would have come to you. I was ringing you to see if you were okay.'

I had briefly discussed with her my visit to Father Carroll when I returned home the previous evening. I could see resignation in her eyes. She recognized that my destiny was now ordained along a certain path - a path that had suddenly become radically different to her own.

She blankly observed the evolving scene in the garden as the rising sun began to cast a golden sheen. Her mind no doubt churned with the alternatives to the mission I had sworn to undertake.

For me, there was no other option. As I revealed what I had learned, she looked to me, and her expression frowned with abhorrence.

'It's our father, Ally. He is the cause of Martin's pain. It's got to end. And only I can end it. That's why I've been having these bad dreams. The priest said that it was Martin calling for me. It all fell into place last night. I saw it happening in my sleep, Ally! They're up in Blackpool. I know exactly where they are.'

I detected that Alex was hearing me, but barely listening.

'What are you talking about? Why…Blackpool? Of all places?'

'It's where my father went to when he left us. It's his hometown.'

There didn't seem to be any further visible reaction in Alex. I had certainly roused her with my revelations, but the implications didn't seem to register with her straight away.

I continued to explain my motives.

'It all fits together, Ally. Mum's last entry in the diary. The lights, screaming, the tower. It's all Blackpool. How I didn't realise before I don't know. So obvious. I'm sure that's where they are. And that's where I've got to be as well.'

I could see an emerging grimace of steely determination in Alex's features. I expected emotion from her. Or perhaps even a constructive or obstructive reply as per normal.

But I certainly did not expect the response she eventually offered.

'Well, if you've made your mind up that you're definitely going, then I'm coming with you.'

Her declaration was something I had not foreseen.

I expected tears, tantrums, pleas for me to change my mind. Threats to break up. Anything but the decision she determinedly issued. Alex had confounded me once again. Evidently there were aspects about her mindset I did not yet know.

Yet again she had seized the opportunity to show me the depth of her love and loyalty. She had watched me get this far. Alex evidently wasn't going to walk away from our union now.

That's when I was once more smacked in the face with my old friend - irony. Whilst initially I was taken aback by her wish to accompany me, I was also gratified.

Then after a few minutes of digression, I realised that my protective instincts toward her should be heeded. Despite her instinctive whim, she *couldn't* come with me. It would be unworkable and unthinkable. It would be nothing less than total upheaval. She had school to think about. She had a future. A family. A home.

I had those things in a sense, but they were not my priority. They weren't instilled as my foundation. Not as they were in Alex's life.

I offered my viewpoint as she continued to sip her drink and gaze through the glass doors to the rear lawn.

'Ally, I appreciate your support, but this could cause more trouble for you than it's worth. I don't know how long I'll be gone for. It could be days, weeks, even months. I don't know. All I know is I've got to go. You *haven't*. Besides, I don't think your parents will approve. As much as they've helped me, I'm pretty sure this would be a step too far, even for them.'

I watched Alex in profile as she quietly contemplated the brightening vista outside. She looked immaculate - even first thing in a morning. I so admired her poise. She carried such class for one still so tender in years. Her soft freckled skin; her furrowed features. She was wearing Mickey Mouse pyjamas.

Strange what stays in the mind, isn't it?

Then the picture of tranquillity became tainted by the onset of tears as she rose to her feet. *Her* tears for once - not mine. Now it was *my* turn to do the comforting. I stood behind her and held her tightly. Yet she did not weep openly. It was more through frustration than sorrow. The wave of emotion dissipated as quickly as it had descended.

A slightly sullen minute passed as we stood in mutual silence.

Then she turned to me.

It was at that moment I knew that I loved Alex more than anything in the world.

'We can talk to whoever we need to, Jay, and they can say whatever they like. But I *am* coming to Blackpool with you. However long it takes. I don't care. I want to be with you wherever you go. Please don't leave me behind. Say you'll take me with you.'

We embraced again with conviction being our bond.

Yet both knowing full well that revelation of the development to her parents was a very daunting prospect.

But for now, we were adamant and united.

And prepared for the opposition that lay in wait.

*****

'What the do you mean you're going to bloody Blackpool? What the hell for?'

Kevin Lawley, quite predictably, did not react to our proposal in the upbeat manner his daughter had hoped.

'Don't get angry, Dad. Jamie wants to see his brother. That's all.'

It's a strange truth, but I've found over the years - through my limited experience - that most domestic arguments tend to occur at the dining table. It's the time of day when the family can get together and relax as they replenish minds and bodies. But the flip side of the coin is, that by teatime people are generally weary and considerably less tolerant.

Her father smashed his cutlery down causing the salt and pepper pots to up end themselves.

'How long are you planning on going for? We're supposed to be going abroad soon, you know!'

'I don't know how long, Dad. I've no idea.'

Alex didn't like to annoy her parents. It wasn't a regular occurrence, so when it did occasionally happen, she became readily upset.

But I couldn't see her father being appeased in this instance.

'*Why* don't you know how long for? How do you know Jamie's brother is even *there*? It's a bloody ludicrous idea, Alex! What about school? What about Cyprus? What about your mother and me? Do we not deserve some consideration in all this? You youngsters make me sick. It's all take, take, take!'

Fortunately, I was at work when Alex broke the news to her parents. It came as no real shock to me that it was not well received. Though I wasn't there to feel the full force of Kevin's reaction, Alex informed me when she met me at the end of my shift that her father not only got angry – but went reliably up the wall.

And probably rightly so.

It was to be expected. There was no easy way to tell them that I was dragging their only daughter off on some wild goose chase and we'd be back whenever. What self-respecting parent *would* take it lying down?

On our eventual return to the house, the atmosphere was as cold as ice. There was no sign of Sarah. Apparently, Alex's mother had opted to take a back seat on the debate and that meant that her husband's word would be law in this instance.

Kevin had already been seething for an hour or two when he took his chance to confront me in the hallway as I shut the front door.

Alex scampered upstairs for cover amid a flood of tears. It was an understandable reaction considering her predicament, if perhaps a little cowardly.

Her father stood at the bottom of the stairs to obstruct my path, with his clenched fists resting on his hips.

'After all we've done for you, Jamie! You're just going to desert us, are you? Just because of what some bogus priest has told you. Look, I don't care what you must do to make *yourself* happy, but why drag Alex into it? I don't like the sound of this little excursion. In fact, I'm worried sick already! But it doesn't matter. Because she's not going. End of.'

There seemed little point in trying to argue. I knew precisely how Alex's father would respond. It was an unavoidable collision of interests. I tried to offer Kevin the honest explanation.

That being I didn't want Alex to give everything up for me. I hadn't asked her to put her life on hold. It was *her* choice. We were a team and had been for almost a year. She wasn't prepared to split the team up. It showed great commitment to our relationship.

But far more potent in my eyes was the fact that she was now risking her relationship with her parents.

That issue concerned me more than anything else.

As I withstood Kevin's tirade in the hallway, my mind was elsewhere. The opinion of others was not significant enough to draw any diversion on my part.

The decision had been made *for* me. Not *by* me.

Unlike Mum, I would follow the ordainment.

Life with the Lawley family was distinctly rocky from that moment on. Kevin and Sarah felt that I was needlessly putting their beloved daughter's future in jeopardy. I totally sympathized with their standpoint.

They felt let down by me and were at odds as to my future potential as their live-in guest. It was made quite clear that should I decide to venture on my quest, with or without their daughter, I would no longer be welcome in their house.

To quote Kevin Lawley directly, they had 'accommodated my hang-ups for long enough.'

I willingly took that statement directly on the chin, even if it did crush my heart to hear it. Needless to say, the whole situation was now greatly upsetting for Alex. I could see that she had become a torn young woman. She loved her parents. She loved me.

Why wasn't life simple?

Well, dear reader, I'm sure you know by now that I of all people am not in any position to answer *that* question.

Whilst Alex deliberated the matter with her parents for the following few days, I stayed firmly in the background and rankled with another issue. July had rolled quietly into August. If I was going to Blackpool, it would have to be sooner rather than later. The place would be teeming with visitors, especially with a Bank Holiday on the horizon. I had to get there, and fast.

I made a tentative private arrangement with Alex.

I would be departing on the second Saturday in August. This would give her a few days to seriously consider her own position on the matter. The by-product of this was that my presence with the Lawleys in Cyprus was now severely in doubt.

I required no further thought on the issue. The sudden coldness from Alex's parents only served to fuel my resolve in leaving as soon as possible.

So much so, that I opted to move myself out of the Lawley home before I was put through the indignation of being asked to leave outright. But it was not a knee-jerk reaction to Kevin and Sarah's anger. Their views did not affect me one iota. It was simply the best solution for all concerned.

This was not as drastic a course of action as one might imagine. I didn't have many belongings to shift. It was a matter of a walk across town with a couple of hold-all's.

There was only one destination I had in mind.

Glenfield Avenue. To Henry.

*****

My sudden farewell to the routine I had come to know with the Lawley family was fuelled by regret and earnest emotion. From my own point of view, the upset caused by my departure to Henry's was tempered evenly by the conviction that I was making a step forward in finding my brother.

However, the untold distress I had caused Alex still managed to cut deep wounds of remorse into my conscience.

Kevin and Sarah had justifiably said their piece and made their position perfectly clear to me. In some respects, I agreed with them. But still they would not understand that Alex's wish to accompany me to Blackpool was entirely of her own will.

It seemed futile trying to argue the facts of the matter. So, I didn't bother. I figured I would need to conserve such energy for another time.

Being brutally honest and possessing the luxury of hindsight, I now find their approach to the whole scenario rather exaggerated.

Blackpool was not the end of the earth. It was a three-hour train ride away.

But her parents realised as I did, that Alex was prepared to place herself in a potentially dangerous scenario. They had every right to defend her against such a threat. They knew my family history and the potentially harmful scenario I wanted to gate-crash.

They did not however, hold the right to blame me for the existence of the situation.

And so, Alex and I hatched a plan to try and appease her mother and father.

She agreed to lie to them.

It was that simple. If she truly wanted to be part of my quest, then fooling her parents was the only alternative. She would pretend to surrender her argument in wanting to come with me. To ably convince her parents she had relented to their concerns.

She would also claim that our loving relationship was over.

What can I say besides expressing my amazement?

The plan worked. To a degree, anyway.

She had managed to dupe her mother and father into believing that she had opted to end all association with me. I had remained firmly inconspicuous for the few days it would take for the seeds of her announcement to take root.

To Kevin and Sarah Lawley, my final appearance on their driveway was to say a fond farewell to their one and only daughter. In truth, Alex and I were carefully arranging a secret rendezvous for the following Saturday morning.

Yes, I agree with you, dear reader. It was a ludicrous scheme that was doomed to fail. But at that moment, we both believed that it was the way to go.

We embraced on that hazy summer morning as though it would be the last time we would ever see each other. I was aware that Alex's mother was watching from the front bedroom window. Looking back, it was a very sad way to separate from the Lawleys after all we'd been through together.

The adage about blood and water is ever potent, however. I was now an outcast. And if Alex insisted on coming with me to the coast, then the act of deceit had to be persuasive.

Outside her house, under covert scrutiny of Mother Lawley, Alex cried authentic tears, though. The premise of betraying her parents was not an easy burden. But it appeared that to her that I was worth it. My cause was worth it.

After a few moments of feigned consolation, I broached the details of the imminent journey.

She stared into me with her moistened, white-blue eyes. For the first time in our relationship, I sensed that the light in those eyes had diminished slightly. In retrospect, I should have been wise enough to have heeded that sign. But I didn't see its true meaning until later.

I knew that Alex was in turmoil over her prospective actions, but it was imperative that we stayed focused on our objective.

‘Are you okay to get to Notts station on Saturday morning?’

‘Yes…Mum thinks I’m going shopping with Clair Richards.’

‘Good. We leave Nottingham at nine-fifteen, and we change trains at Crewe. I’ll be waiting for you in the station foyer at nine.’

Alex again succumbed to her emotions.

Her eyes had become reddened by persistent rubbing. I had to stay strong for the pair of us. I whispered reassurances as her mother continued to spy on us from behind the curtains.

‘Everything will be fine, Ally. Your parents will be fine. They understand. They’ll always understand. It may all be over by this time next week, anyway. You could be standing right here with me again.’

With a distinct strain in her voice, Alex reminded me of our plot.

‘I can’t be seen with you after today, you fool. Have you already forgotten we are supposed to be finished with each other?’

Yes. I had forgotten. Hands up.

I had foregone that part of the arrangement already. It was a pivotal aspect to matters to let slip from my mind.

There seemed little more to be said at that moment.

It was time to part.

‘I’ll take care of everything. We’ll find digs easily enough up there. I’ve got some money saved. We’ll buy extra stuff when we get there.’

Letting go of her hand that morning was the most difficult thing I’d had to endure during our year of love. To be truthful, despite her pledges of loyalty, I honestly didn’t know at that moment if it would be the final occasion I’d ever *see* her again, let alone touch her.

I walked to the end of the driveway and turned to Alex.

Her flawless features were racked with pain.

It was not pleasant to see.

It was definitely time for me to go.

‘Until Saturday, then. I love you, Alex Lawley.’

She did not respond.

I briefly glimpsed her mother prying at the top window before I turned away and headed for Henry’s.

The image of Alex standing alone at her gate has never left me.

Many would say it was me who had pressed her into an uncomfortable, no-win situation. They can say what they bloody well like. Outside opinion never swayed me from my own stance.

*****

I entered Henry's front door and made straight for his whisky bottle. He didn't touch it much, usually preferring his rum as a night cap. Even at my tender age I wasn't averse to a drop of Scotch when needed. He had given me his spare key should I need entry in his absence.

Surprisingly, he happened to be absent.

He didn't go out often, but when he did, he normally told me prior to the event. And before you start thinking that I was turning to booze to calm my nerves, let me inform you that a mug of coffee with a drop of whisky in it makes a wonderful soothing tonic.

I had been in half an hour and was rinsing my mug in the kitchen when Henry finally arrived back home. It was around dinner time. I glimpsed the taxi pulling away as he shut the front door behind him.

I watched him literally fall into his favourite armchair. He looked unusually tired for the time of day. I enquired as to his whereabouts as I made him a drink.

'You never said you were going out today.'

There was no response from my friend.

I had shouted through from the kitchen. I suspected that he hadn't heard me properly.

'Do you want me to make you anything to eat, Henry? Where have you been?'

Again, silence followed my query.

Whilst I had presumed the opposite might be true, I had come to suspect that Henry was also somewhat disapproving of my planned venture to Blackpool.

He didn't try to talk me out of it when I revealed the news three days previously, but he was openly concerned as to what I might find when I got there.

During the short time I had been living with him he had been rather quieter than usual. I had put it down to my impetuousness. He was worried and, as I can vouch, worrying is a tiresome occupation.

I entered the lounge to see what was wrong. The expression of despair on his face indicated I would not be hearing good news. It was then that Henry dropped a bombshell of his own.

He looked me in the eye. The typical rosy colour in his cheeks had vanished. It had been replaced by a pallid, wrinkled complexion.

There was an unusual atmosphere between us which although revealed nothing, had naturally set my instinct into overdrive.

I knew he had something to tell me. Something he had known for a while. Yet, I was the only person of significance left in his life. I was the only one he *could* talk to.

It transpired that unbeknown to anybody, Henry had been for medical tests earlier in the summer as he had found it increasingly difficult to breathe after his fits of coughing. He had ventured to the hospital that morning to get the latest set of results.

He ordered me to be seated.

Catching his breath in between intermittent splutters, he summoned his words to the fore.

I watched wide-eyed and attentive as he revealed his discovery.

'I didn't want you to know about any of this, Jamie. You've got your own troubles. But seeing as your back here, and you're leaving on Saturday, it only seems right to fill you in now.'

My temporary secondment with the Lawley family had eclipsed my relationship with Henry to a large degree. Firm friend that he was, he had welcomed me with open arms when I asked to move in with him.

He wanted to know everything that had been occurring in the most recent chapter of my life.

I was now about to play catch-up on six months' worth of *his* personal strife.

Typically, he went straight to the point.

'I'm dying, son. I've got cancer in both lungs. They won't operate because of the risk to my immediate health. They believe it's probably through smoking my pipe.'

Henry coughed heartily once more as a shadow of dread cast itself across the room.

He looked me closely in the eye as if to assess my reaction.

'There…that's it. You know, now.'

I was stunned.

I literally did not know what to say to my oldest friend in his hour of need. I'm ashamed to say that my thoughts were immediately selfish.

Something along the lines of *what fucking inconsiderate timing.*

My eternal accomplice, Mr. Irony, duly appears once again to rain on my parade!

I simply moved over to Henry's chair and held his hand. It was the least I could think of doing. I asked the inevitable questions. When did his breathing begin to falter? How long had the doctors given him?

Why the hell didn't he tell me sooner?

Then I remembered about seeing the blood on his handkerchief earlier in the year. I got the distinct impression that Henry wasn't particularly interested in debating the issue any more than was necessary.

His next move I have never forgotten. He asked me to pour him a large, neat rum. As I did so, he contentedly stuffed his pipe full of tobacco and lit up.

Henry noticed my look of disbelief as he started to send smoke rings toward the ceiling. I placed the tumbler on the small table beside his armchair.

'Don't bother lecturing me. The horse has bolted, Jamie my lad. May as well leave the stable door swinging in the bastard wind now, eh?'

He chuckled and turned on the TV. We sat together for the rest of the day in front of the screen, both getting slowly drunk.

Afternoon evolved into evening, which eventually turned to night.

And cruel reality dawned.

## 17
## A TRAIN RIDE

It was Saturday morning on departure day. Eight o'clock precisely. My mind was in disarray. I had not slept a wink. Not because of nightmares, though. I attributed it to a steady flow of adrenalin combined with stirring anticipation. So much had happened in the past week or so.

Too much to take in at once.

I reluctantly rang John at the supermarket to confirm that I would be away for the week. A week was probably a conservative estimate, but it would suffice for the time being. He was reliably fine about things and told me to enjoy myself.

Ideally, I hoped my trip to the seaside was going to be short and fruitful.

In my heart, I focused on the pending journey with a growing sense of dread.

I had washed the breakfast pots as Henry shaved in the bathroom mirror. I had observed his restful night without moving from his side. He seemed a little more upbeat than the previous day. I assumed it was because he had unloaded some of his personal trauma. He felt better now that I knew about his prognosis.

In fact, he was now surprisingly enthusiastic concerning my mission.

A taxi was due at half past eight. It would easily get me to the station for nine. Whilst Henry got dressed, I flicked on the TV to be greeted by the news bulletin.

Another war; another murder; another plane crash. It depressed me to watch it. It would be the last time for the foreseeable future that I would be sat in front of Henry's television.

It was this thought that suddenly rendered me feeling so sad.

My thoughts turned to his physical condition. It had been explained quite frankly to him that nothing could be done. Both lungs were riddled with disease. If such cases are caught early enough, then one good lung will suffice. However, it was too late for Henry.

He had received the verdict with far more grace than could be expected. It hurt me to think of him staying at home, suffering alone. Sure, he had one or two contacts through the community club, but he was not one for talking about his private business with them.

Only one kind of people wanted to know anything about him, he always claimed. And their kind were nosey bleeders. I found it hard to argue which such logic.

He tottered into view wearing pressed white shirt, brightly coloured tie, and rather dapper trousers.

His grey hair was combed and lacquered.

'I'll look bonny walking through town like this, eh lad?'

I looked at him in mild amusement.

'What do you need to go into town for, Henry? You don't need anything, do you?'

The expression on his face as he turned to me conveyed a combination of puzzlement and disappointment.

'Why…to stand on the platform and wave you both off, of course!'

He knew in an instant that his presence would not be necessary.

I felt terrible having to pour water on Henry's selfless, considerate plan. Then I explained to him that the whole idea was that Alex and I leave in secret. No fuss. Our journey was supposedly covert.

I was never very good at goodbyes anyhow.

'That's why we aren't getting the train from here. I'm meeting Alex in Nottingham.'

I let Henry down as gently as I could. He was as understanding as could be expected, seeing that the need for secrecy was more important than the actual emotion of a fond farewell.

It was not goodbye forever, anyway. I would see him soon. I promised that much to him as the taxi pulled up outside the house.

'He's a bit early, our Jay. Tell him to hang on a minute.'

I opened the front door and gave the driver the thumbs-up. I positioned my sports bag in the porch way so as not to forget it - which could easily have happened considering my erratic thinking.

Henry had disappeared into his bedroom. When he emerged, he was holding a small brown envelope, which he duly handed to me in the doorway.

'Here, take this. It'll keep you in digs until you're ready to return.'

I presumed - although I didn't open it there and then - that it was some money and was genuinely overwhelmed by his generosity. I had already disappointed him by refusing him the chance to accompany me to the station. Turning my nose up at his gift would have served to rub copious amounts of salt into an obviously open wound.

He looked at me sternly as I took the envelope.

'Be careful. lad. You're going into the unknown. And take care of that young lady of yours. Are you listening to me, Jamie? She's only doing this for *you*. Never, ever forget that!'

I simply nodded as a considerable lump formed in my throat.

'I'll be back here as soon as possible, Henry.'

Old friends shook hands.

Henry pulled me close and whispered a final offering.

'I will say this much, Jay. You're an incredibly brave lad for your age. Watch your back, though. There are some nasty buggers about. Good luck. I love you, son. And don't forget your bag.'

As Henry and I embraced, the taxi driver sounded his horn as a reminder of more pressing matters.

As the car pulled away, I waved to my dearest friend through the passenger window until we disappeared from each other's view.

*****

I stood in the entrance to Nottingham railway station watching the gradual influx of Saturday morning shoppers making their way hurriedly towards the town centre. The large clock in the roof displayed a time of five to nine. I fumbled in my back pocket for the train tickets. Two singles to Blackpool. I also pulled out the envelope that Henry had given me. It seemed appropriate to open it whilst I waited nervously for Alex.

It's not every day that you stand in the middle of a city holding a cheque in your hand for one thousand pounds. I nearly fell over in shock as I counted the noughts. It was the most money I had ever been entitled to call mine. Henry had signed it directly to me. My priority would be to pay it into my current account at the first opportunity.

Even now I struggle to comprehend his copious gesture as he simultaneously dealt with his own fate. With the benefit of hindsight, I can now see that it was effectively a form of inheritance.

I since learned that Henry was on marked time when he handed me that gift. I am eternally grateful that he chose to present it to me for the right reason.

He wanted me to utilise it in a way that would help.

I can never thank him enough.

My thoughts teetered on the threshold of melancholia.

I was distracted by the station addresser announcing the train delays in typically inaudible fashion.

This diverted my attention to the clock once again. It was now five past nine. Our train was due to depart in ten minutes.

There was no sign of Alex.

For the first time since I announced my planned trip to her, the seeds of doubt had begun to encroach. Maybe Alex wouldn't be coming with me, after all.

We hadn't spoken since parting on the driveway of her house a couple of days earlier. Negativity bombarded me. If she wasn't by my side, would I be capable of dealing with things alone?

Up until that moment in the bustling station foyer, I had not actually contemplated confronting my destiny as a lone crusader.

And it hit me squarely between the eyes that it would be a considerably more daunting prospect without the woman I loved fighting the cause alongside me.

The large clock ticked on to ten past nine. It was now plainly obvious she had changed her mind. I had to make the decision to wait no longer. Retrieving my bag from the floor, I slowly moved to check the bank of monitors to ascertain the platform I needed to be on.

I started thinking selfish thoughts about Alex and her parents. Maybe they had talked her around to their way of thinking. Made her see sense. Perhaps she had decided to stay at home after all.

One by one, these distracting possibilities fought for pride of place at the forefront of my conscience. I was almost in a state of panic.

Then suddenly, I saw her in the distance.

My fears were instantly allayed. She strode tentatively through the sliding glass doors of the station entrance, and I was completely in love once again.

She was there! She had come! Alex had arrived.

I can remember my instant elation at seeing her walk toward me. The woman I cherished was here by my side once again. I smiled and waved and moved to meet her. Just to feel her embrace once more would be heaven. The past two days had been agony without her soothing presence.

Then I identified the look of utter sorrow in her face.

An expression of dejection and guilt, that one only feels when letting their loved ones down.

I noticed she carried no handbag. No luggage. She was dressed in casual jeans and t-shirt. She was not prepared to travel at all.

She began to weep before I had even got close to holding her. She held her sides with her elbows and covered her features as the tears cascaded down her elegant face.

And then, I saw the reason for her state of desolation.

Alex's father walked in through the sliding doors. He stopped in his tracks and watched his daughter say a tearful goodbye to the man she once said she adored.

Nothing further needed to be said by way of explanation.

Alex had evidently made her decision.

It was time for me to make mine.

I held her and I looked into her eyes. Those incredible eyes that I firmly believed there and then I would never have the chance to become lost in ever again. I couldn't cry.

I was too numb. Numb with anger, disappointment, and shock.

But also, I sensed a pang of placation.

An underlying, relieving knowledge that in fact, Alex had made the just and correct choice.

I quickly glanced to her father, who stood a short distance away, surprisingly respectful of the scene playing out before him. He watched without word.

If I was honest, I could not ask Alex to lie to her parents. And I'm glad she didn't. They were precious, honest people. She was lucky to have them, and she loved them dearly.

I let go of her hands and backed my way slowly toward the platform steps.

Her tears continued to fall as she mouthed the words.

'I'm sorry.'

My response was heartfelt and genuine.

'I'm sorry, too.'

We continued to remain engaged in each other's thoughtful, remorseful gaze.

Alex then said what I really needed to hear at that precise moment.

'I still love you, Jay. Come back to me, won't you?'

My reply required no deliberation.

'I will. I promise.'

Eventually, we turned away from each other and followed our separate paths.

Alex back to the comfort and security she was accustomed to.

My own route would again be taking me into uncertainty and trepidation. Facets of life that I was more than familiar with.

As I sat in the train carriage and felt the engine grind into life, I was sure I heard the distant calling of the woman I loved.

The woman I had opted to leave behind.

Now apart, we were left to contemplate our mutual, overwhelming sense of loss.

I pledged to myself that I would make amends.

My heart broke as Nottingham was left behind.

And the unknown lay ahead.

# 18
# NEW REALMS

I sat in silence observing the world through dirty glass as it passed me by. Landscapes changed by the second. Strangers sat alongside and opposite one another, not once acknowledging anything beyond their own immediate space.

I was stunned to be sitting on the train without my beloved and trusted companion. I looked at Alex's unused ticket. I felt the urge to rip it up in anger, there and then. Instead, overriding compassion defeated my despair, and I slipped the little piece of card into my wallet for safekeeping.

Despite my ulterior motive for going to Blackpool, I had thought surprisingly little about the search for Martin over the past couple of days. My mind had been preoccupied with the matter of severing ties, as opposed to the equally daunting prospect of discovering a long-lost brother.

The first half of the journey endured in the blink of an eye. As the train driver announced the approach to Crewe station, I thought of Henry. Ringing him was to be one of my first tasks on reaching my eventual destination.

It had seemed like an age since I left Nottingham nearly two hours earlier. I wondered what Alex would be doing and thinking. Telephoning her was not an option for the foreseeable future. I could have messaged her but there seemed little point. I knew in my heart that communication with her was strictly out of bounds.

Blue skies greeted my arrival at Crewe. I was hungry, and with an hour to spare before my connection departed, I made a rapid route for a cheeseburger. I watched the myriad of faces through the restaurant window as I devoured the food. It was welcome sustenance.

Many people outside wore shorts and flip flops. It was decidedly warm even for the middle of August. It reminded me that Alex and her parents would be departing for Cyprus the following week. I should have been going with them. Guilt again accompanied my walk back to the platform. I mulled over my decision-making once more.

Should I have left Nottingham? Should I have abandoned the woman I loved with all my heart? Maybe, maybe not. Perhaps Alex was sitting at home staring at my redundant plane ticket, just as I had done with hers.

*****

It was just after two-thirty p.m. when the train finally pulled to a halt at Blackpool. Alighting from the carriage, I could immediately smell the salt in the air, although I couldn't decide whether it was originating from the ocean or the scores of fish and chip shops. Squawking seagulls floated high above on strong coastal gusts, eyeing up free morsels before robbing them from unsuspecting diners.

I made my way to the promenade. The plethora of happy holiday makers could be seen and heard all around. Everywhere echoed with shouting and laughing and screaming and music blaring from open pub doorways.

It was a perversely jovial backdrop for my indeterminable journey.

I had not decided on where I was going to stay. I had never been to Blackpool before in my life. I figured that heading to the sea front was as good a place to start as any.

There was a hive of activity all around. Families formed convoys with pushchairs. Gangs of fancy dressed girls and gangs of lads hogged pavements, obviously out for a good time on their hen and stag parties. The eternal droning of the many amusement arcades backdropped as a soundtrack.

Many of you will be totally familiar with the setting depicted. Hopefully you will by now understand that I was not. By no means was it an unappealing display, but one must remember that I did not arrive in Blackpool for a vacation.

I remember being relatively impressed with the spectacle of the three piers and the tower. That famous old tower - the symbol that had seemingly haunted me for an age. Standing so tall against an azure sky - proud, reliable, and distinguished. It had become a prominent landmark from my own perspective as well as the town's.

I wandered along the promenade for a good hour, soaking up the sights. I had never witnessed so many avenues of fabricated fun. Yet I had no desire at that time to indulge myself in the delights on offer. I had to find some lodgings.

A hotel, a bed and breakfast or even just an en-suite flat. I didn't care. But choice looked to be minimal.

I was primarily focused on what I'd left behind at Nottingham as opposed to what now awaited me in Blackpool.

No doubt the casual observer would question my sanity in choosing to begin my search for Martin without the slightest clue as to how to undertake such a challenge. I will admit now that I must have been a pretty determined young man to have discarded the routine I knew for such a potentially unrewarding - not to mention dangerous - pursuit.

Yet, since the day I met Father Carroll at the church, I felt that I had made a connection with a guiding force. I had recognised my destiny in a most profound way.

It had taken me a while, but I believe to this day that the spirit that encouraged me to follow my true path was the same unseen spirit that had tried to convey the message through my dreams.

I did not initially recognise the overriding supernatural guise that my life had embraced. To me at the time, everything was happening in my mind and at such a pace that to try and attain true perspective on things was not a possibility.

It could be no coincidence that my final acknowledgement of this destination was in parallel with the end of my mental torment. The picture became clear because for the first time, I was able to see it without interference.

It had always been accessible, but I had to learn to interpret such things adeptly. Father Carroll was absolutely correct in his analysis of the situation. Martin's strength of will had guided me through a process of education.

He had informed me to come to Blackpool.

He would continue to draw me closer still to his very being.

Regarding the search for accommodation, my timing could have been better. Being a speculative visitor at the peak of the holiday season was not conducive to finding a bed for the night. After trawling the streets looking for vacancies, I eventually booked myself in at a block of self-catering apartments named The Sandbar.

It was about a fifteen-minute walk from the north pier - the slightly more sedentary end of Blackpool's frontage. As I stood outside the apartments and squinted back along the coastline, the distant yet enormous rollercoaster dwarfed the pleasure beach opposite the south pier. It struck an imposing, although less inspiring silhouette to bookend with the tower.

I paid a week's rent in advance.

The elderly hotelier was pleasant, yet somewhat wary as she looked me up and down.

Her broad Lancashire accent hissed a warning through crooked yellow teeth.

'One rule. No others in the room with ya. If they aren't paying guests, they aren't coming in. Okay, lad? No second chances. And no money back.'

She was a grumpy so and so, but I paid it no heed. She obviously realised that I was not from the area. The room was adequate, with a nice view of the multi-storey car park opposite.

Still, beggars can't be choosers.

I unpacked my few belongings and decided to make my way to the town centre to telephone Henry. I could have used my mobile but wasn't sure how much credit I had left. Alex had all the info on that kind of thing. I really was useless when it came to mod-cons.

I pulled the door of the phone kiosk to enclose myself and suddenly felt great trepidation as I punched the number onto the keypad.

I was thankful that his tone of voice when he answered was very upbeat.

*'Hello, Jay. You got there, then?'*

'Yes, Henry. I arrived here about two o clock. How are you?'

*'Oh...fine...missing you already, though! Have you booked into a hotel, yet?'*

'Yes. Cut it fine, though. Most places are full. I found some apartments eventually. The resort is packed out! It'll do for now. Henry...I can't thank you enough for the cheque. You've been fantastic through all of this. I'm going to put it in the bank first thing on Monday morning.'

I can remember how strange it felt having to speak to my dearest friend on the end of a phone. I'd gotten so used to seeing his face and watching him talk.

Listening to Henry through a wire was surreal.

*'That's a good lad. If you ever get short, don't hesitate to ask for more. I can post it to you.'*

'If I'm here longer than expected I can find some little job somewhere, I'm sure.'

I can recall Henry's slight pause as if it were today.

Instinct told me what his next question was going to be.

*'How's your young lady taking to Blackpool? Does she think she'll like it up there?'*

The emotion that cursed my body as I tried to respond to Henry's perfectly natural question is as painful in memory today as it was in that phone booth back then.

It was like a healing wound suddenly being ripped open.

The priority of the day had been to reach my destination. Alex had been placed on the back burner to a degree.

The subsequent conversation with Henry had brought to light the fact that I had left behind the one thing in the world that I would have willingly died for.

Striving for composure, I stared in trembling silence at the flow of buoyant tourists beyond the glass.

I was alone in the phone box.

I was alone in Blackpool.

The stark realisation of the situation induced an unrelenting wave of tears.

I could not speak or listen. I bowed my head and held the receiver by my side. A minute or two passed before the tone sounded to remind me I was running out of money.

I fumbled for change and rammed it into the slot.

Henry was still on the other end listening to my upset as I tried to talk.

*'Jay, son. Whatever's the matter?'*

My tears subsided a little. My voice reduced to a whimper.

'She…she didn't come, Henry. She…stayed at home. I'm up here on my own. I'm sorry for crying on you. I know you wanted to hear a happy voice.'

There was no hesitancy in Henry's reply.

*'Shall I come up tomorrow? I can get the first train.'*

'No…Henry…you're in no condition. Stay at home. I've paid a week's lodgings up front. I don't know how things will pan out. I'm okay.'

Henry's concern was understandable and appreciated, but I opted to end the conversation at that moment.

There would be better times to speak. I pledged to ring him the next day and placed the phone back on the hook. The dual sense of solitude and isolation as I pushed open the kiosk door was unbearable.

My mind again whirled with the scathing possibility that I had made the wrong choice.

Should I have left Alex and Henry behind?

Should I have even come to Blackpool?

As I walked aimlessly along the row of small shops leading to the high street, my upset was gradually balanced by the memories of what I had been through in the past six months.

The events and circumstances that had led to me being there in the first place.

I managed to convince myself that was not wrong in wanting to respond to my instinct. I felt sure that I was justified in the way I had handled things back home. Unfortunately, the Lawley family would no doubt interpret my motives as highly inconsiderate.

If truth be known, I had never taken the selfish option in my entire life. How I wished for a day that I could freely please myself and do things in accordance with my own desire. Nevertheless, I wanted Alex with me so badly. I hoped the hurt would recede in time.

The clock face set into the Town Hall showed the time to be four-thirty. The August sun was high and warm.

I tried to change my mood by observing the humorous actions of others.

Children throwing tantrums at being denied their umpteenth treat of the day. Fat men in tiny vests cramming hot dogs down their necks. Women counting change for the slot machines. A hundred different movements in the blink of an eye. I was literally surrounded by thousands of strangers in the busiest holiday resort in the country.

Yet I felt as though I was on an island, just like Mum used to feel.

I decided I wanted a drink. A bloody good one. A gallon of ale and a greasy supper to take to bed. It seemed like a grand idea. Until the thought crossed my mind that I would perhaps need some ID. Never needed that in the Tiger Inn back home.

I scoured the nearby streets for an inviting watering hole. There were dozens of pubs to choose from. My thirst began to rage as my mind became more attuned to the idea of getting ridiculously drunk.

The eventual place I decided to sample stood on a corner with several scruffy benches positioned outside. From this front section of the building the north pier was just visible if you craned your neck.

I do not know what drew me to this establishment out of all the pubs in the town centre. The green décor of the exterior looked fairly appealing. Patrons outside seemed relaxed and unruffled by my presence.

To the unwitting observer I was a nobody.

And that would do me just fine.

The jukebox echoed around the bar room and my sense of comfort dwindled slightly as I entered. I was greeted by a few furtive glances.

Judging by the grimaces on some of the faces, the more sociable drinkers were convened outside. Inside appeared to be full of locals. You can just tell, can't you?

Still, the place looked hospitable enough and I offered a smile and a nod to one or two of the curious onlookers. Then the thought struck me that they were probably gawking at me because I looked comparatively young.

Thankfully, not too young to be refused a pint.

The barman looked to be in his sixties. A tall, thin balding man who said hello and made positive predictions about the weather. It must be something that all men like to do as they reach a certain age.

I responded with courtesy, but to be honest I couldn't have cared less about the bloody weather at that moment.

I leaned against the bar and let the cool beer trickle down my neck. I flicked through a couple of newspapers that lay on the side of the counter and reluctantly exchanged intermittent pleasantries with the barman.

I think eventually he realised that I wasn't feeling overly talkative and gradually he resigned himself to giving up trying.

Nobody bothered me for the rest of the afternoon.

The pub remained semi-full. The music continued to drown out any nearby mumbled conversations. I didn't attempt to mingle.

I drank, and sat, and drank some more.

After a few hours of worthy self-indulgence, I happily downed my last pint and staggered from the premises around nine that evening.

I considered contacting Alex.

I quickly talked myself out of the ridiculous idea.

The unplanned yet much welcomed nourishment duly came in the form of a spicy kebab from a chip shop next door to the pub.

I can't remember walking back to the The Sandbar, even though somehow, I managed to recall where it was located.

The landlady was hovering in the hallway, no doubt checking I was unaccompanied.

'Don't make a mess with that grub, son. Or there'll be a cleaning bill coming on top.'

I simply nodded to her as I staggered upstairs, entered my room, and collapsed gracelessly onto the bed.

I stared into the darkness, cramming the dirty, cold doner meat into my mouth.

Reality engulfed me once again.

The craving for Alex could not be erased even with the considerable help of alcohol.

I threw the remnants of my food on the floor and sobbed myself into a deep sleep.

# 19
# THE CELTIC ARMS

I was in no hurry to prise myself off the mattress the following morning. The hangover was offering a resentful persistence. I laid with my head on the pillow desperately wishing I had placed two aspirin and a glass of water on the bed side cabinet.

The strong odour of the previous night's take-away filled the tiny room. Not to mention the aftertaste coating the inside of my mouth.

Even the thought of movement was enough to trigger waves of beer-induced pain around my skull. It had been quite a while since I had downed so much booze - probably not since my first term at Sixth Form. Still, I figured it was well worth it for one night.

I squinted as the sunshine streamed through the flimsy curtains. There seemed to be plenty of activity down below in the street judging by the sounds of squawking kids, screaming mothers, and screeching cars.

With the minimum required effort, I raised my forearm to my face. My watch proclaimed the time to be approaching half past ten. I was prostrate and without enthusiasm for the day ahead, until my throbbing headache demanded I go in search of a remedy.

An hour later I was up, showered and buying paracetamol and a newspaper from the nearby newsagents. My body gradually began to feel partially alive once more. I remember having the strangest desire for a Sunday roast.

Well, not such a strange whim as it was Sunday after all. But I had gotten used to them in regular supply courtesy of Sarah Lawley. Prime sliced beef, Yorkshire pudding and thick gravy quickly consumed my thoughts and kick-started my appetite.

Despite my veins still being diluted with alcohol from the previous day, I decided to go to the pub for dinner. And to save time searching for somewhere suitable to eat, I figured yesterday's haunt was going to be convenient enough.

Recalling its precise whereabouts would however be a stern test.

I walked for half an hour looking for the elusive street corner before finally re-discovering where it was situated.

Unlike yesterday, I made a point of registering the name of the place to memory.

The Celtic Arms didn't seem as busy, but then it was still just about Sunday morning. The billboard proclaimed that roast lunch was served between Noon and three. Happy days. I was right on cue.

My mouth was watering as I entered the bar for the second time in less than twenty-four hours. The combined fragrances of stale tobacco, spilled booze and furniture polish instantly filled my nostrils and temporarily invigorated my receding hangover.

The balding steward from the previous day appeared from the rear of the counter and seemed relatively pleased to see me.

'Bloody hell, lad! You've a thirst and no mistake. Lager, is it?'

I smiled and scanned the enticing array of illuminated pumps.

I made the decision that I needed food first to line my shredded stomach.

'I think I'll settle for a coffee if that's alright.'

The barman laughed.

'Still a little tender, are we? You put some back yesterday. Mind, I wish all my customers were as thirsty. Some of them sit on the benches outside and get their own flasks and picnics out! How cheeky daft can you get? Did you want a cup or a mug, lad?'

I watched him place the requested mug under the percolator, which hissed and whined and steamed as it produced its mixture of brown froth and hot water.

'Here you are. On the house - in sympathy for your undoubtedly pounding head!'

The barman chuckled once again. I didn't pick up on it on my first visit, but he came across as a very capable and amenable host. A naturally jolly chap that enjoyed his work.

The thought struck me that I should have been more sociable yesterday, but it obviously hadn't bothered him to any degree.

He rapidly proved to be the kind of guy you didn't mind having a chat with at all - if one was in the mood, of course. It made a refreshing change from all the ignorant sods I'd observed since arriving.

I felt justified in asking a few friendly questions as my backside perched itself on a stool.

'Nice place this. Do you own it, then?'

The barman was hanging up bags of peanuts and pork scratchings as he swivelled his head to reply.

'No! If only! I'm just the duty manager. It's co-owned by three local geezers. They know how to run a pub, mind. Not the sort to mess with though, if you know what I mean. I'm the friendly face of The Celt. The owners are definitely *not*!'

I sipped the coffee which quickly restored function to my taste buds.

The lounge room was empty aside the two of us. I watched him as he checked the optics and put mixers in the fridges. His evident curiosity ensured that our conversation continued.

'You're a stranger in town then are you, lad?'

Credit to him for guessing correctly. Must have been my Midlands' accent. I thought about what kind of answer to give him. Was he just being affable, or was this another of those nosey buggers that Henry always warned me about?

'Yes, I'm up here for the week I think.'

'On holiday with family?'

'Well, sort of. Visiting family, actually.'

I drained my mug and placed it on the bar, as a hand of greeting was offered from the other side.

'I'm Ken. Ken Tatham. Pleased to meet you again, son.'

It was unusual in my experience for someone to be so outwardly amiable. He reminded me of Henry in some ways. Totally committed to talking straight. Yet he seemed genuine enough and I had no reservations in shaking his hand.

'Hi, Ken. I'm Jamie.'

'You up here on your own then, Jamie?'

'Yes, my girlfriend was coming but couldn't make it.'

Ken smiled and stared at me as though I had just revealed some wonderful secret.

'Really? Where have you travelled from?'

'I live in Nottingham. Like I say, I'm up here to see someone.'

I couldn't avoid noticing the now enormous grin plastered across Ken Tatham's face.

'Wait until Roberta gets a load of *you*! She'll be dropping plates all afternoon!'

He laughed out loud in response to his own quip.

No doubt my subsequently perplexed expression encouraged his amusement.

Naturally, I enquired as to the reasons for his sudden bout of mirth.

'I'm sorry? Who's Roberta?'

Ken began to unwrap the cellophane from a stack of new beer mats as he gestured behind him with a nod of the head.

'Runs the kitchen. She does some cooking, table waiting and washing up for me. She'll be out any time. Especially if she hears there's a good-looking lad like you on his own in the pub! She'll be in bloody heaven!'

I smirked along with the jape and ordered another coffee.

A couple of other lads of similar age to me entered the premises and ordered pints of bitter. My stomach turned at the very thought of booze, which reminded me why I was there in the first place.

'Is it too early to order a roast dinner, Ken? I'm famished.'

Ken nodded and disappeared through the back of the bar.

I presumed he had gone to check with the kitchen. Seconds later he reappeared with a very striking-looking woman of about twenty-five, donned in a white caterer's hat and apron.

Ken put his arm around her shoulder and pointed my way with a bony finger.

Evidently, she was intrigued as to the identity of her first diner of the day. No doubt the manager had encouraged her to come and give me the once over. She was not backward in coming forward either, to put it mildly. She took one, long look at me.

An intense yet captivating, brown-eyed stare that seemed to last for a full minute.

Finally, she spoke in a broad Irish accent.

'He wants me to cook dinner for him, does he? Sod *that*! Let's just go to his place for the afternoon! Time's wasted on eating, so it is!'

The manager's resulting laughter echoed around the pub. I looked across at the other two drinkers who were thankfully no longer in earshot. Untypically, I felt stark embarrassment as Ken offered some welcome reassurance.

'Don't worry, Jamie. She's mad as a hatter! Ignore her!'

However, it was obvious from that first encounter that it was going to be very difficult to ignore the girl from the kitchen. She pretended to avert her gaze, but she was obviously impressed with me as her eyes flitted back and forth in my direction and she gently chewed her lower lip.

I told you I could see the signs.

So naturally I decided to try a little bit of my East Midlands' charm on her.

‘I take it that *this* is the lovely Roberta then is it, Ken?’

He was still chuckling to himself as he replied.

‘It is, indeed, Jamie. It is indeed. A bloody nutcase, she is! Crackers! Great cook, though!’

I didn’t have time to make the obvious joke.

Roberta got in first, again leaving Ken in hysterics.

‘Erm, before you get any ideas, lover boy…he did say a great *cook*, by the way!’

She studied me from under the peak of her catering cap. I confess I was struck by her dark looks and slightly rosy cheeks.

The rest of her form was draped in white linen, so first impressions were fairly limiting. She spoke in a constantly loud voice as though she was permanently trying to shout over a crowd of people.

‘Do you want beef, chicken or pork, my darling Jamie?’

I considered the options for a minute.

She could not resist another tease at my expense.

‘Hurry it up, lad, it’s not a bloody quiz question! I turn the oven off at three, you know!’

Her easy smile and ready wit were instantly addictive.

I contentedly watched her expression as she waited for my decision, impatiently swaying with her hands on her hips. Obviously, I had made some instant mental comparisons with Alex.

Roberta was the other end of the spectrum in terms of her appearance. She was probably a size twelve to fourteen, whereas Alex was an eight to ten. Roberta’s features were more rounded and glowing. Full of life and vigour. Alex carried a more refined, demur profile with mainly unblemished colouring.

I found myself smirking back at Roberta as she feigned impatience.

‘Beef, please. And plenty of veg!’

It was an easy task raising a smile from this girl.

‘You’re a cheeky bleeder, that you are!’

With that parting comment, she returned to the kitchen.

Ken could not help but continue to be amused by the charade.

‘I told you she’d take to you. I bet you a tenner she starts asking about you when I go round the back!’

Ken served other incoming customers at the other end of the bar, but soon returned to recommence the questioning.

Suddenly, I felt quite at home in this foreign place.

It had an atmosphere that comforted me.

Ken resumed his interest in my arrival.

'So, who you visiting then, Jamie? Family, you say?'

I deliberated on my answer very carefully. I don't know why, but I felt strangely vulnerable when talking about my true intentions.

As though I was some undercover secret agent.

My mission was supposedly covert until then, but I figured it made sense to start putting some feelers out to see what I could rake up.

Looking back now, the events that transpired were beyond incredulous.

But I'll leave you in suspense, dear reader.

Trust me.

You do need to see the whole story unfold to disbelieve it.

'Well actually, I'm not entirely sure where my family is. I'm trying to find someone.'

Ken began to wipe down the counter surface as he listened.

'Oh really? A special someone would they be?'

'Well, yes...I hope so.'

He looked puzzled at my reply.

I could detect the cogs turning inside his head.

'Male or female?'

It was a curious feeling talking about my plans. I had only really conferred on them with one other person. It was like submitting vital information piece by piece. I was careful not to disclose too much in my answers.

Yet I was also aware that I may just make some useful contacts for myself if I revealed just enough.

'Male...actually...my older brother.'

At that moment, Roberta pushed open the kitchen door to interrupt and she flashed her cheeky smirk my way.

'Ten minutes until food, handsome! Better find your backside a seat at a table. I'll bring the cutlery and condiments to you.'

With that, she was gone again. I observed her curvaceous rear view as she disappeared back through the swinging door. Ken continued to serve the steady influx of customers yet kept his concentration firmly centred on me.

'Where shall I sit, Ken?'

'Oh...anywhere, Jamie. No one owns a seat in this place.'

I could sense that Ken was more than a little interested in my motive for being in Blackpool.

Again, I couldn't decide if he was just being friendly.

The scrutiny continued as he put change in the till.

'You don't know where this brother of yours is likely to be, then?'

I sat myself down at a nearby snug before answering.

'I don't even know if he's in the area. I'm working on a very wild hunch. I've got no details of his whereabouts at all. I'm not even sure what he looks like these days.'

Ken appeared to be fascinated by what I had to say in general, but when the conversation encroached onto my brother, his curiosity was unrelenting.

I explained that I hadn't seen my brother for a decade and that likely it was he wouldn't even know me by sight, either.

I showed him the photo that Alex and I found in her father's garage - the one of Martin when he was in his school uniform. I had kept it folded up in my wallet ever since that day.

'He's a looker 'n'all, isn't he? Your parents must be proud. How old do you reckon him to be now, then?'

I looked to the ceiling and did a quick mental sum as Ken studied the boy in the picture.

'Oh, I suppose about twenty-six, twenty-seven. Obviously, he doesn't look like that kid in the uniform, now.'

Ken continued to stare intently at the photograph. He didn't say anything. His naked eyes scanned the still. Pursing his lips, he handed the picture back to me.

'Well, I hope you find him, Jamie. What's your brother's name?'

The photograph had instilled a reaction in Ken that wasn't overly definable at the time.

I'm not saying he recognised the little boy in blazer and shorts, but I watched his face as he digested the image. There was certainly a flicker of familiarity in his eyes, though neither of us mentioned it.

However, when I revealed my brother's name, Ken's eyes seemed to light up. He was deliberating on *his* thoughts, now. I was tempted to ask him there and then if he could possibly help, but it seemed like too much of a shot in the dark.

Our conversation was interrupted by the arrival of dinner. As the aroma of food wafted under my nose, it was countered by the scent of recently applied perfume.

'Thanks, Roberta. It looks great.'

She placed a knife and fork and salt and pepper before me and promptly parked herself across the other side of the table.

'Would you be needing mustard and the like?'

'No thank you, Roberta. This is just fine.'

Smiling from dangly earring to dangly earring, she watched me scan the plate of hot food as she talked.

'Did *he* tell you to call me Roberta?'

I began to sprinkle salt and pepper on my meal.

My headache was thankfully clearing.

'Did *who* tell me?'

'The boss. The bald eagle over there.'

I smiled at her mocking reference to Ken.

'No. He just said that it was your name. Why, don't you like it? I do…its very unusual.'

She inspected her royal blue nail varnish as I arranged a wedge of mash onto my fork.

'Well, I'm not overly keen. I like to be called Bobby. Bobby Jones…to give you my full title. It's kookier, don't you think? How's the grub, handsome? Can I get you more gravy at all?'

I swallowed another morsel and found myself becoming quite attracted to this very forward young lady - even if she might be ten years older than me.

I had become accustomed at school to the theory that it's the males that always make the running with girls. Not that I had any experience.

Yet I felt I was being slowly pinned down by Bobby. She was a great looking woman, and she knew it.

She most certainly did not belong in a kitchen.

There was something very individual about her. Obviously, I liked the attention she was affording me. Maybe it was because I was a new face in the pub. I don't know even now. But we struck a chord with each other. It was comforting to think I was making friends on only my second day.

We nattered as I consumed dinner. I was concerned that I might be distracting her from her work.

'Shouldn't you be cooking…or something?'

My gaze followed hers over to Ken, who stood chatting to a couple of rough-looking men on the other side of the room whose entrance I had failed to notice.'

Her eyes never averted from the trio as she answered.

'Nah…no orders yet. You're the only one up to now. You might be the only one all bloody afternoon the way trade is nowadays!'

'Well, they don't know what they're missing out there. This is great grub, Bobby. Thanks."

Bobby didn't respond.

Her gaze was firmly centred on the discussion in the far corner and naturally my interest was also alerted. The two men talked to Ken, yet they appeared to be looking over in my direction as they did so. I noticed their sharp crew cuts and identical black leather jackets.

The look in their eyes was certainly not friendly.

Evidently, while they were seemingly interested in me, they were not prepared to introduce themselves at that point. Ken did some pointing towards Bobby.

I watched him shrug his shoulders before eventually walking back to the centre of the bar. I continued to watch the unseemly duo for a few seconds before they located their own snug and my gaze fell back to Bobby.

She speculated about their conversation.

'They'll be on about me and you.'

I heard what Bobby said but didn't understand the implication.

I pressed for her to explain.

'What do you mean, me and you? Why would they be talking about us?'

'Those two dickheads…over there in the booth. They'll be wondering why I'm talking to you. They'll probably want to know who you are as well. I'd better get my arse in the back out of sight.'

I was a little perplexed to say the least. One minute Bobby was engrossed in watching me eat my lunch. Then the moment the two strangers appeared she became very nervous. I call them strangers because that's what they were to me.

Evidently, Bobby seemed to know them both pretty well.

My initial puzzlement swiftly turned to annoyance.

'What's the problem? We're just sitting here talking.'

Bobby's eyes didn't blink as she continued to scan the two meat heads in the corner.

She had evolved from a tigress to a frightened kitten in the space of two minutes.

‘Talking is enough to cause a problem for both of us. You’d better go when you’ve filled your stomach. Come back later. They’ll be gone by then.’

I had quickly developed a desire to know what the hell Bobby was going on about. I just looked at her open-mouthed as she stood up and brushed down her apron.

‘So…I’ve got to leave the pub because of those mugs?’

Bobby placed her palms on the table and leaned close.

Her face moved to within inches of my own.

‘*Yes, you fucking do*!’ she replied in a forceful whisper.

‘I’ll see you outside that door at three-thirty. Be there, Jamie! I’ll explain all then. Okay? Just trust me! And I’ll tell Ken that your dinner is on me.’

With that command, she was gone.

It was a crumb of comfort to hear my name spoken by an attractive female again. I had forgotten what it felt like, even though it had only been a barely more than a day since I saw Alex.

I duly emptied my plate, stood up and walked to the door.

As I did so I made a point of eyeing the two men once more as I left.

They both stared back without comment as I departed the Celtic Arms and walked into the embracing sunshine.

## 20
## DUBIOUS ASSOCIATES

After leaving the pub I decided to phone Henry once again. Inevitably, it proved to be a much more upbeat exchange than yesterday's emotional conversation.

He was in better spirits and was due to go on an outing to the garden centre with the community club that afternoon. I was in much finer fettle also. He was pleased to hear that I had made a couple of contacts and was putting my face around the place.

I was desperate to ask him if he had heard from Alex. I resisted the temptation. I knew the answer anyway. I had received no text messages so it was highly unlikely Henry would have had communication with her.

It might have been difficult to openly concede, but in all honesty, I felt that my relationship with Alex was very much in the balance if not over for good. Instinct working overtime, I suppose.

However, I felt better after talking to Henry. Neither of us referred to his illness. It was a positive phone call. I had no doubt in the belief that I had cheered him up, too.

Opting to walk my dinner off I ventured onto the North Pier. It would kill an hour or two before returning to meet Bobby. I looked at the brown waters of the Irish Channel below. God only knows how many shades of shit were swilling around amongst that lot. I slowly weaved around the groups of tourists, simply soaking up the vibrant ambience of a Sunday afternoon in sunny Blackpool.

But after only an hour of seeing the many sights, I was getting bored. I still didn't fancy a pint. The time was slowly crawling toward three o'clock. I made my way back to the pub in anticipation of my arrangement with Bobby.

It was an unfounded suspicion, but I couldn't help thinking that I had been followed whilst on my little stroll around the prom and pier.

It was an inkling that I quickly ignored.

The Celtic Arms sign swayed above the pavement in the stiffening breeze. I sat outside on one of the benches and waited for Bobby. Ken came out front and collected some glasses. He spotted me and could not help but comment.

'I see she's got you hooked already. You must be keen on each other if you've come back!' he chuckled.

I couldn't help but think that he was jumping to a rather exaggerated conclusion about Bobby and me. It never entered my mind to ask Ken about the two guys from earlier on. For all I knew, they could still have been inside.

I was becoming a little impatient when she eventually appeared from the side door of the building. My mild annoyance was soon quashed.

She looked stunning. It was a very warm day, and she had dressed accordingly. Short skirt, cropped low cut top and a wonderfully crazy hair arrangement. It was black, spiky, and tousled, yet very stylish, somehow. The look was finished off with tan leather cowboy boots. Yes, individual was certainly the word.

My compliment didn't struggle to sound sincere as my eyes widened.

'Wow...you look great...so...different.'

Bobby beckoned me to my feet with a curled forefinger. I had noticed that she always seemed to address me with the same gesture.

'Yeah...them fuckin' catering costumes don't do much for fashion stakes, do they? Come on, let's take a walk.'

It felt good to have a female companion alongside me once again. I let the sun beat down on my face and enjoyed the moment. The pair of us had quickly established a rapport. Though believe it or believe it not, the scant possibility of romantic involvement hadn't even entered my head.

Yet the sense of earnest, easy friendship she conveyed was most welcome.

'I'm sorry about earlier, Jamie.'

My disenchantment with the situation had long since vanished.

I was now overcome with curiosity as opposed to feeling slighted.

'They looked a mean pair of sods. Who were they...and what were you so afraid of?'

Bobby continued to look straight ahead as she lit a cigarette.

'You'll think it's so silly. They are the co-owners of the pub. Loz Prenter and Ian Doyle. They know my boyfriend. If they saw me with you, they'd think I was up to no good. They'd tell his father. Then we'd all be in strife. Forgive my manners...you wanna fag?'

'No thanks. I never have.'

For such a vibrant and confident young woman, Bobby was suddenly rendered very vulnerable for no obvious reason.

I tentatively enquired about her boyfriend.

Her face assumed an expression of slightly feigned guilt.

'I suppose I should have told you about that as well, shouldn't I?'

Now was high time for a humorous comment of my own.

'Well, I only felt like you were half leading me on in the pub. I don't fancy you, anyway...Roberta!'

Although I managed to maintain a straight face, I saw from the corner of my eye that Bobby had immediately looked at me and smirked.

We crossed the road and walked toward the base of the tower, which soared majestically above.

'You're a lovely guy and a cheeky git, Jamie. I just don't want to walk into more trouble than I've already got.'

I stopped and placed a hand on her shoulder which could have been considered a bold move.

I felt the tremor of annoyance begin to return.

'Trouble? *What* trouble, Bobby? Why would anybody be in trouble? I was sat having the dinner that you had just served me, for fuck's sake! Hardly crime of the century?'

She looked to the floor as she drew swiftly on her smoke. I hardly knew this woman, yet she had made me become very fond of her in a ridiculously short space of time. However, I sensed that I may have over-stepped the mark with my questioning.

'You wouldn't understand, Jamie. It's...it's not *you* that would be suffering.'

She wasn't making any sense. I wondered if it was worth pressing to hear her explanation if she was so averse to letting me in to her wacky little world. I decided to change the subject.

'What about an ice cream?'

'Great...race you to the stand up ahead on the corner there...last one there is buying, though!'

We scampered along the pavement squealing like children, pushing and shoving one another, attracting glances all around from seated pensioners and wide-eyed toddlers. We both arrived at the ice cream stall together, laughing heartily and panting heavily as we collided into it.

Oblivious to the queue we had just gate crashed, we pushed to the front, much to the disgruntlement of several impatient parents.

I was having fun. I didn't care.

'What flavour, Bobby?'

Again, the wag of the finger accompanied her breathless tones.

'But *you* beat *me*! I've got to buy. It's the rule!'

'It doesn't matter...what flavour?'

Bobby looked to the blue sky above as the impish grin emerged between her crimson cheeks. The forefinger now rested on her chin as she devilishly pondered the choices.

'Erm...excuse me, Mister ice cream seller, sir...but do you sell sausage flavour by chance?'

The pair of us exploded with laughter as the vendor looked on in total bemusement. Ken was right about Bobby. She was bloody crazy, but in a very infectious way. After much deliberation and justified objectionable comment from the other thirsty members of the queue, we bought our cones and settled ourselves on a bench by the beach. It was like being a little kid all over again.

Unfortunately, despite her amusing character, the barriers were still up. I still wanted some answers...if she was prepared to talk to me. Bobby was hiding something. I still wasn't sure it was my place to pry into her affairs. But I did so, anyway.

I know dear reader, that you must be rightly questioning my sanity by this point. You must be thinking, why the hell I was hanging around with a complete stranger in this frivolous manner in this strange place and having deserted the two best friends I would ever have in my life back in Nottingham?

I put it down to one of those once in a lifetime experiences that I seem to have had more than my fair share of. I liked Bobby from the off. It wasn't a sexual thing. It was a person thing. We were compatible souls. It was great being around her, even if I had only known her for three hours. Like it or lump it. That's the way it happened. I was becoming concerned for her and attracted to her friendship at the same time.

I couldn't help it. So, sue me.

'Okay Bobby, if you're here with me, where is your boyfriend now, then?'

'Oh...at home probably. Waiting for me to go round to see him.'

'Will you see go round and him today?'

Bobby glanced at me whilst licking her vanilla flake.

She could not resist a smile.

'Depends, doesn't it...'

'Depends on what?' I puzzled.

'Depends on whether I get bored with *you* or not, doesn't it?'

I was still in the dark as she insisted on hiding behind humour. She was still being very coy about the business in the pub earlier. I attempted one last stab at unearthing what it was she was so fearful of those men finding out.

She thought about her answer as she finished off her cornet.

'I just don't want them telling my other half's dad that they've seen me sniffing around other men. They fuckin' make me angry, though. I'm allowed to talk to other men, aren't I?'

I tossed my unfinished cone into a nearby bin and rubbed my hands.

'I don't know, Bobby...*are* you allowed to speak to other men? Doesn't sound like it from where I'm sitting.'

The expression on her face had become stern. She stood up from the bench and began to walk off. Odd behaviour you may think, but as I would discover, Bobby did have many amazing answers to reveal - but only when *she* was ready. Now just wasn't the time.

I hollered after her, admiring her very shapely legs as I did so.

'Where are you going now?'

Bobby was about twenty yards away when she turned to face me yet continued to walk backwards in the opposite direction.

'The pleasure beach. You coming? Or are you scared?'

It was an intoxicating madness, for sure.

It took us a good half hour to walk southwards along the Golden Mile. The 'Big One' rollercoaster loomed ever larger as we approached the entrance to the amusement park.

Bobby and I stood and looked at the passenger carriage clambering noisily up to the peak of the main drop. Screams from two hundred feet in the air were barely audible.

'You ever been on that, Jamie?'

I took my chance to offer a cheeky reply.

'No, but I've never been to Blackpool before. You ever ridden a big one, Bobby?'

Straight faced, she grabbed my hand.

'Not one as big as *that*...come on!'

*****

I had the best time that afternoon. So much so that I occasionally had to remind myself why I was even there. She had re-introduced me to the fact that there were things in life that were infinitely simple and all the more pleasurable for it.

Bobby was amazed that I had never even been to a funfair before. Yet it all seemed so natural with her. It felt like we had a go at every ride and stall in the park. Very big kids in a very big sweet shop. After a few energetic, adrenalin fuelled hours, I was finally beginning to regain my thirst.

We sat outside a relatively quiet bar across from the South Pier. The summer sun had arced over toward the horizon but still offered soothing warmth. I couldn't help but be interested in Bobby's secret life. Yet somehow, it still didn't feel right to ask.

Anyhow, she seemed to have a great knack for turning the subject of the conversation back to me. She asked how long I was staying and where I was from.

'I'm surprised Ken hasn't filled you in on all the details.'

Bobby sipped her cider as she stared at me.

'He has. I just want to watch you talk, you handsome devil!'

I told her about Alex, but she didn't seem unduly bothered. As I said the relationship between Bobby and I was strictly platonic in the short time it had existed, although thoughts of her mysterious other half would not leave me be.

I was undeterred and ever persistent in trying to get her to speak about him.

'Help me out with something. Shouldn't you be sat here with *your* man instead of me? What if your ultimate fears come true? What if he walks past now and sees us? Will he beat me up?'

Bobby was distinctly un-amused and adopted an air of seriousness for once.

'Don't take the piss out of me, Jamie. It's not funny.'

I had seemingly ruined the mood with my big mouth. Yet I also detected that I had come very close to Bobby wanting to disclose a little information to me.

I watched as she sucked her drink through a straw, quietly contemplating the matter of my potential intrusiveness.

In the end I opted to force the issue. One thing I was not going to endure was the bloody silent treatment.

'For fuck's sake, Bobby! You usher me out of the pub half-way through my dinner; you want to meet me this afternoon and I've got two dumbbells giving me evils across the room. Is your boyfriend the violent sort…is that what you're trying to tell me? Because if it is, you've got to dump him, and now! Women who put up with…"

Amid my rant, I had not detected the onset of tears. Bobby's mascara ran down her cheeks as she tried to stem the emotion. Needless to say, I ceased my insensitive tirade and put an arm cautiously around her.

We drank in resumed silence. It had taken me about six hours to form a friendship with Bobby Jones…and about six seconds to try and destroy it. I silently cursed myself as she wiped her eyes. I didn't know what to say.

Thankfully, at last, she yielded to my concerns.

'My boyfriend doesn't come out with me very often. Not in the conventional sense, anyway. He's…a little…confined…if you know what I mean?'

The look of confusion on my face was enough to prompt her further.

'Well…when I say confined…I mean…he struggles…'

I leaned closer to her. Her voice dropped to a whisper. It was evidently an emotive subject. But she could see that I wanted to hear more.

'His father doesn't like him going out too much. So, he must stay at home most of the time.'

It was a situation I didn't understand despite the constraints experienced in my own upbringing. Why would a grown woman and a grown man let themselves be dictated to in this way? Why was the father so protective of his own son?

I quizzed Bobby further.

'You're a nice girl. Is this guy afraid for his son to be seen out with you?'

Bobby pulled another tissue from her handbag and dabbed her eyes again before replying.

'No. He's not *afraid* for his son. He's *ashamed* of him. He wants to hide him from the world. It's sick, I know. So, I must go to their place if I want to see him.'

My mind tried to un-fathom the riddle that Bobby was relaying.

'So, what's any of this to do with those guys in the pub at dinner? Would they think that you were chatting me up, then?'

'If they told of what they'd seen and it got back to my boyfriend, he'd be pretty upset. They're very close to his father. But that's not the problem. His dad doesn't like it when his son gets upset. He tends to try and shut him up…if you know what I mean?'

'No…I don't.'

'My boyfriend isn't viewed as being much of a man in his father's eyes. The expectations are very high.'

The intrigue and confusion were jointly beginning to overwhelm me, yet I could see that Bobby was becoming upset once again. It was probably time to call it a day. We finished our drinks and I walked her back to her digs which were conveniently situated near the football ground.

Time had flown by. The sun was beginning to drop below the rooftops as the clock ticked towards eight o'clock. I enjoyed escorting her back.

We linked arms and talked of the nice things we'd done during the day.

Eventually, we were standing outside the front door to her flat.

'Are you coming in, Jamie? I haven't any beer, but there's a can or two of coke in the fridge, I think.'

Considering the gauntlet of scrutiny she seemed to be forced to confront on a daily basis, I was more than surprised to be invited inside. I remember thinking seriously about the offer for a second or two, but sensibly declined.

Bobby didn't seem too disappointed.

'Okay…you can get the tram back up to the north end, can't you? It's about a pound I think.'

I didn't really want to leave her at that moment, but the alternative looked likely to cause further distress. I had begun to understand Bobby over the first few hours of knowing her.

The brash, abrasive exterior was a façade. I wasn't fooled. It was an engaging act that masked a private life of evident, considerable misery.

Still, it was her business. Not mine.

'I think I might walk it back…grab a burger along the way, maybe.'

Her mouth spluttered another amusing response.

'Stands need, you fat fucker! Did my grub not fill you, then?'

We smiled at each other.

'I'm sorry for making you cry earlier, Bobby. I hope I haven't ruined our first day of friendship. I've enjoyed it. You're a wonderful person.'

Bobby moved closer to me and pecked me on the cheek.

'I've been desperate for a good time, Jamie. And believe me, it's not *you* that made me cry. It's the thought of the others in my life. Those other controlling bastards. It's really wonderful to have met someone considerate. Come and see me again before you leave...whenever that might be.'

We said our goodnights and I made my way back along the prom. I was tired but it had been a constructive day.

My plan for the following Monday morning was already in place. I was going to go to the bank and then to the council offices. The electoral register would maybe shed some light on my mission.

As I walked, I thought of Bobby's predicament. It pained me to think that she felt trapped in such a mess. She was far too special for such a life. Still, she obviously loved her man dearly. He was a lucky fellow - even if he did sound like a complete wimp. I couldn't imagine living like a recluse because of what people thought of me.

There were some sad cases about.

After what seemed like hours walking back up the eternally busy sea front, I finally arrived outside my own apartments. My second day in Blackpool had been a blast. I considered Bobby's offer to meet her again as I put my head on the pillow.

Maybe I ought not to be involved if it would make life any more difficult for her. The pub was obviously the place where she could be put under constant surveillance.

More questions ran through my mind.

Why would she put up with such a ruling to her existence? Why didn't she just dump this guy if his father was such an intrusive influence?

It didn't take me too long to decide that staying out of the way was the best policy for all concerned.

I was a stranger among strangers.

If my presence was not welcome, I could see that it was best to heed the signals sooner, rather than later.

Another thought occurred as I drifted into unconsciousness.

Perhaps it would be a better idea to only stay the week I had paid for and return home the next Saturday.

I wanted to see Henry. I was missing him.

I needed to be there for him, just in case.

He'd always been there for me, after all.

Fatigue gradually subdued my over-active brain.

The vision of Bobby at the ice cream stall encouraged a semi-conscious half-smile, before I welcomed my surrender to slumber.

# III
# THE RETURN

# 21
# GOODBYE, BOBBY JONES

My first ever Monday morning in Blackpool. I lay in bed until after nine and watched TV whilst slurping complimentary tea that tasted like furniture polish.

In effect, today was crunch day. You will be surprised by a rapid alteration of view regarding my mission. My evolution of thought seemed to have occurred in my sleep. I woke up with differing priorities. I don't know why.

It was as though the gates were already beginning to shut on my hopes. My lack of forethought in racing up to Blackpool may have had something to do with it. Perhaps the fact that I was now sleeping soundly was also a telling influence on my mindset.

The calling had long since ceased. I'd had no bad dreams for over a fortnight. My instincts were telling me to accept defeat.

Plus, I had school, Henry, and a job to consider.

And of course, Alex. Maybe.

I had already resigned myself to the fact that heading home the next weekend was the correct option.

If I could not unearth any leads as to the whereabouts of Martin during the next few days, then I was willing to raise the white flag.

I was in no hurry to leave, but a week is a long time alone and I figured that I would need all I needed to know by the end of the day. I donned a new set of clothes that I had brought with me from Nottingham.

The other set was already needing a wash. If nothing else it looked as though I'd need to go shopping for some new gear before the end of the week, anyhow. As you've gathered, I didn't afford much thought to packing my bag before I left, either.

I queued at the bank for over half an hour watching pensioners deposit and withdraw their pittances. It may have seemed greedy of me to pay Henry's cheque into my account even though I didn't really need the money. Not for the intended purpose it was given, anyway.

With my first task accomplished, I asked for directions to the council house, even though I had probably walked past it several times in the previous forty-eight hours.

A short fifteen-minute stroll later and I was standing outside a remarkable old building fronted by stone steps. Even before entering the place, I did not hold out much hope for finding any record of my estranged family in there.

I asked to look at the electoral register and was shown to a computer. As with mobile phones, computers were a little alien to me to say the least. It goes without saying that we never possessed one at home.

I had briefly used them at school before but thankfully a kindly assistant showed me the relevant website and surrounding districts to type in.

The lady on reception seemed somewhat bemused by my claim to be searching for my brother. I got the distinctly amusing feeling that she thought I was possibly some kind of hit man or something similar.

I looked through the indexes of Blackpool, Fleetwood, Cleveleys, and Lytham St Annes, yet nowhere was the name of Jim Andrews to be found.

You are correct, dear reader, in your initial assumption that without much supportive knowledge and little in the way of positive contacts, my venture was already on a hiding to nothing.

On leaving the council building, I had reached the same conclusion.

Yet, the surroundings still felt to be right. Something kept telling me I was incredibly close to succeeding, though I had nothing concrete to work on and subsequently didn't feel overly optimistic.

It was during the morning that one of those spooky moments occurred. By now I'm sure you will have readily come to associate the paranormal with my existence.

My stomach rumbled in protest, so I contentedly demolished a fried breakfast in the nearest convenient greasy spoon. I scanned a stray newspaper as I ate. I noticed that there weren't too many fellow diners at the time. I'd missed the opening time rush and it was a little early for the dinner time crowd.

When I walked into the café and picked my perch, I briefly noted a figure sat behind me with his back against the wall. A middle-aged man, perhaps in his forties. He had evidently just finished eating and was letting the food settle. I sat a few tables away and tucked into my own feast.

It was the most poignant encounter I'd had for some time. I felt the stranger's eyes burning into me. Right into the back of my head. I didn't look round to confirm the fact, but I sensed the man continuing to stare at me throughout the duration of my sitting.

It was an uncanny sensation, very similar to the one on the pier, yet far more acute. I suddenly felt vulnerable and under observation. I could clearly visualize the expression on the man's face but couldn't interpret it.

I nearly turned around and spoke at one point, but fear of making a fool of myself curbed any ideas on attempting to be sociable. Minutes later, just as my mind told me I'd been imagining things, I heard a definitive scraping of a chair and the slightest, coldest draught as the man got up and walked out of the cafe.

From my seat I could see him exit through the door and I watched him as he strode past the window. I gazed at the stranger's half-visible profile. He did not look back into the café.

Yet I had been so certain that he had been watching me for the past thirty minutes or more. Maybe I was becoming paranoid.

The incident was soon eclipsed by the daunting thought that I was now going to spend the rest of the week in Blackpool for no apparent reason. After breakfast I wandered the shops and arcades alone.

It was inevitable that the premise of perhaps seeing Alex again when I got back to Nottingham had begun to plague me as the main concern.

That's when the whole episode of my journey northwards seemed to lose all significance. It was Monday afternoon, and I was wandering around this strange town without any cause or purpose whatsoever.

A rudderless ship. And look at the upset I'd left behind. I'd given the impression to Alex that I would be gone for a long while, which was why her decision to stay in Nottingham would have been so heart-breaking. Yet there I was contemplating a return within two days of my desertion.

To say I was beginning to feel very frustrated with my uncertain position was putting it mildly. I was kicking my heels and beginning to nurture regret.

That was when I began to think about Bobby's situation. She had been the one positive aspect of the duration of my visit and was the only person that I had made a connection with.

Irony saves the day once more.

She was the only reason I could think of for staying put the rest of the week, and yet she couldn't see me for fear of her stupid boyfriend and his agoraphobic tendencies!

Monday dragged on forever. I was bored shitless - not a term I like to use too often - and I was ready to go home. Whatever or wherever home was at that point. I ambled along the prom looking for potential areas of distraction.

The waxworks would have been a laugh with Bobby. We could have hours of fun in the amusements. We could have even gone to see a comedy show together, just to pass some time.

By early evening I was in a bar on the Central Pier trying to drown my tedium in strong lager. I do not have to tell you, dear reader, that one's mind and reasoning is drastically altered when under the influence of alcohol. I was no different to anybody else. Worryingly, at seventeen years of age my affinity with booze was becoming something I was relying on more and more.

The drink muddled my thinking as planned. I wanted to see Bobby again. And I wanted to see her that night. I was missing somebody I hardly knew. It was madness. The more I supped, the more I was determined to see her.

I emptied the dregs of my sixth pint.

Fuck it! I'd go to her flat and see if she fancied a couple of hours on the pleasure beach. She could only say no, couldn't she?

My usual lazy stroll was nigh on a gallop as I made my way to the south end of the resort. I recalled that her place was somewhere behind the football stadium. It would be easy to find. I'd remember the brown front door with the number thirty painted on it. It seemed like enough of a clue in my inebriated state.

The setting sun encouraged the plethora of neon to acquire increasing vibrancy as daylight gradually diminished. I walked quickly down the side streets that sat under the watchful eye of the unlit floodlights of Blackpool Football Club.

It was as though I was on automatic. I located Bobby's flat off Bloomfield Road without any delay in navigation. I put it down to my in-built radar system.

I knocked on the door and waited impatiently. Seconds passed. There was no reply, and the curtains were shut. I knocked again. I was determined to see her, though admittedly it would have been a better proposition if I had been sober.

My attention became distracted by a barking dog and resultant shouting in the distance. Somebody had obviously let it run loose by accident. Out of the corner of my eye I sensed the curtain twitch at the window in front of me. There was somebody in, after all.

I knocked once more and did something that I would never have done without a drink inside me.

I crouched down and bellowed through the letter box.

'Bobby…it's me, Jamie. Are you there?'

I gave her time to answer.

No response was forthcoming.

I shouted through the letterbox again.

'Bobby…I know you're there…'

I then decided to try and coax her out with a little humour.

'I've been stood out here since last fucking night…I'll come in for that drink now if it's alright!'

I chuckled to myself, even though it slowly became obvious she did not want to speak to me.

Time for another angle of attack. I lifted the flap in the door once again.

'Roberta, will you open this bloody door at once! Do you hear me?'

Suddenly the front door flew open to reveal the inhabitant, who was of course armed and ready with her own reply.

'Don't ever fucking call me Roberta in public, again! Okay? Or you'll be chewing my fist! Have you started drinking without me? Charming, that is!'

I couldn't help but laugh out loud.

'About bleeding time! What were you doing in there?'

The lamp from Bobby's front room was partly cast across her face. I noticed a dark area under her left eye. As she turned her profile in the half light, I saw that the flesh around her eye socket was swollen to the size of an egg.

I became immediately concerned and tried to politely encourage my invitation into the flat.

'I wondered if you wanted to come out to play, tonight. I'm piss bored. I'll buy the drinks if you're skint. Just say you'll come out.'

Bobby fully opened the door.

'Alright, you whiner. Get your arse in.'

I followed her through to her kitchen, trying to catch a fuller glimpse of her bruise.

She mumbled as she led the way.

'Being as you mention it, I *am* skint…but I wouldn't go out anyway. Not tonight.'

When Bobby eventually turned around, I couldn't believe my own eyes. She was black and blue. Her cheek was the colour of a plum. She had several scratches above her eyes and on her chin.

My heart began to race. Sobriety quickly ensued.

'What the fuck happened to you, Bobby? Who the hell did this to you?'

The onset of emotion constricted her attempt to reply.

Without word, Bobby put both arms around my neck and pulled me close. She was shaking like a leaf.

I was upset for her, of course, but anger was my prevailing response.

I demanded some answers.

'Was it your boyfriend? Did he do this? Or was it his father's mates? The fucking Mitchell Brothers? All because you were talking to me in the pub, yesterday? Wait until I get hold of the bastards! They'll wish their mothers had never met their fathers…'

Bobby looked me in the eye as the fear emanated from her vandalised expression. She had taken a proper clouting. It was unbelievable that anyone could inflict such damage to such a beautiful woman. She was evidently frightened to death.

I could tell that she wanted me to be there, and that finally she wanted to talk.

'I have beer now, Jamie. Help yourself. And get me one, please.'

I grabbed us both a can of lager each from the fridge and we sat beside one another on the settee.

She composed herself as I sat looking at the surroundings. She was obviously struggling to make ends meet. The place could've done with gutting and starting again. There was rubbish, dirt, and stains everywhere. The carpet was hardly worth hoovering it was so threadbare.

Still, who was I to judge? She had more to her name than I did.

I held her hand as she composed herself.

'Bobby, what happened?'

She took a swig of beer before enlightening me.

'I didn't want you to see me like this, Jamie. That's why I didn't answer the door. But I'm really glad you came.'

I studied the purple swelling on her face.

She was almost unrecognizable from the fun-loving rogue I had spent most of Sunday with. Her hands trembled as they clasped around the beer can.

'They followed us everywhere we went, Jamie. Yesterday. They watched us all fucking day! Then when they saw you go from my door, they paid me a visit.'

'Who, those two from the pub?'

Bobby nodded.

'I told you there would be trouble, Jamie.'

I could not willingly absorb what she was telling me.

It was like something from a gangster film.

'Why did they do this? Who do they think they are?'

'They were following orders.'

'*Orders*? Orders from who?'

'From their main man.'

My mind was whirring with visions of what I'd do to them both.

Although being only a teenager probably put the odds very much against me and in the favour of the opposition.

Then it dawned on me.

Bobby's condition was mostly *my* fault.

I must have been tailed on the pier before I met Bobby at the pub.

And there was me thinking I was going stir crazy.

And it must have been one of the thugs who sat watching me whilst I ate breakfast that morning.

Yet how would he know that I would be entering that particular café out of literally dozens in the area?

Perhaps I had been followed to the council house as well?

The heat of scrutiny was becoming decidedly uncomfortable.

But at least I now had motive to start becoming paranoid.

Her treatment at their hands was testament enough to feel extremely wary of our thuggish looking observers.

'Who is this main man? Who are they working for?'

Bobby gulped more beer and slowly shook her head.

'It's complicated.'

'Try me. Talk to me like I'm a child, then.'

'The two men- Prenter and Doyle. I already told you their names yesterday, didn't I?'

I nodded, vigorously awaiting further revelation.

'Well, to cut a long story short, they run a protection racket here. They oversee many transactions through many small businesses around town. The man they take orders from is my boyfriend's father. I just get caught in the crossfire every so often.'

I had to confess that none of the story was really making sense to me so far.

'Why doesn't anyone sort these bastards out, then?'

'*Fear*, you dummy. That's how gangland works! The people making real money around here are doing it out of sight. You understand? Under the counter stuff. Illegal shit. With the regular influx of new customers every single week they can't fail to make a regular bundle, can they? But of course, the racket needs policing - that's Doyle and Prenter's role.'

Dear reader, I acknowledge that this may sound like an excerpt from a badly written soap drama, but art is often said to imitate life…and vice versa.

In my council house naivety, I never suspected that such unsavoury practice could be vibrantly operable in real life.

But it obviously was, and it was apparently going on almost everywhere around town and beyond.

'So, what did they smack you around for? Not for talking to someone who's having dinner in their pub. Please say not.'

Bobby fell quiet. She began to squeeze the top of her beer can so that it began to crunch. In the end I took it off her. She was avoiding the truth again.

'Does the main man not like you talking to other guys? Is that it?'

Again, I received the disconcerting silence.

I was now beginning to feel annoyed with her.

'Bobby, tell me…what the hell is going on? What are you caught up in?'

At long last she revealed the truth behind her connection with Doyle and Prenter.

'How green are you, Jamie? I'm a debtor, too! I owe them money. Money that I haven't got. So, they come and throw me around every so often as a reminder of my outstanding invoice. Okay? Happy now?'

I remember needing the toilet at this stage in the proceedings. Standing over the urinal I reflected on the scenario I had unwittingly become party to and began to frantically reassess my position in it.

Beyond the shadeless bulb I looked to the ceiling and the myriad of cobwebs that hung from every available anchor point. Then I looked to the floor and noticed the used syringe that had been thrown behind the pan.

I was simultaneously consumed by waves of disappointment and shock.

It had never occurred to me that Bobby could or would be a user.

Having experienced my fair share of problems in life, I had pledged long ago to steer clear of any kind of drug.

So far as I was concerned, drugs were the work of the Devil.

And here I was emptying my bladder in a junkie's toilet!

At that moment doing up my zipper, I made the decision to leave Blackpool, hopefully never to return to the shit hole again.

What a complete waste of invested time and emotion.

Mostly of my own creation, granted. I'd been a fool.

It also dawned on me that if I didn't decide to get out of the picture quickly, then was highly likely that someone weighing around sixteen stone with a leather jacket and a bald head would soon point out to me that it would be my best option, anyway.

I didn't want or need this negative environment. I was here for totally different reasons. Reasons that I'd quickly forgotten amid all this Bobby Jones bullshit.

I returned to the lounge where she had flicked on the TV and brought some much-needed fantasy into her world of harsh reality.

I thought carefully about making my excuses and leaving.

Yet as I watched her sitting uncomfortably with her badges of misfortune on display, my heart softened yet again. The humorous side of our relationship flashed before my mind once more.

Was it really fair to just bugger off and leave her to it?

The rate she was going she was likely to end up lashed to the underside of a pier as the tide comes in. These people were obviously serious about chasing debt.

That's when the thought entered my brain and tumbled from my mouth before I could even consider another, more sensible avenue.

As she sat hunched up on the sofa with the remote control in her hand, I asked her how much she owed.

Sheepishly, she answered with her own question.

'Why do you want to know?'

'Are you going to tell me?'

'About a grand, give or take. There's no interest building. Just the grand.'

It was a crazy notion, but Bobby *was* crazy, and her craziness was obviously wearing off on me.

'If I pay it, will they leave you alone?'

She averted her gaze from the screen and on to me as my offer slowly registered.

Her unexpected response was like taking a pre-empted punch in the mouth from Prenter or Doyle.

'I'm not your fucking charity case! It's not your problem, Jamie! Thanks, but no thanks.'

Well, you could have knocked me down with a bastard feather. I couldn't believe my ears. The ungrateful little cow! I felt there and then like taking a swing at her *myself.*

In fact, if Prenter and Doyle invited me to her next pummelling, I'd have joined in!

'Well, I suppose I'm no good to you either way, then. I'm off. I'm sorry to have bothered you. Have a nice life!'

I was absolutely fucking fuming. I'd been prepared to hand this stupid girl a lifeline and she could barely afford me the courtesy of gratitude. Well, fuck her and fuck Blackpool. I had made my inebriated mind up. I was on the first train home in the morning.

As I made for her front door, she finally roused herself into action at the thought of never seeing me again.

"Jamie. Please don't go. I beg you. Not yet. Stay a while. I'm sorry…okay...and…I'm bloody scared."

My fingers had come to rest on the door handle at this point.

Yet again I was face with indecision.

I turned on her, fuelled by vexation.

'I'm aware of the fact that I barely know you, Bobby, but you're in my head, okay? That's not my fault or yours. It's plain fact. I want to help you. I care. I'm sorry if you don't grasp that little issue, but I do have concern about what happens to you.'

I distinctly remember the look of consternation on her face when I revealed my intention to go back to Nottingham the next morning.

'But you see the danger I'm in, Jamie. I'm only trying to protect you. I don't want you to stay away because, I care about you also. But you're involved with an idiot – namely *me*! *I* need to get myself out of this mess. Not you. Can you understand?'

She meant every word. It was fear that had made her so reticent to invite assistance. She had learned to life live under a hard rule of self-survival. I had to respect her for that. All things considered, if she couldn't afford to have me around because it was unsafe for us both, then I would have to go.

'Do you have a mobile phone?' I asked.

She looked at me in bemusement, so I repeated the phrasing.

'It's not a difficult question. Do you have a mobile phone?'

She shook her head.

'Christ! I'm not the last, after all! Writing paper, then?'

I adopted a tone of stern assurance as I scribbled Henry's home telephone number on one half of the note paper.

Tearing it off and handing it to Bobby, I told her to write her flat number on the other half, which I then slipped into my wallet.

'I'm leaving tomorrow, whatever happens. I'm pissed off with the way things have turned out. But I will think of you, Bobby. I want you to promise me something. If you need me, you ring that number…you hear me? I can be up here the very next day.'

Bobby Jones nodded her head regretfully.

And I so wished I hadn't turned up with booze inside me.

Parting was not easy, but evidently unavoidable.

I kissed her on the cheek which had escaped a battering and wandered into the night.

Back in my apartment, I crudely crammed everything into my bag.

Ready to depart first thing in the morning.

# 22
# DISTANT DRAMA

Dejection shrouded my journey home the following day. I checked out of The Sandbar with a cheery goodbye to the gorgon of a landlady.

'Christ, lad. Thy's hardly messed the bedclothes and you're off? No money back you know? Your choice.'

It was a choice I was more than happy to make and headed straight for the nearest phone box with the intention of informing Henry of my imminent return. I still hadn't got used to using my mobile by habit.

I tried ringing him three times. There was no answer.

Thankfully I didn't have to wait too long for a rail connection to Crewe, but the time on the train dragged. My mind was filled with Bobby's ordeal, Henry's condition, and the hopeful prospect of reconciliation with Alex.

It occurred to me that amongst all the distraction I had afforded little time for the priority item on the agenda - finding my brother. I can remember instinct telling me that all hope was futile on that score.

Yet I had gone to Blackpool with such a positive attitude.

It just goes to show how wrong your instincts can be at times.

*****

It was a relief to be back in familiar territory. Henry wasn't at home when I entered his hallway. On the worktop in the kitchen, I noticed an official looking letter from the hospital, which detailed Henry's position and suggested several ways of preparing for the inevitable physical strife that was coming his way.

My feeling of depression only deepened. I should never have left him alone. Even if it *was* only four days ago.

Life could be cruel, but the alternative was far worse. Poor Henry didn't want to die, not really. He pretended that to do so would perhaps reunite him with his beloved Doris, but he didn't truthfully have much faith in such a philosophy.

It brought it home to me just how desperate Mum must have been to dispense with her own life so callously.

Many people claim that suicide is an act of cowardice. How can that be? It seems to me that to end one's own existence through a wilful decision must be the hardest and most desperate option that anyone would ever consider.

Thinking about it and doing it are completely different ends of the psychological spectrum. Poor Henry seemingly had little choice in his destiny. The decision had been made for him.

As there was no reason to stick around at Glenfield Avenue I decided to go for a stroll.

I'm sure you can guess the destination, dear reader.

Despite the drama encountered in Blackpool keeping my mind occupied, I had missed Alex deeply. I walked across town to her house with no real guarantee of the outcome of my visit.

As it turned out, I need not have fretted.

I stood outside her front gate to find the curtains were shut and nobody at home. Of course, they were on holiday in Cyprus - as I should also have been.

Kevin and Sarah Lawley must have despised me for my selfish attitude and willingness to sod off and do my own thing. I hoped Alex didn't hold it against me. I realised then - perhaps way too late in the game - that I still needed her in my life.

Whilst it was pleasant to be back, I returned to Henry's with a heavy heart. I had been in the house less than five minutes when the taxi pulled up outside.

He had been to the hospital for a formal briefing about dealing with possible problems he may face in the coming months. I felt such overwhelming guilt that I had deserted him at such a traumatic time. Yet, considering the nature of his visit, he entered the front door in a very jovial mood.

'They even told me that I could carry on smoking! Sod 'em! I would have carried on anyway! It's the only pleasure I've got left in life!'

I watched him as he ranted on about being told what might happen and what might not happen to him and his condition. It was appropriate that I listened to someone else's strife. Lord knows he'd heard enough about mine over the years.

Finally, he stopped to draw breath and gazed up at me. I looked at his face. He was tired and drawn. His brave front was doing a sterling job, mind.

'Do you want a cuppa, Henry?'

'Ay, can do, Jamie. What are you doing back anyway, lad? You ain't been gone five minutes.'

I related my experiences of the past few days and Henry listened whilst filling his pipe. I told him about the fact that I'd cashed his cheque - though not the part about offering to bail out Bobby.

He seemed glad to have me around so unexpectedly. In truth I was more than pleased to be back in Nottingham.

Then of course, my impatience got the better of me.

I had to ask him if he had seen anything of Alex.

'Sorry, son. I haven't. I hope you don't think I'm prying Jamie, but have you two had a falling out?'

I sat across from my friend as he gazed at me curiously and sipped his tea. What could I tell him? I didn't know if I'd had a falling out with her or not.

'She just decided that Blackpool wasn't for her. She wanted to come with me, but I think her parents may have put pressure on her. As it happened, she needn't have bothered coming. It was a waste of time.'

There was no way I could have known at that moment that Alex's decision not to accompany me to Blackpool was one of the vital components in this whole story. I look back now knowing full well that her presence would have dictated a totally different chain of events.

It was the fact that I had ended up going alone which, unbeknown to me at the time, had allowed me to pave the way to achieving the initial stage of my aims.

However, I'll continue to keep you in suspense, for now.

Anyway, back to grounded reality. For the next few days before the beginning of the new school term I pulled in a few shifts at the supermarket. John Harrison was flabbergasted to discover I'd given up on my excursion after only four days.

'I bet the bloody train fare amounted to more than what you spent on birds and booze! Did you crack owt, then Jay-Jay?'

Typical John. Little did he know the true intentions of my mini expedition. But then, he didn't need to know. As August evolved into September, my thoughts became centred on the immediacy of A-levels and work. They were the most important factors in my life.

However, school could prove to be a tricky environment if Alex was intending to remain incommunicado.

Yet I still felt she had no justifiable reason to be angry with me. If anything, she ought to be ready to offer an apology of sorts.

After all, it was her that had backed out on me, not the other way around.

As I half-heartedly began to lay plans for the short term, events elsewhere were about to unfold in my absence.

Had I stuck it out for the week at Blackpool and acquired the knowledge that I have now, I would probably have never left the place.

*****

In my absence, it had been a reasonably busy September Saturday afternoon in the Celtic Arms. Quieter than of late as the main thrust of the holiday season was over.

Bobby Jones had finished clearing up in the kitchen and was getting changed ready for her weekly visit to her boyfriend who lived with his father in nearby Stanley Park.

She had met them both in that very same pub almost seven years earlier. She found it to be an unusual set up, but Bobby took to the son straight away.

He was of similar age to her, extremely handsome; undoubtedly intelligent, yet there was obviously something amiss.

He was awkward in public and frequently temperamental. Not in any remotely violent manner. More like a child. He could sulk for England. But Bobby could sulk for Ireland. She was attracted to him, nevertheless.

She also sensed from the off that her boyfriend's father was keen to keep her at arm's length. But Bobby being the headstrong woman she was had no intentions of giving up on the man she had set in her sights.

A few weeks into their casually friendly relationship, she was permitted a first visit to his home - the very same house that she was about to visit that day. It was during this inaugural call that she was introduced by the father to a couple of undesirables, who promptly got her drunk and acquainted her with the dangerous yet highly enticing world of drug taking.

Whilst not turning into a full-blown addict, Bobby was quickly endeared to the bodily reaction that foreign substances induced. Unfortunately, she was oblivious to the high financial cost of keeping such company and maintaining the habit, let alone the great personal risk involved in this most unscrupulous of pastimes.

The debt mounted up over a period of months. The father decided that rather than try and get blood from a stone, Bobby could work for him at the pub he conveniently co-owned with the other two. Bobby supposed at the time that it would be a good way to repay her supplier.

But despite being streetwise in many fundamentals, Bobby Jones was naïve in this situation.

It was never intended that she would be paid a wage for her duties.

Her destiny lay along another path.

A trail of mistrust, violence and degradation awaited her. And she willingly walked that route in the belief that one day she would be freed of the burden she had incurred.

She still awaits the arrival of that day.

Luckily, her recent bruising had all but subsided. She inspected the remnants of the damage and carefully applied foundation in the backroom of the pub.

The pub's duty manager was fully aware of her current predicament and had developed a fatherly affection for his assistant.

He shouted through the closed toilet door.

'You've worked bloody hard today, Roberta. You paid off them idiots, yet?'

'No, Ken. It'll be weeks before I see any fucking wages. Still, it's my fault, isn't it?'

Waving goodbye to Ken Tatham as she marched through the bar room, she made for the nearest bus stop. It was the bus stop that she always used when going to see the man that she loved. She had made the same ten-minute journey many times over the previous years, yet the feeling of trepidation that accompanied her visits never seemed to diminish.

She recognised every visible landmark along the route as she neared her destination.

Each was a signal for her heart to begin beating just a little faster.

Her legs always felt weak when she got off the bus, as though they didn't want to carry her any further.

Then she would have to prepare for the imminent rendezvous - physically and mentally. Never knowing what she would discover behind that permanently closed door.

The rain began to fall as she knocked three times. The observer may rightly justify a case for her having her own key for access, being as this was the house of her loved one. However, the situation visible to the untrained eye could not see the misery that lay festering behind the door of number twenty-seven, Joseph Street.

Bobby Jones was one of a supposedly privileged few. Entry to this domain was strictly forbidden to the great majority. Yet she was deemed to be an accepted face on entering the vicinity.

Firstly because of her love for the man in her life; and she did, truly love him. But also, because she owed his father money - money that she didn't have.

Money that she would never, ever have, for that matter.

Money that was certainly not needed by her pusher, anyhow. She had fallen into the trap that many occasional users should strive to avoid. Never take drugs without offering the money up front. Cash is an unequivocal settlement.

It leaves no doubt. There is no potential for leeway; money is the currency of absolution.

To strike suitably alternative bargains over drug deals is a route to oblivion. Hence, Bobby Jones was now in a situation of such helpless vulnerability, that she was forced to discharge her arrears in other ways - on a regular, weekly basis.

Dear reader, I trust you will not require any specific expansion on the nature of her repayments. Suffice to say, that the arrangement dictated that she was able to acquire a moderate amount of any substance that took her fancy, at any given time.

Her supplier was guaranteed a more than satisfactory remittance.

The predator's claws were now well and truly sunk into his desperate quarry.

So, as she waited for a response to her knock on the door, one can only presume the terror that awaited her on the other side. For many weeks over many months over many years, Bobby dreamed of a way out of this vicious circle.

Little did she know as she stood waiting outside number twenty-seven on that day in late summer, that she had already encountered the answer to her wish for immunity.

Although a short while ago, she had nothing but fond memories of that handsome, blond haired teenager from Nottingham. His contact number remained safely secret. For who knows what reaction it should provoke if she was found with it on her person.

She had already taken a hiding for spending the afternoon with him. What would be next if she was found to be a willing companion to the stranger from the Midlands?

As her mind pondered the possibilities, the front door of number twenty-seven was opened, and she was ushered in by the older of the two occupants.

The tall, well-built man in his late forties sported a three-day growth of stubble and looked in need of a good bath. He scanned up and down the street for unwelcome onlookers as Roberta Jones - as she was always referred to in his company - entered the premises.

The hallway stunk of tobacco, booze, and a putrid mixture of other various though conveniently unidentifiable exotic odours. The wallpaper accommodated damp. Dirty laundry lay scattered over the stairway and hall carpet.

Bobby's heart would not relent. It beat so hard she could almost hear it echoing. Her eyes moistened as the man placed a gruff hand on her shoulder and pointed up the stairway toward the bedroom.

Words were not exchanged for the duration of the next sixty minutes.

Afterwards, Bobby - as always - felt utterly repugnant.

She pulled her underwear back on as a tear rolled down her cheek. She did not want her loved one to see her cry. She re-applied some make-up in the sullied pit of a bathroom, before waiting on the landing for her boyfriend's father to emerge from his insidious lair.

He walked past her at the top of the stairs and offered a sinister wink and a crooked, gap-toothed smile.

Bobby forced a half-grimace in response.

She was glad that the degrading ritual was completed for another week.

She followed the man downstairs and to a door which was locked. He pulled a key from his pocket and let her in. The lounge room was kept in semi darkness by permanently closed curtains.

The younger man sat in the single armchair in the middle of the room watching television and offering intermittent commentary to an absent audience.

As Bobby entered, the door was shut and locked behind her. At last, she could be alone for a short while with her love. She approached her boyfriend and gave him a kiss on the cheek.

The recipient diverted his attention from the screen to the visitor and presented her with the broadest, most affecting smile she had ever seen.

He pointed to the television once again, identifying the source of his mirth.

'Road Runner isn't clever. It's just that Coyote never learns!'

Back as her preferred personality of Bobby Jones once again, she sat on the chair opposite and looked admiringly at the man that had become the centre of her whole life, the nucleus of her dreams and the sole reason she retained hope for the future.

She smiled adoringly back at him and spoke with a calming voice.

'Hello, Martin, my darling. How are you today?'

# 23
# A PRAYER FOR JAMIE

You will interpret my next move as an act of weakness, and you are fully entitled to that opinion. You would be entirely correct. The first day of the new school year began in early September.

I opted not to attend.

In principle, I was attuned the fact that I needed to concentrate on my education and try and ignore other distractions. But I was not ready to face Alex just yet. I felt bad about the way we had parted. She was in pieces in those last few days. Confronting her so soon would have been awkward to say the least.

Little did I know at the time but again my concerns for Alex were due to be eclipsed by a chain of events that defy belief and encompassed all that fate can deliver.

I had just about settled into a routine that would accommodate Henry's needs and the demands of working practically full-time hours again for John Harrison.

Henry was not dealing with his ailment well. Mentally he was in good fettle, but his lungs were being increasingly ravaged as the weeks passed. Still, he continued to smoke and still he smiled, but the things his took for granted only a few months ago were becoming matters of extreme exertion.

He wanted to prepare the garden in readiness for the onset of seasonal change. It was a part of his life that he loved dearly. The prospect of not even being able to fill his chest with fresh air for the task was one that Henry found both daunting and intensely frustrating.

The slightly colder mornings made it impossible to breathe without irritation and inevitably this begun to affect his energy levels. Having to be careful even for a short time was depressing him slowly but surely. As usual, I was helpless to assist. A knowledge that so weighed me down.

There was another development currently. I had started to have nightmares again. Not as frequently as before, but still filled with the images of pain that flashed repeatedly before my conscience in the dark hours. I felt the calling once more. My being was under summons.

Yet I was still at a loss as to the origin of the distress.

Turmoil was upon me once again.

*****

The younger man looked at the mound of food that he had just spilled onto the kitchen floor. His father's meal was now inedible. The consequences of such an incident would be predictable and inevitable.

Jim Andrews threw the kitchen door open wide to reveal the carnage of his spoiled egg and chips. He looked at the cause of the atrocity. His son quivered in anticipation.

The temper welled within his father just as a rumbling volcano would threaten to erupt.

In anticipation of a cruel retribution, the son began to retreat toward the back door. Typically, he found it to be locked. He turned to witness the raging form of his father.

'You fuckin' retard! Can't do anything, can you? No wonder I have to keep you locked up! You're a fucking liability to the world! Useless!'

The younger man was being goaded. It was the usual game. He would offer his typically intelligent and sarcastic wit in responding to his father's anger.

'The floor is clean. The crockery is dirty. Food good still. Still eat. It'll be okay, Daddy.'

Jim Andrews was not a man for laughing at his son's - or anyone's for that matter - attempts at humour. He certainly did not take kindly to being the subject of spontaneous comment, or perhaps even ridicule.

Especially from the offspring he resented so deeply.

Subsequently, he reacted in the manner of a person whose articulacy had only developed through action of body, as opposed to word of mouth.

Two generations faced each other at opposite sides of the room. The protagonists were ready for battle. There would be only one winner.

The older man made his advance with a familiar war cry.

'You think you're clever, don't you? I'll show you who the clever one is. Fuckin' retard!'

Rooted to the spot by a customary reverence, Martin Andrews felt the vice-like grip of his father close around his throat. Within seconds his lungs became restricted of air flow and the younger man began to panic.

He briefly observed the dimming vision of his father's manic expression.

In desperation he flailed wildly with both arms, catching his father's nose with a loosely directed fist.

A most regrettable move.

It was the first beating he had taken from his father in a few weeks. The continual reign of blows to his head and body more than compensated for the recent absence of such treatment.

As his head lay in the meal that had fallen from his father's plate, Martin cried and whimpered like a lame dog facing the end game.

Jim Andrews only ceased the tirade having exhausted his energy after an unflinching bout of inflicting the paternal wrath. After a short respite, he grabbed his son by the hair and dragged him into the lounge, before locking the door once again.

Jim Andrews then went out of the house, leaving his son to drown in pain and anguish.

Rather than struggle and acknowledge his injuries, Martin remained where his father left him and wept until sleep eased his sufferance.

The last vision he beheld before relenting to slumber was of Bobby.

The woman he loved; the centre of his world and his sole reason for retaining any hope for the future.

*****

Time passed quickly. My longing for Alex had not cured itself. I had not seen her since the summer.

I awoke in the middle of the night. I don't know what time it was or even what day it was. I recall that it was well into October. I had just finished a long shift at work a few hours earlier. My eyes would not focus, yet my mind was concentrated on a sound from the next room.

I attuned my hearing before trying to identify the source of the repeated drone. I quickly attributed the noise to the telephone in the front lounge. I crawled out of bed and first checked in on Henry. He was sleeping soundly. I ventured to the living room where the harsh ring tone called loudly in my delicate ear.

It seemed far more resonant than normal. The face on the mantelpiece clock read at ten past three. Who the hell would be calling at that ridiculous hour?

Tentatively, I lifted the receiver in the murk and placed it to my cheek. The voice that spoke was somewhat familiar, though not immediately recognisable.

Then my responses gradually became alerted to the situation.

It was the last person I had expected to hear from. The accent was broad and brash. Yet the tone sounded reserved and tense.

My docile head was quickly jolted into a state of concern.

'Hello, Jamie…is that you? Please God…I hope so…Jamie?'

I rubbed my eyes and could not suppress a yawn.

'Hello…who is this? Bobby?'

'Yes…it's me…help me…Jamie…I need you to come back…*we* need you…'

My first pointless visit to Blackpool had become a distant, faded memory for me by then. Although it was only two months earlier, it generated little in the way of any positive recollection.

Aside from meeting Bobby Jones.

Her phone call was - if I'm completely honest - something I never expected to happen.

I fully believed that our acquaintance was to be forever confined to those few dramatic hours in August.

However, as I stood in Henry's lounge with receiver in hand, I remembered what I said to her just before I left.

I had instructed her to contact me should she ever need my help. It was a firm offer with an earnest motive. I liked the girl. I had made a point of telling her so.

Evidently, the trouble she faced had become unbearable to face alone.

I would be true to my word.

Her initial call was short and emotional. She did not divulge any detail. We agreed that I would travel up the next day. An arrangement was made that we would meet at her flat. She was to lock herself in and stay put.

I made my promise to ring her as soon as I arrived at Blackpool railway station.

It was to be the most incredulous week of my entire life.

# 24
# A FATHER'S SON

It was a shrill mid-October morning when I stood on the platform at Nottingham train station. Although now a journey with obvious familiarity, the certain aggravation - and undoubted danger - at the other end of the line was a prospect that I did not wish to try and ascertain in advance.

As far as I was concerned, I was going to help a friend. She was a friend that I didn't have three months earlier. Little did I know then of the importance of my imminent reunion with Bobby Jones.

The stark reality and total coincidence of events still confound me to this day.

The pure chance of two souls meeting to confront their individual yet intricately intertwined fates was an occurrence that can only be commandeered by some higher force. Mere mortals cannot have the power to influence events in such a way. But as I said, dear reader, my life and the decisions involved in it were pretty much mapped out for me.

Somebody else always had control. I rarely did so.

I had left a note for Henry as he was still sleeping when I left the house that morning. He had started to have longer lie-ins as the autumn months set in. It was a laborious undertaking for him to try and be up and active every day, and when he did so he would begin a coughing fit that could last anything up to an hour and often longer.

To leave a note may have seemed too convenient a gesture on my part, but I didn't want to worry him. In hindsight it was probably downright discourteous. I swore to myself that I would ring him on reaching Blackpool.

*Déjà vu?* It's my middle name.

The train journey including the connection at Crewe seemed to take far less time that the first occasion. I barely recognized the passing scenery, however. Maybe it was because my mind was fixed on a purpose this time, whereas before I had no agenda to follow, and I could let my attention wander freely.

My eventual arrival in Blackpool was greeted by a severe rainstorm, causing me to find shelter until it eased off.

I rang Bobby to confirm my position and headed for Bloomfield Road.

I can clearly visualize the steamed-up windows of the tram and the crude shapes that had been administered into the condensation.

I think it must have been half-term because there were a lot of kids around for a weekday. Within minutes I was standing outside Bobby's front door. Unlike the first time I found myself in this position, the door was opened within seconds of my initial knock.

As one may imagine, she was more than gratified by my presence. I was thankful to see that her face appeared to be bruise-free, and we embraced tightly for a full minute.

Again, it is almost unreal when I look back on the chain of events. Hugging virtual strangers was not a practice I was familiar with.

Exchanging the usual formalities about trains and weather was quickly dispensed but the true nature of our reunion was avoided. I made us coffee and we sat in the lounge.

I noticed that Bobby appeared to have made attempts to tidy the place up. Bless her. She looked remarkably well, considering what she was about to reveal. Perhaps she had made the effort for me specially. Typically, she tried to dodge the real problem for a while.

Her divertive tactics were quite exhaustive.

'How's school going?'

'Did you make up with Alex?'

'How's Henry doing?'

'Did I still have the supermarket job?'

Responding with short answers to her queries shortened her delay in telling me why the hell she had phoned me less than twenty-four hours earlier.

I rightly expressed my own concerns.

'You sounded very afraid, Bobby. You sounded scared and desperate. What's going on?'

As if I couldn't hazard a guess.

Before she could utter a word, her Irish bravado disappeared to be replaced by a child-like visage. She did not cry; yet I could see that her emotions were on a raw edge.

She hadn't disclosed much information about her boyfriend until then, other than brief and vague references. She began to talk again about the drugs, the origins of her relationship with her boyfriend's father and the mess she now found herself in regarding him. She also spoke of the violence that had been perpetrated unto herself over recent times.

I was literally gob smacked as she disclosed layer after layer of disheartening tragedy.

Yet even all these terribly negative issues were not her primary concern.

'My boyfriend is in trouble, Jamie. I don't know what to do.'

Bobby relayed the scenario. The man she loved was being beaten regularly by his own father. It sickened me to hear it. My preconceptions about the insular and unsociable nature of the man of her dreams were instantaneously reversed.

Action was required, but Bobby felt helpless.

She could not go to the law. Involvement with the police could undermine an entire empire of debauchery that had been nurtured over the years. Everyone would be sunk if officialdom became alerted. The repercussive ripples would be eternal and detrimental.

A lot of people had a lot to lose, including Bobby herself running the risk of jail. Ultimately, Bobby was not looking for revenge.

No. She wanted advice on how to set the wheels of freedom in motion. She told me that she wanted to escape with her man to a better place. Somewhere away from the worry, the suffering, and the constant threat of hurt. A place where she could help her boyfriend to become confident and enjoy the life he deserved. Help him maybe to get work.

She had privately harboured dreams of marriage. Children were a possibility. She admitted that she wanted to start a family one day. Do normal things that normal people do.

Yet there was seemingly no way out from the corruptive and abusive lifestyle cycle into which they had been ensnared.

In short, Bobby had a plan and she wanted me to help her realize it.

I listened intently as she spoke. She was a different person from the brave actress of the summer. A quietly cocky determination had evolved into thriving, relentless necessity of ambition. And she wanted to do all these things with the man she loved.

Yet naturally I had questions of my own.

There were gaps in the jigsaw, and I needed pieces putting in place if I was to be of any real assistance. I conveyed difficult enquiries of my own which received curt response.

'Why does your boyfriend choose to spend his life a recluse?'

The pain in her mind became expressly visible as she responded.

'It isn't his choice, Jamie.'

'I don't understand. Why doesn't he come and visit *you*?'

'He's not allowed. He lives under lock and key.'

My initial reaction of mirth was crushed as the realization dawned that Bobby was not joking.

I probed further into her web of despair.

'Why does his father resent him so much?'

Bobby wiped her eyes and took several deep breaths.

It was evidently arduous to talk about such things.

She had always believed that no one would ever care enough to listen to her. She knew that in me, she had found a true friend. Little did she know how much influence I was about to have in her life. For her to reveal her innermost thoughts openly was obviously an ordeal.

'He has a condition. He was born autistic. His father blames the world for his imperfect son.'

It was difficult enough for me to hear; let alone for Bobby to say it. I considered how to approach things further. Something in the back of my mind was becoming seriously alerted to the forthcoming revelation.

Amid the consuming darkness, I could see emerging shafts of light.

That light was showing the way forward.

I made a demand of her. Her reply to which would change my entire focus in a split second.

It was fortunate I was sitting down when she answered.

'Can you tell me your boyfriend's name? Give me his name, Bobby. If I'm going to help you, you've got to knock down some basic barriers for me."

She paused for a few seconds. In hindsight, I wish she'd have taken longer before speaking.

Yet somehow when the moment happened, I already knew what she was going to say.

Yet even now, I can't determine how I knew.

I just instinctively...*knew*.

'His name is Martin. Martin Andrews.'

My initial, off the bat reaction was to ask her to repeat the name she had just pronounced.

She tentatively complied.

The subsequent shock that raced through my body was comparable to a million vaults of electricity.

Instantaneously my head began to spin, and my heart raced as though it would explode.

Then I began to shake uncontrollably as I sat opposite Bobby in the armchair.

I went to stand. Instead, I fell to my knees and crawled across the floor to where she sat. The tears were unrelenting.

Simply an immense, emotional, relieving release.

I buried my head in her lap and cried in joy; in desperation; and slowly, a realisation of what I had inadvertently discovered - by pure and total coincidence.

Even now, it is exacting and possibly inappropriate to try and paint a picture in words of what I was experiencing at that moment in Bobby Jones' living room.

All I could do for minutes on end was look up through my raw, tear-strewn eyes.

I so wanted to tell her: *that's him, that's got to be him.*

Inevitably and of course, ironically, Bobby was becoming confused at an equal rate to my growing comprehension.

All this time…I had been correct.

The calling; the signs; Father Carroll's forecast.

It was all there. All of it was in place. Waiting for me to open my eyes and discover it. Bobby Jones had been that beacon of light. It had shone bright enough to allow a union that would change our lives implicitly.

How and why, I had happened to stumble upon her through my own free choice on that lazy Sunday dinnertime back in the summer is unanswerable.

For my life to alter so dramatically through the simple act of walking into that pub on that day is beyond reasonable analysis.

That is why I firmly believe that someone else was showing me the correct path. It can be the only conceivable conclusion.

Coincidence is irrelevant and does not even approach a placating explanation. As I contemplated the situation on my knees in front of her, it was as though somebody was finally hauling me from a black hole that I had spent years wading around in, blindly and aimlessly.

As I retained a semblance of composure, I engaged with Bobby's expression. Understandably, she was completely perplexed.

I had gone to help *her*. Inadvertently, she had assisted me more than I could have ever dreamed.

We would need to do some fast talking.

My next question was obvious.

'Bobby…do you have a photograph…of your boyfriend?'

She did not seem to understand the necessity of my request.

My voice trembled with a combination of authority and urgency.

Her blank and soundless response was instantly irritating, and I conveyed as much.

"…a fucking photo…of Martin…get me one…now!"

Bobby jumped to her feet and scampered to her bedroom.

She returned within seconds presenting to me a six by four inch still in a silver frame. I remember snatching it from her and squeezing the pewter between my fingers and thumbs as I analysed the man in the picture.

It was him. There was no doubt in my mind.

I could see the face of the boy I once knew, in the image of the man she now loved.

'This is fucking unreal, Bobby! It can't be happening.'

She continued to gaze vacantly at my frothing visage before her own powers of deduction prompted a query at last.

'Are you trying to tell me that you *know* my boyfriend? You're acting like you've met him.'

I laughed heartily.

I then shook my head as more tears fell and then I laughed some more.

Not in amusement or joviality. But in sheer undiluted, ecstasy.

'Bobby…Martin is…*he* is…the reason I originally came here…'

Her eyes narrowed as a half-smirk emerged on her beautiful face.

I continued to clasp the photograph as unrestrained excitement possessed me.

'Why, Jamie? When have you seen him before? Who is Martin to you?'

For the first time in my life, I experienced what it might be like to feel utter elation.

I put the photo frame down and held Bobby's hands in my own.

I spoke calmly so she would understand me at the first attempt.

'Bobby…the man you love…*he* is my elder brother…*he* is who I've been looking for. *Martin*…is why I am here…'

# 25
# SIBLING LESSONS

My revelation rocked Bobby Jones to her already unstable foundations.

Her eyes widened and whitened as she digested my announcement.

'It can't be. You're being ridiculous, surely? It's beyond belief. Your...*brother*? The brother you've not seen for nearly ten *years*? But Martin has never even mentioned having a brother. Are you sure, Jamie? You wouldn't be winding me up, would you?'

Quite understandably, the reality of the matter did not seem to register easily with Bobby. She desperately rankled with any potentially alternative explanations.

'You must be mistaken.' she claimed.

'Not a chance.' I volleyed.

This was destiny's prophecy being fulfilled.

I had been shown where to look for Martin and I had found him. There was no single strand of doubt in my mind. I didn't want to even acknowledge the possibility that Bobby's boyfriend was *not* my brother.

He was where I had been sent to look.

I had been ordained to find him.

I was now so close to satisfying that wondrous call.

I spent the afternoon with Bobby, discussing Martin and his apparent affliction. So many instances that I recalled from our younger lives together were now woven as the complete tapestry, as opposed to a futile struggle to connect loose threads.

It became painfully clear to me that our father had treated Martin as some sort of alien for the duration of their fractious relationship.

My brother had effectively suffered nearly thirty years of rejection.

The tragic thing was, he would not have known his life to be any different to other people's.

That was why he watched the rest of his family ride the balloon on Wollaton Park, without the merest strain of belief that he too should have been involved and he should have desired the same.

Martin had spent his life stranded as a castaway.

Literally, spiritually, and metaphorically.

My mind again recalled the ingrained image of us hiding in the coal bunker. I finally understood the significance of such an innocuous event.

He was following *my* lead.

Martin saw my way of escape as a respite from the situation he was party to, and he simply copied me.

He was not following his own instincts.

He was following *mine.*

Bobby was spot on. He needed someone special to communicate with. During our childhoods, as my parents' regular and mutual torrents of abuse resonated out of the house and into the street, I had been that someone who showed him asylum.

And so, it would be once more.

I wondered if he would remember me from all those years ago.

The last time he looked at my face was when he was exiled from home and forced to leave Lodge Close. A solemn wave from the back window of a taxicab. Although not that long ago in terms of years, I would not look the same to him. I had developed as an adolescent. Change in physical state is unavoidable.

The boys of then were now grown men.

The prospect of our overdue re-acquaintance was all consuming.

But I had to be patient. The status quo was precarious for all concerned.

I asked Bobby to revive her early memories of Martin. She sat cross-legged on the settee. The smile never faded from her face. I could see the evidently deep affection that she beheld for my brother.

'I remember how so shy he was when I first laid eyes on him. Obviously, I didn't know about his autism then. Nobody told me. Not until I took him to a doctor. I think we were both around twenty-years-old. There or there abouts. I just couldn't believe that such a gorgeous, intelligent man could be so withdrawn and wary. I just wanted to help him out of his shell.'

I smiled as the mental image of them together conjured itself in my head.

'No doubt you gave that your best effort!' I chuckled.

'Yes, but I quickly discovered that it wasn't so much a defective problem that he had. Once that awkward top dressing of his personality was uncovered, he came to life. All he ever needed was someone to relate to. Someone he was comfortable with. A sounding board.'

I couldn't help but chuckle.

I was now delirious with expectation.

'You were his saviour, Bobby. But neither of you knew it.'

'I don't think he had ever had any friends before. Then I appeared on the first night he had ever been to a *pub*! *Me* for Christ's sake! All gob and cowboy boots! Well, I wasn't to know, was I? Whatever chance did the poor lad have? I took to him straight away. And he was very receptive to my interest.'

It was difficult for me to bridge the gap between then and now.

What had gone wrong for them both if their meeting was so inspiring?

'Slowly but surely, I was turning Martin into an individual. Your father suddenly felt threatened by Martin's intellectual progress. And believe me, Jamie - your brother is so very *clever*! But your father didn't trust me because of this. He was scared it would upset his cosy, twisted little existence. Martin and his father would begin to argue regularly in public. He was no longer the tame boy that tagged along with his dad. He was becoming freed of the shackles that he had known all his life. With me around, he quickly realized that he didn't need his father anymore.'

I could not help but feel gut-wrenching sorrow for the solitary existence my brother must have endured.

The further my mind pondered the situation then more pertinent questions began to emerge.

'Did he ever talk about me to you, Bobby?'

'No…not once…he's never mentioned you, Jamie. Honestly. I'd tell you if he did.'

'Did he have any possessions that might have given you some hint to his history? Photographs or the like?'

'No. It was probably forbidden for him to talk openly about his past, anyway. Like I say, when he started to spout opinion on things, your dad only knew one way to keep him quiet."

It was only then that I had started to understand the hatred that our father must have felt for Martin.

As the afternoon wore on, I found myself immersed in total admiration of Bobby Jones. She had been there for my brother throughout the later period of his lifelong ordeal.

And most importantly, she wanted to see him break out from it.

Yet the realization also dawned that reconciliation would not be a simple operation. There were perilous complications.

Primarily the detestable attitude of our father. Not to mention the circle of suspicious and undoubtedly violently defensive cohorts that he had surrounded himself with.

The time ticked on as Bobby and I tossed theories around for what had transpired over the past few years. Our father had never been a loving man. I could vouch for that much. He was overdue some penance for his brutality.

If he had taken to beating his own son, he would need to be confronted head on. If that was the only language he understood, then so be it.

It was a very unpleasant prospect. Yet I was also aware that my uninvited appearance on the scene could severely complicate matters.

I had the chance to formulate a successful solution in the palm of my hand, yet it could so easily go wrong and slip through my fingers.

Bobby's initial disbelief at the sudden revelations didn't wear off for a few hours. Pondering the next move, we found ourselves in something of a no-win scenario. All I could be sure of was that I wanted desperately to see Martin.

How to go about achieving such an ambition required serious thought. But I had to rescue him from this cess pit of a town.

His suffering needed to end as soon as possible.

That was the only certain priority.

'How does Martin feel about spending the rest of his life with you, Bobby? Have you spoken to him about your feelings regarding the relationship? Are you really that serious about him?'

With the umpteenth mug of coffee in her grasp, Bobby thought carefully about her reply.

Immediately I took it to mean that she hadn't broached *any* opinion on any of her future hopes to my brother.

She suddenly adopted a defensive air.

'That was only me messing, you know, back in the summer. I'd *never* be unfaithful to Martin. Even though I'm a born flirt. All eyelashes and legs, me.'

Time for a tease.

'Bobby…I realised when I first met you that you were full of it. I can see you'd never hurt him. You love him, don't you? I *know* you do!'

Her smile slowly vanished as she analysed the scale of constraint that had been placed upon her and Martin's relationship.

'We've never had chance to plan anything! I'm only allowed to see him once a week now, Jamie. If I'm lucky, I get half an hour alone with him.'

The sickening reality of it all fuelled my inner fury as Bobby continued.

'If Doyle and Prenter are around, then I don't get to be alone with Martin at all. It's fucking crap. So, my opportunities to tell him I love him have been minimal. And I would never let them fuckers hear me tell him how I felt. It would really mess things up for us.'

I looked Bobby straight in the eye.

'So, you've never told him that you love him?'

She uncrossed her legs and stood up.

I repeated the question as she averted her gaze through the window.

'No…I haven't. It doesn't seem fair to him. The moment's never arisen when it felt right to do so. It would only cause him more pain. Especially if he doesn't understand.'

Now I was really confused.

'How can that be? You just said that you are best friends. If you want more than that then you must be honest with him, Bobby."

She shook her head.

The atmosphere was becomingly decidedly awkward.

'When it comes to passion, I've only kissed him properly twice. And both times were our first two Christmases together.'

I pondered her plea.

'But you've known him a lot longer than that!'

'Yes…I know I have! But I'm not allowed to see him now, am I? Not even on bastard Christmas Day!'

My frustration was growing by the hour.

The more Bobby told me, the more consuming my desire to put things right became.

Her sorrowful disclosure was never-ending. I could do nothing but listen.

After all, she knew him far better than I did.

'He doesn't understand love as we do, Jamie. Only a comforting presence. He'll talk all day about stuff that doesn't matter. But I can't expect him to know how to love anyone if his family life hasn't presented him with any idea of what it actually *means* to love. You must give it to receive it. How can he comprehend such a policy? How can I open my heart up to him while he's watching fucking Tom and Jerry? He's on a totally different planet most of the time. I just wait for the day when I can be with him on my own terms and not his fucking father's. Then I can proceed to love him as I want to. I'm sorry, but your father is a psycho bastard and deserves to die in hell! Him and his evil mates.'

It had been an emotive afternoon to say the least.

Her tears fell again as she relayed her desperation to me. I was still only just beginning to grasp the gravity of the situation.

Martin was a prisoner. Bobby was a prisoner.

It was a depressing scenario to try and absorb.

I was also effectively a prisoner - of my own upbringing and history. I had never been able to live life as I had wanted. It was always as though I was incomplete in some way. I never felt myself to be a fully rounded person.

There was a persistent sense of injustice, almost a hollowness that followed me everywhere.

The time had come to address the wrong doings that had been inflicted on my brother and me. It was time for some retribution. We had lost already lost Mum due to the burden that Jim Andrews had imposed on his family.

Father Carroll was correct when he said that Mum did not have the strength to fight for her beliefs. She was a martyr that could not cope with the cause.

I considered her death to be a futile act of sacrifice. Losing her would *have* to be turned into an advantageous event to her sons.

I would see to it that even though she was now liberated from a vast sea of wretchedness and woe, her death would not be in vain.

I would avenge her desolation.

I pledged my undying aid to Bobby.

I wanted to make both our dreams come true.

It was agreed there and then that I would stay with her indefinitely.

The talking had at last secured a solution, but our mutually exhaustive game of catch-up had left us dog-tired.

Lying on the sofa I closed my eyes and searched for sleep.

I said my silent prayer for Martin.

I hoped he could hear me.

I was not far away now.

*****

Across town in a darkened kitchen, three men played cards by lamp light and drank spirits. In the adjacent room, the son of one of the men slept soundly in his armchair.

The TV flickered incessantly with a late-night news bulletin.

The card game reached an explosive conclusion, resulting in the table being up ended and considerable verbal dissatisfaction being expressed.

One of the men rose unsteadily to his feet as he ranted.

'Are you fuckers in this together? I haven't won for days!'

One of the seated men urged his friend to calm down.

'Jim…for god's sake…it's only a game, man! It's not even our money we're playing with! Let's play another hand if you're not happy with this one…'

But Jim Andrews' temper was well and truly lost. In his alcoholic daze he announced that they should indeed revert to another form of entertainment.

'Nah! Fuck cards. We are going to play burn the blind man! Great fun! Where's that retard of mine…'

Martin did not hear the key turn in the lock of the lounge door. His state of slumber also nullified his response to the first punch. The large fist that snatched the hair on his scalp soon began to rouse his senses as he was pulled from his chair and into the kitchen.

As soon as his vision cleared, it was hindered again with the use of a tea towel.

Now blindfolded, Martin could only sit and wait for the torture to begin.

One of the men, Loz Prenter, held him fast to the chair by his wrists as the other, Ian Doyle, righted the dining table and firmly held Martin's left hand, palm down against its surface.

Jim Andrews watched with delight as his friends became excited by the prospect of the sickening display.

Their wild cackling and drunken calls of encouragement were only matched by the expectant whimpering of the victim.

That was soon ended as a heavily soiled dish cloth was forced into his mouth.

Martin convulsed in the chair as his father lit a cigarette. Jim Andrews did not like to lose at cards. Martin did not like his father to lose at cards, either.

He could only sit and submit to the consequences, as the aroma of tobacco was eventually mixed ever so slightly with that of burned flesh.

Agonized yet muffled screams were eclipsed by the raucous laughter of the three spectators.

Minutes later, as the cigarette finally burned down to the nub, Jim Andrews was only just beginning to enjoy himself. He watched his son grow limp with pain, as he carefully lit another.

The blindfold became sodden with the tears of desperation.

Martin silently screamed for the game to stop.

When it eventually did so, he was thrown back into his lounge room cell. His head cracked against the hard floor. His hands were blistered and raw; his throat dry and strained.

Like so many times previously in his life, Martin was left to dwell in contemplation of his own pain.

He dared not open his eyes just in case the trio of executioners were in proximity.

His temple throbbed against the rough floorboard.

His heart, although broken long ago, still beat ferociously.

It was then that he sensed a change in the spiritual dynamic.

A new realm was on the verge of being discovered.

From the deep, desperate cavern of his mind, the turgid thoughts of what was possibly still to come suddenly scurried for cover.

No longer was his head full of such chronic infestation.

A light appeared to scatter the perverse and injurious demons that has for too long tormented and dominated his existence.

It emerged dimly at first; then grew gradually brighter.

Then that same light shone the way for an approaching stranger.

Martin opened his eyes to discover his own weeping had stopped.

He now knew his calling had been answered at last.

# 26
# CONFRONTATION

Memory is typically scant, but I think it was a Friday morning when Bobby and I awoke together in her flat. She had slept in her bedroom; I had made do with the sofa.

As I switched the kettle on, Bobby ambled into the kitchen in a pair of briefs and the skimpiest bra I had ever seen. Not that I was a connoisseur in such things. I was almost stuck for words as she defiantly stood right in front of me.

'God, I'm knackered, Jamie. What time were we up talking to?'

I struggled to avoid even the briefest glance at her physical form before ushering her for a dressing gown.

'Put some clothes on, Bobby. You'll catch your death. It isn't summer now, you know! There's tea brewing.'

She chuckled and turned on her heel.

'Well, I do declare that's the first time anyone has hurried me up to get dressed. It's usually the opposite request. You're a strange one Jamie, my lad.'

I smiled to myself as she went back into her room.

We were now a team, united in our cause, yet up until then lacking a coherent strategy for the way forward.

And could now sense that Martin knew I had come for him. He had been remarkably patient. If my expression sounds rather fanciful, dear reader, then I make no apology. I had come to believe that my future by this point was firmly in the hands of the Great One.

I was quite prepared to submit to his prophecies. I was totally in fate's hands. Bobby felt it also, though her approach to the day was rather more direct as she reappeared now adorned by a bath robe.

'When are we going to sort out those tossers then, Jamie?'

After a terminally interrupted night rolling around on the settee, I had not yet formulated any detailed plan of attack.

We debated the appropriate next stage.

I threw an idea into the ring.

'What if we head to the Celtic Arms? Just see how the land is lying?'

Bobby nodded enthusiastically as she sipped her tea.

'Great idea…Ken will know where the pricks are likely to be today.'

It slowly occurred to me that Bobby had no intention of taking the lead in our mission.

I knew she was scared, but I wasn't exactly brimming with confidence, either. Our very appearance together would immediately ruffle the relevant feathers. That is before we could even consider our next move.

As in all cases of doubt, I opted for another cuppa. It does actually soothe the mind. Tea allows the true conscience to become focused.

Besides, I was becoming more than a little reticent in facing the inmates of the pub. Any delay tactic was most welcome.

We eventually dressed and left her flat at around midday. Stepping outside the front door sent a chill down my spine, accentuated by a sharp autumn wind in my face. It was as though I were on a film set. The avenger of wrongdoing ready to embark on his super-hero mission.

We opted to walk to the north end of the resort as opposed to taking a tram. It would help us prepare our minds for the unpredictability of what lay in store for the pair of us. We linked arms for the full half hour stroll. As the tower grew ever more imposing high above us, our touch grew tighter and our pace a little slower.

Nervous was not the word by this point.

I can remember us taking a right-hand turn at the tower base. Along a couple of shopping precincts and across a couple of roads. I could soon see the overhead signage of the pub, being buffeted against the grey October sky.

All parts of my body were reacting in varying resistant ways on our approach to the entrance door. I would rather have been anywhere in the world than outside the Celtic Arms at that moment.

Then quite surprisingly, Bobby suggested that she make the first advance.

'I can go in and say hello to Ken, have a look at what's happening. I'll come back out to you if the coast is clear.'

I stood on the adjacent street corner as Bobby entered the bar. Scanning the area all around me, I backed into a convenient alcove. I hoped that Bobby's show of bravado was not for my benefit. My fingers were crossed that it was an earnest display of fortitude.

The seconds passed slowly. I looked around me once more in all directions. I hadn't yet been detected as far as I could tell.

Then finally, Bobby re-appeared and beckoned me across the road and inside the premises.

The lingering aroma of ale and ash was instantly recognizable from my previous visits - as was the face of the ever-smiling manager, Ken Tatham.

On seeing me he offered his usual greeting. I shook his strong hand in genuine warmth. I quite liked old Ken even though I hardly knew him.

'Well, well…look who's turned up, again. What's the matter, Jamie…you been missing her roast dinners? Shame it's her day off today.'

We chuckled as Ken fixed us a coffee each. Bobby suggested that we perch on stools facing the doorway. At least then we couldn't be taken by surprise. Ken seemed a little on edge as I recall. Not so talkative and upbeat as he had been before.

Whilst he appeared to be concentrating on his work, he would intermittently glance toward the entrance door and then back to the pair of us. After five or so minutes, the silence was screaming to be broken. As usual, Bobby did not need much encouragement in that department.

'Has Jim been in lately, Ken?'

Wide-eyed, Ken observed Bobby with an obvious degree of suspicion.

I could sense his immediate unease regarding the subject.

'Erm…no…can't say I've seen him around, love…why do you ask?'

Bobby slurped her cappuccino and wiped froth from the tip of her nose before continuing.

'Oh…just wondered…what about his mates?'

Ken swiftly realised we were scrutinizing him for a reason. He became visibly agitated, again looking toward the door. For saying he was the manager of the place, he seemed distinctly uncomfortable when discussing the subject of the proprietors.

His resulting attempt to feign stupidity was pretty pathetic to be honest.

'His mates? Who's that, then?'

Bobby was not feeling very patient, and her tone altered to such effect.

'Fucking Pinkie and Perky! Doyle and Prenter! They're always bastard in here checking up. Are they due in today, do you know?'

I wanted to pat Bobby on the back for her sternness.

It almost made me smile, in fact.

'I...I've no idea, Bobby. They like it that way though, don't they. Turning up unannounced. It keeps everybody on their toes. It must be important if you actually *want* to see them. Normally you'd run a mile.'

Bobby was not in a jovial mood. She carried on drinking as I watched the smattering of early doors faces gathering around the counter. Her mind grappled with the next relevant query. All we wanted was a clue to my father's whereabouts.

'We won't hang about. Tell Jim I was looking for him. And be sure to tell him I've got him a new customer. He'll understand. You got that, Kenny boy?'

We both eyed Ken as he grasped for the appropriate response.

However, the honour was taken from him.

A deep, rasping voice sounded from behind us.

It was a tone laced with distaste and suspicion.

Bobby and I were no longer the hunters.

We had suddenly become the vulnerable prey in a split second.

'Did I just hear you are looking for me, Roberta?'

Instantly, Bobby and I spun around on our stools as Ian Doyle stood defiantly before us with his hands in the pockets of his leather jacket. I remembered his face vaguely from the summer. I now recognised him as the man I saw in the café on my first visit.

I observed his crew cut, greyish-blond hair; a few days growth of stubble; one of his front teeth missing. No doubt he carried other reminders of previous unsavoury encounters.

How he had entered the place without us seeing him we couldn't comprehend. It didn't really matter at that point. Adrenalin began to dilute my blood stream.

Doyle looked a nasty piece of work and sounded a naturally vindictive character. The physical image certainly fit with the reputation. Not for the first time in my life, I began to question what the hell I was doing in the middle of such a mess as I fidgeted nervously on the hard wooden seat.

Bobby did not display such reserve, however. She was more than familiar with the menacing figure that stood no more than five yards away. She may well have felt intimidated but wasn't about to show it. Pulling herself gracefully around on her stool to speak to him face on, she folded her arms and offered Doyle a cynical grin.

'I just wondered where I might find Jim, that's all. Do you know where he's likely to be?'

The expression on Doyle's face remained fixed and unemotional. It was hard to decipher what he might be thinking at that moment. He pondered Bobby's query for a few seconds before replying. I found it strange at the time, but not once did his attentive gaze fall to me.

He must have recognized me but didn't even mention my presence.

I was soon to be enlightened as to Bobby's secret little plot.

It was so secret that she hadn't even consulted *me* on it!

'Why do you want him?' Doyle rasped.

Bobby gestured toward me.

I said and did nothing.

At that moment, I was totally under Bobby's jurisdiction.

'I might have another grateful buyer for him, that's all.'

Doyle did not move from his position. Removing one hand from his jacket pocket, he checked the time on his watch.

'He's gone to Manchester for the day. A little deal needed attending to. Can I help?'

Before Bobby could offer a response, another figure entered the fray. Loz Prenter was slightly smaller in stature than Doyle, but the pair of them could have been mistaken for twin brothers. I noticed that they even wore the same leather coat.

Prenter realised that a situation was in development and immediately perched next to his friend and snarled.

'Problem, Ian?'

Doyle shook his head and smiled.

'This little tart wants to introduce the boss to a new client. Sounds a bit dodgy to me.'

Loz Prenter eyed me up from across the room. I could see the flicker of recognition in his eyes. He seemed far more alert to the situation, and he didn't hesitate to remind his cohort.

'This fella here? This is the goon that was up here earlier in the year. Do you remember, Ian? Few weeks back it was. Here in this place. He's got some nerve coming back, I reckon.'

If there was one thing I couldn't stand, it was being talked about as though I wasn't present. My trepidation was becoming balanced by a will to take the pair of them on. I despised their misguided arrogance.

I also despised the way they treated my friend, Bobby. I bit my tongue, hoping that the rush of blood would pass. I listened to the pair and their routine plastic gangster dialogue.

'Can't say I recall, Loz. Did we give him a pasting as well as the tart?'

Why Doyle would lie about recognising me I don't know.

God only knows he'd followed me around enough.

Prenter laughed and looked me threateningly in the eye, as if making a pledge.

'No…not yet…anyway…'

My anger was fighting for an escape route.

It was a struggle to keep myself in check. The odds would have been totally against me, but I'd have had a go, there and then in front of everyone. Thankfully Bobby's next statement served to smother my boiling frustration.

'So, Jim won't be home for a while, then?'

Yet again the gruesome pair glanced to each other and considered their answer carefully. Bobby had in fact played a blinder. They wouldn't be prepared to readily dismiss her story just in case I did happen to be a bona fide user in need of supply.

If the main man knew they'd willingly turned away a few hundred quid, he would likely not be pleased.

I could see where Bobby was taking us with her idea.

Those two dimwits looked like they would take the bait easily.

Doyle speculated in a voice laced with distaste.

'No…it's most likely he won't be back until tomorrow. He'll no doubt get pissed up and sleep over as he always does.'

Bobby was quick on the uptake.

She was ahead of the game at this point.

'So, what do I do about seeing Martin, today? You know that today's my one day of the week to see him, don't you?'

Bobby was running the risk of blowing everything sky high with her direct assault. Still, she who dares…

The less than dynamic duo seemed a little lost without someone to press their buttons, though. They looked at each other, struggling for an appropriate solution to the dilemma.

Their combined brain cells must have had to work very hard to present Bobby and I with what must have been the easiest take in history.

Or so it appeared. Doyle seemed strangely at peace with the way the conversation was developing.

'Well, I've got the only spare keys to the house. The lad's there now. We've only just left him.'

The pair seemed initially amused that Bobby may be deprived of the chance to see her loved one.

But full credit to her. She persevered.

'Yes…but come on guys…do it for me? Will one of you come back to the house with me and let me in? I've not seen my man for seven days for Christ's sake.'

She was brave. So very brave was Bobby Jones. I now questioned whether I was brave enough to keep up the act, myself. More silent seconds passed as we waited for a verdict.

Prenter and Doyle vacantly examined each other yet again for a strand of intellect and slowly shook their heads simultaneously.

The former declared the joint solution.

'We're not going back until later tonight. If I trust you with these keys, will you get them back here by let's say…six o clock? That gives you four hours with Quasimodo.'

I could have walked straight up to Prenter and put his lights out there and then. The humour in his face as he referred to my brother so insultingly was more than enough provocation.

Still, now was not the time. We had the keys. We had succeeded with stage one.

It all seemed too easy. Bobby was a wonderful actress when need demanded.

'Brilliant boys…you know it makes sense! I owe you both one!'

She jumped off her stool and snatched the keys from the grasp of Ian Doyle. Immediately, his free hand came to rest with force on her shoulder.

A move that temporarily halted Bobby's obvious joy.

He stared into her with nothing less than hatred in his eyes and conveyed a whispered warning.

'This is a big favour, Roberta. Don't go letting me down now, will you? Lock up after yourself. I don't want Jim knowing about this. Because if we get any problem from *him* then you know what will be waiting for *you*. And you've only just healed up, too.'

Bobby assured Doyle of her earnest intentions.

His vice-like grip did not release.

He moved his mouth closer to her ear.

'I'm sure if you were to return the favour in some way at some point…? After all, you just said that you owe us *both*.'

Yes, dear reader. My stomach turned at the thought of it.

As ever, Bobby remained utterly composed with her performance.

'Well, being as Jim's not getting *his* today, I suppose I could meet you at yours later. You know…when I bring the keys back?'

Doyle simply nodded and smiled.

'Good girl. Very sensible. Very considerate.'

What I wouldn't have given to have had a baseball bat in my hands at that point.

Utter scum. The pair of them.

I hadn't forgotten what they'd done to Bobby. But she had played them to a tee. They'd get theirs someday.

Kissing them both on the cheek, Bobby beckoned me to follow her.

I didn't look back as we brushed past the brothers grim and made our way from the Celtic Arms and into the town centre.

Now we had some valuable time to consider the next part of the plan.

Bobby and I huddled together and shivered at the bus stop.

As the shuttle to Stanley Park conveniently pulled up, she turned to me and winked.

'Stick with me, kid. We are going places!'

The arena was becoming enticingly dangerous.

The unknown awaited us.

## 27
## THE VISIT

'Well even by my expectations that was a fucking doddle! Like taking candy from a baby!'

Bobby Jones laughed heartily at her own quip as we took our seats at the rear of the nearly deserted bus. Throwing the bunch of keys up into the air, she caught them and instantaneously planted a kiss on my unsuspecting lips.

'How fucking good am I, Jamie lad? Please, just tell me…how good?'

Her conviction in our apparent victory seemed rather premature. I could not hide my reservations about what we were now possibly getting ourselves into.

'They might have been fooled, Bobby. But what happens when they realise they've been duped? Are you in for another smacking? Maybe there's one in the pipeline for me as well? I don't like this at all! It's highly likely they're on the phone already to tell you know who what's cracking off.'

Still, she continued to smile from dangly earring to dangly earring. It was an infectious grin. Mischievously beautiful yet daringly stern. I could not find fault with her cheeky defiance.

Ten out of ten for sticking two fingers up at the enemy.

'We're going to get Martin, for Christ's sake! Can you believe it? You're going to see Martin! I told you we'd do it!'

She was right of course. At least, partly right.

Here I was concerning myself with a couple of dopes who probably couldn't even spell their own names or get their shoes on the correct feet without supervision.

My primary thought should have been my brother.

I gazed at the passing view beyond the bus window. After all this time, here I was, finally about to achieve my ambition. I contemplated the losses I had countenanced in getting this far.

Fleeting thoughts of Mum, Henry and Alex zipped through my mind.

But hell yes, this was exciting.

I was suddenly overwhelmed by the premise of imminent gain that destiny had instructed.

Any reservations were quickly balanced by the most potent sense of anticipation as we neared our destination.

After about ten minutes, Bobby yanked on my sleeve indicating that it was nearly our stop.

We alighted from the bus in the middle of a squalid looking street. The brickwork of the houses reminded me of home. We linked arms again as we strolled along.

For the first time in a very long time, Bobby must have felt quite comfortable in approaching number twenty-seven, Joseph Street.

Being in totally foreign territory, I felt the expectation brimming as we stood beyond the front gate to the property. I looked at the frontage of the house that supposedly contained my brother.

All curtains were shut. A couple of broken windows were unfixed and boarded up. Again, it exhibited more than a fleeting reminder of Lodge Close and the surrounding council estate.

Despite the glib scene parading before us, Bobby was by now full of herself and dished out the orders accordingly.

'I think it best if you wait outside. Let me get in and talk to him for a while. At least then if Laurel and Hardy do come checking up it won't look suspicious.'

My understandable objections to her plan were short-lived as Bobby thwarted my enthusiasm.

'Think about it, Jamie. I don't even know if he'll remember you. Let's tread carefully, eh? Now that we're so close! We don't want to jump in and stamp on the butterfly, do we?'

A wonderful idiom that I'd never heard before. Must have been a Bobby Jones original. Reluctantly, I agreed. I positioned myself across the road behind a hedge directly opposite. I can still recollect the strength of my beating heart at that moment.

I don't know to this day how Bobby managed to stay so relaxed. I wanted to shout from the rooftops and grab my brother and run for it. Instead, I kept a stealthy vigil from behind a shrub.

As ever, Bobby promised to include me when the time was right.

I had to trust her.

I settled down to wait for her call.

*****

It had been nearly an hour since Bobby and I had left the Celtic Arms.

Loz Prenter and Ian Doyle had sampled a couple of pints and made the inevitable enquiries about Bobby's new male friend.

Ken Tatham was as reliably discreet and compliant with Bobby's wishes as ever. Despite knowing my original motive for being in the vicinity, he claimed that I - as a supposed user - needed a new supplier.

Thinking ahead as ever, Bobby had filled Ken in on all he was required to disclose. Doyle and Prenter's undeniable suspicions were appeased temporarily. They talked at the bar, chuckling briefly about the impending sexual rendezvous with Bobby. Their twisted minds contemplated the prospect of sharing her between one another. They wished!

As their tiny imaginations fantasized about the unattainable, reality suddenly came crashing down in the form of a booming voice from the front door of the pub.

Every occupant of the Celtic Arms at that moment turned to see the silhouette of Jim Andrews, bellowing to his henchmen across the room.

'I don't pay you two idle gits to sit around all day, do I? Get your fuckin' arses out here.'

Prenter and Doyle nearly dropped their pint glasses where they stood. Despite their sensible inclination to do so earlier, they hadn't yet opted to inform Jim Andrews that his eldest son was about to receive a visit.

Jim was evidently back from Manchester unexpectedly early. Way too early for everybody concerned. No doubt with the hope of surprising a couple of people. The pair looked to each other open mouthed as they joined the pub's owner in the street, struggling vainly to think of a way out of their little situation as they shuffled toward their main man.

In similar mode to his two accomplices, Jim Andrews was dressed entirely in black, and he sported a short haircut which exhibited several scars around his forehead and ears.

'I thought I told you both to stay at the house until I returned. Isn't that what I said? I'm fucking sure that was the last order I gave you.'

Doyle looked vacantly at Jim as Prenter ventured his feeble excuses.

'We've just come out for a drink, Jim. No harm done. You can't have expected us to stay indoors for twenty-four hours, surely? Anyway, what are you doing back so soon?'

Jim Andrews grimaced and closed his eyes in mild frustration.

'Business was concluded ahead of schedule. I don't like to hang around after I've splattered a debtor against the wall of a public convenience. It tends to help Mister Plod no end if the criminal hangs around at the crime scene. Not the outcome I would have preferred gents, but there you have it. Such is life.'

Doyle and Prenter nodded in vacant comprehension.

Jim Andrews had still not received a satisfactory explanation for their presence in the bar.

'So…if you two chimps are in there supping, then who's watching the retard…fucking Inky?'

There wasn't even time to fabricate a suitably convincing lie.

Jim forcefully pulled the truth from them as though extracting teeth with pliers.

A practiced art, I learned from Bobby, that he was now quite adept at doing.

'Just, don't bother bullshitting me. I can smell it before you even open your fucking mouths. I know the pair of you are fucking useless! I can accept that. Just don't keep *reminding* me that you're fucking useless. Give me the spare keys. I obviously can't trust you two with them. I'm going back home. I'll check the place for myself.'

Again, there was no word of reply from Doyle or Prenter.

Jim looked at the pair of them in expectation as he held out his right palm.

His features furrowed into a mask of aggression as his focus centred on Doyle.

Ken Tatham tried to decipher the muffled exchange beyond the entrance door as he nervously rummaged around behind the counter.

A shroud of fear began to descend around the bar room as the scene outside played its course.

Jim Andrews clenched both fists as he waited for a response.

'Have you gone deaf, Ian? Keys…NOW!'

Doyle gazed helplessly into space as the net drew in.

'What do you want the spares for, Jim?'

The mood had altered distinctly.

Jim Andrews was now a very frustrated man.

After a few reticent, carefully chosen, and honest words of why he didn't happen to have the keys anymore, Ian Doyle duly received a smack in the jaw.

The aggressor momentarily stood over his whining accomplice before leaving.

Fury was now welling within him.

It was disappointing enough that he couldn't trust his counterparts.

But the salt in the wound was that Bobby Jones was at his house unsupervised.

Strictly unacceptable practice.

Ken Tatham watched quietly from afar, secretly praying for the safety of those currently lined up to be discovered.

Doyle pulled himself to his feet and rubbed his mouth, as the sound of Jim Andrews' car tyres could be heard screeching away towards Stanley Park.

*****

Joseph Street. Bobby had only been inside the house about fifteen minutes. My own impatience was getting the better of me. I was just waiting for the owner of my little hideaway across the road to come and usher me off the property.

It was then I saw movement at the front window of number twenty-seven.

Two partially silhouetted figures squinted out into the street. Dusk was gathering. The light wasn't great. I was frozen stiff - like a statue. Not with the cold, but with an elating disbelief.

There, standing next to Bobby behind the glass, was the image of someone I had only seen in my dreams.

A handsome young man in his mid-twenties. He smiled at Bobby as the pair continued to scrutinise the scene through the window.

They kissed one another. She pointed over to my position. I remained hidden from view. The man who was my brother looked a little confused.

Should I reveal my presence, or stay put?

I was not privy to the next part of Bobby's plan. As usual, she was keeping her strategy to herself. I wasn't sure if that was such a good idea. We were supposedly a team, after all.

I was torn between remaining hidden, and obliging my tormenting intolerance and succumbing to an overbearing will to run across the road, kick the door down and embrace them both.

Then, as quickly as the pair had appeared at the window, they were gone again.

I continued to glance toward the house from my secluded position in the foliage. Any sign of activity was minimal. I felt like some covert spy staging a stakeout in a police drama.

I willingly crouched at my post, just waiting for the call to act.

It was then that I sensed something was amiss.

Instinct told me that our luck was about to run out.

Events happened in slow motion from that moment onward. It was even more worrying as my growing sense of urgency could not be conveyed directly to Bobby.

I began to panic. Pending danger was the only thought that cursed my mind. Why that should be the case was not yet apparent. I could not decipher the source of my sudden unrest.

All I knew was that the very recent positivity of our situation was heading for a downturn.

Then, with perfect, relieving timing, the front door of number twenty-seven opened and Bobby emerged. She was smiling and walked to the front gate.

I stood up to acknowledge her whilst glimpsing the figure behind her that waited in the doorway. Then suddenly, Martin slammed the front door shut, causing Bobby to turn around.

Simultaneously, the distant sound of a car engine rapidly closed in on the scene.

Bobby and I glanced up the road to see a dark coloured four by four speeding towards our location. I didn't recognize the vehicle or the driver, but I had a bloody good idea who was behind the wheel.

Martin had evidently recognized the approach straight away and had retreated inside accordingly.

Only on seeing my concern did Bobby also begin to flinch.

Too late to send out a warning now.

And of the three of us, I was the last to realize it was my father.

All I can recall of the car in question was that it was deep blue in colour. It seemed to be anyway as the daylight was dimming.

Jim Andrews mounted it onto the curb and slammed the brakes on outside the front gate to number twenty-seven, effectively trapping Bobby's exit.

She began to stress as the driver emerged and left his door wide open.

As I studied the back of his balding head, I could hear the overly familiar sneer as he addressed Bobby.

'What's all this then, Roberta? Visiting without permission? Who's a naughty girl then?'

I moved from behind the hedge and stood on the pavement a few paces behind my father on the opposite curb. He had not detected that I was over his shoulder as his monologue to Bobby continued.

The smile had long since disappeared from her face to be replaced by a mask of genuine terror. No longer the champion of our cause.

She was the vulnerable prisoner once again.

Though this time, the odds would be decidedly different.

I was there to intervene. I watched my father gesticulate wildly to her from the front of his car as his voice alternated between hissed threats and bellowing fury.

'You know the rules, Roberta. Not unless *I'm* here or the others! Did you forget the rules, Roberta? Shall I remind you of them?'

Bobby vainly began to offer lame excuses as Jim Andrews slowly advanced towards the gate. She glanced past him towards me. Her desperate expression showed that she was at a loss as to an escape route.

This was not totally unexpected. I edged forward. She shook her head quickly, as if to prompt me to make a run for it rather than intervene.

Not a chance.

I wasn't hiding from this bastard anymore.

I'd spent more than enough time in the shadows.

I'd come here to face him.

And face him I would.

Bobby slowly walked toward my father, who was now completely blocking any chance of an evasive tactic for her. His form eclipsed that of hers. He was a big man, indeed. But only in the physical sense. He spoke as though she had done something badly out of turn. As though he was a king whose servant had dropped his crown.

His misplaced sense of self-grandeur was incredible for such a non-achieving low life.

'Let me help you remember how things work around here, shall I? Get in that fucking house, Roberta! Now!'

Her pleas for forgiveness went unheeded. Jim Andrews knew she had easily deceived his friends.

But he no longer cared about Prenter and Doyle's ineptitude.

It was the thought that she would ever try and make a fool out of *him* that sustained his despair.

He now had only one objective in mind.

I had now moved from across the road and toward my father's car. I watched the pair as they moved back up the path to the front door. I was maybe fifteen yards from where they stood. Both were now oblivious to my position.

Bobby vainly continued to justify her reasons for being at the house. Her voice trembled with dread.

'Jim…I…didn't…mean any…disrespect…I'm…sorry…I…'

I watched transfixed as my father drew back his hand and clenched his fingers. The sound of calloused fist on dainty female chin sent a repulsive wave through my ear and into the pit of my stomach. The crack of bone resonated along the front path.

There followed a momentary silence.

The hatred instantly began to surge in me.

Any strand of pity I might have reserved for my father evaporated. Yet I was still undecided as to a course of action. Crazy and pathetic as it sounds, it was as though I was watching one of my own nightmares.

Subjected to this horrible exhibition.

Yet totally powerless to stop it.

'In the house, Roberta. You've forgotten how to behave properly. You need punishing.'

Bobby's emotions had taken hold. She was by now a quivering, wounded wreck. Her resolve had all but vanished as she cowered whilst cradling her jaw. Her voice was muffled and tearful.

'Please, Jim…I just… just wanted…'

He did not wish to hear her reasoning.

A second blow landed heavily on her temple, knocking her backward toward the closed door.

Another deathly few seconds of disquiet followed the second assault.

I could take no more.

My priority was no longer me.

No longer Martin.

It was Bobby.

I had to get us out of there. I looked around for some sort of weapon. Something that would buy us a few seconds of respite.

Then I saw it, nestled under the privet hedge that lined the property.

As my father grabbed Bobby by the lapels and yanked her to her feet, I retrieved the piece of jagged concrete from the floor.

Gripping it firmly between my palms, I made sure the edge that could do most damage would impact first into my father's skull.

Bobby was dragged to the doorway and slapped once again. Her frame was pulled about like that of a rag doll. I began to make my advance.

It was then that she saw me, armed and ready to strike.

Her raised hand was accompanied by a scream of distress.

'JAMIE! NO! NOT NOW!'

Her motive was puzzling to say the least. As I was stopped in my tracks at her tearful request, my father's grip on her released, and she was freed.

I saw a glimpse of blood as she ran toward me and then past me, out into the street and into the safety of a now curious neighbourhood.

Jim Andrews turned and, instead of pursuing his prey, he maintained his position.

The pair of us remained motionless as we faced off.

His focus met mine as we stood at either end of the path.

He at the doorway; me at the front gate.

He glanced at the small boulder of concrete that I held in both hands.

A grim smile encroached onto his weathered features.

The weapon dropped from my grasp.

I'll never forget that look of hateful recognition in his bloodshot, raging eyes. It was then that I saw the true definition of fear. Not fear on my own part but fear emanating from my father's soul.

It was as though he was being confronted by a long dead ghost.

We stared at each other for a few, sinister, indeterminable seconds.

He knew in an instant who I was…and why I had come back into his life.

Then, as he regained his composure, my father uttered the first words he had spoken to me, his youngest son, for the better part of a decade.

Ironically, it was a promise - a solemn pledge.

Now, Jim Andrews was not one for keeping promises - especially to his sons - but bearing in mind the circumstances, this particular statement seemed to be genuine in its intent.

His words were spat through a lattice of gritted teeth and long-standing resentment.

'I suggest... sunshine... that you follow her. For your own good... as well as hers.'

He stood defiantly to his full considerable height and rubbing both fists, he completed the vow.

'You're both going to need the head start. Because I won't be far behind you... and I'll know where to look if you try to hide...'

I was transfixed by the psychotic declaration of the person that stood before me.

I asked myself: does he truly know who I am?

Can he *really* know who he's just threatened to hurt?

I examined his features through the half shadow of early evening. The deep lines on his forehead and around the eyes represented years of harboured bitterness.

As my mind pondered the whole ridiculous situation, I spotted Martin at the lounge curtains again.

He must have witnessed the encounter as it transpired. It briefly occurred to me that he must have been more confused than anyone.

My gaze was torn between the vexed figure of our father and the innocent curiosity of my brother staring through the windowpane.

It was only the distant shriek from Bobby calling my name that quickly re-awakened my senses.

Our father pushed open the front door as I retreated from number twenty-seven and scampered after her.

I heard the slamming sound as Jim Andrews entered the house.

And as I ran, I prayed for Martin once again.

I hoped God could shelter him from what was to come, as I regretfully made my retreat.

# 28
# A REMEDY

Bobby was inconsolable when I eventually caught up with her a couple of streets away. Her permanent state of stemmed devastation had now evolved into total loss of faith. I was supposedly her one and only hope of making our dreams become a reality.

In her eyes, we had failed miserably. Now, so far as she could see, my father was destined to rule her life forever more.

I however, had other ideas.

She could not summon the words to her lips as I held her tightly in my arms. Yet again she had taken a battering and been had been forced to scurry away in defeat.

We walked a little way as the dust settled. The late October air was armed with a biting edge, and we huddled closer as darkness began to descend among the rooftops.

On reaching a bus shelter, we sat out of the cold breeze, contemplating our mutual pain and the imminent, undoubted horror that we had left behind in Joseph Street.

After a few thoughtful minutes, Bobby spoke. Under the minimal light from the shelter, I inspected her cheekbone, which was now swelling rapidly. Her strained eyes were raw, and her inner hope seemingly destroyed.

I cradled her face in my hands as she crumbled under the inevitable weight of desperation.

'That's it, Jamie. The police are our last option. We must tell them everything. It's the only way to get Martin out of there.'

I didn't tell her so, but I totally disagreed.

For the first time in this whole conundrum, I had gained some clarity on my own solution.

Involving the police would only indulge the authorities in producing endless reams of red tape. It would not serve any immediate purpose - aside from possibly getting Jim Andrews in custody until any potential trial could come to the fore.

For a trial, we needed a charge. For a charge to be issued there needed to be a modicum of proof. We had no actual evidence of the persecution that had been occurring due to the insidious nature of the man that was father to Martin and myself.

There were no reliable witnesses to anything that had taken place over the past decade. Indeed, during the entire lifetimes of Martin and myself.

We only had our word.

Based on the excruciating knowledge of the unjust situation that was existing within the walls of twenty-seven, Joseph Street.

The bus seemed to take an age to arrive.

Understandably, the driver looked rather concerned to see me get on board with a dishevelled, bloodied and obviously emotional companion.

Thankfully, he didn't ask any questions as I handed him the fare. I accompanied her to the empty back seat, and she huddled in my arms as we headed back to Blackpool town centre.

As we travelled, I secretly composed my own plan for dealing with my father. I could see that he was physically stronger than me, undoubtedly more aggressive and totally unwilling to listen to reason.

Yet the one aspect that stood out when I saw him at that front door was the reaction in his face on seeing me again.

As if he felt instantly challenged by the very presence of the son he had tried to forget.

Whilst not openly acknowledging the fact, he knew exactly who I was. And it scared the hell out of him. His own eyes revealed his fallibility. That was my key to victory.

To utilise *his* fear to my advantage.

Turn it back on him - make *him* feel the trepidation that he had inflicted on others for so long.

I would make him confront the disorder that he had created and subsequently cowered from all his life.

It was not a plan without a large element of danger, but I would be motivated to face him and present to him what he dreaded being exhibited most of all - *himself.*

Force him to face what he had done to me, to Martin and to Mum.

He wasn't *that* cold and callous.

No man could completely avert his mind from such a trail of desolation.

No man could.

He would buckle. I felt sure of it.

I would weaken him quickly.

My sudden sense of superiority was all consuming as I looked at the poor girl that floundered in my embrace. It was difficult at that moment on the bus to conceive that Bobby was nearly ten years my senior.

But I promised I would protect her from now on.

This was no longer Bobby's private battle.

I would finally unite her with the man she loved.

I would liberate them.

As the bus glided towards the sea front, I silently made my vow.

*****

Martin Andrews screamed into the darkness as his legs were repeatedly stamped on. The sour taste of beer spilled onto his face and mixed with the blood that seeped from his eye.

His father's incoherent, inebriated shouting was more than sufficient to dissuade the casual passer-by outside from interrupting the fracas.

After all, it was an everyday occurrence behind the front door of twenty-seven, Joseph Street.

However, as he lay in his well of sufferance, the light of retribution did not dim in Martin's conscience.

He knew his calling had been answered.

Now he had seen his saviour in the flesh.

Across the street, crouched behind the bush and then on the path, ready to strike at his nemesis.

Martin knew that his chronicle of misery was soon to end.

Fate would bring two brothers back together.

His premise of his salvation glimmered like a flare in a void of blackness.

It wouldn't be long now.

*****

I had settled Bobby to sleep and locked her in her flat. I didn't want anybody to know she was there.

I also wasn't keen on her wandering around looking for me.

I left her a note - a note that I keep safely hidden to this day.

I still see myself scribbling it out on her kitchen worktop. It was growing bleaker and colder outside. I picked up the pen and glanced at the uninviting scene through the kitchen window.

It reminded me of my father.

A black, soulless pit of cold menace.

I can dictate the note for you. The wording did not need much consideration at the time of writing but has gained real poignancy with the passing years.

The sentiments were earnest.

*Dearest Bobby,*

*Sleep soundly, my sweet. Remain here in your comforting retreat. I have returned to Martin. Destiny has decided it must be so. I have no choice. You do. That is why I wish for you to stay protected.*

*Do not follow, for I shall duly return.*

*Please understand. My mission is clear.*
*I shall not fail you, or my brother.*
*Until our reunion*
*Jamie.*

*****

It was nearly seven p.m. No sooner had I left Bobby's, I was on a bus straight back to Stanley Park. Yes, dear reader, you may either fault my stupidity or praise my bravery, but I had decided that to confront my bastard of a father - once and for all - was now the only solution.

Everything looked rather more unforgiving in the evening darkness. The bus route was suddenly rendered unfamiliar. My return to Joseph Street would undoubtedly be a surprise for Jim Andrews, but that would be to my advantage.

At seventeen-years-old, I was about to face the biggest challenge of my life.

My mind and body were focused. I now knew my father was running scared from his own history. His lack of courage would be his undoing.

Bobby was safe. No one could hurt her now. I would be her shield. The human boundary to all her pain and sorrow. It was my ordained path. I would rescue my brother from his pit of woe and avenge my mother's sufferance and ensure that her ultimate surrender to her own frailty was not in vain.

As the bus trundled back toward hell, I tried to ascertain a landmark that I recognised through the murk outside. Thankfully the driver was a willing guide.

I was soon in Joseph Street.

And outside the gate to number twenty-seven, once again.

Two cars were now parked outside. One being my father's jeep. I couldn't tell who the other belonged to, even with the aid of the amber glow of the streetlights. But it wasn't the stuff of Einstein to hazard the correct guess.

There was definitely life inside the house. I could see the rooms upstairs and downstairs were illuminated behind closed curtains.

With a glance up and down the pavement, I took a deep breath and walked through the gate and up to the front door. I don't know why but I briefly felt a compulsion to inspect the floor around my feet. It occurred to me that I may need to bring something to hand in self-defence.

The lump of concrete had seemingly gone from where I had dropped it. I didn't bother to look around just in case. I figured that my father would have far more amenable weaponry inside - just in case of need.

I knocked three times, soundly and firmly. I could hear myself breathing and watched as the cool vapour bellowed skyward.

There was no response.

I knocked three times again.

A few more seconds of silent inactivity followed.

Yet, I did not feel nervous, now.

I felt totally assured.

Then I saw the moving shadow against the tiny frosted porthole in the door. A somewhat jerky, blurred silhouette that advanced slowly down the hallway.

It might sound strange, but Ian Doyle was apparently pleased to see me standing there when he pulled the door open.

Evidently, the afternoon's events had not yet reached his ears.

Nor, thankfully, had my identity.

I figured by then that the guy was too dumb to put on an act.

He genuinely believed I was still in need of a supplier!

*Me*! Of all people!

He was no gangster, though it didn't stop him believing so.

'Bloody hell, youth! You're keen, aren't you? Still interested in our wares? Walk this way, kid. I'll go and fetch the man you need to see.'

I simply nodded whilst maintaining a straight face and did as I was told. Had I been in Ian Doyle's position, I might have not known either that I had just invited the wolf into the fold.

Had I been in my father's position, I would be justified in thinking that my personal bodyguard - if that is what Doyle was supposed to be - was as effective as a chocolate teapot.

The hallway stank. A rotten atmosphere comprising of decaying spirit and dying reputations - the perfect setting.

Doyle shut the door behind us and showed me into the kitchen, where I was asked to sit down at the table. I could detect the muffled sounds of a television from the next room. I presumed my father was in there watching it. I looked at the surroundings. Filth and germs took delight in each other's company, in copious amounts. It was a cess pit.

A hole of merciless, vile disease. It reminded me of a bomb site. Or perhaps more accurately something seen on the news after a natural disaster has visited and passed through.

Only there was nothing destroyed by nature around this place.

The demolition had all been orchestrated by the will of one man.

The welcome I had begun to quite enjoy was abruptly disturbed by a loud thud at the bottom of the stairway. The kitchen door had been left slightly ajar.

My father's booming voice identified the object that had landed heavily on the hallway floor.

'And tell that other useless idiot that I don't want to see *him* again here, either, or he'll get the same. Now get in your car and fuck off out of it! I'll ring when I need you.'

There was another dull thud - which could have been a punch – and then whimpering. I could only surmise the source and cause. The next noise was that of the front door opening and being slammed shut once more.

Then, quiet resumed.

In the adjacent lounge, an active mind stirred.

A mind that had become highly adept at identifying sounds as opposed to images.

His attention was drawn away from the screen, diverted by an unusual presence nearby.

A presence he had never detected within the house before, yet there was something familiar and indeed balming about the unidentified visitor.

Martin reduced the volume of the TV set. He rose from his chair to listen more attentively at the locked door of his living room cell.

I continued to sit at the kitchen table, though understandably after the fracas in the hallway I had swiftly moved position and was now facing the door.

A shaft of light peeped through from the hall, to be eclipsed by the shadow of my father as he shoved his way clumsily into the room.

The handle smashed into the wall behind, knocking a naked girls' calendar from its hook.

There in the doorway, facing his youngest son, stood the tarnished and tempestuous figure of Jim Andrews.

Unworthy father; vile drunkard; natural born bully and local dealer of dubious repute.

Quite a C.V.

We glared at one another in the half light. I immediately detected the anguish in his expression once more. Of all those acquainted with the man, I was the only one who could ignore his domineering façade and see him for what he truly was.

I was also the only soul who could instigate such a reaction of disdain in him.

I watched as he tried to gather and organise relevant thoughts.

His mind at that point must have been a maelstrom of emotion.

Anger; hatred; jealousy; maybe even deep down, a pang of regret.

Though I doubted the latter.

I didn't truthfully know and cared even less.

I wasn't there to pass the time of day with him.

I had come for my brother.

My father swayed slightly under the influence of booze as he issued his introductory greeting.

'You're a brave little boy, aren't you? Following me…here.'

I knew exactly the reply that would annoy him most of all.

I remained seated and calm.

I never averted my eyes from his.

'Hello…Dad.'

The frown lines deepened as his gaze narrowed.

A sly smile of gamesmanship crept onto his pursing lips.

'You're no son of mine, boy.'

He recognized me as an opponent of worth, which of course, I was.

His next query smacked of desperation.

'What the fuck…are *you*…doing *here*…in *my* house?'

I remained focused and forthright.

This was a battle of wits that I wasn't going to lose.

I tried desperately to be sarcastic.

'I've come to see *you*…Dad. After all, I am your son, whether you like it or not. I thought ten years apart was long enough.'

I looked around me at the squalid surroundings, pretending to notice minor details of the room.

'Nice place you've got here.'

I could see him clenching and unclenching his fists in the dimness. I could tell that he was seething, but somehow, he felt unable at that stage to vent his annoyance toward me.

'How did you find me? Was it that slut? *She* told you, didn't she?'

My father began to walk slowly around the table toward where I was sitting. He'd had more than enough to drink.

'If I told you the truth, Dad, you wouldn't believe me. I found you completely by accident. It wasn't Bobby's fault at all. You can't keep blaming her for everything that's wrong in your pathetic little life, you know. She didn't make the shitty bed that you're lying in. *You* did.'

Jim Andrews' voice gained harshness.

His poisonous tongue rarely took prisoners, but I was unmoved by mere words.

'She's nothing more than a cheap tart. Do you know she sleeps with me for drugs?'

'Dad…I know everything…absolutely…*everything*. So, I suggest you take that fact on board. I know far more than you *ever* will.'

By this stage I was surprised by my own bravado. I rose to my feet after noticing that he was in swinging distance of my head. I wasn't going to invite him to gain the advantage, even if I hadn't gone there to fight.

Ultimately, I knew deep down that I would have little choice in the matter. The risks were obvious.

Like it or not, I had willingly walked into the lion's den.

'You haven't changed, you snotty little bleeder. How can you *ever* know more than *me*?'

I looked at his snarling visage. He was a man consumed by mistrust and a penchant for life in the gutter. In fact, he didn't deserve to have a life. I was wasting my breath engaging him with such preliminaries. That much was already obvious.

Though, I would persist in trying to wear him down mentally, minute by minute.

'Did you know that Bobby loves Martin?'

My father stopped his unsteady advance and looked at me as if I had presented him with the genie of the lamp.

An expression of amusement, disbelief, and ultimately, suspicion.

'What the fuck…are you on about?'

I stood on the opposite side of the table, watching his every action.

'Just like I said…Bobby loves him. She wants to be with him. But you don't like it…do you…Dad?'

I was surprised that he maintained his composure for this long. I was willing to goad him for as long as it took. Drawing him in was admittedly a task that was taking longer than I would have expected.

He reverted to the previous element of the conversation.

'I still don't know why you've come here.'

I looked him sternly in the eye.

I spoke clearly so as not to be misunderstood.

'I'm taking Martin away with me. Now…tonight. This is his last hour under your control. Sorry if this is at short notice, Dad, but I'm about to piss on your stinking parade. It's gone on for long enough.'

I had at last touched a raw and highly agitated nerve.

He was beginning to bite. The muscles in his face twitched uncontrollably as he fought to conjure a response.

But I held all the cards, and he knew it.

'Martin stays here, where I can watch over him and look after him. Who the fuck do you think you are? Coming here, messing around with people's lives?'

My unrestrained laughter was a genuine response to his sheer audacity.

It only served to add fuel to the growing inferno.

'Martin has no life here with you. Yet you don't want him to leave you. Because he's an embarrassment to you…isn't he…Dad? You're ashamed of your son…and you don't even know what's wrong with him…do you…Dad?'

My father made a sudden lurch into the side of the table, evidently forgetting it was there. His vision had seemingly become clouded by alcohol and animosity. I side stepped his move and made sure I had further space to manoeuvre.

My father's claims of righteousness left me amused, if almost speechless.

'He's never been a normal boy. That's why I must protect him.'

Again, I could not suppress my pitiful mirth at the pathetic, delusional figure before me. I was ashamed to even acknowledge him as someone I knew, let alone as the man who brought me into the world.

'Is that what you call it? Protection? Locking him up and beating him up when it takes your fancy? Well, watch my lips…it's all over!'

I moved a little further away, noticing as I did so the trivial images around the kitchen that happened to catch my eye as I shuffled.

Odd shoes on the work top; a stale pile of food on the linoleum floor; white powder in small piles on a tea tray; the sink filled to the brim with dirty water. It was all very surreal.

Yet this was the haven of tranquillity that my father was prepared to inhabit. It was a nuclear fall-out zone.

'He's my son. You can't ever change or challenge that fact. You've got no rights even being here, boy.'

'*I'm* your son as well…the little accident…remember? I've got news for you, Dad. I've got *every* right. More rights than you've *ever* had!'

My father jolted toward me once more, his swing only just missing my shoulder. My heart began to race uncontrollably.

Now I felt vulnerable.

It was me and him.

Finally.

Father and son - the chief protagonists - the ultimate meeting of minds.

I continued with the gentle tirade. I felt the momentum building.

'You treated Mum horrendously. She's better off dead. At least she's rid of you!'

He looked perplexed once more.

I was revealing an event that he could never have known about. It was sacred to me until that point. In the drug and booze-fuelled haze of his personal history, he had probably forgotten he was ever married to my mother.

It was something else he had tried to obliterate from his conscience, even though the arrogant bastard still tried to put the onus of failure onto me!

'She couldn't cope with the two of you. She was always tired. She should never have had two babies. I told her so at the time.'

I shook my head as disgust evolved into vexation.

'Oh yes, Dad. You told her plenty of things at the time. You dictated her life right down to the last detail. Even after you'd gone, she lived in fear of you. You stayed right with her, and eventually finished her off. She hanged herself because of you, Dad! She fuckin' hanged herself because of what *you* did to her!'

For the first time in the encounter, I felt my emotions getting the better of me. Talking about Mum was heart-breaking at the best of times. The tears attempted to begin a descent. It was a badly mistimed sign of weakness considering the circumstances.

Now it was my father's turn to enjoy the spectacle.

He emitted an evil cackle as he witnessed the onset of my distress.

His voice became louder - almost as if empowered by my temporary lapse in fortitude.

'*YOU* WERE THE PROBLEM, BOY! THINGS WERE FINE UNTIL YOU CAME ALONG! *YOU* KILLED YOUR MOTHER...NOT ME...DON'T BLAME ME...I WASN'T EVEN THERE!'

Martin continued to listen intently from behind the locked lounge door. His concern was mounting for the unseen situation developing in the kitchen. Something told him that he must try to assist. He would be needed soon.

He had never tried to break out before, but then again, he had never had the inclination before now...before the arrival of his saviour.

The sight of my smirking father enabled me to become angry once again and in turn override the flow of emotion.

I rubbed my eyes to clear my vision.

It was nearing crunch time.

There wasn't much more to be said between us.

'You should never have been given children. You never wanted a family, did you, Dad? Go on...admit it!'

Jim Andrews moved toward me quicker than before. I couldn't evade his grasp in time.

The next thing I knew, I was reeling in shock and pain from his first punch. My resolve was only strengthened by his opening assault.

The gauntlet had been laid down for me to respond.

The second blow caught me on the back of the head.

Not painful, but dizzying.

'I'll teach you about family, boy! You've no fucking idea about me! You've no fucking respect! Well, you soon will have after this.'

He flailed wildly with his foot, which connected with my right kneecap, sending me to the floor in searing discomfort.

Something in my mind told me to stand and fight, but I couldn't.

It was my father. What could I do?

His imposing form now stood directly above me as I looked up, blinded by the strip light on the ceiling.

His fingers clamped around my neck and hauled me back to my feet before I was flung like a rag doll against the wall. My head cracked against the plaster once more as he repeatedly threw me against the chimney breast.

Martin had spent long enough in constraint.

He would no longer bear his father's rage.

He would amend the wrongdoings in his life.

He would help his stricken brother.

He had stored a secret weapon for just such a purpose.

He had covertly retrieved it from the front garden as his father drank himself stupid in the bath upstairs.

It was one of the few times that Jim Andrews had forgotten to lock the lounge door, having just indulged in giving his elder son another good kicking.

Jim Andrews would live to rue that little oversight.

Picking up the piece of jagged concrete that he had seen his brother holding earlier that day, Martin began to hammer it onto the door handle. Time and time again he brought it down onto the brass latch.

As the metal began to fatigue, Martin gained inner strength from his gradual success.

The three surviving members of the Andrews family were on collision course.

The end game was upon them.

*****

It was an instantaneous reaction to the unpleasant sensation of being hurt. I flung a fist in my father's direction and connected with something hard. Now it was my turn to stand over him as he lay at *my* feet, fondling his jawbone.

I remember breathing heavily and hearing a repeated banging sound. It seemed to be coming from the hallway.

I tried and failed to detect the cause.

As I strained to listen, my feet were taken from under me, and my left temple crashed into the table edge.

From this point on, I can only make fairly accurate assumptions as to the events that followed. I recall my father grabbing me by the lapels as he then snatched at my hair. In doing so he wrenched my head backward. He forced my arm up my back as I was then shoved roughly toward the kitchen sink.

I was completely disorientated. Pain was an irrelevant emotion by this point. I was numb and bewildered. I was broken and nearly beaten.

Defeat seemed inevitable. I felt powerless to resist.

There was no waking from this nightmare.

I closed my eyes as my father bent me over the worktop and pushed my head firmly under the surface of the water in the sink. My forehead and nose smashed among the crockery and into the bottom of the bowl.

*****

Something had stirred Bobby from her sleep back at her flat.

Not a dream or a nightmare, but a mystical conveyance from somewhere in her subconscious self.

She sat on the settee with the note from me in her hand.

Her anguish had dissipated. She sensed impending elation.

A vision formed in her mind.

Two brothers, together again; united; liberated.

*****

I could not move an inch. I was at my father's mercy, totally and unconditionally. I opened and shut my eyes to fend off the ever-growing blackness and the stinging detergent in the water.

My feeble attempts to breathe simply allowed poisoned water to flood into my gasping lungs.

With the air supply cut off, my racing heart began to shudder to a nearing halt.

Only seconds of life left now.

My failure was almost near its completion.

Jim Andrews would stand in triumph once more.

As the resistance ebbed from my body, visions from my life flashed through my head.

I thought of Mum; Henry; Martin; Alex; John Harrison and Bobby, and even Ken Tatham from the pub.

In separate and strangely combined montages of what and who I was leaving behind...and what I was about to meet.

Then, my struggle ended.

It was done.

Instinctively, my body sensed that the force restraining it to a certain demise was no longer potent.

There was suddenly...nothing.

The power constricting my being had ceased.

I was freed.

A reflex action abided my back to arch and my head to lift clear of the water.

It was indeed true.

I had not passed over. I was definitely still alive.

My incessant choking and spluttering of blood, vomit and mucus into the sink was proof enough of that.

I cleared my airways for a few seconds, not daring to turn around and face my father again.

Yet...intuition told me it was safe to do so.

Everything was now peaceful.

My father would no longer hurt me...nor anyone else for that matter.

Hauling myself up from the draining board, my sore eyes looked down between my feet and tried to find focus.

There, lying motionless on the floor...was Jim Andrews.

The man who only seconds ago had tried to drown his own son.

On finally accepting the vision below me as genuine, I turned my head to engage with another.

A terrified expression befell the features of the older man by my side as he observed the result of his assist.

He dropped the jagged piece of concrete to the floor, before slowly raising his glance to meet mine.

Standing in his customary void of puzzled anxiety…was Martin.

The man who only seconds ago had saved my life from the destructive, evil intent of a person he could no longer acknowledge as his father.

We stood next to each other and again looked down at the dormant, prostrate form.

Yet there was no sense of victory.

Only dismay at what had happened in the past hour.

And in the past years.

The mutual feeling of nausea was quickly alleviated by the knowledge that we had seemingly ended our toleration of his reign.

Our father's ominous shadow loomed no more.

# 29
# UNITY

A few, savoured seconds of quiet acceptance passed in the kitchen at number twenty-seven, Joseph Street. The minds of siblings assembled events and the ramifications.

Their lives would never be the same again from this day on.

I had just about regained a regular heartbeat. I leaned back against the sink, staring without particular interest at my father's idling form.

Slowly, my gaze turned again to my brother.

Martin looked directly back into my eyes. In his face, I saw a history of uncertainty. A life of undeserved sorrow. It had been a curse placed upon him from birth.

But his emancipation was now absolute. We listened to each other take welcome breaths in that place of malignity.

I saw it in him once more. That little boy from the back window of the taxicab. Only now, there was a thriving spirit inside the body. Not merely a being that would conform to the damaging instructions and dubious ideals of an unworthy guardian.

My brother was now a man. A man who had little knowledge of the fact that he was dearly loved.

Words did not come quickly. I did not force them. Our mutual attentions fixed to each other, allowing familiarity of mind. The enduring seconds of renewed association evolved into a minute or two.

Then, it happened. My brother spoke to me for the first time in so many years. For the first time in fact, that I could remember. He held out his hand, which trembled as I took it in mine.

I could not tell if he was still afraid. I could not tell if he was feeling pleased. His focus never wavered from me as he composed his declaration of liberty.

'We must go…Jamie…Daddy is asleep…can we please go now?'

I couldn't recall telling him my name. Maybe he instinctively knew. Or more likely that Bobby had revealed our plan to him at some previous point.

I did not need any more encouragement to leave that house.

I gripped my brother's hand tightly and led him from the dank, disturbing cave of the kitchen and into cess-ridden corridor of the hallway.

We passed the open lounge door.

He stopped me by pulling at my arm and raising a forefinger.

'Need something. One moment. Won't be long.'

I watched as he walked quickly into the living room. The room that had effectively been his world for God knows how long. I could detect Martin rummaging around out of view.

He wasn't long, as he'd promised.

My brother emerged from the room with two new additions to his being. The first was a warm smile. Bobby was right. He had the dark, brooding looks of a film star.

Then I looked down and saw the reason for his sudden injection of pleasure. Under his arm, he carried a teddy bear. A light brown teddy bear, wearing a red bow tie. He noticed me nod affectionately toward his furry friend. It prompted another remark, and a broader smirk as he made his adamant claim.

'Never go anywhere without Rufus. Never!'

I regained my hold on his free hand once again as we headed for the front door. Stepping from that domain of hostility was the most beautiful sensation I had ever experienced.

Neither of us looked back. There was no need to ponder what we were leaving behind.

I opened the gate and ushered Martin onto the pavement.

He stood tentatively and glanced back to the frontage of number twenty-seven, as if contemplating the possibility that his actions would result in the usual, painful penalty.

A hint of angst sounded in his voice as he urged me to stand still next to him.

Even though he had heard and witnessed the events of the past hour unfold, he was still unsure as to the authenticity of our departure from Joseph Street.

'Daddy doesn't know we're going…does he, Jamie?'

With an earnest expression of reassurance, I attempted to allay his understandable concerns.

'Daddy doesn't matter anymore, Martin. Daddy won't hurt you again. I promise *I'll* protect you from now on.'

He was not immediately convinced. I soon realised why.

'And Rufus? You'll protect Rufus, too?'

I observed the face of the stuffed toy under Martin's arm.

If only it could speak of what it had seen.

I patted its head and smiled at my brother.

'Yes, Martin…Rufus, too.'

The innocent observer at that moment would not have suspected anything could have ever been wrong in the lives of the Andrews brothers.

We walked out of Joseph Street, hand in hand, shoulder to shoulder.

Whilst I had tried to appease Martin's worry, I thought fleetingly of the potential consequences of what had happened that afternoon.

Pangs of trepidation hit me at short intervals as we waited for the bus to Blackpool promenade.

I considered what might become of us when the slumbering giant that was my father regained his senses.

Could there be a chance that he would seek retribution for the desertion tactics of his offspring?

I needn't have troubled my mind with such a trivial issue.

Whatever happened to Jim Andrews now was not our concern.

The future was ours to dictate.

That was all that mattered, for now.

# 30
# ILLUMINATION

Bobby knew immediately. Despite being safely distanced from the action she had suspected the positive outcome of events. The anticipation devoured her as she waited at her flat. The man she loved was coming to her at long last.

For the first time in their relationship, *she* was waiting for *him* to arrive. It was an absorbing prospect.

She checked her face in the bathroom mirror. Foundation would mask the damning hallmarks of the past for now. Soon those painful mementoes would disappear naturally. She showered, changed, and made herself adoringly presentable.

For Bobby Jones, it was like a thousand Christmas Eves in one wonderful night.

For the first time since she could recall, her beating heart was caused by the excitation of romance, and not by the shadow of intimidation.

Her horizon was now purely golden; not shrouded by grey and black. Within minutes she was a beauty once again.

A phoenix from the ashes of a life she had already forgotten.

Tidying the flat of obstacles and discarding several unsavoury items of refuse, she readied herself for the turning of the key in the door.

She had longed for this moment.

This most perfect of reunions.

She nearly jumped out of her skin when she detected that the visitors had finally arrived. A glance at the clock on the mantelpiece displayed the time as just after eight-forty p.m.

It had been a long day.

Yet the new dawn had begun early.

Moving to the hallway, she nervously clasped her hands in front of her. Bobbing up and down on her tip toes, she could barely stand the suspense as she squinted through the small window in the door.

Outside however, matters were stalling.

Martin's amusement encouraged a sigh of feigned frustration.

'Don't tell me, Jamie…let me guess. Keys are lost…I know…just don't tell me.'

I stood outside Bobby's door fumbling around in my pockets.

The wind was icy, coming straight in from the Irish Channel. I smiled in response to my brother's cynicism as I shivered.

My numb fingers could not feel a thing inside my coat.

Martin was enjoying the spectacle.

'Shall I knock the handle off? I'm well practised in the art of knocking handles off doors now.'

My chuckle accompanied the successful extraction of a bunch of keys from my inner pocket.

'There isn't a handle you clown. Right, now I've found them I can't remember which one opens the door."

Martin took the keys from me. Squinting in the darkness, he took one look at the lock and then one look at the keys. Selecting the key that he believed to be the correct one between thumb and forefinger, he handed the bunch back. I thought he was joking.

'You sure this is the one?'

Martin smiled and patted his teddy bear.

'Even Rufus can recognise a Yale forty-two-millimetre barrel. An older, but standard and reliable model.'

I shook my head in speechless admiration.

'Okay, Martin. You step to one side so she can't see you. It will be a surprise for her.'

Eventually after enacting our comical scenario, I placed the selected key in the lock and turned it.

The latch released. The door pushed open.

Martin nodded sarcastically.

And then my breath was taken.

The vision of Bobby that greeted me as I stood in the doorway has remained with me ever since. She had pulled out all the stops.

Martin was indeed a lucky man.

Stepping into the hallway I moved toward her, and my eyes moistened as we embraced. It was reassuringly firm and gratifying.

I held the back of her head gently as though she were my own love.

Eventually, we drew apart.

By then, her make-up had already begun to smudge with her gradual emission of joy.

She looked in the hall mirror and wiped her eyes with a tissue.

Bobby turned to me again and I placed my hands on her shoulders before whispering.

'I've brought someone with me.'

She swallowed, then smiled, then struggled to offer her typically cheeky reply.

'I was hoping so. I'm not letting all this cold air in for nothing!'

We embraced once more and I quickly moved aside, before beckoning my brother inside.

He had purposely stood out of her eyeline as if in recognition of the importance of his arrival.

'Martin…are you coming in, or what?' I giggled.

As if by magic, my brother appeared in the doorway with Rufus secured under his arm. He carried a stern look on his face, which I have since learned to be an indication of slight embarrassment.

I watched as Bobby stared intently at the love of her life. But her mood rapidly switched. For the first time, they were both free. Free to be together to do as they wished. She could have him, and he could have her, without condition; without restriction.

Glancing across to me she was obviously overwhelmed.

She confirmed the invitation for her man to enter.

'Welcome home, Martin.'

My brother stepped inside as I moved to close the door behind him. For a second or two he seemed very unsure of the unfamiliar surroundings. Still clutching the teddy bear in his arms, he studied the walls and ceilings. The décor was strange to him.

He resembled a five-year-old child as his eyes scanned the scene in wonderment.

Finally, he relaxed.

'Nice place…Roberta. Mine as well, now?'

The simple fact that he'd even mentioned her full name was too much for Bobby. Her façade of assuredness fell away once again, but this time for all the right reasons.

'Yes…it's your place as well now, Martin."

My brother's eyes widened as he continued to observe the interior of the hallway.

His gaze settled on the teddy bear.

'Rufus staying, too?

Bobby and I laughed in Martin's blessed innocence, as his face lit up.

'Of course, Rufus too!' she gushed.

‘That’s good. Rufus and I are a good team.’

He pointed to the stuffed toy cradled in his grasp before turning to the woman he adored.

He had more to say.

Bobby and I waited with bated breath.

‘Like us, Roberta. We are a good team too.’

She could withhold no longer and threw her arms around him. Martin responded in kind and the pair became immersed in an oasis of intimacy.

I left them to their reunion in private and entered the living room.

Sitting myself down, I listened to their laughter and their tears.

The note I had written to her earlier that day lay on the coffee table.

Instinctively and without further thought, I picked it up and folded it carefully into four, before placing it into the back pocket of my wallet.

*****

November encroached into our lives almost unnoticed. The three of us spent a few joyous days together relishing the simple passage of time.

The thought that we might stumble on the repercussions of our recent actions was only an occasional blemish on proceedings.

As it was, the spectral ogre that had overpowered our history never ventured to disrupt the close-knit celebration.

It was one of our first aims to take Martin shopping for new clothes in the precinct, where he must have tried on every combination of shirt and trouser in every menswear shop and had great fun acting silly in front of the many mirrors, before repeatedly telling the assistant that it wasn’t really his sort of thing!

We ate at McDonalds where he blew several straw wrappers at the passing staff and spat peppered gherkin on the floor, encouraging other kids in the vicinity to do the same.

He took delight in blowing bubbles in his coke through the straw then proceeded to tell us how much rainforest is needed each year to sustain the paper market for such products.

We walked on the piers, taking in the salty air as though it would erode the clinging debris of yesteryear. I watched the wind blow Martin’s hair as he stared out to sea. He cracked me up with a comment regarding the contents of the water below.

I myself had given fair consideration to the same subject.

'A lot of poo in there, Jamie! No swimming for me! Don't fancy a mouthful.'

A visit to the waxworks turned into a lesson in Twentieth Century culture as Martin identified every single dummy as a prelude to a short resume of their life and career.

His mind was a font of knowledge, most of it absorbed through television and books. Bobby and I never stopped laughing as he proudly took us on his own personal guided tour.

The three of us tried to fit in as much as we could. It was like a timed race to see the sights. Bobby and I concluded that Martin would really be in his element at the pleasure beach. It was an exhausting, enlightening experience.

We must have ridden on everything at least twice. If Martin wasn't sure about a particular attraction, he'd go and ask the stall tender as to his or her opinion. He would study the height limit on each ride before assessing the queue to guess who would fail and pass.

Over those few wonderful days, it was like watching a dying flower gain new life.

My brother was sociable, humorous, intelligent, and eager to explore. We could not hold him back for fear of upsetting him. There were so many things he was willing to partake in.

He spent forty minutes and eleven pounds fifty on the shooting gallery - just because he wanted one of the tacky prizes hanging on the wall behind. Every shot was painstakingly analysed and scrutinized in his efforts to attain the trophy he had set his heart on.

The eventual reward was a poster of two dolphins in a picture frame, smiling eagerly as they arced clear of the water. When he finally held it aloft in triumph, his comment carried incredible potency.

'Look, Roberta. It's you and me!'

Guess who ended up carrying *that* for rest of the day!

Finally, we managed to persuade him to venture onto the biggest ride of all. The Big One. He stood in wondrous awe underneath the structure. He no longer accommodated any semblance of that emotion called fear. There was no challenge too big for Martin. Leaving our day's loot at the entry gate we made our way to the carriage station.

His face repeatedly lit up on hearing the screams of the distant terrified passengers.

After queuing for over half an hour, we finally made our clattering ascent to the top of the first drop. Ten yards from the peak, my brother turned behind to face me and grinned like a Cheshire cat. I shouted to him above the wild chants of the other passengers.

'What's the matter?'

He continued to smile at me as he pointed across the dazzling landscape below.

'Look at the beautiful view! It's like we are in space, Jamie!'

In the next instance we were hurtling down to earth at eighty miles per hour.

Thirty seconds later and with dizzy heads, Bobby, Martin and I staggered our way toward the exit.

Our day at the pleasure beach ended leaving the three of us cold and hungry. We must have been one of the last groups to leave the park.

Bobby and I walked behind Martin as he avidly observed everything in his sight. People eating and drinking in the windows of cafes, hotels, and pubs.

The laughing policeman in the glass box; the hot dog vendor dressed up as Jerry the mouse - a particular point of delight for my brother.

The gates to the amusement park were set a little way back from the sea front. Martin wandered off ahead, inspecting this, touching that, intermittently talking to himself.

I linked arms with Bobby as we strolled a short distance behind. Neither of us could believe how circumstances had changed over the last few days. We were all different people for the experience.

I felt wiser; inevitably hardened and highly appreciative of our new status as independents.

As we walked and talked, neither of us had noticed that my brother had reached the roadside and had stopped in his tracks.

He just stood with his arms by his side.

Like a statue. Stationary, inanimate - just looking.

'What have you seen, Martin?' I asked in all innocence.

By this time the three of us were standing across from the entrance to the south pier. We followed Martin's gaze as he pointed north into the distance.

Then he turned to the pair of us, wide-eyed and evidently excited.

'What is it, Martin?'

Bobby's enquiry did not receive an immediate reply. He simply continued to stare at the source of his amazement.

Finally, it dawned on the pair of us. He was transfixed by the scene along the promenade. It was the last week of the Illuminations. The shimmering Golden Mile looked incredible against the jet cloth of the late autumn sky.

Martin gazed to the two of us whilst continuing to point along the prom. Bobby understood his exaggerated reaction to the spectacle and squeezed my arm.

'He's never seen it before, Jamie.'

I did not comprehend her.

'Never seen *what* before, Bobby?'

'The *lights*, Jamie! He's never, ever seen them. After living here all this time…he's never, ever seen the lights.'

We approached my brother and linked an arm on either side of him, before embarking on our final excursion that day.

Walking the length of the sea front at Blackpool was something that most of us have done and taken for granted.

Martin took *nothing* for granted.

Everything was new to him, and he fully appreciated it.

We reached the tower.

That most significant of symbols that had implanted itself in my conscience for an age. It was sheathed in a million flashing, golden stars. Martin never averted his gaze for a second. Once an icon in a mysterious nightmare, that magnificent glimmering spire that soared into the blackness above was now representative of hope.

Our hope - the hope of brothers that were once estranged.

He never uttered a single word. I had only ever seen him react in such a way before. When he was a little boy. It was on the fifth of November - the first bonfire night I could remember as a youngster.

As usual, we were restricted to watching other people's fireworks from the confines of Lodge Close. It goes without saying we never had fireworks of our own.

I can vividly recall the scene at home from all those years ago. I watched Martin as he sat quietly in his push chair. The face was expressionless as he observed the explosive and enticing view from the window. There was a reflective light in his eyes.

It was a childish, yet intensely invigorating moment.

Now, years later as I watched him study the neon flashing high above, I saw that same light in his eyes once again.

The man was still a child in essence.

A happy, enthusiastic, loving child.

As the Gods above looked down on the myriad of electric colour, there was one light that shone brighter than any other.

It was the energy from a trinity of exempted souls.

A powerful flame that would never fade.

*****

As I am sure you will understand, dear reader, the dramatic experience of my visits to Blackpool had taken clear prominence over every other facet of my life for several weeks.

I awoke in Bobby's flat one morning with a nagging sensation that the situation I had left back in Nottingham was now yearning desperately for my attention.

Bobby and Martin had quickly become accustomed to being with each other on a daily basis. My concerns for them were now secondary. My order of priorities had suddenly altered once more.

Since my departure a month earlier, I had not attempted to contact Henry. The note I had hastily scribbled to notify him of my intentions was all he had to link me and my absence.

I also contemplated the situation at school. I had missed nearly a whole term in my second A level year. I hadn't informed the school that I *wouldn't* be returning, although I held the presumption that word would have gotten around as to the reasons for my non-attendance.

Then of course, there was Alex. God only knows what she must have been doing as I sat thoughtfully in Bobby Jones' kitchen on that early November morning.

Would she even still love me? Would she even recognise me as the reckless idiot who left her standing in tears at Nottingham train station?

At that stage, my reputation with her could only be a subject of rhetoric. I wasn't even going to try and guess.

As Bobby and Martin slept soundly in their room, I plucked up the courage to call Henry. I decided to ring from a public telephone. It would save running up Bobby's bill and I couldn't find my mobile anyway.

On reaching the call box I was shaking.

It was partly because of the seasonal temperature but I was also weighed down with anxiety. Checking the number from the list in my wallet I punched it into the keypad, not knowing what response to expect from the other end.

Eventually, after five or six rings, my call was answered.

An unfamiliar, elderly sounding, female tone.

'Hello?'

I didn't recognize the voice.

'Hello…I'm sorry. I think I've dialled the wrong number.'

'That depends on who you are trying to contact, sir.'

She sounded rather abrupt, but amiable enough.

'Erm…Henry Thompson.'

'Yes…he lives here. He's in the bath at the moment. This is his sister, Eileen. Can I be of assistance?'

I withdrew the receiver from my ear and looked at it in bemusement.

I didn't even know Henry *had* a sister.

'It's Jamie. Jamie Andrews. I haven't spoken to him for a while. I thought I'd better check he's okay.'

The pause on the end of the line was long and thoughtful. She had perhaps already been informed about me. I waited nervously for her response. I couldn't decipher whether she was pleased that it was me or absolutely fuming at the fact.

Finally, she spoke.

'Er…I think it best you speak to Henry yourself.'

'I thought he was in the bath?'

'I'll fetch him…he won't want to miss your call. Can you hold?'

Of course, I could hold.

I suddenly felt incredibly neglectful. He had given me money, a home and shown me love like no other adult was willing to.

For Henry, I could hold forever.

I strained to hear the activity on the other end of the line. There was some muffled talking, then silence, then the painful sound of relentless coughing. It got louder as Henry picked up the receiver.

'Jamie…is it *really* you?'

A lump of guilt swiftly formed in my throat as I tried to speak.

Henry got in first.

'Jamie…I've been so worried. Where have you been until now? Are you okay, son?'

I wiped away a tear as I compiled my response.

'Henry…I did it…Henry…I *did* it…'

His tone became sympathetic and curious.

'You did *what*, son?'

'I got my brother, Henry. I found Martin. He's…with me now. I'm still in Blackpool.'

Henry himself seemed to be grappling with his emotions.

It was a poignant moment for the pair of us.

A short silence ensued.

I heard him take several deep sighs.

'My god. You did it, son. You got him back.'

'Yes, Henry…it's been awful…I miss you…I…I want to come home…with Martin. And his girlfriend. Is…that alright?'

I could hear Henry's voice struggle to maintain composure.

I waited for his answer. I looked out of the phone box at the miserable scene through the scratched and cracked pane.

Our future was not here.

I so hoped Henry would respond positively.

'Do you mean you'll be here for Christmas, Jamie? All of you?'

'Yes, Henry. I want to bring them back to Nottingham as soon as possible. To your house. If that's okay with you?'

'Just a moment.'

Again, I held patiently listening to the crackling void of silence.

Henry was always the foundation to which I had hoped to return when my mission was over.

I mentally crossed my fingers hoping the verdict would go my way.

After an agonizing hiatus, Henry spoke.

'Jamie…can you come home tomorrow? I'd love you to. I *need* you to. Please, say you'll come back tomorrow. All three of you.'

It was the final piece of the jigsaw.

The return to Nottingham was unavoidable and inevitable.

I thanked Henry for his eternal love and returned to the flat to inform Bobby and Martin of what I had planned for them.

Within hours we would have completely severed our connections with Blackpool.

We could prepare to depart and wilfully banish its ghosts.

In readiness to begin the rest of our lives.

# 31
# A HAVEN

Bobby did not take much convincing. She hated her flat. She hated Blackpool and all it stood for. It was only on leaving the place that she told me the terms of her very unscrupulous and unorthodox tenancy agreement.

I offered to pay for any rental arrears.

Her attitude was quite to the point.

'Fuck 'em, Jamie! They'll never find me once I'm outta here, anyways.'

I sympathised, but quickly altered my viewpoint when she revealed that the landlord was a friend of Loz Prenter. Talk about covering all angles. The bastards had her pinned down on every aspect of her existence.

She was even more justified in claiming that she detested the life that she was about to relinquish. Although understandably, Bobby was still reticent in her expectations of co-habiting with Henry. It was something she was going to have to trust *me* on for once.

Martin certainly didn't have any cares. The thrill of his first train ride for years was more than enough of a distraction. His world was now one of untroubled adventure. He had no perspective on what was being left behind in Blackpool and how it would compare with his future.

He was happy spotting cows, horses, and sheep through the carriage window, accompanying his intermittent discoveries with the appropriate impersonations as we went.

Sod the rest of the passengers.

Let anyone dare question his right to pretend to be a farm animal.

It was a most enjoyable journey for me personally.

It was comforting to have company on the train for a change. The three of us sat around the table, reading the paper, drinking a disgusting tasting brown liquid that passed for coffee, and we laughed regularly.

Yet, despite the apparent calm in the storm, I could see the doubt in Bobby's eyes.

'Do you think he'll mind me tagging along? You haven't told him about me yet, have you, Jamie?'

She was taking some convincing, was Bobby Jones.

'Look…he knows you are coming with us. Henry has been the only family I ever had next to Mum. He thinks of me as his own son. Don't worry…there's no problem. He begged me to come back as soon as possible.'

'Yes, but…he's bound to want to take you back with Martin, isn't he? He has no obligation to me. He doesn't know he's got to find room for *three* lodgers! And you say it's a two-bed bungalow? Christ on a bike!'

I shook my head and gazed through the window as if to end the conversation. There was nothing more to be said on the matter as far as I was concerned.

Time on the train passed rapidly and the change at Crewe was conveniently swift. I suppose it made all the difference having my brother at my side. Not to mention the fact that I was pleased to be going home again at last.

Climbing out of the taxi outside Henry's was one of the most satisfying moments of my life. I felt like an explorer who had just returned from navigating the mountain or an astronaut who had returned from the moon.

Placing our minimal luggage outside Henry's front door, I beckoned Martin to stand in front of me. He insisted on carrying his bloody teddy bear. With Bobby positioned next to him, I stood behind them both and knocked on the door.

When he answered smoking his trusty pipe, Henry's face became a picture of relief and delight. The welcome was predictably warm and genuine.

'Well, well, well. What have we here, then? Three lost pups that have found their way back. Come inside, please, everyone…come inside.'

And it was as easy as that.

*****

We slotted into life at Glenfield Avenue as though we were always meant to be there. That little bungalow became alive with animated tales of where the three of us had been and the sights we had seen.

We skipped the gory details, though.

There was little incentive to recall too much of what had transpired during the past month.

Henry took to Martin and Bobby straight away.

Of course, they began to regard him with great affection within a matter of hours. The reunion was idyllic.

The only matter that wasn't mentioned was Henry's illness.

I could see he had deteriorated rapidly during my absence. He looked to have lost weight and his cough was disturbing enough to wake the birds before dawn. Still, he kept smiling throughout.

It was a few days before I managed to catch him alone so he could explain the state of play with his own situation. We were both up early one Sunday morning.

It was a couple of weeks before Christmas as we stood in his kitchen, admiring the frost tinted view of his garden through the back window.

'Well, Jamie. You've done your brother and his girl a great service. You're a hero…and nothing less.'

His voice wavered ever so slightly as he looked me in the eye.

'I'll be honest, though. I never believed I'd see you again.'

I thought it a strange comment at the time. After all, I wasn't at the other end of the Earth. But of course, it would have seemed so to dear Henry.

I offered a woefully weak attempt at excusing myself.

'If you'd have called for me to return, I would've come, Henry. I'm only sorry that I left it so long.'

He lit the large tuft of tobacco protruding from his pipe and sucked vigorously.

'No matter anymore, Jamie. You're all here now. Safe and sound.'

'Yes, but even so…I didn't know what to do for the best, Henry. I didn't want you worrying about me. I hoped a note would be enough.'

He created rings of aromatic smoke that partially hid his tired face.

I saw a gentle smile emerge as he clasped the pipe between his forefinger and thumb.

'Me Jamie? Me…*worry*? I don't think so, son. I don't do that nowadays. Too late for me to start whittle-arsing, isn't it, lad?'

My mind recalled the phone conversation that I'd had with his sister. He hadn't mentioned her since we got back. To be honest, it hadn't entered my own head again until that point.

Henry's sheepish response saddened me.

'No, you're right to enquire. I never spoke of my sister before, Jamie. That's because I haven't got a bloody sister! Well, not a real one, any road.'

He continued to smirk as my face became distorted with wonder.

'The morning you phoned I was having my weekly check-up. You know, lung capacity, that sort of thing. The woman who spoke to you was a nurse from the hospital. I told her that as a cover to any cold callers, I wanted her to pretend to be my sister.'

I observed his wizened features, bemused by the whole charade.

'Well…you know that I don't like to answer the phone at the best of times. It's always con men and nosey bleeders. So, whenever the phone rang, she would scan any calls by putting them off the scent. You see?'

I did understand, although it seemed so unnecessary. The silly old sod.

'So, you were never in the bath then…when I rang you?'

'Nah…that's just a ploy to get them to go away. Make 'em think they've caught me at a bad time. Besides, I can't physically get in the bath these days.' he chuckled.

My head was still grappling with Henry's little game.

'Obviously you told this nurse that if I phoned you would take it?'

Henry looked to the ceiling and rolled his eyes in mockery.

'Now he gets it…now the penny drops.'

It concerned me that he was prepared to cut the world off from his own plight. What if something important cropped up, and they needed to talk to him urgently?

'Jamie, my lad. In my state…nothing seems that important anymore. You're the only person in the world that means owt to me. I don't owe a penny to anyone. I've got no true friends besides yourself. I don't need to see anybody but you, anymore. I sleep well enough at night, thanks.'

I tentatively asked about his treatment and the current forecast for his long-term health. He paused before answering. Several deep puffs were taken on his pipe.

It was ironic that inhaling smoke was the best way to calm his ailing lungs. If ever a coughing fit encroached, he would instantly reach for his pipe and light up as soon as possible.

Finally, his eyes diverted from the back garden and met mine once more.

'You know I said I was glad to have you back for Christmas?'

I nodded without a word. I listened without interruption. He had my full attention.

‘Well…that’s because…this Christmas…will be my last…’

He must have felt like thumping me.

I heard what he said, but the implication of the words did not immediately register.

My reply was oafish at best

‘So…what does that *mean*?’

He continued to create great plumes of smoke as he spoke.

‘It means…’

I watched Henry’s calm manner crumble a little as he revealed the latest prognosis.

‘It means…Jamie, my son…that I won’t be around this time next year. That’s what it means.’

I thought I was hearing things. It couldn’t be true. It couldn’t be. I fought a compulsion to hold Henry and weep for him. I didn’t want to accept the prospect of losing someone so dear to me when I had spent weeks rescuing the one other person in my life that meant anything.

I wanted to know, in the bluntest terms, how long I’d got left with him.

‘Between four and six months. Tops. Might be less than that.’

I argued with him as upset verged.

‘But it *might* be longer. *They* might be wrong.’

‘Yes Jamie. They *might* be wrong. They can’t accurately measure how quickly the cancer is spreading. Only by the symptoms I show can they estimate where it has moved to. That’s the problem when it’s caught too late. They can’t just open me up and have a look inside. It’s not as simple as that.’

Our emotive discussion was interrupted with the sudden appearance of Martin at the kitchen doorway. Henry and I turned to see his stubbly features framed by an unkempt mop of black hair.

He shifted weight from foot to foot before producing the teddy bear and smiling.

He had evidently overheard the conversation regarding Henry’s health.

‘Rufus says that the chances of surviving such a condition depend heavily on the intake and settlement of nicotine deposits on the lungs. That contributes greatly to cell destruction and the body’s ability to deal with invasive non-performing foreigners.’

Henry looked down at the billowing pipe between his lips.

He could do little else but smile as he addressed my brother.

'Well, young Martin… I do declare that Rufus is spot on…and I'm a stubborn old man.'

Martin seemed content with the reply and made for the bathroom.

Henry glanced my way and removed the pipe from his mouth.

'Maybe he's right. Maybe I should stop. Yes, I'll stop.'

Henry ran the cold tap and extinguished his pipe.

I questioned him on his unusual actions.

'You don't have to stop smoking, Henry. Do you actually *want* to stop? You said it didn't matter anymore.'

'I've realised Jamie, that I've been fooling myself all this time. The one thing that matters at the end of the day…is being alive. It appears I've foregone that privilege. I don't want to die, son. Not at all. But we all must go when our time is up.'

His thinking had certainly altered since we last spoke on the subject. I couldn't resist mentioning his late wife.

'But what about Doris? You said that dying will bring you back together. That's what you hoped for, isn't it? That's what you've wanted from death.'

He laid his dripping pipe on the draining board and spoke conclusively as to his feelings.

'No, Jamie. No. It's not going to happen. Death is the end. There's nothing afterwards. Fate doesn't provide a happy ending.'

After the events of the past couple of years, I could not agree with him. I believed that destiny had been favourable to me in the end.

The trials I had face along the way were a stern test for sure, but ultimately, fate *was* kind.

'You're wrong, Henry. Keep the faith. If you stop believing in your dream, you can be sure it won't happen. *Never* stop wanting to meet Doris. If you give up, it's a certainty that you never will.'

He did not argue.

Reluctantly, he placed his pipe in the kitchen drawer and turned to put the kettle on.

It was the last time we conferred on the issue.

*****

The prospect of losing Henry burned heavily within my heart. Even so, the days still passed quickly with other distractions.

We were now into the third week of December.

Bobby had taken Martin into Nottingham on his first ever Christmas shopping trip. I had opted not to go with them. I felt I had other pressing matters to attend to.

They would be fine together. I gave her a bus timetable and a few quid to spend - well, it was actually the remains of Henry's generosity. To see her beaming smile as she escorted my brother down the road that day, complete with his oversized woolly hat and gloves, was a pleasure in itself.

Other issues had begun to fight for attention at the forefront of my mind. I had made my mind up that I was ready to go back to school. Previous circumstances had dictated otherwise, but now I wanted to resume my A level studies.

In fact, I needed to. I was still an intelligent, capable young man who was in grave danger of missing out on important opportunities.

Opportunities that may not come my way again.

The day that my brother and Bobby went shopping, I decided to go into school to arrange a meeting with the Headteacher and the head of the Sixth Form. It was of paramount consideration. I needed to secure permission to return straight after the Christmas break. It was an idea I had nurtured over several weeks, usually during those lonely little moments in Blackpool.

Now was the time to stop thinking and start acting.

It was an incredibly strange sensation walking back through the school gates for the first time in nearly six months.

I received calls of recognition from various familiar faces as I made my way to reception and asked to speak to the relevant people. I had to wait over an hour before both the Headteacher Geoff Davies and my Head of Year Alan Steele could make themselves available. It didn't matter to me how long they took.

I would have willingly sat and waited all day.

They shook me firmly by the hand and the three of us convened in a small office adjacent to the staff room. Coffee was served and my nerves were slowly settled.

I was ready to go on my knees to them if necessary.

I just wanted a chance to get back to school and catch up.

The Head didn't say much at first. He was taking his lead from the response of Mister Steele, who understandably wanted to know where the hell I'd been for the last term.

I explained in relevant detail the situation that had arisen. They listened for nearly half an hour as I recalled the events of the previous four months. I couldn't decide whether they believed me or not. All I could do was to state my position and await their response.

The Head eventually began his response by slapping my wrists.

'It would have only been courteous for you to have enlightened the school as to the probability of your education being disrupted. People have spent valuable time trying to locate you. A weekly phone call would have sufficed. Having considered the upheaval you have experienced, I'm not convinced at this stage that you are fully committed to a return to school.'

Admittedly, the reaction from Mister Davies was not exactly welcoming. Thankfully, Alan Steele was more of a soft touch.

'You've missed a lot of vital lessons, Jamie. It's going to take great effort from yourself and your subject teachers to get you back on track.'

I sat up in my seat. I could detect positivity around the corner.

'I'm aware of that, sir. I'm ready. I can do it. There are no more distractions now. I'm focused. I want it so badly, sir.'

Still the verbal tennis continued. I could play this game all day if it got me what I wanted. Mister Steele continued to state the obvious.

'You've managed to miss the most important term of your A level courses. And you've missed your mock exams. Any other period lost would have been manageable. I don't know if I can pledge the school's support whilst you fill in all the gaps. It's going to take many long days of hard work.'

The Headteacher interjected with a suggestion.

A suggestion that I really did not wish to hear.

'What if you forget about this year and come back to complete your second year next September? That would be better for all. You can slot in with other classes quite easily.'

I wasn't in favour of any unnecessary delay to my ambition.

'No! I...I mean...no...I really need to do this *now*. *This* year.'

Mister Davies was not easily swayed.

'I can assure you that re-starting the academic syllabus with fellow second year A-levellers would be preferable to playing catch up in the

New Year. It would be far easier for all concerned. Unless of course, you try and get in at a local Sixth Form college.'

I became agitated, beginning to sense that they may not want me back at the school at all.

I played along with the digression.

'Another college wouldn't take me though, would they?'

My feigned interest in the Headteacher's' alternative proposal was a mistake. It led to a revelation that sunk my heart.

An unexpected kick in the guts.

He continued with promoting a placement elsewhere. I listened without genuine interest until he mentioned the one person I secretly wanted to see most of all.

'Oh yes, they will. Most local colleges will gladly accept stranded ships such as yourself. They receive extra bursaries from the council for doing so. In fact, we had one pupil leave us earlier this term to do exactly that.'

He glanced across to Mister Steele for confirmation.

'Wasn't she in your maths class, Alan?'

The Head of Sixth Form nodded in the affirmative.

Then he said that name.

He may as well have hit me on the back of the head with a mallet.

'Yes, Alexandra Lawley. She just decided to leave after only two weeks of this term.'

The Headteacher diverted his attention back to me.

'I believe you know her quite well, Jamie.'

I felt anger breaching the calm.

It was as if they were aware I would be moved by such news.

My reply was amazingly composed.

'Yes…we know each other…*fairly* well. So…is she no longer at this school then, sir?'

'No. She claimed she couldn't settle down after the summer. Shame really, bright young lady. Very capable brain. A sad loss.'

I couldn't agree more.

My mind whirled in response to what I had just learned.

I couldn't fucking believe it! It was as though she knew I'd be coming back and had moved on just to spite me! The selfish bitch!

I wrestled with the premise of Alex being elsewhere, as the teachers impatiently awaited my decision.

I struggled to concentrate for a moment as another question came my way from the Headmaster.

'Have you considered where your A-levels may lead? Did you intend applying for university? If so, then that process will need to begin in the New Year. You're taking a lot on your shoulders.'

I had always nurtured the vague dream of being a journalist.

A degree would be vital in pursuing that field.

'Yes, sir. I intend to go to Uni next September - after passing my exams of course!'

My enthusiasm alone had finally managed to convince the pair that I was perhaps worthy of the opportunity.

'Okay, Jamie. We are prepared to give you the chance to prove your capability and determination. You sound like you've had a rough ride lately. No reason for us to heap more disappointment onto you. Are you sure about this?'

I retained my temper enough to confirm a rational decision.

Fuck Alex. I couldn't go chasing her round the district just because I loved her. I had my education to think about.

'Yes, sir. Definitely. I want to come back here next term."

The Headmaster looked across to his colleague.

'Are you happy with that, Alan?'

Both teachers eyed me with the merest hint of suspicion. I felt the need to eradicate any doubt in their minds - and my own for that matter.

'I won't let anyone down. I promise. I'm not playing to lose. I'll show you all.'

At last, the Headmaster smiled and offered me a hand of welcome.

'Well, there's little more to be said on the matter. Report back on the third of January, Jamie. We look forward to seeing you.'

Despite my success in attaining readmittance, I left the school grounds in something of a mild fume. It didn't dissipate until I'd gotten home and told Henry I'd enrolled back into Sixth Form. He was absolutely overjoyed.

'You're too smart *not* to be bothered about qualifications, Jamie. I'm so glad you've made the right choice.'

My mind was assured in the fact that I had achieved what I set out to do that day.

My heart was not so enamoured with the scenario.

It was a day of accomplishment, slightly tinged with doleful resignation.

I had been given little option in the matter.

I would just have to put Alex out of my mind.

*****

It was around teatime when Bobby and Martin returned from their shopping trip. Armed with several carrier bags, the pair confirmed they had never had such a wonderful time before.

The delight in their voices edged out my own disappointment of earlier.

Martin was typically full of childish enthusiasm as he entered the house.

'Hey, Jamie. I had a conversation with Santa Claus today.'

I could do no more but play along.

'Really, Martin? The *real* Santa Claus?'

'Yes. In the Victoria shopping arcade. I don't think he understood my request, though.'

The thought of my six-foot-tall elder brother sitting on Santa's knee in a grotto flashed through my mind.

I looked at Bobby as she mockingly winked back.

'What puzzled him, Martin? What did you ask for?'

Martin's expression exhibited no emotion.

It was evidently an earnest conveyance of his true wishes.

'I just said to him that I'd finally got everything I ever wanted for Christmas. And I made him promise not to take it away again. I didn't even take the sweets he presented to me. Bobby ate those.'

I watched my brother as he removed his coat in the hallway.

My hero.

# 32
# REMEMBRANCE

The twenty-second of December. Twelve months since I said farewell to Mum. The anniversary of her actual passing was a couple of weeks earlier, but I didn't feel content in commemorating her surrender. Not just because of the upsetting nature of the business generally, but because I still felt aggrieved that her passing should have been avoided in the first place.

Her willingness in sacrificing herself was still not a decision I could accept. And so, I deemed that acknowledging her burial instead of her death was a slightly more palatable choice.

I hadn't spoken to Martin about Mum or the way in which she died. It didn't carry any relevance to our relationship at that time and I certainly didn't want to drop any upsetting flies into his currently idyllic ointment.

He was very happy with Bobby. Possibly even in love with her although his kind of love may have been different from the conventional kind. Though we never talked about that, either.

Her loyalty and commitment to him were undoubted. I didn't feel happy throwing a blanket of sorrow over proceedings.

One afternoon as he watched television, I told him that I would be attending Mum's grave and in doing so presented to Martin the option of him accompanying me.

I didn't think he'd heard me. His eyes never left the flickering, jabbering screen in the corner. His expression never altered.

I asked him again just in case his attention hadn't been captured by my invitation.

'Martin…I'm going to see Mum tomorrow…at the chapel cemetery. Do you want to come?'

Again, there was no verbal reply. He rose from the armchair and moved to turn off the TV set. I thought it to be a strange reaction. I had never seen him willingly switch the telly off before. It had been the centre of his life for so many years. His own personal channel of commune with civilization.

To suddenly see him dispense with his favourite source of entertainment came as a something of a surprise.

What followed was even more unexpected.

I prompted him to indulge me.

'Martin…I'll understand if you don't want to come. I know it might be hard for you.'

He sat back down and stared at the grey screen he had just disconnected.

He then looked at me.

I couldn't tell if he was afraid of the prospect of seeing Mum in her place of rest.

I guessed that he may have felt a sense of honour in being asked.

His emotions rarely conveyed themselves for open interpretation.

Sadness and happiness were not parameters in Martin's life.

Peace and disquiet were the benchmarks he had always abided by.

His view on the issue at hand was startlingly brutal, yet somewhat tragic.

'I can't go with you, Jamie. It would be disrespectful. To me, I mean.'

He didn't make much sense at first.

I needed to understand his feelings about Mum.

He alternately clenched his fists inside one another and began to rock gently in the armchair as he relayed his thoughts.

Staring intently into space, his honesty was a smack in the face to me.

'I have never forgotten, Jamie. I begged her. I *begged* her not to. I was terrified, but still, she did not listen to my plea.'

I assumed it must have been painful for him, but Martin's face remained a picture of indifference as he opened his heart to me.

I still couldn't understand his viewpoint.

'What do you mean, Martin? What didn't you want Mum to do?'

The light in his eyes was cold and unmoving as he leaned towards me from his seat.

There could be no doubting his sentiment or motive.

'I was banished, Jamie. I was sent away against my will. That is what I remember my mother for. The woman who spurned me. Threw me to the dogs. She chose another life instead. I pleaded with her, but she still chose her own preference.'

For Mum's sake, I tried to defend her actions.

'But she regretted it for the rest of her life, Martin. She wasn't happy about any of it at all.'

My brother's composure was unwavering.

'Her regret…I shared. But the burden was far more mine than hers. Believe me.'

I knew what he was saying and knew why he might have nurtured such resentment.

Realistically, his opinion was his right to hold.

I had little time to think of persuading him otherwise.

He got up and switched the television back on with a final declaration.

'Countdown. The semi-finals. Exciting! They won't beat me, though!'

And that, dear reader, was Martin's final word on the issue.

I did not discuss the matter with Bobby or Henry in any detail.

Both were too respectful of two brothers who had obviously experienced different consequences of the family break up.

We had dealt with things over the years as individuals and I decided that was the way it should be left.

After all, we had led mostly separate lives. We were now both adults, entitled to feel what we did. We had no right to expect anything of each other. Although bonded by blood, we were of course different in our outlook and judgements.

Nobody was in any position to say that Martin was wrong for feeling the way he did.

I can now see that such a relationship between siblings is perfectly acceptable and normal.

*****

I walked the three miles to East Park. To the tiny chapel and surrounding burial plots. The sky was clear azure on that crisp winter morning. I enjoyed the stroll. The air inflated my lungs as I soaked up the familiar sights along the route.

Alone in the graveyard, I assembled my thoughts.

It had been a year since I first stood at Mum's headstone.

A small, black granite affair inscribed in gold. I chose it with Alex and her parents.

According to her it was stylish, as if style was ever a relevant criterion for such things.

I read the epitaph to myself.

*Elizabeth Andrews.*
*Born 25 August 1959*
*Died 3 December 2003*
*May you rest in peace.*
*Your ever-loving sons*
*Martin and Jamie.*

In my moment of recollection, I thought of the torrid times she had endured, and happier times that she would never know of. I did not openly speak, for I did not truly believe that she would hear me.

Not even in spirit.

My contemplation remained silent, to be hopefully carried on the waves of the subconscious now I knew there was such a thing.

The minutes passed as I immersed myself in reflective solace. The bell in the chapel rang out once to announce the time as eleven-thirty. It didn't disturb my concentration.

Nor did the approaching footsteps of the diminutive figure that stood respectfully behind me.

Only when he vocally disclosed his presence did my attention become diverted.

'Her passing was not a waste, my son.'

I recognised the voice.

The earthy north-eastern accent.

Authoritative, yet gently consoling.

He continued with his appraisal.

'Do not mourn her absence. Time has proved you more than worthy of her departure.'

I turned slowly to see Father David Carroll standing at my side.

He offered a hand in greeting, which I reciprocated. Although we had met only once before, it was as though I was suddenly in the presence of an old friend.

I could not conceal my astonishment at his attendance.

'Father…what are you doing *here*? This is a fair way from your usual place of residence.'

He smiled as if expectant of that very question.

'I like to get around. I perform my duties near and far.'

I glanced down to Mum's grave.

'I thought it best to come and see her. It's been a year already since she was laid to rest, you know.'

He placed a hand on my shoulder.

'Yes, Jamie. That is why I am here, also. I thought I'd find you paying your respects.'

It surprised me that he would remember this day of significance, considering the amount of death he must be confronted with on an annual basis. Yet, I was most glad of his company. He carried a soothing air around him.

It was nothing to do with his profession, though. It was his persona.

He was continually insightful.

'It's no coincidence that you happened to be here then, Father?'

A slight smile emerged underneath his white beard.

'There is no such thing as coincidence, young Jamie. I would have thought you of all people would have learned that for yourself. Your brother would certainly vouch for the fact.'

I nodded in agreement. My experiences of the past few months had certainly taught me that much. Then my mind focused on what he had said a moment ago, regarding my worthiness of Mum's passing and the reference to my brother.

'How do you know about Martin? Do you know that I've brought him back with me?'

His smile had now fully broadened, accentuating his scarlet hued cheeks.

Folding his arms across his chest, he observed me with warmth in his eyes.

'You wouldn't be here now if your mission had failed. The sufferance would be in continuation. Your torment would not have ceased. I can see that calm is your companion now, as opposed to anguish. You've done well, my son.'

I hesitated to bring Martin's opinion into the conversation, but it was relevant to the conversation.

'My brother doesn't see things the same as me. He feels bitterness that she acted as she did.'

Father Carroll's eyes narrowed as his face came closer to my own.

His whispered tones carried a veiled yet definitive slant of foreboding.

'Yes Jamie, of course. But ask yourself this. Is he angered by her death…or by her life?'

His features became contorted by inquisitiveness as he continued.

'Your brother is attuned to the attitudes he has grown up with. His opinion will have only been entrenched in the company of other, similar minded souls.'

'Are you saying its right for him not to be here with me now? That it's correct if he chooses not to care about Mum?'

The priest shook his head and pursed his whiskered lips.

'I am no judge. I am simply an observer. But if the demons he carries within him are not vanquished by his own will, they may never leave him. Indeed, he may give them sustenance if he harbours their influence.'

I was becoming more than a little alarmed by the implication of Father Carroll's words.

'So, what do I do to help him overcome these negative thoughts?'

He raised a forefinger and began to move away, as though to offer one final, parting lesson.

'You may have liberated your brother in the physical sense, but his spiritual being will provide a separate challenge, personal to him. You can have no jurisdiction over the minds of others. Not even your dear brother. Nor can anyone else who ventures to love him and protect him. Be aware, Jamie. Be aware, my son.'

He offered a hand of farewell.

I was stupefied by his counsel, yet also grateful for his presence for those few brief minutes.

'Thank you, Father Carroll. For everything you've done.'

As he shuffled away between the headstones, he turned with one last sermon.

'Do not fear the future as you did the past, young Jamie. Prepare for it and oppose it if you must. But do not fear it. I bid you and your family every health and happiness.'

With those confounding words, he swiftly made his exit.

It was an encounter that still amazes me to this day. He had such a grasp of the situation I was immersed in. It's an incredible thought that someone who has barely had contact with you can predict so much about your life.

I never anticipated that I would see Father Carroll again after our first encounter at his residence. And I don't suppose I will now, after our second meeting effectively drew a line under events.

Only the passage of time will prove if his insight gains true potency.

*****

I returned to Glenfield Avenue feeling suddenly shrouded by uncertainty. Bobby and Henry were at home. They were understandably surprised to see that Martin was not with me when I walked into the house.

'We assumed he was at the cemetery with you.' Henry proclaimed.

Bobby was becoming visibly distressed.

'But he's been gone ages! Where could he have gotten to? He'll end up so confused. He could be anywhere!'

I began to lose my temper.

A sense of immediate concern descended on the room.

'For fuck's sake, Bobby! I can't believe you've just let him wander off! Get your coat on. We need to go looking.'

I stormed out of the house without a single idea as to where to begin the search. Martin was not exactly a danger to himself or others whilst out alone, but he could become disorientated quite easily. The thought of him being lost and upset was an image that I fought to place at the back of my mind for the time being.

Henry appeared in the doorway trying to appease a coughing fit.

'I'll wait here, Jamie just in case he decides to turn up.'

I nodded in appreciation whilst wincing at the sound of his barking chest. Bobby followed me out of the front door.

We both stood silently on the pavement. I was angry with her.

I was in the wrong for feeling that way, I know. But she had to understand that Martin effectively needed twenty-four-hour supervision.

'Three days before Christmas and I've lost my brother again!'

She pulled her gloves on without responding.

My tirade continued.

'Where do we start then, clever clogs?'

If Bobby was perturbed by my attitude, she wasn't showing it.

'Calm down, Jamie. How far could he have got? It's not like he knows the area, is it?'

I looked at her in disbelief.

'I suppose that's meant to make me feel better, knowing that he's totally unfamiliar with his surroundings?'

Bobby looked at her watch.

'It's only ten to three. Let's try the village centre. He might be exploring.'

My temper was getting the better of me.

'Oh yeah…in his pith helmet and rucksack! Jesus Christ!'

I'm glad Bobby laughed out loud at that precise moment.

It reminded me how distracting she was in a crisis.

Subsequently, I was instantly dissuaded from landing a fist squarely onto her nose.

I tried to chill myself out and counted to ten.

'Stop fretting, Jamie! He'll not be far.'

'Okay, but we'll walk. It's quicker than waiting for the bus. And we might bump into him. Come on.'

I strode on ahead, forcing Bobby into a half trot to keep up.

The minutes passed as I tried to think about where Martin might have gone. Then I thought of what Father Carroll had said, about the possibility of my brother having to face his own challenges in the future. I supposed it wasn't a specific warning regarding any impending event. More an overview of what might be in the future.

I tossed alternatives around inside my head as we approached the main road to the town centre. It was the doctrine that Father Carroll had pronounced on our first encounter. The signs were there. I just had to see them for myself. That was the most important lesson that he had taught me. Learn to interpret what happens rather than cower from it.

If Martin had decided to wander off alone, there must have been a specific reason.

He must have had a destination in mind, otherwise it would be an aimless meander.

Rather like the one I was experiencing at that very moment.

I turned the mental wheels of logic and reason. What did it mean? It reminded me of before, trying to attach definition to the images in my dreams.

I glanced back at Bobby, who obviously had no idea of my brother's potential whereabouts. Come on, Jamie, I said quietly to myself.

*You know it. You know it.*

We'd been walking for about fifteen minutes when the answer finally hit me.

Yes, of course. It was obvious. If you could read the signs, that is.

I stopped dead and started to walk back the way we had just come, which only added to the confusion that Bobby was feeling.

'Jamie, what the hell are you doing?'

'There's no time to explain. I know where Martin is. Come on.'

I began to jog. Bobby began to run. Although satisfied that my instincts would be correct, there was an accompanying perception that I may need to rescue Martin all over again.

I hoped he hadn't gotten himself into any strife.

Within minutes we were running back past Henry's and further into the estate.

My guess was proven right.

Bobby required a little explanation as she began to grow short of breath.

'Where are you going, Jamie? Why would he be down here?'

I did not answer. I knew exactly why Martin would be there.

Entering Lodge Close, I glanced along the pavement to number fifteen. Outside was a police car, next to which I observed two or three irate looking neighbours, two policemen…and my brother.

I slowed my pace and tentatively approached the group, all of which stopped their heated exchange and looked in my direction.

Bobby had opted to stay some distance behind.

The policemen did not look particularly disgruntled, which was more than could be said for the female member of the throng.

Martin noticed my advance and smiled to me as I entered the fracas.

I tried to lighten the tone of the scene.

'Officers…I apologize for any distress. This is my brother, Martin. Has he been up to mischief again?'

One of the policemen turned to me and flipped open his note pad.

'And your name is, sir?'

'Jamie…Jamie Andrews.'

The officer explained that Martin had been seen outside the property at number fifteen for nearly an hour.

The inhabitants had obviously taken him to task.

'Loitering is the term, sir. Only when the occupants confronted him about his intentions did he tell them that this was *his* house and that they shouldn't be there. He asked to speak to his mother. He then refused to move on. Hence, we've been called to assist. Can you throw any light on the matter, Mister Andrews?"

I eyed Martin, who had now diverted his gaze to the pavement.

'We both grew up here, officer. Although, that was a long time ago. I think he just got a little bit homesick, that's all. He seems a little confused. There will be no further disturbance. I apologize for the inconvenience to you all.'

The second policeman beckoned me over and whispered under his breath.

'Is he…is he *alright*, sir? It's just that he seems a little bit oblivious to the issue he's caused. He keeps mumbling about wanting to see his mum. He says he's seen ghosts at the windows and that the place is haunted. It's been quite unnerving for the occupants. We haven't had the chance to breathalyse him yet. I hope for his sake he isn't drunk, sir. It is now a criminal offence, you know!'

I turned away in growing frustration and beckoned to Bobby who came and took Martin by the arm to lead him away. My brother appeared to be getting upset. A sight I didn't appreciate seeing.

The officer continued, though I was no longer really in the mood to listen.

'If there is any repetition of such an incident then we will have to treat it officially as disturbing the peace. We can't have folk wandering the streets annoying neighbours, sir.'

My anger with Bobby for letting him go out alone in the first place had not subsided, so when the police implied that Martin may be placed under arrest for harmless curiosity, my vexation reared its head once more without restraint.

'Why don't you two pricks go and do something useful, like have a fucking tea break…or maybe even catch a few *real* criminals?'

Oh dear, Jamie Andrews. A bad move.

Sitting in the back of the police car with one officer at my side and one in the front, I wished my mouth was a little less reactive.

What a bleeding spectacle! I looked through the window at the small crowd that had amassed in the gathering dusk. Bobby and Martin stood wisely out of sight. My rage was at boiling point.

It was an effort to play the game with Mister Plod. as he duly read the riot act.

'Let me make it quite clear to you, Mister Andrews, that your brother posed an unknown potential threat to these people, and it is our responsibility to investigate the matter until we are satisfied of its conclusion. Is that clear?'

I nodded at the copper's reddening features.

'Furthermore, if he insists on telling his neighbours that their houses are haunted, we can only consider that to be an incitement of affray. That is a criminal offence under the public order act. Do I need to make myself any clearer as to the position he may find himself in if you don't take him home?'

I had to concede defeat, though I offered one final parting shot as I got out of the car.

I couldn't help but smile as I said it, either.

'He's right though, officers.'

Simultaneously, they looked up as I walked away.

'Number fifteen *is* haunted. I can guarantee you that much.'

The group dispersed as I walked to the end of the road where Bobby and Martin stood waiting. They watched with open-mouthed vacancy as I brushed past them on route back to Glenfield Avenue.

'Let's just get him home, Bobby! I almost got myself arrested over a fucking ghost story!'

Understandably, she was perplexed by the whole affair, to which I felt obliged to explain the origins back at Henry's.

Martin sat in silence as I spoke of the life we had known together at Lodge Close, and the memories it evoked. I didn't even know if Martin truly believed that our mother was no longer with us.

I was torn between ramming the point home and leaving it alone, hoping that Bobby could make him understand.

Eventually, with an expression of scant remorse, my brother offered an opinion as to his little game that afternoon.

'I just wanted to look around, Jamie. That's all. Just look. My home too. When did Mum leave?'

The message did not seem to be getting through. I could not make it plainer to him, but at the same time I was averse to distressing him about what could not be changed.

I had interpreted his opinions to be his own. I mistakenly believed he hated Mum for what she did to him.

It was at that point that Father Carroll's words gained resonance.

I recalled the point about Martin's opinion possibly being influenced by other souls. Maybe he was simply regurgitating my father's attitude.

After all, it was a theory that fitted the facts.

Our father was undoubtedly bitter about being cast from the family home. The sentiments expressed by my brother may have been heard elsewhere. Almost second hand.

Perhaps my brother *did* love Mum after all.

The possibilities needed examination. But then wasn't the time or the place.

I was more concerned with the premise of him being banged up for disturbing the peace.

'Martin…do not go to that house ever again. It's all in the past. You don't live there anymore. Do you understand me?'

My brother lifted his gaze and looked me directly in the eye.

His words carried ulterior meaning, the significance of which did not fully register at the time.

'Oh yes, Jamie. I'm the only one that *does* understand. The *only* one.'

# 33
# HAPPY NEW YEAR

Christmas came and went, thankfully without further incident regarding the local neighbours. It was a time to rejoice; to wallow in a family environment at last.

Martin was in his element. Henry was in good spirits. Bobby had devised most of the festive schedule with all the acumen that females seem to genetically attain in the business of organising males.

I had tried to omit the previous few months from memory. There was little positivity from the year that I wanted to take with me into the next.

My main objective was to get back into my schooling.

The first week back in Sixth Form was hectic, but by the end of January I had established two workable timetables. One was for daily lessons. When that concluded, my second itinerary kicked in at home and often tailed off indefinitely into the night.

My subject teachers and fellow pupils were most helpful in their ambition to get me back on an even keel by half term. Basically, between the beginning of January and the end of February, I was working a fifteen-hour academic day.

A lot of work I could do at school, but inevitably, much more needed to be accomplished at home with the cooperation and understanding of Henry, Bobby and of course, the ever-inquisitive Martin.

My brother seemed fascinated by the fact that I was suddenly confronted with such an intellectual challenge. There was so much information to write down, learn and absorb. The route to success would now take weeks of dedication. Yet I was determined to achieve my mission.

Bobby was playing her part too, bless her. She had secured herself a placement with my old boss, John Harrison at the supermarket. She was determined to contribute to the household coffers.

I've never forgotten the never-ending consideration that John afforded me throughout my life.

Just as he had assisted me over the years, Bobby was also privy to his friendly and trusting nature. With typical application, she was working as many hours as he could throw at her. She loved the job and welcomed the money, but most important of all she was finally doing something that she *wanted* to do.

Pleasing herself was a privilege that she had never been accustomed to.

There was never any doubting her capabilities.

She had only lacked the freedom to express herself before now.

She was content, decisive, and engineering her own life instead of accepting the hand that fate dealt.

There was no stopping her.

*****

It was two weeks before Easter that poor Henry was admitted to hospital for the last time. Considering the prognosis given some months earlier, he had done extremely well to endure his sufferance for so long.

A message to phone Bobby at home had been passed on by the school receptionist, who eventually found me whacking a football around the playground at morning break. If I ever found my mobile phone, I suppose it would have solved a lot of trouble in the interim.

I instinctively knew that Henry's time was now at a premium. Every visible symptom of his condition had accelerated dramatically over the past month.

Back in the administration block, I was shown to a private office.

From there, I dialled Henry's home number.

'Hello, Bobby? It's me. How is he?'

She sounded in control, but her voice was trembling.

'He couldn't get his breath this morning. They've taken him in. I know nothing more than that. I'll stay here with Martin while you go to hospital. No problem. Take as long as you need.'

'But what about work?'

'I've phoned John and explained. Nothing's a problem for him where you're concerned, Jamie.'

Bless you, John Harrison.

I felt myself becoming overwrought with anticipation as I fought for some reasoning to all this. Everything was going to plan in our lives for once. There was only this one black cloud lingering on the horizon.

Evidently, the storm was now upon us. Why did fate never give us a bloody break? I knew the situation with Henry was imminent, but it didn't make it any easier to face.

'Okay...I'll go to him now. You sure you're both okay?'

It was a silly question, really. Bobby Jones was never more assured as she crossed her fingers and prayed for Henry.

'Just go to him, Jamie. I don't think he's coming home. Give him our love.'

I put down the phone and asked the receptionist to book me a taxi.

I suddenly felt numb and soulless.

It was the same reaction I experienced when I found out Mum had passed.

The harshness of life's cycle rarely incites a flood of emotion in me as it does in many. It was as though I was still going through the motions.

A well-rehearsed scenario of tragic, unwarranted loss.

*****

I cannot remember the taxi ride, or my inquiry at the hospital admissions desk, or even my anguished search to locate Henry's ward. I knew what was waiting for me. I was in no rush to advance the sequence of events.

When I finally engaged with the sight of my friend on what was likely to be his death bed, it angered me.

Despair and sorrow were my chief accomplices on arrival.

Yet again, I was in receipt of the duff hand from the dealer.

Yet again, the shitty end of the stick was pointing in my direction.

Jamie Andrews - full time hard luck story, griever, and resident martyr for any cause.

The consultant noticed me standing at the end of Henry's bed and offered some words of condolence. I heard what the doctor said, but it meant too little, too late. I offered no reply. I needed no words of explanation for the sight before my eyes.

The sedated form of my dearest friend was the starkest analogy of the truth.

I lay by his side for the whole night on a camp bed. My only companion was the intermittent droning of the life support machine.

By morning, Henry's vital signs had not improved - only deteriorated.

I had not slept a wink and sat up in a chair contemplating what the day might bring. I did not have to wait too long. The moment of reckoning dawned as the morning ward manager poked his head through the bed dividers.

I attempted a smile in greeting him but could not rise to the challenge.

I simply went straight to the point with my questioning.

'It's not good, is it? It's near to the end, isn't it?'

The nurse moved closer and shut the divider to enclose us once more.

He crouched and lowered his voice to a whisper.

'Henry's organs are now failing, Mister Andrews. We have tried to contact his next of kin, but it seems that you are the closest we will find in that category. There is minimal chance of him regaining consciousness. I'm so sorry, but the situation is dire for him now. It may be the case sooner rather than later that the question will be put to you.'

I was puzzled. No doubt my expression confirmed that.

'Question? What question?'

The medic did not waver as he expanded on the next stage.

'It's very likely we will need your consent to terminate Mister Thompson's life.'

I don't know if such phraseology is commonplace around the wards of death in other hospitals, but I couldn't swallow the callous approach of the nurse who shocked me with such a sentiment first thing in the morning.

Rubbing my eyes to disperse the remnants of disbelief, I looked up to the figure in the green tunic holding his clipboard.

Unfortunately, my inherent cynicism came to the fore.

'Why do you need *my* consent?"

The nurse seemed surprised by my perfectly reasonable question.

'I'm sorry?'

I purposely wanted to sound annoyed.

I repeated my query in a sterner tone.

'Why do you need *my* consent to kill my best friend?'

'It's…legal procedure, sir. A lawful requirement. We cannot make that decision whilst there is a party present who assumes authority. It states quite clearly on his records that the next of kin has power to authorise after appropriate consultation.'

I was in no mood for this bullshit.

'So…asking my permission is a matter of right and wrong, then?'

The nurse was now visibly discomforted by my attitude.

'Well, yes, sir. Technically, legally, and morally. Yes. You are correct.'

I rose to my feet and pointed to dear, helpless Henry.

'Well, why don't you ask the poor bloke who's about to have his electricity cut off, instead of asking me? I'm the one person in the world who desperately wants to keep him *alive*, for Christ's sake!'

An uneasy silence prevailed as the ward charge collated his thoughts.

I turned my attention once more to my friend.

That man who had been a major part of my life for so long. I had offered him nothing in return for his time, his interest, and his concern over the years.

And now he was about to be banished with all the other rotting souls that would make a mockery of his unprecedented contribution to my existence.

Finally, I acknowledged the hovering medic.

'Just do what you must do. I'll sign all the necessaries later. If his condition is not retrievable…then my answer is academic.'

Of course, my preferred approach to the procedure of ending Henry's life was not agreeable, just as I suspected it wouldn't be.

'I'm sorry, sir. This is official binding documentation. It must be dealt with *before* the event.'

My heart was suddenly an empty shell. My mind in paralysis.

I signed on the dotted line and cast my pal adrift on the ocean of nevermore.

Resigned to a life without Henry, I turned away.

Ever resentful of my continuing misfortune.

With tears fighting for public exhibition, I said goodbye my friend.

And I say this hand on heart now.

I didn't deserve him.

And he certainly didn't deserve my bad luck in his life.

I hope Doris is up there waiting somewhere.

*****

Unbeknown to me, Henry had already organised and paid for his own funeral some years before his passing. Apparently, it is a common but sad facet of modern times.

Still, I understand why he would feel compelled to do such a thing.

And I was quietly relived I wasn't charged with carrying the responsibility.

I appreciated his forethought. It would have been a burden I was not willing to shoulder.

That's two funerals in succession I hadn't had to organise.

Lucky me.

But strangely enough, Henry had not specified a final resting place.

So, the only choice bestowed upon me was where to lay his honourable form.

After a few days of sincere consideration, I thought it appropriate to set down Henry next to Mum at the local cemetery in East Park.

They would both have appreciated that, I'm sure.

*****

There was just the three of us in attendance at his final departure. It was disappointing to note that not even one of his fellow community club members came along to pay their respects - the miserable old sods.

It perhaps will seem natural that I didn't feel the need to inform Alex, either.

Nor any of his home care team, even though we had no need for their services once the three of us moved in with him.

But then I suppose in some eyes Henry was a miserable old sod as well. He was never one for socialising to any exerting degree. I think he viewed other people as little more than unnecessary interference.

In commemoration of our joint farewell to a dear friend, Bobby, Martin, and I went for a drink at the Tiger Inn to toast Henry's passing. Of course, the lunch time tipple turned into an all-out piss up as the afternoon went on.

It was nice to see friends showing their faces as they dropped in after school. I introduced my brother and Bobby to those in the bar room, both of whom it seemed got on famously with everybody.

The day had started with ungainly sorrow and had concluded in the immersive joy of camaraderie. We laughed together, staggered around the pub lounge, and drank to our heart's content.

In the end the Tiger was veritably brimming with my fellow Sixth Formers, sharing jokes, berating unfortunates, and generally making the most of the unplanned yet brilliantly upbeat party.

My suit and tie also came under some humorous scrutiny once the intake levels had permitted.

As I am sure you will understand, dear reader, alcohol always induces honest emotions to the fore.

Unfortunately, as ever, mine got the better of me toward the end of the booze session. At one point I found myself sitting next to a very pretty fellow pupil named Clair Richards who seemed to take particular interest in my brother.

'Martin's lovely. Where have you been hiding *him* all this time?'

It was a poignant query but of course she wasn't aware of the story.

'Before you tell me you fancy him I ought to let you know that firstly he's ten years older than you and secondly his girlfriend is with him. I haven't been hiding him, Clair. Believe me…anything but. He took some tracking down though. I can tell you that much!'

Clair blushed slightly and chuckled.

I recalled that she was fairly close to Alex at school and she didn't hold back in asking me about my feelings regarding our absent mutual acquaintance.

'We all know you loved her, Jamie. I was as surprised as anybody that she left so suddenly. She didn't even tell *me* she was going until the day before. I thought we were better mates than that.'

I didn't really want to divulge anyone in the subject of my private relationship with Alex, but under the considerable influence of export lager, I couldn't help myself.

'Did she mention me before she left? Did she ever talk to you about what had happened last summer?' I stammered.

Clair looked me sternly in the eye as she answered.

I took her response to be earnest. I had no reason to disbelieve her.

'No, Jamie. She didn't even say that she'd finished with you.'

I was more than a little taken aback by Clair's wild assumption.

'We haven't *finished*…not as far as I'm concerned, anyway!' I snapped back.

'Okay, calm yourself down! I don't know the full story, do I? All I'm saying is that Alex was certainly headstrong. And she was obviously pretty adamant that being at school with you was going to be nigh on impossible. So, she upped and went. Strange decision, really.'

Initially, I didn't find it overly difficult to talk about her. But as the conversation with Clair continued, I began to realize how much I still loved Alexandra Lawley.

I was really slurring my speech by this point.

'Do you think her parents pushed her into leaving the school and going to the college?'

Clair scrunched up her nose and looked up to the ceiling whilst debating the possibility.

'I can't see why her parents would have any objection to her studying here. Maybe there is an underlying reason. Why did you ask about last summer? Did something happen in the holidays, then? I thought you both went to Cyprus with her mum and dad?'

I was almost drawn into revealing the events of the previous months. Thankfully, I glanced across to Martin and Bobby and saw how devoted they were to one another. It was a welcome instance of joy as I gamely battled to remain composed.

As it was the conversation was briefly interrupted and I opted to say nothing in the end.

I had experienced enough heartache for one day.

But then I conceded to my lack of will power.

There was one final query that I posed to Clair.

'Do you ever see Alex around and about?'

She sipped her drink and took a deep sigh.

'No. No one has seen her since the day she walked out of school. There was talk that she had moved districts, but I don't know how reliable the rumour mill is on such things.'

Clair emptied her glass and looked at me quizzically.

'So…if you're still an item, how come *you* haven't seen her for so long?'

If I wanted the answer to that question, all I needed to do was look in the mirror. I knew deep down that I had possibly thrown true love away.

My eyes moistened as I gave Clair the most honest answer I could think of.

'I really don't know. I don't suppose she wants to see me again, now. Not after all this time.'

'So why not just go around to her house and see if she's still there? You know where she lived, don't you? You could sort things out, I'm sure. She wouldn't be able to resist your charms, Jamie!'

Clair must have been reading my mind.

I looked at the fresh pint of beer that Bobby had very conveniently placed on the table and thanked her with a thumbs-up.

'I...I can't go to her house. I didn't part on the best of terms with her parents. It's best left well alone, I think. I haven't set eyes on her since last August. It's been a long time.'

Clair was apparently surprised by the fact that I could still be even slightly interested in rekindling any relationship with Alex.

'Jesus Christ, Jamie! That torch you are holding for her should have gone out by now. What a waste of valuable time! They're queuing up to go out with you at school! Emily Watson almost fainted on the spot when she heard you had come back after Christmas!'

I laughed along, but only in mock disbelief, of course!

'Yeah...well...they'll just have to stay in the queue for now, won't they?'

I poured some more lager down my throat as without prompt Clair suddenly leaned over, kissed me on the cheek and whispered in my ear as she got up to mingle with the others.

'Listen. Make sure when you finally *do* come to your senses over Alex, that you give *me* first refusal and not Emily!'

I smiled at her as she wandered off.

It was certainly food for thought. It was also time to cheer up.

Looking back, I felt I had given Henry a brilliant send off.

Assured in the knowledge that he would have watched and enjoyed the scene with us as we got drunk in his honour, it was my first real overindulgence in alcohol for months - probably since Blackpool. I must have orchestrated three cheers for him at least ten times during the afternoon!

I like to think that from his vantage point in heaven he smiled as much as we did.

I loved Henry like a father.

And it goes without saying that he was the finest male role model that a boy could ever have.

And I wish so much that I had told him so.

*****

I can vividly remember the hangover the next morning. I only realised I'd got one when I felt Bobby's hand on my shoulder trying to coax me into life.

Yesterday was spent trying to eclipse the passing of my friend.

Today I felt like death, myself.

'Jamie, wake up…there's a man on the phone. He wants to speak to you. Now! Shift it!'

I fell out of bed and crawled into the lounge. My head felt as though it was about to explode. My stomach lurched with every breath. My tongue felt as though it was made of carpet.

Grappling for the handset, I finally managed to position it within adequate proximity of my ear and acknowledge the caller.

'Yes?' I heaved.

'Mister Andrews? Good morning, sir. This is Steven Wilkinson from Simpson and Grade Solicitors. We need to arrange a meeting with you about the estate of Mister Henry Thompson.'

In my semi-inebriated condition, I was in no mood for anything remotely approaching a serious conversation about anything.

'Can you call back next year? I've got a headache today! Thank you!'

The next thing I knew Bobby had snatched the phone from me and continued the conversation on my behalf.

'I'm sorry, Mister Wilkinson. He's…rather preoccupied at the moment…with symptoms of…a migraine. Yes, he's got a migraine. Can I pass a message on?'

I watched Bobby as she indulged in a short exchange with the caller. Her eyes widened as the dialogue ensued. It appeared that the mysterious Mr. Wilkinson was relaying some very positive information. Bobby's smile directed itself towards me as I lay in a dehydrated heap at her feet.

After a couple of minutes, she replaced the handset and began to walk into the kitchen. My vision fixed vaguely in her direction as I beckoned for some clue as to the nature of the phone call.

'Oy! Where do you think you're going? Come back here and tell me what he wanted!' I slurred.

Bobby was in a particularly teasing mood as she replied through a huge smirk of self-satisfaction.

'I thought you were more interested in nursing your headache?'

My attempts to stand up resulted in an unbearable pounding sensation throughout my skull.

My legs did not wish to abide my wishes either.

'What…ouch…was all that about, then?'

She stood in the doorway with her hands on her hips. It was a reminder of the first time I met her, standing waiting for my order for Sunday lunch at the Celtic Arms.

God, it seemed like a lifetime ago. Although amused by her little game of secrets, my curiosity was becoming empowered by slight annoyance.

'Bobby! Tell me!'

She placed a finger to her lips and rolled her eyes as if she held the key to eternal knowledge.

Finally, if only to shut me up, she relented in the game.

'This afternoon, you are going into Nottingham, to meet Mister Wilkinson. I have made the appointment for you. He has in his possession Henry's will…and you are the sole heir and benefactor!'

My mouth dropped open as the welcome process of sobriety suddenly gathered increasing momentum.

Simultaneously, we began to smile at each other, which evolved into giggles, ending up in fits of wild, shrieking laughter as arm in arm we jumped up and down in the kitchen.

'You've got to be joking, Bobby! Tell me you're joking!'

'I'm not fucking joking, Jamie boy! You just heard the call yourself, didn't you? I suspect some money is coming your way!'

Martin heard the din and emerged from his bedroom.

I told him the news.

At last, the dealer had offered me a decent hand to play with.

Fate had finally sided with the virtuous.

# 34
# THE MEEK SHALL INHERIT

'Good afternoon, Mister Andrews. Please, sit down. I'm pleased you could attend at such short notice. I take it you've been informed of the nature of this meeting?'

Sitting across from the solicitor, I gulped in trepidation.

'Y-yes, sir. It's about Henry's will.'

'Please, call me Steven. We like to keep the formalities as informal as possible. You are quite correct. I realise that Mister Thompson's funeral was only yesterday, but I felt no need to delay matters any further.'

I was nervous. I can remember looking around the walls of the office. Everything looked so official. Steven Wilkinson continued in his introductions.

'Mister Thompson has named you as sole benefactor. As there are no contestants, I see no reason to withhold any of the details from you. I have a copy of the will here. Do you wish to read it, or shall I dictate it to you first and explain as we go along?'

'I think you had better read it, don't you?'

I was in the building of Simpson and Grade for less than an hour. I left through the tinted glass front doors in a state of utter shock.

On the bus back to home I turned over the revelations of Henry's last wishes in my mind. Even on turning the street corner into Glenfield Avenue, the reality of my award had not sunk in.

The dealer had presented me with four aces!

Bobby opened the front door. I wandered in like a zombie before collapsing into Henry's armchair. I stared vacantly into space. I couldn't bring words to describe the sensation of suddenly accumulating such financial security.

Bobby handed me a mug of coffee and sat opposite with Martin by her side on the settee. They both stared at me with bated breath. They did not need to ask. They simply waited for me to speak.

After a few sips of caffeine to re-sharpen the senses, I summoned the wherewithal to disclose our newfound position.

Slowly I opened the envelope containing details of Henry's wishes.

Bobby was becoming impatient. Martin remained calm yet curious as he cradled Rufus on his lap. Finally, I announced the news as I read directly from the will.

‘This house…that *was* Henry’s…is now *ours*. It’s estimated as being worth between one hundred and seventy and two hundred thousand pounds. It is now our property to do with as we wished. This bungalow belongs to *us*!’

Bobby grabbed Martin’s hand and stamped her feet excitedly. Her cries of joy must have been heard down the street.

Martin smiled, simply because his loved one did so.

She could barely contain her elation.

‘Fuck me, Jamie! He’s left you his *house*! Fan-bloody-tastic!’

I raised my hand as if to call for hush.

‘There’s more. Brace yourselves. You haven’t heard the best of it, yet.’

Silence eventually resumed. You could have heard a pin drop.

And when Bobby Jones is in the room that never happens.

‘As you know, his life insurance policy covered the cost of the funeral. But Henry also used his insurers to set up a savings plan, many years ago. He has left the proceeds to me as the one and only beneficiary.’

Yet again, Bobby was like a kid at Christmas.

‘How much, Jamie? How much?’

‘One hundred and thirty thousand pounds.’

The casual observer would perhaps be justified in thinking that our vocal celebration of becoming over a hundred grand richer in the space of a few minutes would seem to be a rather callous treatment of Henry’s memory, especially when considering the fact that he had only been in the ground for less than a day.

However, bearing in mind the sufferance that Martin and I had endured in our lives, this dawn of prosperity was more than welcome.

Henry would not have felt dishonoured by our happiness - not at all. His gift was motivated by a will to *ensure* our happiness.

The three of us were in full agreement.

This development called for another party!

*****

Our celebration part two at the Tiger Inn that same evening knew no bounds.

God knows we had every right to be happy and contented. Martin, Bobby, and I were making the most of it. We had earned our long overdue taste of good fortune.

I for one would relish every second of the resultant jubilation. As the jukebox vibrated, I downed my umpteenth pint and watched Bobby and Martin dancing in the corner of the room.

I felt strangely mixed emotions. Partly because of the previous day's booze intake and the fact I was now topping it up.

Obviously, I enjoyed the sense of unbridled contentment at the way our lives had altered so drastically over six months.

It was nothing less than undiluted pleasure at seeing Martin growing, adapting, and changing every single day. His new life was now his to dictate - with Bobby's consultation of course!

But I was also envious of my brother. He was loved and he was in love. The intimacy he was able to convey to Bobby was almost spiritual and that sensation was something I missed.

Although my head was attuned to being single, my heart was secretly yearning. I wasn't going to be the wet blanket, though. Too much good was coming our way to cast any shadows of my own.

In terms of practical arrangements, we now had a permanent, reliable roof over our heads and money in the bank. I could not have dreamed for a more rewarding outcome for the three of us.

All in the garden seemed rosy.

I felt that nothing could interfere with our oasis of contentment.

# 35
# A BROTHER'S WISH

During the months that Martin and I spent in renewing our fraternal acquaintance, I had given little consideration to what might become of him in the long term. This was not purposed negligence on my part. I was simply keen to take his rehabilitation one step at a time.

The fact that he was back under the protection of a loving household environment was initially satisfactory for me. I was available to be with him out of school hours, whilst Bobby preferred to work her supermarket shifts in the evening so she could be with Martin during the day. Even when Henry's money came our way, this situation did not drastically alter.

Yet, to our discredit, neither Bobby nor I offered much thought as to Martin's personal ambitions and desires. Despite his autism, he was bright, charming, and intelligent. He could now mix socially - albeit under the watchful eye of yours truly - and he welcomed anything new into his life with relish.

No challenge was deemed insurmountable by my brother. He absorbed anything and everything in his perpetual quest to learn that which he did not already know. His thirst for fresh understanding and enlightenment on all levels knew no limits.

It was during my A-level exams in the early summer that he broached the subject of going back to school himself. It was not a total surprise to discover that he had been impressed with the way I had disciplined myself into the rigours of lessons and intensive revision. He could see that I was applying my mind to something incredibly positive.

He wanted to follow suit.

The concept of school obviously appealed to him. He had been unwittingly deprived of such a privilege years ago. I believe that he had already mentally conquered his own afflictions. The symptoms were barely noticeable to the uninitiated onlooker.

His strength of character was to be admired - even emulated.

I thought I was mentally strong, yet Martin possessed personal resolve and fortitude that was beyond belief at times.

By the time I sat my first A-level paper in the June, I had put in nearly six months of hard work to make sure I could give the exams my best effort. Anything less than my best would have been unacceptable to me.

My brother had been most gracious in allowing me quality time at home to attain the necessary level of commitment.

There was a major factor in Martin's wish to return to study. His condition was not as severe as other autistic cases. He beheld a curious yet passive approach to most aspects of life.

Bobby had undoubtedly been a major influence on his development over the years. Many affected by the condition find typical interactive situations uncomfortable.

Any overbearing physical or social manifestation of his autism would have been a massive stumbling block to his ambition to enter a state-run comprehensive school.

Bobby revealed that she had arranged for Martin to see a specialist when she first met him all those years ago. The doctor claimed at the time that despite the comparatively mild symptoms on display, he saw no reason why Martin could not attempt to lead as normal a mainstream life as was possible.

Sadly, at that stage in his mid-teens, my brother was under the direct influence of our father. Any chance of even a strand of personal independence was unattainable.

Yet evidently Martin had nurtured this wish for many years.

Only now, as a liberated spirit, did he see his opportunity for education as a real and accessible option.

Bobby was correct when she ascertained his main problem as being a lack of ability in conveying relevant thought. He was certainly not a nuisance to himself or others. Yet I could readily identify his rate of improvement after living with him for several months.

He had quickly discovered his own identity and wanted to establish his own place in the great scheme of things. He had gained supreme confidence to judge and convey his own responses. In short, he had learned when to offer his opinion and when not to.

His level of articulacy was never in question, nor was his appetite for knowledge. His foundations for trying to claim a place at school, even if he was by this time twenty-seven, were all in place. He was part of a stable family unit once again. He had matured and mellowed as an individual.

He did not need to argue a case to me about his proposition. I had every confidence in him. So together, we pledged to arrange a meeting with the school and convince them of Martin's prospects and potential.

The Headteacher Geoff Davies was very sympathetic toward my plea for Martin's circumstances to be heard. He was also very appreciative of my own personal efforts in the build up to the A-level exams.

He had taken a gamble on me, and it paid off.

So, it may perhaps have been my direct intervention that succeeded in getting the initial meeting arranged for Martin. On the other hand, I may have had not a jot of influence.

And on yet another slightly cynical hand, Mister Davies may have decided to seize an opportunity for the school to gain some plaudits, in employing the equal opportunity policy on behalf of the local education authority.

But if the proposal had the potential to prove mutually beneficial, then Martin and I weren't going to complain, were we?

Either way, the meeting was arranged.

Martin and I were invited to discuss the situation at the beginning of July when all exams were completed. This would give the relevant bodies the chance to prepare for Michael's arrival - should he be accepted - at the school for the following academic year commencing that September.

As you may correctly assume, dear reader, our anticipation of success was balanced by the very real possibility of failure.

But such a thought was banished from any conversation regarding the subject prior to the big day.

*****

On the chosen date of our summit with the school dignitaries, Martin and I entered an argument as we donned our suits.

'Why can't Rufus come?'

'Because today is important, Martin. Today is the day to act like a grown up if possible.'

'I can't act grown up without Rufus beside me.'

'I don't think the people we are going to meet at school will understand that logic.'

'But Rufus is always with me.'

'Not today he isn't. He can guard the house with Bobby while we are out.'

'I think Rufus will be jealous if I leave without him.'

'Rufus will understand. He is your best friend. He won't mind. Bobby, can you help Martin with his tie, please?'

We were under orders from Bobby regarding dressing to impress. Her nerves were uncontrollable as she waved us off on that wonderful summer morning.

As we walked, Martin kept checking his suit and glancing at his shoes. He repeatedly fiddled with his shirt collar. It was very warm and top buttons and ties were only adding to the nervous perspiration.

He noticed me watching him and I smiled.

He shook his head and grimaced.

'She makes the top knot too tight. I need to loosen it up a little.'

'Okay, bro. But you need to tidy it back up when we get to school.'

As we entered the gates to the school car park, I checked my brother's appearance and gave him the thumbs-up.

We made our way to the admin block to check in, the butterflies in my stomach now feeling like bats.

'How do you feel, Martin?' I enquired as I opened the reception door for him.

His response was deadly serious as he stared ahead and strode confidently past me.

'How do I feel? I feel deserving.'

I couldn't argue with such a beautiful reply as the receptionist asked us to take a seat in the waiting area.

The Headteacher appeared after a few minutes and warm introductions ensued. We both stood to greet the man who could pave the way for my brother's future success.

'Hello, Martin. Jamie has told us so much about you.'

My brother gazed forlornly at the pair of us before answering Mister Davies.

'Well, there's much more about me to know. I'm really hoping you want to find out.'

Geoff Davies smiled politely.

'Yes…yes of course. This way, gentlemen.'

The main consultation room was occupied by several unfamiliar faces around a large table. Mister Davies cordially announced their names and positions of authority.

My recollection of those present around the table is rather sketchy, but I'll have a go.

There was the Deputy Head of the school, Miss Thraves. Two representatives from the school's parent-teacher association. A director from the Midlands Education Board of Governors. The school's appointed doctor was also in attendance and there may have been one or two high brows from the local council authority.

In all, over half a dozen influential figures that would have a say in determining the outcome of events.

Martin entered the room, waved, and smiled handsomely.

'Hello, everyone! I'm so glad you didn't start without me.'

It was an opening gambit of genial quality.

The ice was instantly broken.

His confidence and humour won them over from the off.

Although none of the group had met him before, Martin's background had been made clear to them prior to the event. That was my main contribution to the agenda.

Quite rightly, his family history never came up in conversation during the actual meeting.

I am eternally thankful for Geoff Davies in ensuring that the focus of the morning remained firmly fixed on the future instead of the past.

Once momentum built, questions were fired at him left, right and centre.

But Martin never wavered with his responses.

He never dodged a single issue.

He was asked why he wanted to go back to school. What he hoped to achieve. Where he thought his future lay in terms of employment. Which subjects was he most interested in doing? Did he hope to do A-levels after his GCSE courses has ended?

I was made aware that the financial burden in accepting someone of Martin's age into the school would be considerable. As a mature student he would need to partly fund himself.

But the priority for now was they wanted meet Martin and ascertain for themselves just how much he wanted the chance of a placement and whether they felt able to accommodate him with his condition.

It was notable throughout the consultation that the appointed medic said very little at all.

In all, I felt that the two-hour discussion had gone very well.

Martin's evident ease in the company of strangers was also a latent factor in how the decision would fall.

As the Headteacher called the meeting to a close, he addressed my brother.

'I want to thank you so much for coming today, Martin. It's been a pleasure talking to you for the first time. We admire your courage and ambition. Without giving too much away, I hope that this board can come to a decision which acknowledges and rewards your undoubted determination and commitment.'

My brother unexpectedly rose to his feet and spoke to the officials in response.

'I would like to thank you all for listening to my case. I hope all your fingers and toes are crossed on my behalf.'

Leave 'em laughing. Good lad, Martin!

When the chuckles had subsided, Mister Davies pronounced the next stage.

'We will now have a secondary meeting this afternoon to discuss your case, Martin. You will be informed of our decision within seven days. Is that okay?'

My brother's honesty shone as always.

'That is absolutely fabulous, everybody!'

There was a smile on every face as Martin and I walked out of the meeting room, through the reception foyer and towards the school gates.

As soon as we were outside the premises, I gave my brother a hug.

'I'm so proud of you, bro. You did great in there.'

He returned the embrace with a pledge.

'Thank you for everything, Jamie. I won't let you down.'

*****

Every morning for the next seven days, Martin was first to pick up the mail that dropped on the doormat. Bobby and I had warned him to be patient. It might take ten or even fourteen days for the letter to arrive, even if the school predicted seven.

But Martin didn't want to be patient.

He had spent the thick end of thirty years waiting for his chance.

He was more than ready.

His heart was set on a positive outcome.

Then, on the eighth morning, the letter arrived.

The sun was high and warm once again, set against a beautiful cloudless July sky.

The three of us sat in the lounge.

Martin was visibly shaking as he held the unopened envelope in his hand. He began to rock slightly as his nerves got the better of him.

It was crunch time.

'I don't want to open it. Bobby, you read it to me. Please.'

She shook her head and wagged a discerning finger.

'Not bloody likely! I'm shitting myself more than you are!'

I laughed as Martin's gaze quickly fell my way.

'Please, Jamie. I can't do it! Please. You reveal the decision.'

It was the least I could do for my brother, wasn't it?

I sincerely hoped that breaking the seal would deliver the right answer for him. I can recall the exact content of the letter.

I think Martin may have kept it safe somewhere.

I noticed the school's distinctive motif as I unfolded the white, headed note paper. The wording was short and sweet. I read it through first to myself, trying desperately to hide any subsequent reaction.

Bobby exhibited her usual feminine impatience as she studied me studying the text.

'For fuck's sake, man! The suspense is killing us! Read the blasted thing, Jamie!'

Taking a deep breath, I relayed the conclusions of the board of officials that we had spoken to just over a week earlier.

My heart pumped vigorously. It felt as though it was about to explode.

*'Dear Martin,*

*Thank you for your attendance at the meeting held on the seventh of July.*

*After due consideration concerning all aspects and implications of your proposal to attend our comprehensive school to study at GCSE level, it gives me great pleasure to accept your application forthwith.*

*It has been ordained that your initial term of entry to the school will begin on the seventh of September of this year. Please bring this letter with you and report to reception at 9a.m. for your personal induction.*

*We can finalise any further necessary details on the day.*

*Should you have any urgent or general queries regarding your placement in the school, please do not hesitate to contact me at the number above, or feel free to make an appointment with the school secretary before the beginning of the new term.*

*On behalf of the staff and myself, we dearly look forward to welcoming you to St. George's Secondary.*

*Yours faithfully,*
*G Davies*
*Headteacher.'*

Suffice to say, the three of us went to the Tiger that evening to celebrate.

# 36
# PROSPERITY AND AFTERMATH

Collectively, that summer was the best of our lives. The weather was gloriously hot throughout July and early August. Life at Glenfield Avenue was just about perfect. I had resumed some hours at the supermarket, though I was effectively working an opposite shift to Bobby.

Even though Martin had achieved so much and come such a long way in such a short space of time, neither of us felt totally confident in leaving him completely to his own devices.

However, our faith in his development was growing by the day, and it would only be a matter of time before he would undertake sole responsibility for his routine.

Luckily, he wasn't patronised by our loving concern. Quite the contrary. He was more than happy to be in the company of his loved ones at every available opportunity.

He didn't sit idle, either.

Due to his increasing poor health, Henry had neglected the front and rear gardens. Martin readily applied himself to becoming green-fingered and was soon an expert in the art of potting plants and cutting grass.

He also gave one or two rooms in the bungalow a facelift via a fresh coat of paint. And most of it ended up on the walls, too!

I wasn't sure how or when he acquired his sudden sense of house pride.

It certainly wasn't inherent, but he revelled in the satisfying process of home improvement.

In fact, he was thoroughly enthusiastic in all aspects of his newfound freedom.

Since learning of his placement in school, Martin instantly gained wings. He became a different person.

Focussed. Self-assertive and confident.

Ready to navigate any hurdle.

And despite his years of comparative isolation, he adored socialising. I invited friends from school – yes, via text messages! - for a day of barbecuing and boozing. Martin joined in as though he had a lifetime's experience as the congenial host and resident cook.

It came as no surprise to me that one or two females paid more than a passing interest in the good-looking dark-haired hunk that was supervising the burgers and sausages.

During those few weeks of unbroken sunshine, the three of us worked, rested, and played to our hearts' content. Nothing and nobody could stop us wallowing in our duly earned happiness.

As the middle of August encroached however, my nerves began to fray a little.

On the third Thursday of the month, the A-level results were released nationwide.

My prospective place at Swansea University was dependent on at least three C grades. I was hopeful, of course. I had fulfilled my pledge to knuckle down and give it my best shot.

It was now out of my hands.

Fate was once again in control, and I didn't appreciate it one iota.

When the day of judgement finally arrived, my routine was the same as two years earlier when I had gone for my GCSE results. I had taken the day off from work.

I was grateful for John Harrison's bear hug for good luck the day before.

But it did nothing to alleviate the pending sense of dread that I felt on entering the school reception area.

It was nearly lunch time if my memory is accurate.

Many pupils had arrived early, received their grades, and already left. Judging by the feedback from the handful of teachers that were present, it seemed that very few students were disappointed with what they found inside their envelopes.

One of the first faces to greet me was that of Clair Richards, who beamed an intoxicating smile across the foyer as I walked through the door.

Her apparent air of satisfaction prompted my query.

'How did you get on, Clair?'

She batted her eyelashes and bounded over to convey her news.

'Three B's, Jamie! I'm off to Bristol! Isn't it fantastic?'

We embraced in celebration of her achievements.

I couldn't remember the last time I had been so close to a female.

Yes, it felt great.

Then it was my turn.

I took the brown, sealed envelope from the receptionist and seated myself in a quiet corner of the room. Clair did not leave my side as I fumbled clumsily for the opening.

I glanced at her as my racing heart thudded.

She was nearly as anxious for me as I was!

'What do you need, Jamie?'

'Three C's. That will hopefully get me into Swansea to do journalism.'

Clair playfully squeezed my kneecap, moved even closer and squealed childishly in my ear.

'Here goes...fingers crossed! Promise me you'll come to the pub afterwards, Jamie. Whatever your results I'm buying you a drink!'

I nodded silently as the computerised piece of paper emerged.

With shaking hands, I opened it out and without further thought, scanned the subject grades that I had been awarded.

English Literature – C; History – C; Art – B.

My heart jumped into my mouth. I thought my eyes were deceiving me. I began to squeal myself and jumped up and down.

I felt like Charlie Bucket when he discovered the last golden ticket.

The sensation was incredible.

A mixed feeling of immense personal pride and utter bloody relief.

Clair planted a kiss on my cheek as I stood up again and danced around the foyer like some demented idiot.

Finally, genuine, liberating laughter ensued.

The Headteacher had noticed my jubilation. He walked across reception to offer a hand of congratulations.

'So, Jamie. You're off to Swansea, then?'

'Yes, sir. I can't believe it. I'm over the moon!'

Geoff Davies smiled and placed a hand on my shoulder.

'You've more than warranted the placement, son. Never forget that. I didn't think you'd manage it having missed an entire term last year, but I'm so glad you've proved me wrong. Well done!'

It was inevitable that I would bring Martin into the conversation.

'It's *me* that should be thanking *you*, Mister Davies. You've given me and my brother everything we could ever wish for.'

'Well then...we're all happy. Don't worry, Jamie...we'll look after Martin. You can rest assured of that much. You must make the most of your own opportunities now. There's nothing stopping you.'

Clair had hardly stopped giggling since I opened my envelope.

Her long-term secret affection for yours truly was something she no longer seemed prepared to conceal.

And I didn't mind one bit.

Quite a throng had gathered in the meantime, as several other arrivals had come to claim their results.

Clair leaned closer and whispered in my ear.

'Jamie…I really need to ask you something…I was going to wait until later when I was a little bit drunk…but I *can't* wait any longer!'

I was understandably confused.

We both walked outside to continue the chat.

She seemed very excitable about something.

'What's the matter, Clair?'

She took a deep sigh, looked to the ground, then reverted her focus directly into my eyes.

'Well, you know that I said I wanted first refusal when you become…you know… available?'

I found Clair very attractive, although I had never dared to admit it before that moment. I was gradually becoming enticed by where this conversation was leading.

She continued, not a little embarrassed by her unusually forward approach.

'Well…I was just thinking…that maybe we could…you know…'

We were only inches apart. I could detect the fragrance of her perfume.

It was a great chance to tease, though.

'…we could…*what*, Clair?' I smirked.

'Well, it seems silly to wait any longer. Why don't we make the most of our time together before we shoot off our separate ways?'

'You mean…go steady? As a couple? Just for three or four weeks?'

She smiled from ear to ear.

'Oh yes, please.'

It sounded like a good plan. My enthusiasm grew by the second.

We moved ever closer as our first kiss became imminent.

However, the episode was instantaneously tempered by the sudden grimace that etched itself across Clair's features.

Naturally, I enquired as to the source of her evident discomfort.

'What's up? You look like you've seen a ghost!'

Her response was honest, though I hoped in all sincerity that she hadn't seen something from the netherworld.

I'd had enough of the supernatural to last me a lifetime.

'I think I just *have* seen a ghost!'

'I don't know what you're on about, Clair,'

'Forget it…just forget it, Jamie. I'm sorry. I've made a fool of myself. We never had this conversation, okay? I thought it was too good to be true. I'll perhaps see you around! Good luck at Swansea!'

With a swish of her golden ponytail, Clair Richards was gone.

My own emotions were unsure of how to respond to her dramatic and short-lived performance.

As a male of the species, I was of course more than pleased that she had shown interest, yet quite saddened by the fact that she had opted to withdraw her proposal almost in the same breath.

Then I started to become a little angry.

Was she deliberately trying to piss me about, or what?

Then the reason for Clair's rapid climbdown soon became all too clear.

I must admit that I was taken completely unawares just as she was.

It was initially an undetected approach which came as a wonderful, pleasurable, mind-numbing shock.

The cause of Clair's retreat made herself known with that familiar voice of hushed velvet that I hadn't heard for an age.

'Who's a very clever boy again, then? Congratulations, Mister Andrews!'

Time seemed to freeze as I stood rooted outside the school reception.

The sudden presence behind me was no ghost, but it was definitely from the recent past.

The tone was instantly recognisable.

The statement delivered I had certainly heard before somewhere.

Yes - it was two years ago exactly.

It was the first time that I spoke to…no…surely not.

It couldn't be…could it?

I turned around to identify the owner of that wondrous sentiment.

My eyes willingly registered the holy vision before them.

Yet, my brain would not readily identify the beautiful truth of its form.

Alex stood before me.

Natural, gorgeous, annoying, incredible, mystifying…Alex.

*My* Alex!

For once, I was speechless.

I scanned her image avidly without word. Was this another dream?

Her hair was much longer than before and less wavy. She wore a little more make-up than was previously her custom. She was dressed for summer in t-shirt and shorts.

My heart flexed, my stomach lurched, and my legs trembled.

I finally managed to summon a reply to the woman that I hadn't seen for a year.

Eventually, I acknowledged her as she posed radiantly in the sunshine.

'Jesus H Christ! What a surprise this is! How are you, Ally?'

The smile never left her tanned face. Those crystalline eyes were more sparkling than I had ever known. She was obviously pleased to see me, though there was an inevitable feeling of awkwardness between us.

Barriers had gone up over time.

A lot had changed during our twelve months apart.

'I'm good thanks, Jamie. I'm very good. You?'

I didn't want the rest of the school gawking at us.

It was a perplexing enough sensation as it was, without nosy parkers spectating.

'I'm good…in fact…I'm great. Do you want to take a walk?'

In the next instance, Alex held out her gentile hand for me to place in mine. The rush of potentially renewable romance flooded my veins.

I'd totally forgotten how good it felt to be in love. It was then of course that I realised I had never stopped loving her in the first place.

In truth, our estrangement had only served to fuel my resolve in wanting her back. It was fate that she should be there, at the school, on results day.

I had so many questions, but I couldn't summon any of them to mind.

All I knew was that having her next to me and physically touching her was the best feeling in the world.

We strolled along the canal almost as though the past year had never happened.

Yet, perversely, conversation did not come easily.

Despite my overwhelming inner joy at beholding her again, there was a detectable void between us.

I had loved this woman; I had *made* love to her and *lived* with her, yet I felt as though we were on our first date.

We were strangers once more.

'Did you get your results today as well, Ally?'

'Yes. Three B's. I'm going to Nottingham University to study Economics Engineering in September. You did very well, considering! A little bird tells me you'll be fleeing the nest soon, yourself.'

Then it began to sink in.

The horseshoe always hanging around my bloody neck.

My old friend irony was back to haunt me once again.

Alex was back on the radar, and there I was about to disappear from the scene!

My elation at our reacquaintance was suddenly overshadowed by the reality that it would be all too brief.

'Why did you come to the school today, Alex? Honestly.'

There was a silent pause as we continued to walk hand in hand by the canal. I had no idea what she would say in response.

'To see *you*, of course! I kept in touch with Tracey Jones. She told me you'd gone back to school after Christmas. I didn't really know if you would want to see me after all this time. So thought today would probably the ideal day to take the chance and find out.'

The vision from twelve months earlier recurred.

The sight of an emotional Alex torn in pieces at the railway station formed again in my mind. Guilt shrouded my conscience. I moved in front to stop her stride.

Taking her other hand, I looked into her eyes.

I had missed her so much it still hurt.

I felt like crying for the past there and then.

The next words rolled off my tongue without thought.

'Ally…I'm so sorry about last year. Eternally, dreadfully sorry.'

She seemed a little unsure of my motives for saying so at that moment.

She appeared almost detached from the conversation I wanted to broach with her.

Something was amiss.

Her reply was distinctly unemotive.

'It's all history, Jay. Life goes on. People change. I couldn't go to Blackpool with you. Not when it came to the crunch. And when I realised how much that decision would upset you...well, I couldn't stand it at school any longer either. I couldn't face you so soon after letting you down. But there was nothing easy about it. Believe me. I missed you too...for a long time.'

I suddenly sensed her discomfort as we stood face to face by the canal on that idyllic sunny day. She obviously wasn't the Alex Lawley that I thought I used to know.

No longer the Alex Lawley that I used to love.

The light in her eyes was there, but it didn't seem to reflect her mood any longer.

I found myself struggling to judge her signals.

I soon deduced that the wondrous crystalline pools were no longer shining for me.

Yet my heart continued to open itself up to her.

'I've missed you like crazy, Ally. Not a day has passed when I don't think of you. I don't know where we go from here, but I want you to know here and now that...that I still love you.'

The hidden truth that tormented me was about to be disclosed.

Alex removed her hands from my grasp and began to march back toward the school.

I knew then that her heart was no longer in tandem with my own.

I became alarmed and confused.

Upset began to simmer at the thought that perhaps Alex had come to tell me something I did not want to hear.

I watched her stride in the opposite direction before trotting up behind her.

She glanced over her shoulder, but only briefly. It was now plainly obvious that she had come to see me for a reason other than to see my results. I observed her run her hands through her luxurious, brown locks.

Her evident unease was also now mine.

I needed to know how she felt.

My uncertainty in that instance was agonising.

But the certainty that followed would cut far deeper.

I had to end the charade.

'Alex...what's the matter? What's happened? Why did you *really* come to the school?'

She did not look at me as she pondered her response.

She kept on walking.

I persisted.

'I've just told you that I still love you. I was expecting a similar response. Is that too much to ask? Is it too late for us?'

She stopped herself and finally gazed upon me.

I could see the hurt welling in her hypnotic eyes.

'Yes…yes, it is, Jay. It is too late. Because…'

The suspense was unbearable.

'…because *what*, Ally?'

She sniffled and wiped away a tear of possible remorse.

'…because…I've met someone else…and…I love *him*.'

The way she said the words was more torturous to me than the meaning they carried. She was calm, and somewhat relieved to have finally informed me just how much she had 'changed'.

Maybe I should have been angry.

Maybe I should have gone down on my knees there and then and pleaded with her to have me back.

I should never have left her alone last summer.

Henry was correct.

Look after her, he warned, because if I didn't then somebody else would.

That is exactly what happened - to the letter.

Damn you, Henry! Why did you have to be right all the bloody time? I had made the one cast iron mistake that you warned me against.

I had fallen into the trap of taking her for granted.

Foolishly, as is the case with all spurned lovers, I wanted to know more about this other person in her life.

She walked off again at a faster pace.

I was struggling to keep up, mentally and physically.

'Who? Who is he, Ally? When did you meet him?'

She then became annoyed.

Probably rightly so. After all, it was technically none of my business.

Her voice was now laced with despair.

'What does it matter, Jay? It doesn't concern you anymore, does it? I just wanted to see you again, that's all. Just to see if you were alright. I can see now that I shouldn't have come. My mistake. I apologise.'

I was now becoming furious.

I wasn't buying the concerned old friend act.

'That's *bollocks*, Ally! You turned up to break off with me. Just fucking admit it. Neutral territory. No hassle. Well, thanks for ruining another fucking good day.'

We had now left the canal side and reached the school gates.

I fired one last shot into the air as she approached the road.

'That's it then, is it? Hello and goodbye? After all this time?'

The stony expression in her face was unyielding. She did not seem at all sorry. Indeed, Alex now appeared to be gratified it was out in the open. She must have been harbouring a long-standing sense of guilt.

Today's release was her therapy.

Fair play to her. It was a brave move to do it the way she did.

Standing at the kerbside in her orange flip flops, she faced away from me and gave a signal to a black sports car parked opposite the school entrance.

It pulled up beside her and the front passenger door duly sprung open.

I could not see the driver through the dark tinted windows.

No doubt he could see me, in all my tearful distress.

Alex walked around the front of the car.

My sorrow was now loud and clear for all to witness.

As I vainly made my case, I remained fixed to the spot, as though accepting the crucifying truth that if I really cared about Alex Lawley, then I must allow her to walk out of my life.

I sobbed as my latest grapple with destiny rendered me empty-handed.

'Don't do it like this, Ally. I want you back. Please. Don't go.'

She offered one last crumb of comfort before getting in beside the driver.

'I loved you too, Jay. I honestly did. Please forgive me.'

The passenger door slammed shut on my hopes once and for all.

As resignation streamed down my face.

The black sports car carrying the woman I adored sped off into the distance.

I felt helpless and desolate. Raw and paralysed.

Half an hour earlier I had been standing with the key to my future in the palm of my hand.

The joy of passing my A-levels had suddenly been eclipsed by this episode of unexpected heartache.

The hand of fate had dealt its perennially shitty cards once again.

And once again, I was deemed the loser.

It has remained one of the most distressing recollections in my life.

Strange that our story was all over as quickly as it had begun.

To finally let go of Alex was something over which I had little influence.

It wasn't my choice.

Small consolation, eh?

It only occurred to me some time afterwards that she never even bothered to ask me about the search for my brother.

That was, after all, the cause of our initial separation.

It was likely she would never now get to know Martin.

That was something of a tragedy in itself.

All she and I had shared, now meant nothing.

For all I knew, I would never see my beautiful Alex again.

# 37
# THE FUTURE?

The time to leave Nottingham for Swansea arrived soon enough. Martin and Bobby claimed things at Glenfield Avenue would be rather different without me around to boss them about.

Similarly, they were optimistic about my departure. Firstly, because they were delighted for me. But also, because it would give them the chance at long last to establish a life of their own as an orthodox loving couple.

My destiny was now taking me along a different path.

To a new environment. Away from my roots.

Although, *roots* is a loose term.

Once settled in Swansea, it didn't take me long to realise that university life would suit me just fine. I loved the studies; I made friends quickly and the social scene was fantastic.

And of course, the ladies were queuing up!

But tarnishing this newfound Jamie Andrews' experience, was the fact that I really missed my brother and Bobby. It was an unavoidable sacrifice that I would have to come to terms with.

Living in students' quarters in Wales, I could not exactly pop home every night to watch his own progress at school.

I made regular daily phone calls, though admittedly, I should have made more effort to go and see them. But that was the whole point, really.

I had done my bit. He didn't need my guiding hand anymore. He didn't require supervision. He was an independent young man with a loving home and a woman who thought the world of him.

Any contribution I might have made since leaving him to his own devices would have been comparatively minimal. Perhaps he may have even resented any further intrusion on the routine he could now officially call his own.

Bobby would assure me many times over the course of several weeks that he had nestled into St George's seamlessly. Martin himself would proudly read extracts of homework over the phone.

He had rapidly become very assured of his own intellectual abilities.

In turn, I was completely satisfied that my absence was not having any negative effect on his outlook or progress.

Bobby was certainly enjoying her time at the supermarket, confirmed by the news of her promotion to assistant shift manager in less than eight months of working there.

All things considered, life was brilliant.

On the surface, it appeared that all three of us were flourishing simultaneously.

*****

Christmas would eventually present the chance for Martin, Bobby, and I to spend some valuable time together back at Glenfield Avenue after our first academic terms concluded.

We drank plenty, ate more than was good for us and shared stories about our newfound educational ventures.

But for those few days of the festive holiday, I noticed that Bobby seemed a little evasive.

She was quieter than her usually chipper vocal self.

She appeared comparatively withdrawn from her normally vibrant personality.

She looked tired as well.

I could not ignore the issue.

One evening before New Year as Martin dozed on the settee, I felt obliged to ask her if all was okay in the world of Bobby Jones.

Her reaction was instantly guarded.

I had become accustomed to Bobby telling me what was on her mind, whether I asked her or not.

Yet that night, it was as though she didn't want to talk at all.

But she knew that my instinct in such matters was now finely tuned.

Making sure Martin was not stirring I switched the TV off and asked her to join me for a coffee in the kitchen.

I wanted to know outright if she was still happy about life with my brother. I felt fully entitled to ask the question.

Call it fraternal concern if you will. But she had become as near to a sister to me as I would ever get, and my natural affection for her was automatic.

I was intrigued by the implicit changes in Bobby's mood.

'So, there's nothing worrying you, then? If I can help, then I want to. I'm going back to Swansea next week. I can't do much when I'm two hundred miles away, can I?'

She cradled her mug and continued to look at the dark, dank scene beyond the kitchen window.

Self-imposed silence was not one of Bobby's typical practices.

I would not back down, though.

The less she said, the more I wanted to know.

'Is it the supermarket? Are they working you too hard?'

At last, she offered a little smile but shook her head.

I was perhaps pushing the issue too hard.

But nevertheless, I guessed again.

'Is there a money problem? You just have to say, Bobby. I'll sort it out. We've got plenty. It's a nest egg for a rainy day but we don't need to be struggling to count the pennies.'

Still, she would not open up to me.

I changed the subject to Martin as he snored his head off in the next room.

Little did I know I was getting closer to the truth as I gestured toward my brother.

'It doesn't look like *he's* got any troubles! Listen to the lazy sod! He didn't get up until dinner time and he's fast off again! You're not keeping him up all night are you, Miss Jones?'

Thankfully she let slip a semblance of amusement, but her face soon dispersed the smile and reverted to a mask of worry. Her frown had been present for most of the holiday. She was acting way out of character.

Eventually and without a direct prompt, she decided to join the conversation.

'Jamie…there's something you need to know.'

My suspicion suddenly veered toward excitement.

My gob ran away with my brain and beat it to the finish line.

'What? Are you pregnant?'

It wasn't an unreasonable question. But Bobby looked horrified that I could even suggest such a thing.

'No, you silly arse!'

'Okay then. Second guess. Martin's proposed, hasn't he? Are you getting married?'

Again, the expression of feigned indignation was her reaction.

'Er…no!'

Okay, a light-hearted shot in the dark.

'Are you buying a puppy?'

Bobby openly smirked at my attempt to lighten the evident shadows around her mind. But the grin was swiftly banished once more.

'Jamie, just listen. I don't really want to tell you, but you deserve to be informed.'

Now I was confused and curious.

I opted not to continue with the jokes. I could see that Bobby was not in a particularly jovial mood.

When she began to reveal the source of her unease, my act as court jester was cut to the quick by encroaching dread.

'Martin is tired out, Jay.'

Admittedly, my brother's fatigue would not normally be something I would concern myself about. I suggested a viable reason.

'I can see that, Bobby! But so what? He's had a testing four months at school. His life has changed dramatically. He's entitled to be tired, isn't he?'

'No...I mean...generally...all the time. He's flaking out at five o' clock after school every day.'

I could not resist the chance to tease her once more.

'Bloody hell, Roberta! You'll really have to leave him alone at night!'

Placing her coffee mug on the dining table, she leaned forward as though to enable her voice to carry in a lower, whispered tone.

She glanced through to the lounge at Martin before continuing.

'Look...Jamie...this may be of interest to you, so listen! It's not *me* keeping him awake at night.'

My instinct writhed in fear of her pending revelation.

I tried to remain unmoved.

'Okay, okay! So, tell me! Why is he so tired all the time?'

'He hasn't had a good night's sleep since you left for university. At first, I thought it might just be restlessness. You know? He's perhaps worried about where you are and why you aren't living here anymore.'

I moved forward in my own chair as Bobby spoke.

Martin continued to snore as I reluctantly became ever more immersed in her imminent disclosure.

My façade of composure remained intact.

'Well, that's natural, I suppose. But I still don't see a major problem for you to worry about.'

'Neither did I, Jamie. Not at first. But he has started to wake up in the night.'

She must have felt like smashing me in the face.

I honestly did not grasp what she was trying to say.

I needed it spelling out.

The joker in me briefly returned.

'What then…toilet trouble?'

Bobby looked angered by my flippancy.

She adeptly wiped the smile off my face.

'No! For fuck's sake! Nightmares! Every other night! He's waking up screaming his fucking head off! It scares me, Jamie. I don't know what to do about it.'

I could hear my own heartbeat.

Chills shot down my spine.

I could suddenly detect the feint calls of a thousand ghosts.

'What sort of nightmares, Bobby? What happens?'

Again, she checked on my slumbering brother.

The trepidation in her eyes was now readily visible.

'He's being chased. He fears for his life.'

It dawned on me at this point that despite all the positives of the past four months, fate might not be affording me total liberation after all.

'Chased by *who*?' I demanded.

'He doesn't know who is in pursuit. All he knows is that he must keep running from them.'

Instantly, I understood.

I understood all too well.

The bottom fell out of my world at that precise moment.

In my absence, Martin had succumbed to the demons that Father Carroll had warned me about.

I was no longer my brother's protector if I wasn't there with him to fend away the evil that lurked in the back of his mind.

I dare not share my sinister thoughts with Bobby.

What could I do to make her feel better? I couldn't just change the subject. I had to play along, even though I was all too aware of all the symptoms and causes.

I couldn't indulge Bobby in the truth.

Not then, not ever.

I feebly attempted to allay her obvious concerns.

Experience should have dictated that my suggestion was the very last resort to plunder.

'The doctor will sort him out. First thing after New Year, make him an appointment and get a prescription for some sedatives. He'll be fine. Believe you me. Don't worry about it, Bobby. It will pass. It's just a phase.'

I retired to my own bed that night with little choice but to embrace the possibility that the past was not quite behind us just yet.

*****

Once the holiday period was concluded, Bobby obliged my advice and made the appointment at the doctors. Martin was promptly issued with a month's supply of sleeping tablets.

The quack claimed that my brother's change of lifestyle had rendered his physical routine out of synch, and that once he started to sleep properly at night, everything else should fall back into place.

I did not tell Bobby that the diagnosis was terrifyingly familiar to my mother's.

And mine, for that matter.

I hoped that in time, Martin's strength of character would allow him to rise above the nagging skeletons of our history.

In hindsight, that most futile of human mechanisms, it appeared that nobody was listening when I prayed for my brother all those months ago.

I reluctantly returned to Swansea with a heart of lead.

Preparing to battle the offerings that fate may throw my way.

I spoke to no one about the things that Bobby had said to me over Christmas.

I convinced myself not to inform her of the suspected reasons for Martin's growing unrest.

I hoped in time, that my brother would defeat the evil apparitions that had implanted themselves and now visited his subconscious each night.

But who was I trying to kid?

I sullenly returned to Swansea and resumed my studies.

Waiting for the calling once again.

# EPILOGUE

The mature student threw his sports bag over his shoulder and departed the school premises. Another successful day had endured. He had received top marks for a German language test and was feeling rather pleased with himself.

Considering his lack of sleep the previous night, he was buoyant.

The one hundred percent result was an amazing accomplishment.

Joining his younger friends outside the gates, he zipped up his jacket to keep out the chill of that cold February evening.

After several bursts of conversation amongst the group, they went their separate ways home.

The man was tired but content with almost everything in his life at that precise moment.

But he missed his younger brother dearly.

He wished he could see him every night.

Especially since the visions had begun.

The images that formed in his mind's eye as he slept were still devastating enough to wake him on a regular basis.

Those same demons stayed with him all day, every day.

There was seemingly no respite from the entity that now plagued his newfound solace. For instant comfort and ease of distress, he always thought of his beloved partner, Bobby.

As he trudged wearily along the canal towpath, he suddenly needed to visualise her once again.

He closed his eyes briefly and re-opened them, as if to check that the trailing phantoms had been dispersed.

Satisfied they were vanquished once more, he continued to walk.

Amid his misguided and temporary appeasement, he did not see the figure in the shadows a few paces behind, observing his every step.

Martin had not yet detected the true cause of his horrendous nightmares, because the chief tormentor was satisfied to remain exactly where he was for the time being.

Under cover of darkness.

Not yet ready to be revealed.

But once more, ever present in the minds of his two sons...

...TO BE CONTINUED...

ACKNOWLEDGEMENTS

I wish to thank the following people for their invaluable expertise and support in helping this book gain wings:
Samantha Thornton; Hannah Bliss; Charlotte Wilson; Robbie Wilson; Carole Thornton, Chris Bliss; Charlotte Bliss; Jeanette Taylor Ford; Sue Hayward; Ford Wood and last but certainly not least, David Slaney for his superb cover design.
I couldn't have done it without any of you.
I am forever indebted.
RJT

Also Available on Amazon
by Richard John Thornton

DELIVER US FROM EVIL

AT HELL'S GATE

THE SWANS AT CLEARLAKE

WITHIN THESE WALLS

Printed in Great Britain
by Amazon

11531239R00187